HANGED BY FATE

By Rowan Wolf
Rare: A dark anthology of unusual secrets
Contributor with the short story "*Remedy*"

Coming Soon
Canvas Black
Summer 2026
Canen Dera Book 2
2027

Also from Alex Parker Publishing
The Light of Lúnasa by Laura Foley
Gas Giant Gambit by E.S. Raye
Rare: A dark anthology of unusual secrets edited by June Visosky and
Stephanie Vislay

HANGED BY FATE

ROWAN WOLF

ALEX PARKER
PUBLISHING

WWW.ALEXPARKERPUBLISHING.COM

Book Cover Design by Story Wrappers

Map Design by Tiffany Munro

First edition 2025

Alex Parker Publishing

16755 Von Karman Ave, Suite 200 Irvine, CA 92606

www.alexparkerpublishing.com

This book contains depictions of extreme peril, death, violence, gore, kidnapping, imprisonment, abuse, manipulation, ritualistic practices, and inferred sexual assault.

For Uncle Dan—
Your early encouragement meant more than you will ever know.

N
W
E
S
TENUAL
GAULLE
GEN REAON
HANIELLE
GRANATH
HILLS OF TESSIRA
WERILYN
LEVILLE
ESCENONE
TEVACAS
WESILEA
CESURE EACE
JAISETT
MT. OHBROLIS
VAER GOUN
VAELSOVE
ILNEM RENON
TEMISSE
HELT ESON
SAULLE
MADINNE
THE BLACKWOOD
DHENPARA MOUNTAINS
SAY LIVORE
FELREAON
AROUN VAER
MT. RELDOR
HILLS OF MINUAL
ELLACE
VACKEUS
TANES
KABIRIL
DHAESREAON
ISLAROURNE
NYARUSE
VANENOR
BILTAK BAY
THE SOUTH SEA
LAKE KAILAEL
NIERA
THE ADLEAN SEA
TAMILIE
QABRIAH
WASUREN
BERR ISLAND
BERRIS STRAIT
LACASLA
DACKENE
MT DEENE
CASCANVORE
MT DIRE
MYRE FACE
THE LAND OF
MONERA

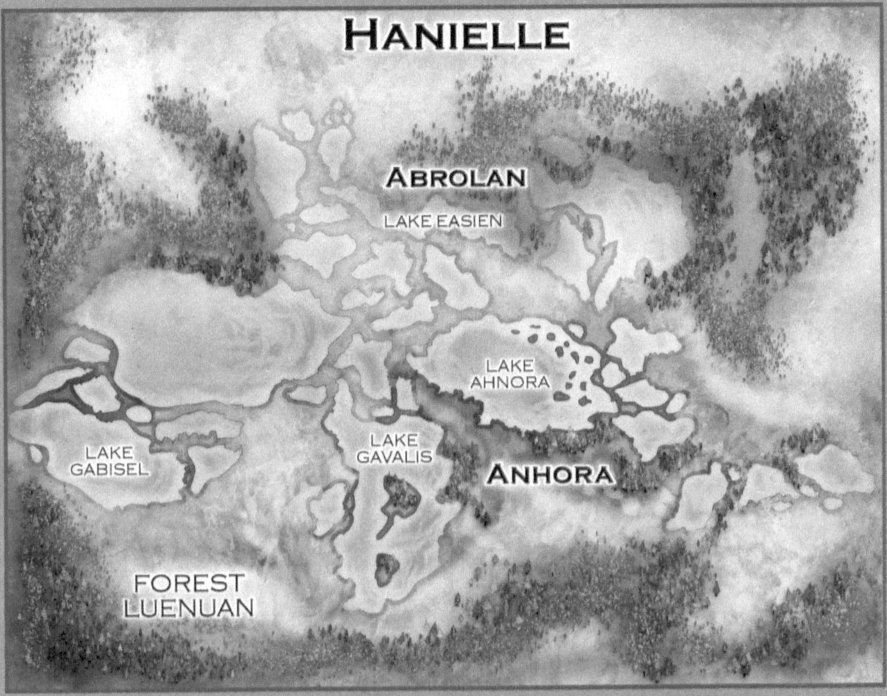
HANIELLE
ABROLAN
LAKE EASIEN
LAKE AHNORA
LAKE GABISEL
LAKE GAVALIS
ANHORA
FOREST LUENUAN

SUS' GACETEO
SUS' ESON
SUS' ABARELL
SUS' ABROLAN
SUS' LELORA
SUS' NECALLE

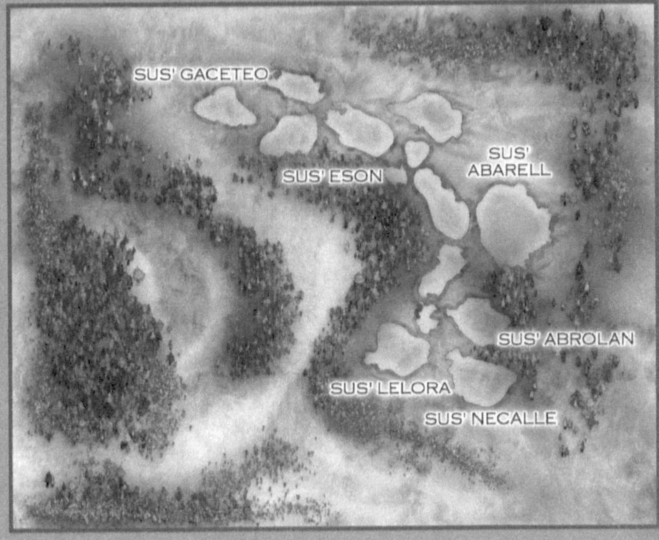

AUCTION

2177

ere tetem let anoisirie dere eti tevis roscem
ougesau nas iltem eti nurorar marisu rim gean aurum ere felren
ere qi laneviu aere kestem bavage gean daurum tecu le
- *The Book of Kings*, Entry 620, Year 841 of the Golden Age

Ariaas leaned over the cliffside in the black night, his torch angling over the abyss and reflecting orange on the stone edge. Rumors swirled about the winds and the fall below the edge of his worn boots. He outstretched his torch, tilting the flame over the darkness. He nudged a rock.

The stone tumbled, whistling until the sound sluggishly faded, never meeting the earth below.

His stomach sank.

A plummet from this height had no discernible end.

The torch's slim, circular glow hindered his vision. He dropped his only light onto the stone ground, stomping out the flame. Perhaps the whispers of the Forever Fall were true; however, his curiosity refused to hold until dawn to glimpse the prison.

As the blanket of stars brightened, far from his edge of the void, the silhouette of the hanging cage materialized. Jagged edges and nothing more across the dark chasm.

The Reldory.

The prison had no bottom, no legs, no arms—a mere black, rugged moon hanging in the emptiness, stalactites dripping from the base. The presence of captives weighed in the air—weary, hidden traitors, liars, and witnesses none could speak to, all silent, dangling in isolation.

Two rumors had been correct thus far: the depth of the abyss and the hanging cage. If the third held true, the *goods* would arrive at his side of the chasm for auction at dawn. The *goods*—Ariaas's confidante's words—if she could even be called a confidante. Perhaps she was onto something; he would call them *goods*, for assigning another word today would bring a far too personal a price to this task.

Ariaas wedged his body between a boulder and an old tree stump. It would be a pity if the winds shoved him over the cliffside before anyone arrived. Without reason, the winds whispered, then intertwined in his hair and slapped his face. He clutched his blade as if the savage gusts might yank it from his grasp. The dagger in his left boot and the needle-sized blade in his right comforted him.

In his opinion, one could never be too handsome, have too much food, or have too many weapons. The type of weapons was negotiable, but he preferred blades. Since he'd eaten all his provisions and his hair was ravaged, he leaned into the third option, planning on slaying as many vile Southerners as his blades would allow.

His tattered appearance could be used to his advantage. Endruas, his dominant lineage, granted him the gift of laggard physical maturity. To the unknowing, Ariaas was a simple pale man in his third or fourth decade. His general appearance and skill with a blade never alluded to his actual years, and he either concealed or gloated over this fact, depending on the day and to whom he spoke.

He rubbed his fingers into the creases between the rocks, gathering dust and rubbing his palms together like he might create fire. When they congealed with the sweat, he pressed them into the delicate tucks of his brow and into the crow's feet at his eyes, squinting and opening to layer the muck deeper into his fine lines. He wiped the rest of this damp mess on his trousers and drew fresh, dry dirt into his hair, pulling his hands through his scalp to sully his chestnut locks. He coughed and spat as the dust entered his lungs.

This auction required finesse.

The auction also required lies and acting skills, which he possessed in equal quantity as weapons and dashing looks.

Now the *goods* needed to arrive safely. And he needed to buy every single *good*.

He had sold all that time allowed: two paintings of geriatric people he didn't know, the silverware, the fine porcelain, pots and pans, the tables and chairs. He hauled them to Ellace on his neighbor's carriage and sold them for measly silver. He practically gifted the chickens, but those buyers were as dumb as the fowls, who would depart their new confines in a week or two and wander back to Aroun Vaer. However, the one item that allowed him to believe on this starry night that he might be able to purchase the *goods* was his late wife's aquamarine and gold necklace. Though it pained him, his memory of the trinket would fade just as her memory had faded over the years.

Because of that necklace—and the additions of his wares—he held forty-one gold coins. *Forty-one.* He still scarcely believed it. He felt like the wealthiest man alive, perhaps even more affluent than the queen.

Only a few more hours of agony.

He reminded himself to forget what the *goods* were, or he'd crumble into searing pain.

Two female Xentirie arrived on foot, wearing anemone pins and holding honed spears. Three men in gray and black uniforms appeared when the sky brightened to plum. No one spoke. Ariaas removed himself from the rocks, curving his spine and slumping his shoulders to appear feeble.

When the sun peeked over the jagged rock, a carriage arrived from Qabriah. More gray and black-clothed soldiers arrived, then lastly, a glass carriage with two prominent men with gruff brows and fur-lined cloaks lumbered the incline.

The throng waited in tense silence, eyeing one another, surveying weapons, evaluating wealth. Finally, a wooden carriage lumbered up the incline with the eight-sided star of The South Sea.

Ariaas's heart eased. The *goods.*

A middle-aged man dressed in an ashen cloak sprang from the carriage, smiling broadly. "Thank you so much for your attendance." The auctioneer pulled at the lapel of his jacket, wide-eyed and smug, like a man who had solid reason to suspect he would soon swim in gold. Perhaps he dreamed of retiring in the countryside and buying himself a woman, horse, or whatever his ugly heart desired.

The smug auctioneer nodded at the female Xentirie. "You will keep the winds at bay while we host our business, yes?" Without waiting for a reply, the auctioneer clapped his hands ceremoniously. "The children have arrived."

Nausea swelled in Ariaas's stomach.

The children. The word *goods* brought him far less internal turmoil. They were so much more than bodies. They had names, parents, people who loved them. They were *not* anonymous goods for auction. They were *his.*

"Today, we bid on three."

"Three?" shouted Ariaas, his voice far harsher than he intended. "There are supposed to be four."

"Three's all that's here." The auctioneer shrugged. "Can't create somethin' from nothin'."

The children were removed from Ariaas's protection for a mere month, and this is what happened. *This?* Their father had assured him they would be safe, and then they were taken and sold on the black market. Ultimately, it was Ariaas's good fortune: the auctioneer didn't know what they possessed, otherwise, he would be facing a far different battle.

From beyond the rocks, a familiar olive-skinned man arrived. Ariaas needed a moment to recall the name associated with the sloping shoulders and the beady eyes.

"Rarrk?" Ariaas whispered harshly. Not the Yurelan he expected to see. Surely, they would send someone to the auction, but why this heavily tattooed man with straws for legs? All would know he was Yurelan immediately. "Where's my daughter?"

"Grieving."

Ariaas's heart clenched. Certainly, he could empathize; four of her children had been stolen. "And the children's father?"

"They hadn't found his body when I left. Not sure if he survived the raid."

Ariaas struggled to land on an emotion for the news: pleased, saddened, unmoved? Either way, he could have used the extra arms. He exhaled through his nose. This straw man Rarrk, this *one* Yurelan, would not be enough if blades were drawn instead of gold. And truthfully, though Rarrk stood against The South Sea, the man's alliances were not exactly aligned with his own.

Ariaas closed his eyes. He could win the auction if he were smart about it. But he would struggle to bid on three children when the others came for them, too. They are *goods;* keep a level head, he reminded himself, just *goods. Wares* like the porcelain he himself sold in Ellace.

But which of his grandchildren was missing?

Rarrk surveyed him from boot to dirtied scalp. "You look terrible."

"If you told me I looked nice, I would've slapped you."

Why did they send this man? Were the Yurelan really that injured after The South Sea stole the children that they could send no one else?

Ariaas rubbed his brow. He stood at this precipice with half an ally.

"How much gold did they send with you?"

"Nine coin."

"Nine?" scoffed Ariaas. Nine was all the Yurelan could fork up for their prized possessions? But a measly old man from Valesove could fork up four times that? Ariaas pinched the bridge of his nose. Pacing on this precipice would be frowned upon.

"And if we combine," asked Ariaas, "where do the children go when we leave? They'll come home with me, yes?"

"Yes." Rarrk nodded. "The new king agreed they could go home with you. They'd be safe."

Ariaas contemplated asking who this *new king* was before he stopped himself. He didn't care. He had all the new information he could handle today: his daughter lived, her husband unaccounted for, his captive grandchildren—minus one—moments away from being in his sight line, and if he could buy them, they could all go home to Aroun Vaer with him.

Finally, some good news. One less person against him.

"We go back and forth. Don't bid against each other." Ariaas instructed Rarrk below his breath. "I'll give you the coin if you go over. I've got plenty. Stand on the other side. Don't speak to me again until it's done."

Nodding, Rarrk departed Ariaas's side and perched himself on the far side of the cliff. Ariaas surveyed the other bidders. Whether they came to sell his family or buy them—they were monsters regardless. Every last one.

The auctioneer addressed the bidders in carriages. "Introduce yourselves. We don't deal with unknowns."

In turn, they bowed their heads, hands on chests, showing silver pins, providing names and titles. Someone from Qabriah, as Ariaas suspected. Only the old gods knew why; Qabriah had no power or wealth. He should have listened more intently when the two lumbering men from Mount Ohbrolis in Dhaesreaon introduced themselves. When the bidder spoke, Ariaas saw a bull wearing fur with a toothy mustard-yellow smile.

The auctioneer turned to Rarrk. "And you?"

"Nobody. From nowhere."

"A nobody from nowhere! Ha!" barked the auctioneer, slapping his thigh. "Very well, Nobody from Nowhere, do you have gold? No point in bein' here if ya don't. Silver ain' for today."

Rarrk patted his jacket, metal clanking.

Pleased, the auctioneer turned his sights to Ariaas. "And you, old man?"

"Does it matter?"

"Does it matter! Well, we have a *Nobody from Nowhere* that thinks we can't see plain as the sky he's Yurelan." He gestured to Rarrk, performing a show for the nobility, before waving his weak arm to Ariaas. "And a *Does It Matter*."

They laughed.

This auction provided joy.

This morning entertained them.

Ariaas clenched his fists. His ears pounded.

The auctioneer slowed his pride. "Yes, old man, it does. I want your name. Full name and titles."

"Ariaas. Ariaas Haran Ebronds. Tu'dende. Dominant of the Endruas."

Should he have used his real full name? Probably not. Should he have shared he was Tu'dende and not a pure blood Sengura? Probably not. Should he have told them his lineage? Also, probably not. But he didn't have the wherewithal to think of another surname of the Endruas. He could use this to his advantage if they knew he was older than he appeared.

The auctioneer pinched his lips and regained his jovial tone. "And what's your age, old man?"

"Much older than you, boy." Ariaas snickered, joking and leaning into his theatrics.

The more people spoke, the more certain Ariaas became that everyone on this peak should die. They came to sell his family or to buy them, except perhaps Rarrk. He had yet to determine if the tattooed man was beneficial or a dolt.

"By the way, where'd you get 'em from?" Ariaas knew the answer but performed with the naivest inquisitiveness he could disguise behind his gritted teeth.

"Bought 'em off a royal carriage. The royal carriage stole 'em off that lot," he gestured to Rarrk. Ariaas's grandchildren handed from one group of idiots to the next. "We sell 'em today, or they get tossed in The Reldory. I've got my stay there until next Uen'can."

Ariaas rubbed his lip with his thumb. "What's your breakeven?"

"We paid three gold."

"*You paid*—" He restrained his sudden harsh tone. "You paid three gold coin? One for each?"

"Yeah. Three's here, ain' they? What you wanted five? *Ten?* Surely, you ain' got enough money for all that." The man winked, curling a wicked grin. "What're you gonna do with 'em anyway?"

That's a question Ariaas hadn't thought to answer—his motivations shouldn't be questioned in a simple purchase. A better answer would be to tell this bumbling idiot that he would slit his throat for selling his grandchildren like meat at a market. Blood pulsed through his brow and ticked at the vein in his forehead. Instead, he released the muscles in his center, wincing, cowering his shoulders, and further curling his spine. At the hip, he turned his left leg inward, to where his foot appeared lame.

"Got lots a' land. Need some strong young ones to pick up after the horses. Tend to the gardens, ya know?"

"Ah, yes," the auctioneer sympathized, "such a task must be difficult at your age."

At his age. Was it possible to hate someone more than this idiot? He could dance circles around this wide-eyed man, especially in a reception of swords. Those children were worth far more than three gold coins.

Ariaas whispered under his breath, "Certainly don't know what you have, do you?"

The auctioneer tilted his head. "Hm?"

"Just wishing my back was as strong as yours, lad." Lies smooth as butter. "That's all."

Three children exited the carriage in days-old, dirty clothing. Arienne, less than four feet tall, draped her arms lovingly around her two brothers; her yellow hair had been cut to the scalp, her violet eyes met the floor, and her lips pulled taut. A crown of lavender blooms adorned her brow, dried and wilted. Thealor, like his sister in height, buried his face into her shoulder. Brenor, a diminutive copy of Thealor with richer hair and deeper skin, wept.

Where's the baby? Arienne would hold her sister; she wouldn't leave Lenora.

There *were* only three.

Ariaas's stomach sank for the second time.

Arienne hushed Thealor as Brenor raised her ivory dress, burying his face. Ariaas licked his lips, pursed, and whistled a low song against the breeze. As the winds shifted, Arienne's shoulders perked, and her eyes suddenly raised, wide, searching. A breath skipped in his chest when their sights met. He raised a finger to his lips for silence. Arienne understood. She pressed Thealor and Brenor closer into her embrace.

The next part required this family to be strangers.

The precipice weighed with a density of inarticulate hostility.

Four parties came to purchase three *goods.*

Gesturing at Brenor, the auctioneer began, "Do I hear one coin for the boy aged three?"

Crickets.

The groups then chattered amongst themselves. A boy of three brought more problems than solutions. What a terrible auctioneer. He mentioned no redeeming qualities for Ariaas's grandson whatsoever. No mentions of his abilities, his strong verbal, and coordination skills. His love of animals. Of course, the boy wouldn't sell high. A diamond necklace might not sell in the hands of his man.

Ariaas shrugged, performing a beautiful insouciant opinion. "One?"

"I hear one," the auctioneer paused. "Who has two?"

No one bid for a few moments, then a woman from Qabriah raised a hand.

The man from Ohbrolis asked snidely, "Is it house-trained?"

"Is it *house-trained*?" the auctioneer repeated, shaking his head. "I wouldn't have the foggiest."

The bull from Ohbrolis pursed his lips as if he tasted something he didn't quite like. "Three."

Ariaas groaned, grasping his low back, grimacing, and playing further into his fragility. "Four. Highest I'll go. Don't want to house-train it, though."

No further bidding.

There appeared to be silent agreement amongst the crowd—no one wished to house-train a young child. When the auctioneer motioned toward Ariaas's win, the bull chuckled. "Seems you added more than helped, old man."

"Mr. Ebronds owes us four. This strapping young man, aged five years, will be our final bid. We expect him to grow to be quite strong." The auctioneer preened; this auction was worth his while already. He grasped Arienne by the back of her neck, morning sun glistening off the chopped edges of her waves. "Now, on to the second. The girl, aged seven. From what I've been told, she's quite ... pleasant. Oldest. Cares for the younger ones."

The navy man from Dhaesreaon gestured to her frail arms. "Will she be strong, too?"

"Hard to say." The auctioneer spread her arms wide like a bird, then turned her around and kicked her legs open. The sun gleamed through her ivory gown, revealing the thin outline of her thighs. He tilted his head as though he evaluated fine art he didn't quite understand. "She leans more … meek at the moment. I don't know lineages on 'em though."

The bull from Ohbrolis leaned down into Arienne's face. Ariaas could only suspect how foul his breath smelled at his proximity. The fur atop his shoulders tickled her nose, her face crinkled, and she sneezed. "You know your lineage, girl?"

Arienne's brows pressed. She shook her head.

Ariaas bit his tongue.

The bidding commenced. Between Qabriah and Dhaesreaon, they drove the price over nine before Rarrk closed, buying Ariaas's eldest grandchild for eleven gold coins. The auctioneer swelled. "Nobody from Nowhere owes eleven. Now, onto our final bid."

Ariaas exhaled. This auction was unfolding better than he expected. He'd only spent fifteen, and Thealor remained. Between him and Rarrk, thirty-five gold coins remained for Thealor.

Take three home today. Worry about the baby's whereabouts tomorrow.

The auctioneer shoved Thealor before the throng. The boy fell to his knees over the loose stones, weeping and holding his skinned palms. Arienne aided him to his feet, evaluating the cuts on his hands.

"Back up, girl." The auctioneer shoved her, and she stumbled, landing on her rump.

Thealor sobbed louder. Two guards in gray cloaks grasped his arms and legs, holding him wide, displaying him. Thealor dribbled and howled, flailing futility against the strong hands of grown men like a carp on a hook. Reeled and wriggling, he clamped his teeth toward the guard's forearm, his deep-set eyes wild.

The cliff air tensed.

The boy may be strong, but he wasn't easy to control, was he? Ariaas's insides tightened. *Leave him be. Just get this over with.*

The bull shouted, "Can't you get it to shut up and hold still?"

A guard struck Thealor across the cheek. He wept more, smashing his teeth, and babbling uncontrollably.

Ariaas thumbed the hilt of his sword. Rarrk issued him a knowing glance. Ariaas taught Thealor that maneuver. When weaponless, *bite hard.* Then *bite harder.* Bite hard enough to return with a flesh prize. Thealor's action both pleased and nauseated him—pleased the boy remembered in a state of duress, nauseated he would have to use it at all.

Rarrk stepped before Thealor. "Shut it, boy!"

When his words failed to work, Rarrk spat in his face.

"Look at me." He hissed through gritted teeth, *"Shut your stupid mouth!"*

Ariaas's cheeks flushed red, seething. What was the Yurelan doing? He mustn't kill the only half-ally he had on this cliff. Perhaps this was part of Rarrk's theatrics, just as Ariaas had his.

But this was all wrong.

When his sharp words didn't calm the boy, Rarrk grasped Thealor by his scalp, lifting him into the air. Thealor fumbled, holding tight onto the grasp through his hair. The guards retreated some steps, allowing Nobody from Nowhere his stronghold. Desperately, forcefully, Ariaas sought for Thealor to meet his eyes, to recognize him.

The Yurelan shouted, "I said *shut it.*"

He rattled Thealor. Hard.

Theatrics or not, half-ally or not, this was all too much. Abuse for silent recognition. The auction. The biting, the weeping. Everything was too much.

Abandoning rational thought, Ariaas left behind the voice of the feeble old man, and regained that of his usual strengthened self, bellowing, *"Leave him be!"*

Startled, Rarrk dropped Ariaas's grandson. Thealor scurried to his rump, containing himself to a mere whimper. Thealor turned his warm scarlet eyes upward. The bidders stepped backward at his appearance. While they saw unbound feral fire and fear, Ariaas saw the warmth of blooming roses and a bushel of apples.

The boy became feral only when he was afraid.

Where Rarrk had hoped Thealor would know him, Ariaas hoped the opposite. The dirt in the creases of Ariaas's wrinkles, the wrap around his eye, the crick in his spine made no difference to these children. They *knew* him. They knew his voice when he shouted when they didn't come in for supper. They knew his stance, his voice, his mannerisms, his smell from working in Aroun Vaer's fields—probably more so than their own mother. They had spent most of their years with him.

Thealor exhaled every ounce of breath in his lungs. His shoulders curled—an exhale of worries, abandonment of fear, a revival of hope, his burdens suddenly lifting. He sobbed differently now—out of relief in place of fear, weeping with outstretched arms, reaching for Ariaas's familiar embrace.

Through his tears, he choked, "Papa."

The cliff silenced.

The bull from Ohbrolis turned suddenly, swiftly interested, his sunken eyes wide with dark pleasure. His mustard smile on full display, he cackled and slapped his knee. *"Papa?"*

The cliffside filled with sudden foreboding laughter. Apparently, Dhaesreaon found familial relations humorous. Ariaas's age and his family were court jesters.

"I'm buying the last one, old man. Doesn't matter how much you got." The bull spat. "I got a gold bar. I know you ain't carry that on you."

Suddenly ecstatic, the auctioneer asked, "Are you bidding a bar?"

The bull ignored the auctioneer, pointing a wayward hand between Ariaas and Rarrk. "And don't think I didn't see you two talking. You can't have 'em all!"

Ariaas's cover was blown, and so was his half-ally. No use in playing a lost game. He reached deep into his pockets, tossing his coins to the stone ground. "Take the money. Just take it. I can get more."

"Your money ain't no good, old man."

Ariaas shoved the coin further with the edge of his boot. "Perhaps you should return with more money than you left with, and your lady will buy you some new teeth."

The bull's smile faded.

Rarrk mouthed, "Get it together."

But Ariaas no longer cared for theatrics. He lost caring about the bull from Ohbrolis and acting old. He no longer cared for those who laughed at him for his curved spine or age. Age was a number and nothing more; if one man could prove such a thing, it was him.

The bull grinned wider. "Brouvergs don' want coin. They got plenty of coin. They need some strapping young men to guard those treasures."

Ariaas straightened his spine. "He's five."

"And what when he's ten? Twenty? He'll be stronger than me, I'd wager. I'll pay all I've got just to see you not get them. Not my money anyway." The bull from Ohbrolis grasped Thealor's shoulder.

The auctioneer cradled the gold bar, eyes glimmering, appearing to see heaven itself. He waved them idly away, needing nothing further for their purchase.

The bull shoved Thealor into the confines, practically salivating. When Thealor was secured, he moved over Ariaas, wafting the scent of stale fish with each word. "He's mine now. He belongs to the Brouvergs. He belongs to the Mountain."

Ariaas reached for the hilt of his blade. Before he could remove his steel from its sheath, the arrogant bull butted him, his broad forehead crashing into the bridge of his nose.

The world pirouetted for a moment.

Suddenly, the Xentirie fled, and the winds sprouted legs and a whip with means to crack against him. He drew his blade, charging the man from Ohbrolis, meeting his drawn shield. The bull slammed Ariaas back, slicing through his arm to the bone and pressing him until he was forced to stumble backward.

How did I not see that coming?

An arrow hummed past Ariaas's face, landing on a rock at his backside. Was that Rarrk? Who was to say? A woman from Qabriah struck him, and he parried her attacks from the ground before his blade sliced through her shoulder. An arrow grazed his ear with a *whoosh*.

The bull ran.

Good, Ariaas thought at first, until he realized he ran for the carriage lumbering down the hill with Thealor still inside. Ariaas lurched to his feet, the earth spinning, clutching his wound, searching desperately for today's half-ally.

Coins littered the stone. Brenor cried amongst the chaos while Rarrk battled guards in gray and black for Arienne.

The earth rang into Ariaas's ears. The sky settled slowly.

Ariaas grasped Brenor, calming him amongst the clatter. "It's alright. It's alright."

The carriage rumbled the steep decline, swallowing Thealor, his breath fogging the glass as he wailed. Ariaas's stomach dropped, searching for a safe place for Brenor to hide.

He shouted for Thealor, "I'm coming, boy! I'm coming!"

The auctioneer seized Arienne, dragging her backward, his dagger to her throat. "Open the bridge!" He yanked her petite frame, hoisting her from the ground, her bare feet dangling in his grasp as he forced her into The Reldory.

Arienne screamed, a cutting, tenebrous sound Ariaas had never heard from a human, let alone this child. The shrill voice tore through him like shards of glass, rippling through his head and into his gut. Her lavender crown fell into the void, the winds holding it gently for a moment before tearing and shredding the dried leaves, suddenly wrenching it into the black abyss below.

Ariaas forced Brenor headfirst between the rocks, covering his vital organs; the boy flailed and squealed. Brenor shouldn't lose a leg, but certainly, it was far less important than a head. Ultimately, he whimpered and stopped fighting, conceding to this hiding place. Figures rushed in a flurry, clashing blades shimmering against the new morning sun. Ariaas planted his foot firmly on one rock and raised his sights to see who remained.

Rarrk lay on his stomach, left leg twisted at the knee, beady eyes open wide in shock, unmoving.

Ariaas settled himself down next to the boy. Now, the only ally on his side was a whimpering toddler. He grimaced, clamping his free hand into his fresh wound, blood seeping between his fingers. Brenor murmured terrified words Ariaas couldn't understand in the deluge.

"Quiet, boy. And close your eyes."

When Ariaas glanced again, the bridge to The Reldory retracted, decaying, shrinking branches of a tree, devouring Arienne. Now she hung in the dark moon with all the traitors, liars, and spies.

Thealor's glass cage lumbered the decline, and the bull from Mount Ohbrolis trailed on foot, his blade ready for any who might dare follow.

Would Brenor stay in this place if he chased the carriage? Would he remain? Would he hold silent? Brenor half-listened in duress for a boy his age, his eyes clamped, though he sobbed audibly, uncertain what he witnessed, why he wasn't in the warm arms of his mother, sister, or brother. The boy certainly wouldn't stay put if Ariaas left. He would wail if left alone.

No matter how many gold coins littered the ground, Brenor would be taken or killed—this much, Ariaas could feel in his soul.

What to do? What to do? What to do?

"Song of the Sunrise" floated in the air, whistling, dancing across the abyss. *Arienne.* He choked at her futile plea from the hanging cage. How could he keep Brenor safe, cross the chasm to The Reldory, and rescue Thealor from the glass carriage? How could he be in three places? He struggled to find air at the altitude on his inhale and pursed his lips.

He would come back for her. He *would* come back.

But no sound came between his ragged breath to assure her.

Ariaas collapsed through the rocks, boots slipping and sliding on the unstable stones—her fear, his failure—choking, rasping in his chest, and demanding every ounce of his attention.

One. He arrived at this precipice for four and would leave with *one.* He grasped Brenor, yanked him into his chest, holding him tightly.

He never should have trusted anyone but himself.

RUMORS

2177

Ariaas trekked past Aroun Vaer's rotting spilt rail fence, one arm in a sling he had crafted from vines, the three-year-old boy on his opposite shoulder. The day had grown hot and balmy while he made his way to the destitute castle he called home—now bare of paintings, porcelain, silverware, and chairs.

After settling in the library, he splayed a handful of nuts and berries onto the table for Brenor. When the boy began to eat, he realized he fed the chickens the same way.

Giggling, Brenor grasped the laces of Ariaas's boot and untied them.

Ariaas exhaled, rubbing the bridge of his nose. "Stop touching things."

He'd repeated this phrase countless times on the journey, with the poison oak, the loose gravel at the edge of a gorge, and a rattlesnake, but the boy didn't listen. The phrase now sounded ritualistic instead of commanding. Brenor didn't bite like Thealor, but he certainly didn't mind, either. In the short time they'd been apart, Ariaas had blocked out how much small children have no concept of danger or death.

He stretched his left shoulder. The joint cracked, shooting a pang of pain from his neck to his elbow. That shoulder might never go back the same way again.

A woman's voice, older, worn, projected through the empty castle walls. *"Ariaas?"*

Damn. I'd forgotten.

Thaesla claimed she would be no help with the auction—her own words—but stayed at Aroun Vaer to watch the land for intruders or if the children's parents or the Yurelan returned.

Ariaas preferred solitude.

He called from the library, "In here." This one room still held intact where much of the rest of the castle felt naked and forsaken.

Thaesla pressed her way through the grand double doors, her brows raised in concern. As much as he preferred isolation, his unease settled at the sight of familiar coal-colored eyes, her pointed chin, the long emerald skirt she seemed to live in, her sienna skin.

She grasped Ariaas's blood-soaked arm and squeezed. "Where are the children? What happened?"

How to answer such a question? *Well, I lost my granddaughter to the cage, a madman that looked like a bull took five-year-old Thealor while he screamed my name, Brenor hasn't stopped crying for hours, my left shoulder burns from carrying the lad, I've barely eaten scraps for days, and blood stained my favorite shirt.*

Ariaas smiled pathetically. "I got one."

And, at that, he wasn't sure he'd ever be able to hear the word *Papa* again. Thealor's screams had rung in his mind the entire trek down the mountain, echoing against the rumors swirling about the three captive children. Thoughts reverberated so swiftly, he couldn't land on a single one to home in on.

Thaesla rushed to Brenor, pushing the uncut wavy hair from his brow. She exhaled in relief. "Brenor. Oh, thank the stars."

Thank the stars, what? That I got one? Or that it was Brenor?

"The rumors ... were all true. They had been stolen in the raid from the Yurelan," Ariaas explained. "Taken by the queen's men."

Thaesla kept Brenor at the edge of her sight. "And ...?"

"The Yurelan sent some idiot who got himself killed. Well ... honestly, he botched the whole job. Jolted Thealor around. Made him cry."

"Where are the other three?"

Ariaas's eyes welled with tears far beyond his control. A solemn shake of his head and his eyes meeting his boots was all he could manage.

"Do they know who they are?"

"No." He swiped the evidence of his tears away. "Idiots. All of them."

He hated the Southerners. He hated the Yurelan for sending one dimwitted aid.

"How do you stretch yourself into four places?" And perhaps even more important, how do you choose which one draws the most importance?

He groaned. The turmoil, the separation, Arienne's forlorn song, Thealor's screams. His daughter's grief. "Can you search for them? Can you search for them every day?"

"Ariaas, I can't search every day." Thaesla's shoulders stiffened. "The act alone will wither me into nothing."

"How often then? Each week? Each month?"

Her lips drew to a thin line. A month was a stretch, wasn't it?

Brenor tugged at Ariaas's trousers, asking, "Theo?" Though he struggled greatly with the *th;* the sound came out as a simple *t* and *o*. The boy loved his brother and wondered where he was. What answer could Ariaas provide that would appease a three year old?

He grasped Brenor, wincing, and moving him to a far corner of the library. He tossed one book, then another, piling a small stack before the child. "Stay here."

Ariaas stomped back to his old friend, losing the slim grasp of his marginally stoic mood with each step. At the lowest volume he could muster, he shouted, "The Canen Dera is nothing more than eight pictures. Eight stupid archaic images. They are older than the world, practically!" He rubbed the bridge of his nose. "Why does everyone think such prehistoric idiocy is relevant today? Why?"

Those images haunt this family. He pulled his hands through his dirty scalp. *'Children of the Canen Dera will bring ruin to the world.'*

While Brenor didn't listen much, he certainly wasn't the dark one the Canen Dera predicted him to be.

All powerful? Certainly not.

Dark? Also, no. The boy cried when he stepped on a snail in the garden and broke its shell.

The Bringer of Death? Ariaas audibly laughed at that one. What a joke of a prophecy.

But rumors were swift. Rumors bore more rumors and spread like running ink, branching through the creases of a worn palm, leeching into each surface, growing more dominant, cultivating armor with each passing moment. Once the rumors reached the outskirt cities, the children might as well have horns of the devil himself. And rumors of the children of the Canen Dera had existed for a millennium.

They are just children. But how many variations of them existed in the minds of this idiotic world?

"People like a good story," added Thaesla. "But more than that ... people fear what they don't understand. If I burn down your barn, wouldn't you want to know why? But if I told you the barn was full of diseased men without a cure—a disease that infected all—you would wish to watch the walls burn to ash with all inside, yes?" She raised a brow, seeking confirmation. "The knowing would see justification. The unknowing would see madness."

He could poke innumerable holes in her theory but instead focused on the point she alluded to. "Does that mean you don't believe in Canen Dera? Not as plain as it was seen?"

"It means I understand answers without proper questions are useless."

Now, she spoke above him. He was a simple man, thrust into a complex situation he had never asked for.

"It isn't just the prophecy … there is more to it. I think Canen Dera is the dumbest thing I've ever heard. Predictions that these children will bring an end to all of us. Rubbish. But it affects this family. It runs in our blood, and it changes our trajectory. How are we supposed to live—just *live* when everyone is fearful of our every breath?"

"You think it's a farce?

"I think the depths of imbecilic imaginations run deeper than The Reldory's abyss."

Thaesla cracked a simple grin. It was such a small act, yet amid inevitable failure, it brought peace he had no idea he had misplaced.

But there were so many varying tales of his grandchildren. So many pictures, stories, monuments, and scribblings. And where time stood, it was impossible to tell what tales of the children were rooted in fiction and which were grounded in factual prediction. Certainly, the version from eight hundred years ago where Brenor grew horns and a tail was fairly comical. The tale of them from four hundred years ago as beasts in war—as tigers, wolves, and bears—was also preposterous.

Perhaps, however, some were rooted in truth?

No. He retracted his own thoughts—they were all inane. They suggested his grandchildren were evil, feral creatures, and that was all the proof he needed to toss these notions into the fire and never think of them again.

Compassion of people's idiocy went against his basic instincts. He wanted blood. He wanted death for The South Sea's crimes against his family. And now, more than anything, he wanted the death of a bull in Mount Ohbrolis and a bug-eyed auctioneer. He wanted to watch as he plucked their babes, one by one, from their mother's arms and tossed them into a hanging cage, just as they had done to his.

"You forget." Thaesla's words drew him from his plots of revenge.

"What do I forget?"

"You forget that visions are there for a reason—that we might prevent acts of great destruction or understand what it is for. That we aid those who need us, or that we stop evil from coiling around us all."

"Yes, and if people make choices based on what they think the children will become, they will make monsters out of babes. They will determine their fate for them! You know this as well as I!"

"Calm down, my friend."

"Visions are nothing but a bunch of old, dead men deciding our future. Deciding a future for a world they'll never see! Who knows how much has changed since then? Since any of them offered their unsolicited advice on their foolish pictures?"

"Then do what you do best—toss it in the trash and do what you want."

Ariaas exhaled through his nose and tightened his eyes. "Why do I suspect you don't mean that?"

"Because I don't."

"You're confusing me. I don't know what you want me to do."

"I want you to follow your instincts. I want you to listen to what the world is telling you. Then ... listen to what your soul tells you and decide for yourself what the truth is. You and I both know that there is something beneath the surface that we do not understand here."

Yes. There was much he had yet to understand. And learning would misplace his vengeance. Ariaas paced, slumped into his chair, and stood to pace again. He raised his hand to his jaw, rubbing the tension away.

Thaesla eyed him warily. "There is something you aren't telling me. I can feel it. I don't know what it is, but I know there is something. Like I can feel when the winds are about to change."

Thaesla possessed wisdom beyond her years. Still, there were many things he hadn't told her. *Much.* He hated that she could read between the crooks of his brow and see to the depths of his mind as plain as he spoke the words aloud.

But today—today especially—he needed her. He needed someone in his corner where there currently was no one but a child and a dead half-ally. "Tell me, do I get to choose which rumors I believe and which ones I sweep into the flame at my bedside?"

Atop the desk sat an obsidian box with a soft brass lock, thick with raw and carved dagger-like spines. Ariaas opened the latch, revealing shelves nestled with papers and novels by Faiseus Rancesla Auro. The eight books slept, meaningless at the moment.

Ariaas fumbled through the loose pages.

"What do you need those for?" asked Thaesla.

The passage was in there somewhere. There were so many words, so many pieces of this puzzle his brain couldn't reconcile.

"It's here. You'll see." He scuttled the pages, then handed her a poem, pressing it out of his hand and into hers as if the page were ablaze and burned him.

She read the words, her lips mumbling as she trailed her fingers.

Scattered twenty-three western winds,
Confined for yet-committed sins
Of captive children, three remain,
Old man for years attempts in vain.

Pursue me, alter weary fate,
I'll lead you to the gilded gate,
Of captive children, three remain,
The unfound babe breaks captive reign.

To change their darkened, weary fate,
Hunt bordered code and gilded gate
Of captive children, three remain,
By force, the unrestrained attains.

Reclaim our darkened, weary fate,
Solve riddles, stars, and gilded gates
Of captive children, two remain,
Whom unlocked cages cannot contain.

Reclaim our darkened, weary fate,
Seek truths beyond the gilded gate
Of captive children, none remain,
All now released from tortured pain.

Now go, the freed, journey in haste!
Seek me, the stars, and gilded gates!

Three captive. The words echoed like a dream within a dream within a dream. Something far away, so far away he could scarcely grab hold, but he *felt* it the entire mountain descent. Nagging. Pulling at his innards. *Something.* Something was there in the recesses of his mind. *Children captive ... three remain.*

His captive grandchildren.

But he refused to listen to any more archaic predictions.

"Captive children, three remain. The *unfound babe.* Far too much to be a coincidence. The *old man.*" Thaesla cleared her throat. "Twenty-three western winds. The winds only blow west once a year. In the spring." She raised a weary hand to her lips. "Lenora is unfound. All three ... *captive ...* imprisoned twenty-three ... *years?*"

He watched her brows as she solved the puzzle before her, her coal eyes widening with horror. "You know they are children of the Canen Dera. One of the only that knows fate is fickle and not always as seen," he said. "Is it that far stretched that this stupid poem also predicted their capture? Their length of imprisonment?"

Thaesla's head shook idly. So much information sitting in her hand: how the children would be captive, when they would find freedom, and, more importantly, what they must do when freed from their chains.

She met his eye, echoing a line on the page in her hand. "The old man for years attempts in vain?"

Ariaas tugged on his collars again. Why did he even open that box all those years ago? Why did it haunt him? This stupid poem, these words on a tattered piece of paper, older than all the people in this room combined, would have no bearing over his future. Ariaas gazed into the mirror, dusted the remaining white matter from his hair, and straightened his shirt. "Well, I don't look old, at least. Right?"

"Ariaas. This poem says ..." She glanced at the tattered page. "The children will be separated for twenty-three years."

"Well, I don't believe in Canen Dera, and I certainly don't believe that, either. I might have a bad shoulder now, but I'll find my way to that mountain one way or another. And to the other mountain. And to the unknown whereabouts of Lenora."

"I'll leave in the morning." Thaesla stood, clearing her throat. "My sands are in Wesilea, and that is where I need to be to search for Lenora."

"No." Ariaas rubbed his temples. Exhaustion was threatening to take hold. "No, I need you to stay. Just for a little while."

"Why?"

"I need you to watch the boy. I need to leave."

Thaesla bent over Brenor, this small child, covered in Ariaas's days-old blood and reeking of rotting clothing worn weeks too long. He pinched the skin at her cheeks, cackling at the taut nature of her features.

She smiled, adopting a kinder tone. "But you only just got back. What will I do with him?"

"I don't know. Feed him fruit, let him play in the fountain and with the horses. Let him sleep in the barn for all I care." He flipped the pages seeking answers, then met her eyes again, suddenly concerned. "Don't really leave him to sleep in the barn."

The crook of Thaesla's brow pressed—as if she would ever do such a thing. Ariaas started to make for the kitchen. He needed a hearty meal in his stomach.

She trailed him, asking, "How long will you be gone?" When he didn't reply, she grasped his arms, pleading, "*Ariaas,* if this author claims you attempt in vain for twenty-three years, you can at least sleep the night."

Sleep the night? How would he ever sleep again? His worst nightmares walked out of his subconscious directly into flesh and blood reality: his daughter, gone with the Yurelan, grieving. He lost Arienne. He lost Thealor. The baby, Lenora, was God knows where. Their father was likely dead. Some lunatic, long-dead author is giving him instructions on how to live his life, not mentioning nearly how handsome he is for the years he's lived and merely calling him *old.*

How would he return to the abyss, cross the bridge over the Forever Fall, the bridge that did not exist until someone called it from its resting home? How would he save Arienne, a promise he made to himself and, in some ways, to her? How? How would he find Lenora?

What to do? What to do? What to do?

And what of Theo? What of his indenture to guard treasures for the Lady of the Mountain?

Thaesla interrupted his anxious rumination. "I'll make you the hand pies Idith used to make. I know it's your favorite." The thought of anything related to Idith warmed his soul. But knowing Thaesla, she would lace this pie with some herb to make him sleep for two days. Admittedly, this would help his body, but his mind would never allow it. "Fine. Deal. I'll stay until sunrise. But I'll sleep when I'm dead."

Prognostication would be his ally when it pleased him and at no other time. And waiting twenty-three years certainly didn't please him. Over two decades was far too long, even for a man who was slow to age. Those children would never be lost for long.

Ariaas grabbed a book on Mount Ohbrolis, licked a finger, and thumbed to the page on Brouverg Castle.

He had a bull to kill in the morning.

RUN

2200

Ibigael Rackard Nasalorn, High Born Tu'dende of the Remerard, The Dark
Warrior of the South Sea, The Jaguar
Born: First Month of Spring, 2048
Deceased: Second Month of Spring, 2132
Children: Two

- Official Ledger of The South Sea

It would have been a beautiful blue day in Valesove, amongst the whispering winds of spring, had someone not stolen from her.

Birds twittered in the forest while Anseurea dug her hand into the moss-covered stump, searching again and again. She pressed her fingers against the damp innards, woodlice scattering, mud seeping underneath her nail beds.

Empty.

She slumped to the forest floor, wrapping her arms around her knees. The trinket she sought was no priceless heirloom by any means—yet still irreplaceable. A small token of joy where most around her felt false. More so than false—quite frankly, boring.

In twenty-three years, her mother and uncle had never allowed her beyond the northern forest. Jaguars roamed to the south, east, and west. Whether or not that was true, Anseurea had long since mapped every branch, stone, and patch of moss in the northern woods—so familiar, she often thought of naming them.

Through all her days wandering, shooting, and exploring, she'd never once seen another soul—only her dad. So who, if not him, could have taken it? Not a ghost. Not a beast. Certainly not a passerby. Who would bother with an old bow, garish with faux gems and feathers? It wasn't worth stealing, and besides, she and her dad had hidden it well—deep in the forest, beneath the roots and bramble.

Critters didn't take off with weapons. That bow had to be there.

A sharp crack of footsteps snapped through the trees, crushing brittle branches beneath heavy tread.

Her dad walked like his boots were filled with boulders. Even if she couldn't hear the man clearly from Ellace, he was the only person who would know to meet her beside the place where they once stored their treasure.

When he met her side, breathless, he said, "A full week you've been comin' out here expectin' that thing to be full again."

Had it been a week? It felt like both a year and a day. She yawned. "I thought Mom sent you on an errand."

Warm aromas of sweet bread, butter, cinnamon, and apples ripened early from their orchard wafted from his bag. Anseurea rummaged for his latest creation.

"I'm takin' some apples and muffins into town." He shrugged. "She wants me to give a gift to some kids she knows who got engaged."

His words reminded her she had no partner—not that she wanted one anyway.

Nothing could be accomplished alone, certainly not a house, a home, a plot, a business. How would one tend the fields and the horses and the meals and the cleaning and make money for clothes? And what did she have? Nothing more than apple trees her parents cultivated and grew from seedlings. That, and her family. She had her parents, of course, and her aunt and uncle a short stone's throw away at the other side of the orchard, though not by choice.

Somehow, they made *alone* seem quite appealing.

Once, she stumbled upon a young man at the outskirts of town who thoroughly intoxicated her. They spent time together in the forest. He challenged her to a wrestling match which at first, she found quite exhilarating. Perhaps it was his way of laying his hands all over her without actually needing to show any fidelity. Though, when she pinned him for the third time, she lost all interest in his company. The least he could do was try to put up a fight.

Apparently, he had very little fight in him to speak of.

Luckily, her parents placed no pressure on her to find a partner. Not like the young adults in town, whose mothers and fathers played matchmaker. Anseurea's family never even introduced her to a potential partner. They were quite content to have her live with them indefinitely.

"Do you want to come with me into town?" asked her dad.

She hesitated. The answer was yes and no, all at once. Worry washed over her. "But—Uncle Ebigan won't let me. He said not to go into town without him."

"What, is he your dad now?"

Sometimes it did seem like she had two sets of parents. The set she lived with—those who doted on her, who loved her. And the other set, who lived not a hundred yards away, whom her mom allowed free reign to discipline her even at her current age. And yes, she would like to go into town and see something, anything, that would distract her from the loss she felt. The stolen slice of rebellious freedom wrapped as a family heirloom.

Perhaps she needed to find a partner. Move a little further from them. Probably better living with the boy who couldn't pin her than the uncle who struck her for disobedience.

Her dad pulled her from her musings. "We can see if they have a bow, eh?"

"We can't afford one."

"I didn't say we'd buy it, I'd say we'd see. Just look at it. Longingly, you know?" His eyes twinkled. "Ask how much it is, pretendin' we have the coin."

She suppressed a laugh. The thought alone hurt her heart. There wasn't much to be seen out there—and besides her dad and mom, the bow was all she had and now it was gone—leaving her feeling both violated and disheartened.

"I'm sorry," he said, dropping his jest and wrapping his arm around her shoulders. "I know it meant a lot to you."

"One day, though, can you make another? A real one. Like the one we lost?"

"I wish I had the skills. My father made that one. Ebigan had no idea, that's the only reason we could keep it. If I made you a real one, he'd see that I suffered a swift death. You know how he feels about weapons."

How had her uncle governed all their lives so long? Even the life of her dad who married into this family?

"Ebigan would travel to The South Sea and find someone of a lineage who could wake me from the dead just so he could do it twice," her dad continued, dragging a thumb across his throat, jesting at the exaggerated form of death. "He'd never allow someone else to do the job he's been dreamin' of for decades."

"Certainly, he doesn't hate you that much." She laughed and pressed back, "If you died just once, I think he'd be fine."

He narrowed his eyes and grimaced his teeth. "Ebigan and Dyan want to speak with you tonight. Wouldn't tell me why. Perhaps afraid I'd tell you before they could."

The hair on her arms rose.

What an odd feeling. Even far away, even out of earshot, the simple mention of her uncle and aunt requesting her presence sent her insides fleeing. She squashed the sensation. She barely knew anyone in this small corner of the world. She shouldn't hold disdain for half her social circle.

"When you left, how were they?"

"They seemed ..." Her dad's round face scrunched. "Happy?"

A cavern splintered in her stomach. "Why does that make me feel worse?"

"A letter came. A courier from The South Sea in gray cloaks. Ebigan worked for Queen Navaera before she died, you remember." He shrugged. "He didn't say, but it might be related. They both smiled like they won a gold bar after."

Anseurea mused at the possibility. "Maybe a new position to take him far from here?"

He raised a brow that she swore said, *perhaps.*

+ ——————— · + · + · + · ——————— +

Aunt Dyan wrenched the door open. "Come in. Come in. We're celebrating!"

Her aunt's cold hands wrapped around Anseurea's shoulders, ushering her to the sofa. "Eran, go to the kitchen and make something sweet." She snickered to the stark room. "It's a wonder I still fit in these old gowns with your baking."

Despite her tease, Aunt Dyan never ate more than a bite of her dad's cooking—a minuscule taste of buttered roll torn between two bony fingers and chewed between red-stained lips.

She beamed, her craned neck held high. "Ebigan and I are finally traveling."

Uncle Ebigan perched as a bird on the edge of his wife's chair. She giggled, drumming her feet on the floor. "We depart for Islarourne at first light. We'd hoped you'd join us. See some of the beauty of The South Sea."

Anseurea's chest locked like a fist.

She and her dad had spent such a nice, quiet afternoon in the forest, eating, talking about everything and nothing at all. And now, the moment she walked in her own home—this?

The sudden baffling request left her slack-jawed. They wanted her to join them? The same woman who refused Anseurea's company when she went to town? The same woman who wished her to fetch her tea and tend to the fields far from her so they wouldn't have to speak?

Anseurea did her best to cover her shock. She had not even greeted her mom, and now she must create lies on the edge of the moment. "I ... thought ... The North was known for its beauty."

"We can visit the king's castle. See the fallen city of Niera and the cliffs over the sea at Biltak Bay." Aunt Dyan insisted. "Please say you'll join us. The journey will be nothing without you."

Her aunt had never been quite so happy, and briefly, her red grin reminded Anseurea of a marionette with strings.

Anseurea remembered the one lesson Aunt Dyan passed her of any merit. Gratefulness. "Thank you. The offer is extremely kind. Though, I would prefer to stay in Sanrial."

She lied well enough, at least better than her dad.

"A mere year ago, you pressed to travel on your own."

"My wishes have changed."

Another lie. Anseurea had wished to see the fields outside her home for years. She would start with the forest to the south, east, and west once she figured out how to handle the jaguars and found a weapon. The world was a dangerous place. To many people with powerful lineages of which she possessed none. Then, maybe she could see the mountains. Or perhaps, if she became far braver, one day, the sea.

At their empty stares, she continued, "Mom might wish to join you instead."

Her mom did not reply to her suggestion. She fixated on the floor, tresses of her auburn hair falling around her cheeks. Her knees twitched while she gripped her hands atop her black skirt as if in prayer.

Aunt Dyan's marionette-like lips still formed an upward angle, mimicking a smile, but something darkened in her eyes, an expression Anseurea could not place. "Don't be ridiculous. Everyone wishes to travel. See the world."

At the word *ridiculous*—the way it tugged, the sheer shock dripping from the edge of the *ous*—the hair on Anseurea's arms stood on end. Her mom's hollow expression, her aunt's strange behavior. The oddness of it all.

"You have never ventured more than a few hundred yards from your home, yet you wish to go on a months-long journey." Anseurea attempted to conceal her distrust, planting a pleasant smile across her cheeks. "Tell me, if everyone wishes to see the world, why now? And why so far?"

Uncle Ebigan draped his hands over his wife's shoulders. "Always the curious one." His scalp had conquered much of his forehead, and he had slicked back his black hair to retain visibility of the narrow pass. His pinched lips and weak chin unnerved her, especially when he carved a false grin, requiring her unwavering alliance and gracious acceptance. "I'm called away on business matters to Islarourne. We thought it might be a good opportunity to spend time together."

"The business of apples calls you to the king's castle?" The words poured out far harsher than she wished.

His smile stiffened, and his voice deepened. "I did not always tend to an orchard."

Anseurea clutched her cool ceramic teacup. She leaned over, whispering, "Mom?"

Had her mom not heard the request? Had she been so dragged into her own thoughts that she could not save her daughter from this *ridiculous* request?

"Mom?"

Her mom kept her gaze fixed on her black leather shoes while her dad tasted batter in the kitchen from a wooden spoon. She was on her own to refuse this off-putting endeavor.

"We will delay our journey by a day," said Uncle Ebigan, regaining his positive tone. "Give you a chance to reconsider."

"Thank you, though, that won't be necessary. Again, thank you for the invitation. I wish you safe travels on your journey."

Anseurea stood, wishing to shake off whatever vile mood settled over this room and run like hell for the trees. "Please excuse me; I need to check on Arylana. I don't believe I properly secured her reins when we returned this afternoon." Another lie.

Voices came from behind her—rebuttals, ignored. She slammed the door with sharp ferocity, hoping no one would dare follow. Outside, she released the air in her lungs with a huff. The tension in her shoulders eased. She would never travel with her aunt and uncle to The South Sea or anywhere else; the matter needed no further consideration.

I can't imagine. Trapped in the confines of a carriage for weeks. Forced conversations. Life lessons.

Shuddering, she departed for the one place she knew no one would search for her.

+ ——————— · + · + · + · ——————— +

Anseurea sat with her knees bent up below her aunt and uncle's kitchen window, plucking blades of grass. Certainly, her dad would search for her. Whenever she was not by his side, he looked for her and, more often than not, found her.

After the less-than-desirable interaction with her extended family, the hours passed like molasses, and soon, a dirt hole rested where the grass once lay. The alone time she craved was now tainted, filled with a repetitious loop of the conversation and looming invitation she couldn't forget.

Each passing moment, she expected Aunt Dyan's shrill voice behind her or the back of Uncle Ebigan's hand across her cheek. Perhaps this time he'd use a closed fist instead. The punishment would come; it was only a matter of time.

After long hours in the grass, the door creaked open, then closed. She resisted the urge to peek. They'd see the whites of her eyes.

Uncle Ebigan's voice reverberated through the wall. "It'll be fine."

Aunt Dyan responded—Anseurea knew the piercing edge of her voice well—but she spoke too low, too fast.

Something was missing. Something was wrong. Her aunt never smiled quite like that. She never wanted to spend time with Anseurea. She never wanted anything to do with her.

"A thin provocation is all I need. Thin as a hair," assured her uncle. "In the morning, it'll all be over."

The two shuffled from the kitchen to the bedroom, their dialogue melting into muffled tones. Their line of conversation did nothing to dissuade

Anseurea's suspicions. In fact, now she had much more for the gears in her mind to churn.

Across the lawn, her dad held a torch above his head, leaning into the orchard, speaking halfway between a yell and whisper. "Anse? Where are you?" Sweat beaded his brow against the orange glow. Momentary guilt passed for making him search in vain. She expected he would have given up his pursuit by now, taken to bed, knowing she didn't want to be found.

"Dad," she whispered. "I'm here."

He rushed to her side, his round face dense with fear, his chin quivering. "Where did you go?" He shook his head, correcting. "Doesn't matter. Somethin's wrong." He took her hand, pulling her toward their home. "Your mother. She hasn't moved. When I came home, she wouldn't move. She's in the chair all frozen like a statue. Just said, 'Find her. Now.'"

The hair on her arms lifted.

With every step, her fear mounted until she pressed her way into her home, finding her mom wide-eyed, staring blankly at the cold fireplace. Her lip hung open ever so slightly.

"Come inside," she muttered, "quickly, now." Her body moved in stark contrast to her rushed, panicked voice.

Her mom had lit no candle or fire for light. The room darkened into mere shapes of gray and navy silhouettes.

"Have you moved since I left?"

"You must listen." Her mom perched on the chair edge, leaning a worn empty teapot, filling her cup with fresh air while steadying the lid against her trembling fingers. "Act normal. Act as if all is well." She was no bold woman—never one to speak out of turn or offer orders. She grinned widely, her teeth gleaming against the dark. "They watch you."

Anseurea's stomach plunged.

The words hung in the air, like breath suspended in the stillness.

Giant tears coursed her cheeks, black paint sinking upon her lashes. "They most likely watch now as I speak. You must act as if all is well." She inhaled, securing her facade. "The letter Ebigan received from Islarourne. It was from King Barrard. My brother was not the one the letter summoned." Her mother met Anseurea's eyes with a firm and unwavering intensity. "The king summoned you."

The room chilled.

The words her mother spoke must be untrue; she must be confused. But ... why else would her uncle insist Anseurea accompany him on his journey?

Why else would her aunt wish to spend weeks in a carriage at Anseurea's side?

And yet—why would the king summon her?

"The king means to reclaim his property. To do the work his mother was not bold enough to do. The order was plain—if you do not go with Ebigan and Dyan of your own free will. Ebigan has direct orders to execute you on the front lawn by any means necessary."

The words impaled her like a steel blade to the chest.

The cold room now appeared foreign, the empty hearth, the smell of baked muffins in the kitchen—all as if she had not lived there her entire life. The shadowed, tufted chairs were suddenly not the ones she snuggled into as a child when reading. Her uncle, often unkind, seemed incapable of such a thing. Or was he?

"The South Sea isn't safe for you. Never has been. Never will be," continued her mom. "The old rulers of Rabinor and those who believe in the old ways won't care for your safekeeping. I know in my gut they wish to see your heart torn from your chest—no matter if they say they want to see your true nature. They have no mind of their own. They'll only believe the old stories. The rumors. They'll believe you're vile and always will."

Vile? Me?

"No jaguars live in this forest, not the kind with fur, at least. Hunters guard the forest to the south, east, and west, tasked to your watch and you alone. They have always been there. Since the beginning. The reason you have never been permitted there. The reason I only allow you north. Always watching."

Why would they watch me?

Her mom glanced over her shoulder. Her dad sat at her side, his breath irregular, a hand over his chest, wearing a gaping bottom lip.

"They stole you and the others. The soldiers. From your parents in The North when you were a baby. Gave you to Ebigan. They were meant to raise you themselves, my brother and his wife." Her lips scrunched, and she shook her head at the foul thought. "Dyan couldn't do it. She wished you dead, even as a baby who couldn't sit unassisted. She marked you from birth. They all have. They're afraid." Her tears began to dry, and she whisked a hand across her cheek.

Anseurea swallowed. *Stolen from my parents when I was a baby? Wished me dead?*

Her mom's shoulders perked with pride. "I took you from them."

Anseurea's mind swarmed with thoughts so tumultuous, she could not land on one question to speak aloud. She sat motionless, chills upon her spine, a stone statue upon a worn sofa in the darkness.

"You leave the moment I say. Do you hear me? Take nothing. If you see Ebigan or Dyan, say you lost your journal in the forest. You're going to look for it. Walk as you would normally. Pack no bag. No food. I untied Arylana. Her reins are looped over the fence beside the barn, and she wears her saddle."

Her dad shook his head, speaking through his confusion. "Areya, you sound insane. What are you sayin'? Ebigan found her abandoned."

"No. No. That's the story they told you both."

Her mom did not divert her eyes or listen to her dad's pleas—first hushed and then escalating in volume; she continued, undeterred, "Go due north. Your dad has taught you to watch the stars, yes?"

Anseurea nodded—a slow and heavy weight to her agreement.

"Don't stop. Don't even slow. Not even for sleep. They won't yield. You won't yield, either."

Her mom issued this statement as an order, perhaps the first order in her meek life. Or, now that Anseurea knew her mom took her from Ebigan as a baby, the second.

"Do you understand me? *They know who you are.* Who you are meant to be. Go north until you reach the forest's edge—then due west toward the setting sun. Ride until you are far from sight unless you hear the bells. When the bell rings ... the order has been given."

What order? Why will they not yield? Who are they? But more importantly ... who am I?

Her parents began to argue, their words muted into mere silhouettes hissing in the darkness.

Anseurea righted her posture, taming her thundering heart. The matter of acting normal brought the nuances of her body into focus. She repeated to herself, whispering while her brain reconciled the details in the dark. Her fingernails tapped the ceramic with each passing thought. *Run now. Run north. Don't turn around. Arylana. The saddle. The king. Property. Bells.*

Execution.

Her mom clasped Anseurea's hand, and the world regained focus. Their eyes caught, her mother's chocolate eyes lost to the darkness.

"You must know I've loved you profoundly. It never mattered that you didn't share my blood. The name of your birth—Lenora Ebronds Varan. Repeat it to me so you don't forget."

In between names, she muttered in uncertain tones, "Lenora ... Ebronds ...Varan."

Her mom commanded, "Again."

"Lenora Ebronds Varan."

"Again!"

"Lenora. Ebronds. Varan."

"Remember it well and never repeat it to a stranger. Find your family. Rumors speak of an older relative of yours west of here. I know nothing of the other children." Her mother embraced her. "And hide your eyes."

An older relative? Other children? How do I hide my eyes?

In Anseurea's confusion, her haze of information, she sank into the warmth of her mom's embrace. The background faded. Her dad's shouting, her rapid pulse thundering into her ears, her new name, her fear—all melted away. This same embrace, felt last at this depth in childhood when she scraped her knee climbing trees, and her mom's arms were all she needed to feel whole again.

She should withdraw from the peace and follow the instructions given. Should they truly watch, they would see out-of-character intimacy. But before she could unwind, metal rang in the distance, dense and reverberating in an otherwise still night.

Gonnnggg.

Ebigan and Dyan.

If she felt her mom's strange behavior, they certainly felt it, too. They suspected she would betray them.

Her mom's face contorted at the sound as metal shards coursed through her heart. Her mom held her tighter, tighter, tears soaking her auburn hair until they could not tell one from the other, trapping salt against the skin at her shoulder.

Breathe.

Emotions coupled with her feeble understanding of the instructions became irrelevant when the bell rang; the execution order had been given.

Her mom gripped her cheeks. "Never listen to what they say of you. You are curious and smart and wonderful. You'll never be death walking amongst the living. Run! Now!"

Without thought, she obeyed, flying through the threshold in a blind flash.

Gonnnggg.

She dashed from the dirt path, through the apple trees, her focus homed in on the forest break and her untied black mare. Shouting faded. Stomping faded.

Gonnnggg.

As she rose atop the saddle, she dared to glance south. In the distance, watchers scurried, and harsh cries resounded. Orange flames lit the distance. Archers on horseback charged from the forest, primed for the bell's resonating call. An arrow landed on the ground, a body's length away. Arylana pranced on panicked hooves while her dad scampered through the mayhem.

Gonnnggg.

She spurred Arylana.

Why had she hesitated? When her mom said she should run, she should have run at that moment. Why had she held her embrace so long?

As Lenora breached the wall of northern trees, arrows whistled as they split the air, metal cascaded into the dirt, a broadhead slammed into her open flesh, and blood poured.

CAVEATS

B renor tucked beneath his wool blanket in his trousers and thread-
bare boots, pretending to sleep. The prior two evenings, Ariaas
had opened his bedroom door, closed it, and left the groundkeeper's
cottage without a word in the black. Each one of those nights, Brenor
had been too laggard in dressing himself to catch his grandfather's
sneaking. The man rarely shared much with Brenor; his secret dealings
were yet another in a long line of mysteries.

The room lay dark, aside from the faint gleaming of stars. Winds
rattled the window, demanding Brenor's attention, and he shoved the
pillow over his ears. He groaned. While he lay awake in the nonrhyth-
mic clatter, he assured himself he'd secure the window at sunrise. As
the rattling eased, the old door to his room creaked on its brass hinges.

He meant to attend to the door as he meant to attend to the window. Between Ariaas's endless combat training, building the perimeter traps, cooking and cleaning—very little time remained for home
improvements.

On the other side of the door, feet shuffled, cloth moved, and the
front door to the cottage opened and closed with a *thwump.*

Curious.

Tonight is the night. He won't slip away.

In the living room, Taren groaned and stretched his paws, his
milky fur tangling into the fibers of the sofa. The dog swelled with
snores, followed by sputtering. Brenor chuckled. Taren must be chasing something nimble in his dreams. He draped a bit of leather over
his bare shoulders as a cloak. Spring had not driven out the southern
winds of winter from the mountains across the sea, and he knew better
than to be caught outside in nothing but his skin.

Outside, Ariaas had vanished.

Silently, Brenor glided toward the stables, pausing only to adore the vast presence of Aroun Vaer's worn castle. Even in her state of neglect, foliage creeping into the windows and wooden boards barring the door, Brenor found her magnificent. The sight filled him with awe no matter how many vines coiled into her towers.

Ten minutes into his pursuit, Brenor's stomach soured.

His first and most formative lesson from Ariaas: *always listen to your instincts*. He closed his eyes, breathing in the damp night air. The tugging pulled away from the castle. He drew the leather tight over his shoulders, turning toward the northern trees.

Of the four Varan children—two brothers, two sisters—only Brenor remained free. Though, *freedom* was a relative term. His legs strode Aroun Vaer unshackled, true. He ate whenever he wished. He remained un-enslaved. He evaded torture, at least in the traditional sense, unlike his brother and sisters, or so he presumed.

Brenor, himself, struggled to believe the prediction. However, those ancient stories had grown fangs. The fangs grew claws and legs to stand on. Some days, Brenor was uncertain if he was inherently a good man by birth or if determination alone would make it true. The prophecy could never come to fruition if he studied how to be kind, know right from wrong, and be a moral man.

But the swelling guilt that plagued him kept him in chains.

The whispers said he would be incapable of reason and unable to be tamed. They neglected to specify a date, only repeating the terms: savage, brutal, wild. Today, Brenor was no Monster of Havoc. And waiting for this demon to arrive—to consume his very being—ate him alive every night and again each morning.

Today, he was just ... *him*.

Through the edge of trees, frail moonlight diminished under the roof of heavy oak branches. Leaves long dead and dropped to the forest floor ground into the dirt, returning to soil again through the few snowfalls of winter.

Brenor navigated the intertwining branches with vast strides, careful not to tumble in the darkness. He scolded himself for forgetting his balanser, the light he purchased from a traveling Jolisard in Ellace some years ago with his last gold coin.

How could his grandfather gain so much ground on him in such a short time? And in the darkness?

He tilted his head to the side. At the far edge of his sight, a silhouette moved against the night.

Finally.

Ariaas wandered into the long grass, shifting clumps of dried mud and shed leaves with his boot.

When Brenor approached, Ariaas shouted into the darkness, "You shouldn't follow old men. I keep a dagger in my sock even while I sleep for such instances."

Brenor chuckled. "And you should not spy on grown men as they sleep. How often do you do that?"

Ariaas rested his elbows across his bent knees, the deep crease between his brows scrunched. "Not much. Only five or six times a night since you were three."

Brenor gazed into the starry night. "Do you sit this way often?"

"Only when I feel like pondering the meaning of our vast solitude," jested Ariaas. His tone grew solemn. "No. No, I do not. The spring winds are here—the twenty-third western wind. I can't sleep. My hope rises with the warm air and disappears the same. It's playing cruel games."

"We are awake for the same reason, then. I could not sleep through the pounding of the winds on the window." That and an overprotective grandfather checking on him like he was still a toddler. He was a man, after all. Wasn't he?

Brenor nudged a rock with his untied boot, feeling the movement of pebbles beneath the thinning sole; he knew they both kept tight words they were not sharing with the other.

"Thaesla will search for them in two days. Every month, without fail." Ariaas claimed they would free Brenor's siblings the twenty-third spring—a matter he repeated many times throughout the fading decades. However, his grandfather had not traveled for many years to Mount Reldor to see a glimpse of Arienne in her chains or Mount Ohbrolis to see if Thealor was still alive.

"But Thaesla has never found anything. Please tell me why you believe we will find them now. When the spring wind changes on the twenty-third year?"

Ariaas's face crinkled, searching for an appropriate answer. He shrugged. "Wishful thinking."

Brenor bit back a groan, searching for a way to reword the same question, hoping for a different answer. Certainly, Ariaas possessed more information than mere wishes. His grandfather was snarky, hungry, fearless, grumpy, and a hardened guardian of his grandson—but never wishful. And never so oddly specific.

Brenor gripped his hair and tugged. "Have we lost our minds?"

Ariaas snorted a laugh. "I lost my mind and my heart some decades ago! Scattered it like salt all over—Lake Kailael, Mount Ohbrolis, Mount Reldor ... Wesilea." He sighed. "All we have is a thin hope to cling to. A singular hope I have been holding onto for decades."

"Hope, yes, and four horses," Brenor prodded. "And vast amounts of land to our name. And a sad, broken castle." He gazed at the pale reflection of blackened sky and stars on the castle's high windows.

"We are no more insane than those who took you. They believed the prophecy of the Canen Dera would come to pass. They believed you would destroy us all. Ha! Fools." His grandfather spoke as much with his hands as his projecting voice. "Their belief was never based on logic, only power. The reason most people do anything is for more power, more money, more land. They wouldn't let any of you rise and threaten such a thing. Even when four were born, not five. Fools. Such idiocy can't be rationalized with."

Brenor slumped onto his back on the grass. Throughout the years, he heard plenty of his grandfather's opinions on the matter. He would rant for hours if given a stage.

"I've chosen to believe their freedom will soon be upon us," Ariaas continued. "Too much has happened throughout the years I couldn't ignore. Even if I wished to. I'm telling you—you must trust me. The winds have changed. So will their fate. We'll soon find a way to free them."

All Brenor knew of Arienne, Theo, and Lennie was rooted in the scattered stories Ariaas told when the whiskey numbed him enough to speak of it. Even the memories of those stories faded now, as a dream he had not dreamed in many moons: giggles in the garden's late afternoon sun, hiding in the brush. The scent of lavender and rose refused to fade even when he passed the gardens now, dead and blackened like charcoal. Brenor suspected his grandfather's stories convinced him he smelled the long-dead flora—or perhaps a tiny root held onto life when all else around it died.

"Soon, we'll stop sitting idle. As I trained you, we'll train them, so they won't be captured again. The South Sea and the Yurelan will leave us be at Aroun Vaer. Never the wiser."

"We will have our family home." Brenor allowed himself a moment to bask in the hope offered. His life might truly begin—all of theirs, really. "Perhaps we can fix the castle when they come home? We could live there once more." His excitement rose at the prospect, glancing over the high walls.

Ariaas nodded. "Thealor would be happy."

In the black night, a white silhouette displaced the long grass. Tall shoulders slumped with an exhausted gait as Taren slogged through the field. The enormous dog's face drooped. He thrust himself between Ariaas and Brenor, dropping his weight onto the ground in a *thud*.

Brenor wiped fur from his tongue, moving to avoid a heavy elbow in his side. Taren acted unaware of his space and size, a herding dog made for the mountains. When Brenor found him in the snares, he was no more than a cotton ball of fur the height of his hand. Taren's good fortune was that Brenor had built the traps to ensnare something much more significant.

Ariaas closed his eyes, again whispering to himself in the Old Tongue, "kalilar laneviu te thevay. ere untem gean thero dih larardone rhineru." His words could be a wish on the moon or a prayer, should he be a praying man.

The wind taunted. Gusts pressed Brenor's skin, western and warm, for an instant before they died. The three sat this way for some time in silence. Silence, crickets, and the heavy snores of Taren while the wind played its cruel games.

Brenor wished he knew the cadenced language. "What words did you speak?

Ariaas stood, brushing the dirt from his trousers. "Worries for another day. Come on. Let's go home. We may get a couple of hours of sleep. The winds just changed today, and the wait is already torturous."

"I'll check the northern traps on the way," Brenor suggested. "Less to do tomorrow." Hopefully, that meant Ariaas would sleep when the sun arose, and they could both take a day of rest.

His grandfather had built the interior perimeter in his younger years, swinging blades and snares spiked with toxins to protect Brenor from the hunters. He never knew how many hunters came and never asked Ariaas where the bones went. He only knew poachers arrived at their lands when Ariaas returned home bathed and in fresh clothing, and Brenor had to swallow the lump in his throat, knowing another life had been lost in the pursuit of his.

When he grew old enough, Brenor became a skilled inventor. Now, his creations spanned the exterior perimeters. And since they had been built, years passed since they had found a body.

Brenor dreamed the world forgot him.

However, this did not deter their dutiful rounds.

As they traveled, Brenor checked the steel frames, the teeth strong enough to catch a grizzly and snap bone. Along the shallow northern break of trees, these traps were random, not circling their home as the other two boundaries. So long as he did not witness the act, he rationalized death by this nature—when the hunters passed well beyond the signs, blades at their belts were meant for his heart.

Above the hill of long grass stood a lone sycamore. Birds shrieked and cawed, scattering in varying directions, fleeing on furious feathers. Brenor rushed toward their location, carefully avoiding the wired lines he knew so well, ducking beneath the low-hanging branches and gliding beyond the rocks in the long grass.

Silence.

The grass rustled in the night breeze, and dots of black wings fluttered against the sky.

At the edge of the breeze, the air tasted of iron, and his pulse hastened.

Ariaas dashed toward the lone tree.

Brenor was unable to force his legs to follow. The world accelerated and slowed all at once. He heard no screams, witnessed no torches for light, or smelled the burning flame. But there was blood on the air, of that much, he was sure. Had the hunters found him again?

He forced himself to trudge forward.

Ariaas extended his hand as he drew close. "Don't go further."

Brenor rubbed his lip and pressed his hand against his chest as if it could slow his pulse. "Did someone get caught in the traps? Is it a person? A soldier?"

Ariaas shook his head, his bristled brows tightening over his eyes.

What was worse than a person?

Brenor pushed past while Ariaas cautioned, "Brenor—don't go further. Go home, boy!" His grandfather gripped his arm, securing Brenor's attention until he shrugged him off.

Ariaas implored, "I need to end her life quickly. She's suffering."

Air rushed from Brenor's lungs.

She?

Brenor had a complex relationship with death. He could set a snare for food and justify if his dinner received a swift execution, but he could not watch it die.

Taren whined inches from his heels examining the blood-smeared, flattened grass. Whatever left the signs of struggle was large, be it woman or beast. His thunderous panic would not leave the incident to the imagination.

Some steps further, he found her—a doe.

She lived, though she lay split open, a wound by slashing claws and teeth. Organs of her abdomen splayed across the crushed golden grass, tufts of hair smashed. Brenor rushed to her side, touching her wounds as if he could stop a rushing river. A fly landed atop her pupil, refusing to move no matter how she twitched.

Lions of Dhaesreaon's mountains did not often make it so far east; bears, the same. He did not suspect them, lest their cubs were threatened. Only a few animals prey on a doe in these lands. Only a few passed beyond the exterior perimeter and into the fields. Whoever attacked her did not matter; she would die regardless. They would die, too, a predator who wandered into the wrong land.

"It won't corrupt you to end her suffering. We can use the rest of the meat."

Death at his hands would be mercy. His childhood vow not to kill should not pertain in this instance, not while she suffered, not while she lay wounded beyond repair.

Brenor hesitantly nodded. *Mercy.*

The doe eased under his quivering palms, her low groans and minute movements waning. He drew a dagger from his belt, light steel with a brown leather grip.

"You won't be in pain soon."

When he began training at five, Ariaas gifted him this blade after he boarded up Aroun Vaer Castle and left her to nature's claims. Brenor still recalled the echoes of Ariaas's hammer against the iron nails, the closing of the colossal building, and the horses scattering into the fields. They had walked straight to the stables when he finished. Ariaas placed the heavy dagger into his hand, saying, *'You will make it part of your arm if you wish to survive.'*

The blade rested before the doe's heart while Brenor trembled.

"I am a gentle man," he whispered, "This ... is mercy." Though he stuttered when the *m* quivered from his lips. If he repeated the words enough times, he might begin to believe them, though something inside twisted violently.

The shaking dagger held the position before Brenor released his grips, dropping the blade in the grass.

Death at his hands would have been merciful.

"Go on. Go home," Ariaas uttered. "I won't let her suffer further. Leave if you don't want to see it." Brenor waited for his grandfather to chastise him for his weakness, the pristine blade in his blood-stained hands, though no other words came from Ariaas's lips. Perhaps he would save his lecture for the cottage.

Brenor loathed death: the concept, the fact, witnessing, sadness, grief, the end. A mercy killing should not turn him into the darkness he feared, but he could not help but worry. *What if I like the feel of death on my hands?* He shook his head. *No.* He would not give himself the option.

He dashed toward the trees, wiping his cheek across the fabric at his shoulder and removed the muddle of blood, sweat, and tears beside his eye. His fingers stretched wide, not to feel the warm flesh sticking together.

Beyond the forest break, he came to a small stream, washing the blood from his hands, careful not to glance into the water and his reflection in the starlight. No part of him wished to see a mirror. He did not want to be reminded of what his vibrant blue eyes meant. His gaze would not meet his hands either, the blood drying brown and floating as paint across the rippling water. Instead, he examined the branches above, the breeze swaying them across the canopy and brushing into one another while he tried to control the lump rising inside his throat.

There was something about the moment with the doe—the lack of control, or too much control, or too much deafening silence in the field, or the blood—he could not decide. Something was all too much, all at once.

Brenor repeated, "I am a ... *gentle* ... man." Ripples of red blood lapped the pebbles below his boots. "I. Am. A gentle man."

He would repeat the words as many times as it took to believe them without the twisting feeling.

However, his body knew his mind spoke lies.

Ariaas returned to the cottage bathed, in a fresh cotton shirt and trousers. In silence, the two finished a stew of rabbit and cabbage. Brenor rocked in his chair, on the same legs Taren gnawed as a pup to near nubs complete with teeth marks and splinter shards.

Ariaas dropped his plate onto the kitchen counter, wiped his beard on a cotton cloth, and tossed it onto the plate. "I've been thinking about your vow."

"Can we please not discuss this now?"

"I only mean to say there should be certain allowable caveats. More specific details, you know?" Ariaas spoke with calloused hands, eyebrows, and brown eyes, as much as his lips. "A blanket remark, 'I shall not kill.' It's a little ... broad. At least broad for someone in your particular position. If you refuse to defend yourself, you'll make the hunter's job much easier."

Ariaas wandered beyond the small sofa, a low-smoldering fireplace, the table, and two imperfect chairs. Books lay on the shelf on their sides in horizontal stacks, unorganized to the unknowing. His grandfather found what he searched for, handing Brenor a quill and blank paper rolled and tied with tan grosgrain ribbon. He removed Brenor's unfinished plate from under his chin and tossed it clattering into the kitchen.

"We'll make it more reasonable, don't you think? Your vow not to kill."

His grandfather nodded at the page; he would dictate, Brenor would write. "I shall not kill for fun," he jested, pointing a wary finger, "certainly should be first."

Ariaas paced, adopting a level of professionalism to his task. In his hand, his own quill. Perhaps the action made him feel important or helped him generate ideas. At Brenor's lack of urgency, his grandfather pointed the wooden quill at him. When he still did not move, Ariaas ushered him with his hands the way one would shoo a stray cat from the stoop of their porch.

Brenor began to roll his eyes before he stopped himself. He should oblige. Ariaas was relentless with this manner of thing. The only way out was through. Though he had made it the entire day without the lecture he had been waiting for, he couldn't determine if this was better or worse.

He picked up the quill and wrote, *'I shall not kill for fun.'*

When Brenor raised the quill from the paper, Ariaas continued, "I shall not kill a captive without asking a specific line of questioning first." He watched the ceiling, his fingers pointing as if the line of questioning was written upon the wooden beams. When they failed to appear before him, he waved the thought away. "We can write the questions when we finish here."

"Irrelevant. I would never take anyone captive."

"What if someone told you they didn't like the silly swoosh of your hair? Or ate all the breakfast and did not leave any for you? That justifies some minor level of captivity." Ariaas redirected his attention, deep in his task. "Moving on—*it's all right to kill for mercy.* If severe illness or suffering is involved."

Ariaas did not mention the doe. His knowing nod was enough.

Brenor muttered, "All right," writing in smooth ink along the parchment.

The cottage did not allow much space for his grandfather's pacing. He traipsed between the kitchen and the back of the sofa before turning around again, a few steps between the front door and back to the bedrooms with one additional oversized stride over Taren, who found the most inconvenient places to lay.

Ariaas aimed his quill at Brenor once more. "I'll put my grandfather out of his misery when his looks begin to fade."

Brenor stared at him, refusing to laugh.

"Write that. It's a good caveat." Ariaas stroked his salt and peppered beard. "One you'll never have to use." Between gloating and concealing, today was clearly a gloating day. The Endruas of Valesove matured slowly, in more ways than appearance.

"What of the people we find on our land?" Brenor asked. "The traps are not all lethal."

"Quite obviously, that depends on the path they arrive on."

"How is the path they arrive on of any consequence?"

"Should someone seek us via the fields or the forest, they have undesirable intentions. No one seeking to capture or kill would travel to their intended victim via a road. Especially not people seeking this family. You can't stay hidden on the open road—it's pure lunacy. If anyone is searching for this family with ill intent, they would stay hidden. Try to stay out of sight in the trees. The only possible exception would be if they tried to pretend they were of reputable means, only to be found later to be of terribly unreputable means—liars and spies. Then, I'll finally get to use the table you built for me. Where did you put it, by the way? I keep thinking of names for it. I'm currently going with *ere dere.*" Ariaas smiled with a devious grin. "It means 'The Terror' in the Old Tongue."

Brenor frowned. "I know what *ere dere* means."

Ariaas was so excited at the ridiculous prospect of a torture table, he never noticed Brenor never built it—or agreed to. Each time Ariaas mentioned it, he wished it to do something else fantastical; the far-off dreams of a tormented mind allowed too much time to wander. At one time, he wanted a tower of flames and gears for lowering scorpions from the western desert. Brenor waited until Ariaas's attention diverted elsewhere, much as a small child distracted by a shining toy. *Yes. Scorpions. Poison. Flames. Understood.* Months would pass before his grandfather returned to the idea of his torture table.

"And what of people seeking us with reputable means?"

"Impossible."

"You believe with unwavering certainty that no one will ever simply ... walk up the road?"

"Correct. Those with reputable means know not to come at all, and those with unreputable means would never take the road."

A laugh escaped Brenor's lips as he clasped his hand over his mouth. "You know the words you are speaking are nonsense, right? They will arrive however they arrive—via small caravan, the road, the forest, an army marching through the field."

"If anyone finds us from the road with honorable intentions, I'll dust off the finest whiskey I have." He returned to his pacing. "Next caveat: *it's all right to kill to protect myself or someone in my family.*" He stretched his arms over his head, exhausted from his deliberate pondering. "That should do for now, though we may need to add more later."

Brenor set the quill on the table. "I will add these caveats and do my best to abide by them. However, there is a condition ..." He crossed his hands over his chest. Perhaps he could get his way with the old man. "You must follow them, too."

"Me?"

"You kept me alive as a child when I could not defend myself. You have trained me. I can care for myself now."

"No." Ariaas's eyes widened. "No, no, no. Depth of training doesn't matter when you refuse to use it."

"Ah, but now you have given me good reason to, should someone need my aid." Brenor stared at him, a grin painted across his broad chin. He had Ariaas, and he knew it. "And with my new caveats, I will never go dark should I need to take a life by these means."

"Absolutely not. So much no. How do you expect us to bring Arienne, Thealor, and Lenora home? There will be death when we find a way to free them, that I'm certain."

"Your concern appears to be covered by"—Brenor trailed his finger across the dried parchment—"caveat number five."

"I'll kill the guards at The Reldory who keep Arienne without hesitation. And I certainly cannot be held back by loopholes when I blow a hole under Mount Ohbrolis." Ariaas eyed the whiteroot hanging in the kitchen. Brenor had heard him repeatedly plan to tear Thealor from the glass castle before he lit it ablaze and watched the mountain crumble. "We've never even found Lenora. I'd kill someone for her location, which isn't a caveat. *Oh,* actually, write that one, too."

Brenor crossed his arms over his chest, exaggerating a look of sympathy. "Sorry, killing for coordinates does not make the list."

"There are scenarios we are not thinking of," Ariaas pressed. "This is for you. I can't be tasked with your protection when I'm held back by such nonsense."

Brenor pushed the page toward him, a coy look in his eye. "Put your hand on the paper."

Ariaas shook his head.

At times, Brenor disliked his grandfather's banter, his pride, and joviality at the exact wrong moments. However, his thoughts drifted from the doe, the prophecy, and his brother and sisters. There was one final thing he knew his grandfather could not go without.

"Very well. Tonight was the last meal I make until you take the vow. Cold beans and raw tomatoes are all you get."

Ariaas scowled. "Is there any almond bread left? I can survive on almond bread for a week at least." He roamed to the cabinets in the kitchen. The spring air had not warmed enough for the berries to blossom this year; otherwise, the old man could have lived on those for a long time.

"You ate it all this morning after breakfast."

Groaning, Ariaas gathered his book from the side table and plopped into his worn chair.

Ariaas's stomach remained empty for two days until he found Brenor in the training grounds. He cupped his hands around his mouth, shouting so his voice projected across the distance between them. *"Fine!"*

Brenor smirked to himself. Food always did the trick. Ariaas maintained a good fight, but he knew soon enough hunger and rage would grow too much to bear.

"Fine, what?"

"I'll follow the vow," Ariaas roared, "loosely!"

BLOOD IN THE RIVER

He tossed an ashen curl back from his brow. "To rewrite the most weary
fate ... take haste now ..." His eyes filled with deep tears. "I wait. I am
present. Draped in grief, shadowed by silence."
She left the withered figure of a man and turned for the highlands.
He shouted at her back, "The hills are steep."

- *What Lies Beneath*, Faiseus Rancesla Auro, 1831

A riaas held his worn hands in the air. "I yield."

Brenor wiped sweat from his brow and adjusted the rolled-up cotton of his sleeves. "You are going easy on me today."

His grandfather rose from the dirt, dusted himself, and plucked a blade of grass from his teeth. His eyes bore heavy circles below them. Brenor had awoken the prior night to Ariaas leaving the cottage again, though Brenor had not been able to find him in the fields.

"Where do you keep disappearing to?"

"Problems for the old."

Brenor chuckled. "What does that mean?"

Ariaas turned toward the stables. "I was trying to sound wise and hope you did not ask any follow-up questions."

"It must be your exhaustion making you go easy on me!" Brenor shouted after him.

"Must be."

Brenor followed, returning his sword to the sheath and placing the brown leather on the table. He idly examined a clamp on the iron-barred trap Ariaas had found disturbed by a fallen branch two days prior, pretending he should be there. The trap gaged weight and stride length, ignoring anything smaller than an adult or large as a bear. Brenor prized this snare above all others, appreciating how even if built of metal springs, it seemed to possess a consciousness. He never wanted to find a ball of fluffy fur hanging amongst the sharp blades again.

He fiddled, attempting to repeat his query. "The winds changed days ago."

Ariaas wiped his blade with a dirty rag.

Say something. Say anything.

No question meant no answer—and Brenor meant to ask Ariaas a hundred questions, a thousand, perhaps. *What makes you believe we will save them? How? What are you waiting for? What are you not telling me?* Ariaas was rare to volunteer information, and he would bar the words sharply as the steel spikes of a trap when hounded.

Brenor needed to approach him delicately, though he grew tired of polite requests. He repeated, "Where do you go at night?" his voice dancing at the edge of pleading.

"ne'las lea mertes." Ariaas's reply was smooth and effortless, like melted butter. He repeated in the common speech, "Not your concern."

"Does Thaesla still search for Theo, Arienne, and Lennie?"

"Yes, and I told you this two nights ago." Ariaas's sharp voice insinuated that he would answer no further questions. He dropped the rag.

Brenor's heart sank as he watched Ariaas disappear along the dirt road.

That evening, Brenor sat in his frayed armchair, his stomach grumbling for a second supper.

The two hadn't spoken a word since the stables. Brenor hated the dense void between them. He licked his lips, choosing a topic he knew he might regret.

"I heard odd conversations in Ellace yesterday. Those I did my best not to pry, but wished to hear, nonetheless." Brenor idly flipped the pages of his long-worn book. "Talk of battles in the northern lands; King Barrard leaving the armies of Hanielle to their own devices though they request aid."

Ariaas's eyes remained locked on his novel. "And whom might I ask are the Northerners battling against? *Themselves?* Too much pride and too much anger in the north of Monera."

"Not amongst themselves. Their lineages have long been at peace. They say ... the Yurelan. They have means to move against the Gen Reaon."

"They're nothing more than a small band with radical ideas. Not enough to take over the Northerners." Ariaas chuckled. "You should've seen the stick of a man they sent to help me rescue you at the auction. The Gerideard named it the Gen Reaon for a reason. It's the *Iron Realm.* They're perhaps even stronger than the warring lineages of The South Sea, stubborn as they come, but most skilled with a blade and a bow. After the siege left you and the others gone, the Yurelan were depleted of their numbers. The Army of The South Sea crippled them. The Gen Reaon will hold strong, and the Gerideard will not tread lightly on them should they rise against them."

"Yet people talk, nonetheless. Their ideas grow roots from somewhere," Brenor cautioned. "And the Yurelan were crippled twenty-three years ago. What do you know of their numbers now?"

Ariaas fixated on his novels, for once, he opted for *What Lies Beneath* by Faiseus Auro instead of his traditional favorite, *Revenge and the Long Lie.*

Brenor swallowed a growl. "I cannot help but feel a darkness as of late." He probed for further words, hoping for a crumb of information to cling to. "Something's moving I cannot understand. The night rains feel heavy and the day sun bright, but even the sun cannot shine bright enough to erase the feeling looming over me."

Ariaas stirred in his seat.

"Is there a chance you are a long descendant of the Meiderie?" Brenor pressed. "The reason behind your belief we will find Arienne, Lennie, and Theo?"

"I'm not a Meiderie. And if I was, I would need to *sleep* to have visions in my dreams."

"Then there is no other way for you to know this is the year we will find them." Exasperated, Brenor leaned forward in his chair, unable to control the agitation in his voice. "I appreciate your wish to offer me hope, but this, too, has roots somewhere. All I can do is wonder where you find this information."

"Then, for the foreseeable future, you should be filled with enough wonder to forget the darkness you're feeling."

Should Brenor allow an audible growl, he would expect extra combat training and hours in the stable yard. Instead, he concealed his disappointment as best he could, blurting out what came next into his mind without thought of the consequences. "Do you think Canen Dera will come to pass?"

"If I had a gold coin for every time you asked me that—"

Brenor knew Ariaas's answer, yet he couldn't help but let the fear creep in little by little, day by day, like water seeping into his ears and filling him ever so slowly until he heard his reassuring words again.

Can I watch blood spill and keep my heart from spoiling? Will I ever need to?

Brenor's neck began to itch, and heat rose from his throat to his chin. His breath hastened. Every second Ariaas didn't reply with a proper answer, the worry crept from his stomach into his scalp; he expected to burst until his grandfather's words reassured him again.

"No." Ariaas seemed to sense this internal spiral. He sat forward in his chair. "You hear me? No. I never thought the Canen Dera would come to pass. *Never.* The original predicted five Masters of Death, bringing Monera to an end. Remember? And there are only four Varan children. From that matter alone, the prediction is hogwash. Not to mention you couldn't even kill for mercy." Ariaas winced at his own words.

The flooding anxiety abated, if only for a moment, though new worries were added while others vanished. He had wanted to save the doe from the final moments of pain. He had.

"Thank you," he replied. And mostly, he meant it.

A picture he had drawn as a child sat on the mantle. A family as he wished them to be, hands held between his sisters and brother, Ariaas in the center. Brenor trailed his fingertips over the stick figures, outstretched, hand in hand. Oddly, he never wished for his mother or father. He had no memory of them. Ariaas was both and everything. He always had been every day Brenor could recall.

What would a normal life feel like? A normal life with his brother and sisters? Any life other than one marked him from birth?

Brenor bit his lip. His children might have a different life ... if he had children. At twenty-six, he neared the age most married, and he had never laid eyes on a woman outside of those in Ellace and their closest neighbor, Mrs. Ebrolie.

"Do you expect I will marry one day?" Brenor asked this same question a year ago and the year prior. Brenor remembered his grandfather answering, *'It's better not to have divided attention.'*

Ariaas remained quiet, brows creased, and his drawn sights fixed on the flame.

A twisting feeling rose in Brenor's stomach. "You do not believe I will live long enough, do you?"

His grandfather stood, a deep sadness to his eyes, a finger held between the pages of his novel. He took in a deep inhale as if he might speak before he swallowed it, and left Brenor alone with his thoughts.

The flames danced in the hearth.

Perhaps one day, Theo would be home. They could check the perimeter traps together and carry Taren home when he tired. Perhaps Arienne would run into the garden again and care for him as Ariaas said she had. Perhaps one day, he might meet a woman, and she would see him for something other than what he was predicted to become. Perhaps a woman with dark wavy hair and dark eyes.

A flame burst above their caimeres, the vase crafted by Thaesla's hands decades ago. Cracks ran across the center, painted with scarlet and plum aurum blooms. The air above the vase grew orange, then black, the winds wiping into a hurried tempest until all became still.

A folded silver parchment with a crimson wax seal hung on display above the clay pot, indifferent to the laws of gravity.

Thaesla's seal.

Brenor's stomach rolled.

"*Ariaas!*"

His own voice frightened him. The world seemed to stop entirely in the time it took Ariaas to return to his side.

"It is the middle of the night." Brenor shook his head in disbelief. "Thaesla's letter should not be here until tomorrow."

Her correspondence had arrived so punctually it could time their day. Each gold scripted letter read the same: *The first, no change. The second, no change. The fourth, no location. All else is well in the West.*

They both stared slack-jawed as if the note was a viper that might inject them with venom.

"Read it," Ariaas urged, *"quickly."*

Brenor grasped the envelope from its perch and broke the crimson seal, tearing it without care and reading as if his life depended on the letters he would find.

"Rapidly the fourth races east to west. Hours to your north. Go immediately. You must meet her crossing before she breaches the River Realm. When she is safe, and all well, ride for Jaisett. I fear the West is no longer free."

His large hands held the shards of the envelope and let them drop onto the floor. Thoughts and words escaped him while his chest tightened into a knot. "Lennie?"

Ariaas grabbed his cheeks to garner his sole attention. "Do not think. *Move.*"

"You ... knew."

"Go, boy!" Ariaas shook him, his voice quick to snap him back to reality. "Now!"

The two scattered. Ariaas to the swords, Brenor to the horses.

+ ———————— · + · ✦ · + · ———————— +

Brenor and Ariaas galloped north furiously through the black night, beyond the border to Aroun Vaer, and well into the fields south of the Oak Forest. Hours passed before they reached the sloping hills and open plain.

Brenor tugged Belcen's reins. The stallion stirred beneath his saddle, prancing in the spring grass.

"How will we know where to find her?" Brenor's pulse raced. "Northern parallel is not exactly a precise location."

"*Not. In. The. Least,*" Ariaas seethed. "The letter said *she races*. It's reasonable to assume she's on the run. She would stay hidden. She wouldn't travel through the fields." His eyes ran over the grass and the bushes in the starlight. No land was suitable for a mile or more. "She runs east to west. Coming from where I wonder?" He dragged his hands over his cheeks. "That matter would've helped a great deal, *Thae*."

Brenor turned north. Barely visible through the rolling hills, he caught sight of the edge of a thick forest. "Say Livore."

"I hadn't realized we'd ridden so far. The Oak Forest is thick. It would provide cover," agreed Ariaas. "We split. You head northwest. Go deep into the forest. I'll go northeast and stay closer to the southern edge of the trees."

They nodded to the silent accord, separating without a further word.

Once parted, a tense search proceeded throughout the day, well beyond dusk and the departing sun. A sea of oaks blotted sunlight through the canopy of their branches.

Brenor stumbled upon a small, abandoned cave and a few animals, but no signs of a woman on the run.

How many hours until I find a genuine lead? How many hours could Lennie be on the run?

Brenor whistled a long *tru-lly* bluebird call while darkness surrounded. If he could locate Ariaas, they could rest in turns.

Silence.

An hour after he sounded the call, worry reared: no torch, light, food, and no map to know if he was even in her vicinity. He brought nothing to track Lenora with but hope and innate instincts. Now he would be awake for two nights. Brenor clenched his jaw. He forgot the balanser and the firestarter.

He should have been more prepared.

A line of orange flames freckled the black distance.

Lennie. Where are you?

Brenor crouched beside a thicket at the base of a fir root. A half dozen scouts searched to his north. Each man twenty paces from the next, their footsteps broke no branches, their breath silent. They trailed the length of trees in tight formation, torches illuminating their path.

Through the far trees, a man rode on the back of a dark stallion, long hair tied behind his back. He held large bundles wrapped in canvas fabric, replacing the archers' arrows. Belcen's neighs merged with their stallions' nickers, his deep coat blending into the night.

Once the hunting party was beyond earshot, Brenor whistled again: *tru-lly.*

Ariaas returned the call—two long bursts followed by the sounds of chirping—from the south, close to where the men with torches arrived. Brenor held his position.

Some minutes later, Ariaas found him, taking cover in the same thicket.

Brenor whispered, "Archers. They have restocked their supplies. Their quivers were empty. They have not captured who they sought." They would soon close in on their prey. He could feel it as confidently as the passing of time. Brenor's blood thickened. *"They are hunting her."*

Ariaas nodded in agreement.

For hours, they trailed the archer's flames in the black. In a clearing, the hunting party paused, the light from their fire forming a circle within which they rested.

Amongst the damp brush and heavy roots, Brenor surged to sleep against his will, jolting awake abruptly, finding Ariaas idly sharpening his blade. How long were his eyes closed against his wishes? His grandfather stood, gathering himself. Had the man slept at all?

The cold night smelled of fresh horse excrement and wet oak. Brenor pointed to the northeast, a cloud of his breath on the air, indicating the path Ariaas should take, still in the blackness. Heavy with exhaustion, Brenor handed Ariaas both reins. He was faster over rocks and fallen branches without the stallion.

Brenor trudged alone for hours, bound northwest as the sun swelled into the sky. Desperation spurred him, driving life into his weary legs. The fresh smell of the morning trees began to twist into the taste of stale and new blood in one.

The early sun peeked through the clearing of branches, illuminating the impression of a horse's shoe, fresh by a few hours in the muck. Brenor sprung over the rocks, scouring the forest floor. With each passing moment, the archers drew closer—this knowledge flowed like a current through his limbs. *I'm closer to Lennie than they are. For once in my life, I have the upper hand.* He sealed his eyes, concentrating on his instincts and the forest's thrum.

Breath.

Nickering.

Not a quarter mile ahead from her tracks, a black-haired mare at the edge of a stream.

The mare remained at the water's edge, not fleeing from his swift advance. When he arrived, he found blood dampening her dark hair, and four arrows wedged into her hip. Thick, brown blood smeared the saddle. Brenor trailed his fingers over her shoulder to the saturated brown leather. The archers hadn't missed their mark when they emptied their quivers.

"Not all this blood is yours."

He played through the scenarios—an injured woman would seek a place to hide. But a clever woman would move in the stream if she could walk.

He treaded into the stream, facing east. The feeble current flowed away from him. The water would only carry the weight of a body a short distance.

He would have seen her—he'd followed the stream for a mile or more. Brenor groaned and tugged on his cheeks.

Again, he whistled four high-low short bursts.

He waited and listened. His instincts wouldn't lead him astray.

He closed his eyes and breathed.

At the lack of reply, he turned west and trudged upstream. Perhaps this decision was the only thing in this life he was confident of. As he trailed her, the trees grew denser, and the folding hills steepened. He marched this way for some time, treading through the stream, ascending the rocks and short waterfalls.

Above him—a figure appeared through the young winding trees.

She'd avoided the thicket as he suspected, trudging through the shallow stream. She grasped her lower back with one hand, a heavy pressure against an arrow wedged in her flesh. A rock the size of a melon nestled in the crook of her other elbow, her deep chocolate hair in a mess of knotted braids.

Lennie.

His sister, lost for two decades, now stood before him, bleeding profusely into the forest.

INSTINCTS

"It is significantly more complicated than that," I replied. "You forget. I'm a ghost."

     - Diary of Daisirie Cabredd Mire, Volume 7, Entry 230

Lenora homed in on the footsteps—swift and light—a thin sole between the wearer of the boot and the brush of the ground through the damp morning of the forest. She raised the rock she'd stored in the crook of her elbow above her head, quivering. An embarrassing excuse for a weapon, certainly, but she was not in a position to be selective. The man lifted his arms in surrender, a sword secured at his belt, his back void of a bow.

Her heart thundered. Even if she could get a decent shot while light-headed, he was out of easy range.

The man appeared younger than the archers in Sanrial—not much older than she, with the strange brightness to his eyes she thought only she possessed. His clothing, tan and leather browns, as most in Valesove wore—though hunters had clever tricks.

There was only one certainty. Stopping meant dying. Dying by way of the arrow still wedged in her left flank, claiming the last of her blood, or by the archers' fresh supply.

Her mother's words echoed: *Don't stop. Don't even slow. Not even for sleep. They won't yield. You won't yield, either.* Though, now, against her will, she had indeed slowed significantly.

But she hadn't stopped. And in no world would she stop, even her sluggish gait, to consider this stranger's intentions.

She returned the rock to the crook of her arm. He could speak as she walked if he wished. With each step, pain seared from her rib to her leg. She limped, the jolting wood splintering with each step. Her heart bled for Arylana. If the mare had been able to carry her, she would have been far from the forest by now.

The man asked, "What are you doing?"

"What does it look like I'm doing?" she huffed. "I'm fleeing."

"Fleeing generally implies some level of ... haste."

"This is as much *haste* as I can currently muster."

"The archers will return soon," he pleaded. "I have seen with my own eyes six walking in lines in the forest before me. They rested for only a few hours, after searching most of the night. Their quivers are full once more."

What could this man possibly know about the archers? Unless he was there the night she was shot.

Lenora countered, "By my count, there were at least twelve."

"Then they split. If there are two, even more likely they will find you at this pace. You cannot hope to escape them."

"What would you have me do? I hid in the holes in the rocks until they passed." Perhaps not the best solution, but the best while options were minimal. Though getting into the crevice hurt something wild. She heard the archers and smelled their burning torches long before she heard this man. "They won't double back for some time."

"You hid until the first group passed, and you hope they will not double back for some time. The six I spotted were headed this direction."

Lenora's festering wound ripped open. The arrow had been wedged in her side for two nights and the brown stains on her shirt hardened. Her body trembled from the lack of food, and with each step, the trees moved before settling back where they belonged. The canopy taunted her, branches rustling with the wind and dropping foliage.

"My name is Brenor. Please. I know you do not know me, but I have come to help you. You can go wherever you wish once we are safe and out of the Say Livore. I will explain everything. Once you are safely away from the hunters."

Truthfully, she had no destination aside from heading west at a glacial pace. She wished to take any aid but also never considered herself a naive woman. How had she not known? How had she not seen it? Why did she ignore that screaming in her gut when Dyan and Ebigan were near? Had her father known or pretended to be shocked at her mother's revelation? She would be furious with herself if she trusted the wrong person when she needed aid in the forest. Suppose she walked right into the enemy's hands like a young lamb?

But who was the enemy, anyway?

Brenor followed one step to her sluggish four. "We have spent decades searching and failing miserably. *Please.* I will not let you die in the forest the instant we *finally* find you."

Lenora stopped her wading. He had spent decades searching for her? Who was this man? Again, she took notice of his eyes recalling the shallow sea and ice, should water find a way to burn. He appeared almost pained by her lack of response.

Around Ebigan and Dyan Uloen, she had a near constant sense of unease, whoever they were to her now. But there was never the opportunity to unearth why.

Do I trust a stranger in the forest when my life hangs by a thread? I can't make another mistake. Though something about him seems ... familiar.

"You should trust your instincts, listen to them," he said, as if he knew where her mind wandered. "They will not lead you astray."

"Tell me your name again."

"Brenor."

"No." It wasn't that she had forgotten in the short time; instead, she needed his truths, to see if her stomach twisted with his lies. "Your entire name."

"Brenor Ebronds Varan."

Ebronds Varan. The name Areya had given her as her own. The surname of one parent and the surname of the other.

Her brother—should he be truthful.

Her lip quivered. Did she truly have a brother?

Forcing away surfacing emotions, Lenora focused on her body. She investigated her injury; the arrow's tip, smaller than most broadheads, had torn through her hip above the bone, the edges flared at the end, meant to ravage the flesh should it be pulled backward. The arrow wedged in a tight space. She jostled it slightly to grasp a sliver of the pain her body would soon feel, nausea rising as a stone in her throat. The black feathers vibrated a hair.

Again, she took in the nuances of Brenor's creased brows and square jaw.

"If you have spent decades searching for me, you know my name." This was a silly question, and she knew as much. The archers knew her name, too. But would they go so far as to claim familial relation? Would they not simply execute, per their orders?

His hands outstretched; he stepped closer. "Lenora. Lenora Ebronds Varan ... just as mine." He did not break eyes with her. If he was lying, he was doing it rather convincingly. "I called you Lennie growing up. The *ora* part was hard for me."

Lennie.

She shook her head. The truth of his words, his relationship to her, and her trust in him was too difficult to determine when her life was at stake. Instead, she listened for her instincts among the soft sounds of the stream and the moving water. The smell of fire was further than when the archers passed but not gone altogether. If they caught her trail, her choice of weapon would do little to dissuade their orders.

A sudden idea came to her. "Will you remove the arrow?"

The blood drained from Brenor's cheeks. "I do not think that is wise."

"Please."

"You will lose a lot of blood."

"I can't go anywhere quickly—with you or otherwise—if it's still wedged in my side."

Brenor grumbled under his breath. He rubbed his lip, seeming to weigh her request. For a moment, Lenora suspected he might vomit on his boots. Then he tore the sleeve from his shirt and handed her the tattered cloth.

The blood slithered up her side, rising high on her brittle blouse. She inhaled deeply, unwilling to allow her thoughts to turn to what she'd lost and who this man standing before her was.

Don't think. Just breathe.

Birds chirped.

Brenor corresponded with the winged creatures, whistling a long sound of a bluebird in rehearsed melody. The song from his lips was indistinguishable from the birds perched outside her bedroom window. With one hand, he steadied the arrow's spine at her back. With the other, he carved at the wood with a dagger she hadn't realized he'd been carrying.

Pain surged with every blink, threatening to take her from consciousness to black while he carved into the arrow's spine. Footsteps drew near through the thicket. Horseshoes. Eight. Lenora raised her rock overhead, the same stance she took with Brenor, when a second, older man came into view.

"It is all right. He is with me." Brenor paused his carving to reassure her. He placed a hand on her shoulder and stared into her eyes. "Take a deep breath."

She inhaled through her nose. Brenor yanked the metal broadhead from her torso.

Lenora recoiled—her teeth gritted, muffling her shriek, before she covered the pouring blood with his cloth. Above her, another man held the reins of two horses, taking in her appearance. She choked down the bile in her throat, raising her weapon again, tilted to one side like a pot pouring tea.

The man attempted to retain his amusement. "What exactly is the purpose of the rock?"

"That I might defend myself," she sputtered through gnashed teeth.

"Do you mean to deflect incoming arrows with it? Personally, I would have gone for a large stick."

"Seems I lost the large stick back where I got shot." Lenora tightened her hold, though her arm weakened. She hadn't had all the time in the world while running and bleeding to survey the land for an appropriate weapon. "I'm certain the rock has many uses, some of which I haven't determined."

Brenor sighed under his breath. "After all these years ... that is the first thing you wished to say to her?"

Lenora asked, "What's your name?"

"Ariaas."

"Full name."

"Ariaas Haran Ebronds."

Ebronds. Her father, perhaps? Uncle? She shuddered at the thought of any man possessing the title uncle. Not the older relative to the West; he bore the looks of a man in his fourth decade.

Ariaas seemed to notice her contemplation, continuing his introduction. He placed his left hand over his chest, bowing theatrically. "Of the Endruas. The Enduring Body of Valesove. First and only son of Fabirin Sarvor Ebronds and Lanealyn Dackene Ellnas."

Brenor interjected, "He is our mother's father."

There it was. *Our* mother. *Our* grandfather. Lenora's sharp eyes eased. An Endruas. He *was* the older relative Areya mentioned.

Brenor packed the two sides of the arrow in his pack and scanned the area to ensure they left no trail. He grabbed a clean cloth from his satchel and handed the tattered rag to her. "Will you go with us?"

"I haven't decided."

Rustling leaves drew her attention. "There are only the two of us in these trees," Brenor assured her, "any other voices are not of our allies."

"I passed several at their backs not long ago. They've separated, making grid patterns from what I can see. I suspect they know you're injured, or they would've moved out of the forest by now." Ariaas added, "I left many tracks in varying directions. If fate is on our side, it'll confuse them for a bit."

"I will not beg you to leave. Though I will tell you, we are not leaving without you, and I do not want to fight these soldiers. We have weapons, yes, but—"

"You're injured and only have a stone for a weapon, and Brenor took a vow not to kill. Which is abysmal timing, should you ask me," Ariaas interrupted. He casually picked his teeth. "Which caveat covers being ambushed in the forest?"

"Not the time," Brenor growled.

"Well, they'll certainly find us with you two bickering about." But perhaps staying amongst the trees was unwise. "Where will you take me?" The answer was of no real consequence, should she be away from further harm.

Brenor was correct—whomever he was to her, brother or liar come to claim her—she could not outrun the hunters at the pace she took. "South."

"That's all we can tell you now," Ariaas interjected. "Should you be captured, I don't want you knowing our exact whereabouts."

"Ariaas," Brenor implored.

Lenora almost laughed at the irony. "Do most archers shoot arrows into people they intend to capture?"

"Torture can come in many forms! Torture of the mind is one ..." Ariaas's hands gestured wildly to accentuate his tale. He spoke far too loud for those avoiding detection, pacing between the shallow clearing of trees.

The forest swayed with each blink, and the branches taunted her while he spoke of poison, slim knives, and fingernails. The rant was torture all on its own.

"Are you going to stay here for this?" she asked Brenor. "Certainly, they can hear him?"

"No," he replied. "He could go for hours." Brenor clasped his hands, creating a step onto the back of his stallion. Lenora tenderly grasped her left side. Raising her leg was unbearable, and she retched over the saddle and wiped her cheek clean. Brenor balked at her open wound, saturating the fabric further in deep red.

"You are losing too much blood," The world blurred. His voice faded. "We need to get home."

DENMERO

ere untem nir'aurum aryusone ere gesaur wahrs hes theroone irs
ere un se aurumnet ere iltes lain nothad hes sentamerone laneviu
                    - *The Book of Kings,* Entry 4103, Year 997 of the Golden Age

S issel lingered in the doorway. Her grandmother's worn face reflected in the mirror, her fingers spread to brush paint over the creases in her cheeks, her veins visible through her thinning skin. She wore an expression of pure disappointment—in her body, perhaps, for her lack of control over its muscles.

A cloud of the last months of life hung in the air.

Death was a new concept for Sissel. She had never witnessed death before, not except knowing one person from town, but one day, he just wasn't at the market anymore. She hadn't seen his final moments.

These days, her grandmother left her bed on rare occasions. Today was one of them. They could not be far from the threshold of her final years, or final months, or final days.

"Are you almost ready?"

Her grandmother smoothed a short white curl at her brow, attempting to adjust its position, but it sprang back into a tight coil. She cleared her throat. "Yes, dear."

Sissel clutched the older woman's arm, intertwining their fingers, helping her to her feet. The two descended the stairs, her grandmother's right foot leading each labored movement.

Sissel's silk dress, blue as the sky and the sea depending on the light, was a gift from her grandmother the year prior. Long and fitted at the waist, dangling with pearls and gold jewels draping her open back. The dress was far too lavish for the occasion, creating a beacon in a city that called for invisibility. Something about the gown made her grandmother smile, so Sissel wore it regardless, letting her hair cascade over her shoulders. If this was to be their final outing, she would at least like to bring her grandmother joy one last time.

Once they departed the southern alleyways to the usual afternoon bustle of Wesilea's market, each merchant shouted, offering them fruits and spices.

Sissel softly replied, "No, thank you." Her voice extinguished as the merchants called out to the next likely customer.

Bound for the western gate, Sissel had a distinct mission this afternoon instead of their typical afternoon wandering.

"Where are we going?" her grandmother asked. "To see Thaesla?"

Sissel could not hide the grin rising on her cheeks. "I already told you it's a surprise."

Her grandmother patted Sissel's hand. "I am an old lady, my dear. I don't deal well with surprises."

"You'll like this one. At least, I hope you will."

Beyond the crowd, the alleyway narrowed, adorned with elaborate, vibrant tiles. Further from the market, the noise faded to a hum, and the tiles lost their pristine presentation. They arrived at a cherry-colored wooden door, the well-worn paint allowing glimpses of the natural oak below. The outskirts of the city were far less concerned with appearance.

Mr. Baradelle answered, hurried, his glasses sliding from the crook of his nose. "Sissel, it is so nice to see you! And you must be Idith." He gripped her grandmother's arm, shaking with rapid enthusiasm. "Please, please, come in."

Lanterns hung in long formations on the ceiling, and he dipped below them, disappearing behind the main counter. "I almost didn't have it ready, Sissel."

Her grandmother remained silent, enthralled by the room strewn with jewels, fine crystals in rows, clocks, and silverware. When he returned, Sissel said, "Grandmother, this is Mr. Baradelle."

"Pleased to meet you," she replied.

Mr. Baradelle winced and smiled awkwardly. "Where are my manners?" he said, shaking her hand again. "So pleased to meet you after all these years. Sissel told me much about you."

"Thank you, Mr. Baradelle."

He handed Sissel a palm-sized emerald box tied with a white satin ribbon.

The shop hadn't changed in the least since Sissel worked there; the same lanterns and crystals for sale coated in dust. One day she would return. When her grandmother no longer needed her undivided attention. The two made matters work between them with saved coins, but it wouldn't last forever.

The hunch in her grandmother's shoulders deepened. Sissel retook her arm, escorting her to a velvet armchair, Idith melted into her seat while Mr. Baradelle draped her in a knit blanket.

When she was settled, Sissel offered her the gift. "I hope you like your surprise."

Her grandmother's hands trembled as she untied the ribbon and removed the lid, revealing an ancient gold pocket watch. Tears swelled in her eyes, and she whisked one away before it dropped to her cheek. Her wrinkles deepened with curiosity. "Where did you get this?"

"Thaesla gave it to me this past winter."

"This belonged to my father."

"She told me. He gave it to her for safekeeping many years ago. She said it was time it was returned." Sissel's cheeks ached, soaking in each joyful nuance of her grandmother's reaction. "I remembered you telling me about it when I was a girl. I brought it to Mr. Baradelle."

"It took nearly six months to refurbish, Ms. Vacarro." Mr. Baradelle twiddled his thumbs. "The gears had to be replaced, but I cleaned and repaired most of the rest. I'm sure you know, it's called a denmero." He opened the watch's right side. "I polished the inside and uncovered most of the inscription, 'What you see is simply the surface.'"

The watch appeared dense in her frail hand, lowering to her lap under the weight. She trailed the golden hinge carved in delicate swirls of a rose.

"Do you like it?"

Her grandmother's eyes glued to the golden face as if she were unable to pry them away; she reached for Sissel's hand. "Oh, my dear, it is perfect."

Sissel's heart eased. She succeeded in getting her grandmother out of the house and smiling again. The day was a shining success.

"It's a unique piece." Mr. Baradelle reached across the void between them, pressing his fingers to the clock's face. "I haven't seen one similar in all my years. The watch counts the descent of time. The longest hand's outermost ring measures the years; the second longest ring, the months. The next, the days, followed by the hours, finished by the shortest hand counting the seconds. It may be the oldest piece of machinery I've ever had the pleasure of witnessing. Might I suggest loaning it to be displayed at some point? It would indeed be fascinating to others as well."

He cocked his head. "I had it for some time in the shop, working on it here and there, and several weeks ago, it began holding time on its own. It's magnificent."

Mr. Baradelle struggled to maintain his giddy voice. Sissel knew that voice from many years past, but he hadn't spoken quite so quickly then.

"Regardless of how often I worked on the gears, they returned to the same time and date. I could not open the back hinges as they appeared to be fused shut. Though, I am happy with its finished product nonetheless."

Her grandmother ignored the jeweler, her thoughts drawn and her vision fixated on the gold hinges and script.

Mr. Baradelle leaned over her to read the denmero's face. "I do hope I'm around to see what happens in ..." He squinted, leaning in to see. "Hmm ... five years, this month." Pulling the glasses from his brow, he peered, reading in drawn words, "Eight days ... two hours. Twenty...twenty-six minutes and about ...forty-five seconds. That would be ... hmm ..." He scratched his temple, attempting to calculate the date the clock predicted. "Well, some years from now."

Mr. Baradelle glanced at Sissel, blinking heavily; he scooted his glasses to their perch. Regaining his chipper tone, he asked, "May I get you some tea, Idith?" He scurried to the small room at the back of the shop without a reply.

Before long, the day slipped away thanks to Mr. Baradelle's prattling. He easily ensnared Sissel in conversation until the sun perched low in the western sky while her grandmother dozed in the chair.

"Oh, look at the time." He bustled to the coat rack, grabbing his jacket. "I have some business to attend to with Miss Genosu. May I walk you back to the market?"

"Of course, we would love your company." Her grandmother could use a hand on the cobbled streets, a familiar arm to squeeze, and stable legs to lean into. Also, Sissel loathed walking through the city center alone, especially in the evening hours and in the silk dress.

The beautiful and polite were tormented in Wesilea, man or woman. When she had to walk alone in the market, Sissel attempted to hide her face, tying her long tresses in twisting knots at the nape of her neck and ducking her chin to avoid meeting a stranger's glance, all the while wishing she could morph into one of the intricate tiles of the alleyways.

In her solitude, when the men left their decorum at home with their wives, she grew to hate Wesilea. Should she be with her grandmother and Mr. Baradelle, perhaps she would be saved from the evening tortures. The men would not call her sweet names of candies, willing her to their bedrooms with unrestrained requests alongside crude smiles that made her stomach curdle.

Sissel's polite *no thank you* only encouraged them further. All the while, her insides screamed more profane replies—words she was never brave enough to allow from her lips. Had she heard them, her grandmother would have gutted them, should she still be able to lift a blade.

They arrived home long before Sissel realized they had walked so far. She shook Mr. Baradelle's arm. "Thank you so much. For everything."

Sissel perched on the windowsill, bouncing her knee while the marketplace bustled below her.

Her grandmother enjoyed the gift with equal parts smiles and tears and had taken to bed without supper. Sissel replayed the moment with Mr. Baradelle, unable to pinpoint where her sense of unease from the day originated. She opened the emerald box, grazing her fingertips over the intricate carved script, the longest hands visible through the golden petals.

Although her grandmother had been a vibrant woman well into her ninetieth year, the last several had seen her deteriorate rapidly, now returning to where nature intended. Her frail body would never survive to see the denmero's conclusion. Whatever it might be.

All had their time on this earth.

Her grandmother lay sleeping in the bed, mint tea and lentil soup untouched at her bedside table, a single, immaculate white curl across her brow. The ending days of her life were far too much for Sissel to bear alone.

Quietly, Sissel dressed in her jacket and brown sandals and took to the alley. At the hour, most men would be unconscious from too much drink by the taverns or the docks or, stars forbid, home with their wives.

Before sunrise, she arrived at Thaesla's. The journey to the roof presented a rare sense of danger, manipulating steep stairs and plodding over piles of rubbish in the darkness, though the minor threat was worth the risk. From the roof, over the buildings to the east, the sky opened to the approaching dawn, the only time of day Sissel smelled salt of the sea. The air felt crisp and cool. Something about the sunrise, the beginning of a new day, the quiet of the hour, brought her ease she found nowhere else.

She calmed while the sky displayed its artwork—first navy and violet, seeping into orange and wild pink, streaked as the hide of a tiger. When the sun burst into the blue morning sky, Sissel returned to the stairs, avoiding the rubble.

Thaesla stood beside the dining table, rubbing sleep from her eyes. She kissed Sissel's forehead. "I didn't hear you come in, dear."

Sissel gripped Thaesla's wrists, drinking in the comfort of her affection. "I didn't want to wake you. I came to watch the sunrise."

In the black pursuit of the view, she'd overlooked the state of the room—broken clay pots and shattered glass. Books were heaved into shambles of tattered pages. The table sprawled across the floor, shattered chairs and splintered wood spilled from the cabinets like broken bones.

"What happened? Are you alright?"

"Yes, dear, I'm alright." Thaesla gathered her skirt, stepping over the broken rubble. "I cleaned the bedroom last night, so I had a place to sleep, but I have much more work to do this morning."

Sissel gathered pieces of clay carved with floral designs, now scattered across the floor in jagged pieces and charcoal ash. "Your caimeres."

"They did not seem to break anything with intention. Instead, just bumbling fools who never held anything fragile." Thaesla examined a rough piece of sage pottery, broken when the hard clay spilled to its side in the shuffle, a large hole where it smashed into the floor.

"Don't concern yourself," Thaesla assured. "I sent two final letters with the caimeres yesterday. The most important I've ever sent. They served their purpose."

"Who did this?"

"There are soldiers from The South Sea in the city; certainly, you've seen their heavy boots trampling the past few days. Snakes in suits. It would seem not everyone in this city is a friend to us. They came seeking evidence I'm not who I say I am."

Thaesla's letters, contents in the Old Tongue, their recipients and destinations, were a mystery she had long kept, but Sissel knew the woman meant no harm. Her aunt for her entire life, as no better term presented itself for a woman so close to family. The blood in her veins was not enough to make her a malefactor. Was being born a mal'soniure such wickedness?

"Don't be afraid; there's nothing to find. They came with suspicions and left the same. They have no proof I'm a mal'soniure. Caimeres are from Tenuel." Thaesla sat on her knees, selecting shards of clay and glass from the floor and placing them into the remains of the basin. Sissel joined her, stacking books into their rightful piles.

The door at the base of the stairs creaked, opened, then slammed closed.

Thaesla left the lock open for Sissel should she need her, but no one else ever used it besides her and—when she could walk unassisted—her grandmother.

A man ascended the stairs, some years older than Sissel, perhaps in the middle of his third decade. When he reached the room, he surveyed the haphazard scene, his large chocolate eyes empathetic and warm. He dressed in white linens cut short at the arms, void of the vibrancy of Wesilea.

Thaesla addressed him with a vague nod before returning to her task. Although his skin was worn as expected from someone her senior, the muscles in his shoulders and arms appeared thin for a grown man. Perhaps he still had room for maturity.

Without a word, the man returned the table to its legs and the drawers to their tracks.

Thaesla asked, "How's Idith?"

Sissel gathered three gold coins from the floor and a broken glass jar, returning them to the dining table.

Why doesn't Thaesla introduce us?

"Worse by the day. I took her to the shop yesterday. Mr. Baradelle finished the watch you gave me. The walk to the shop took the entire morning; then, she needed to rest. We did not even arrive home until after supper, and she went back to sleep. Admittedly, Mr. Baradelle was responsible for some of the hours."

Thaesla halted her cleaning and sat upon her heels—her skirt sweeping in ash. Once she gathered herself from the floor, she clutched the unknown man by the back of his arm, guiding him to the far corner of the room.

They conversed in hushed tones, brows pressed.

When finished, Thaesla extended her hand to guide Sissel toward the narrow stairs. "Let me see you out, dear. There is not much more to be done. My friend and I can finish."

Sissel opened her mouth to speak but misplaced the words. Thaesla never asked her to leave. Now, she ushered her with gentle arms.

When the two approached the door at the base of the stairs, Thaesla held Sissel behind the door frame, glancing north and south to ensure no one moved along the alley. When she determined they had no ears listening, Thaesla asked, "Sissel. Do you think your grandmother is well enough to travel?"

Surprised she would inquire after the recent warning of her state, Sissel contended, "I believe her days of traveling are behind her."

"Let me rephrase." Thaesla held her breath, arranging her words carefully. "Do you imagine she would survive? If she were to travel?"

Sissel's spine prickled. "What are you not telling me?"

"No matter now." A smile grew on Thaesla's rouged cheeks. "Would you bring her by after lunch today? I know she's tired, but I'd love to see her and the denmero. It'll be good for her to get out. She can rest here if she wishes to sleep. I want to see her state for myself."

The thought of her grandmother moving again, at least for a few days, did not sit well. However, she did wish for a second set of eyes to assess her condition. And Thaesla had not seen her grandmother in nearly a week.

"If she is up to it, I'll try. If not, tomorrow."

Sissel departed with a hollow the size of the Adlean Sea in her stomach.

JUST FOR FUN

He won't listen. He thinks I lie.
                    - *Diary of Daisirie Cabredd Mire, Volume 5*, Entry 215

Lenora raised the worn cotton at her hip, studying her wound. Scarring ravaged her flank, rough and jagged from healing outside of binds. The prior evening, Brenor trembled while he sutured her tattered skin. He poured gleaming water from Lake Virdine over the damage, and while it bore a clear luminescence akin to an opal, it filled the room with the stench of sulfur. The arrow pierced all flesh—no organs or significant arteries—but it embedded deep inside her flank.

Tumultuous thoughts ravaged her between fragments of sleep: the betrayals, the strangers she now must call family, the gonging of the bell. She slept and mourned and slept again, her heart shattering in the silence.

Gazing in the tarnished oval mirror, she whispered, "Lenora."

Lenora.

Lenora.

Len-or-a.

Perhaps one day, when someone else spoke, the name would feel like hers. The word belonged to her for such a short time. Although, *Anseurea* felt artificial and strained, even after decades. The name meant *bright light*, as her mother told her, but it twisted when it fell from her tongue.

Through the thin door, Brenor mumbled, "Has she come out yet?"

She heard many of Ariaas and Brenor's conversations this way: how the exchange went when they found her, their concern for her wound, her lack of eating, the archers. Nothing of the situation sat well with them, even long after the ordeal finished. They compared the matter to a man expecting to work his entire life to earn one gold bar. After an hour of work, the man received payment in full for his first month. Perhaps they had been tricked, trapped into using Lenora as bait to find Brenor, capture them both, possibly.

"Well, I purchased her some clothes in Ellace," Brenor continued. "The snares were free. No intruders in the northern or the western perimeter."

Footsteps walked to her door, leaving something before the threshold, then trailed away; the front door opened and closed, leaving the cottage silent.

Lenora gathered the food and clothing, considering what types of snares caught intruders. She forced herself to swallow a few bites of stale bread, grateful for something to eat after her days without. The clothes could fit a woman twice her size; white embroidered flowers graced the blouse across the shoulders, flowing from the sleeves and waist. Grasping the loose cotton, she wrapped the brown leather belt around her waist twice to fit high and tight above her wound.

She mourned her false life enough for her fill and then some. She grieved most for her dad, the unknown status of his alliances and well-being. For her mother and the sacrifice she made for her escape.

The questions shooting through her mind burned.

She needed answers.

Outside the cottage, Lenora shielded her face from the sun. She adjusted to the bright day until a destination presented itself. She meandered to a garden filled with blackened vines and dead leaves, the scent of crisp and sweet rose and jasmine in the air. A few scattered green leaves poked through to find the sun amongst the twisted dead growth above them.

A monumental castle commanded her attention, shadows of the façade casting well beyond the road. Though the stone lay broken and boarded, the edifice demanded reverence.

At the entrance, she trailed her fingers along the rotting wood hammered into the doors, securing them from unwelcome visitors. Lenora tugged on the boards, wishing her hands alone were strong enough to remove them and explore the depth of the castle's secrets—stepping on a floor it appeared no one had been for decades.

Her list of questions grew.

+ ———————— ·+·✦·+· ———————— +

Belcen and Aurometti wandered free through the dirt paths. A cream stallion with a black mane and a deep gray spotted mare followed behind.

They appeared wild creatures, free and meandering by their own will. So different from the tame creatures Lenora came upon in Say Livore.

In the distance, metal clashed. She wound her way toward a vast field, following amplified echoes of sparring.

Behind the stable, Brenor dangled by his heels, ensnared in a rope, precariously swinging from a tree branch. Breathless and coated in a sheen of sweat, he defended Ariaas's oncoming attacks. Despite his curious position, he defended himself quite eloquently.

"You didn't even see that!" Ariaas jabbed between strained breaths, the only of the two on his own feet. "I set it last week!"

Brenor held his attention still for a moment, gathering his strength. Then he pulled himself to the rope, slicing through it with his blade, plummeting to the ground in a *thud*. Dried dirt swirled below him, and he rose amongst the thin cloud. Ariaas did not ease, attacking while Brenor gathered his footing.

Lenora leaned into the shadow of the stables, studying their brawling. Ariaas prodded Brenor repeatedly while Brenor remained stoic. Even for his years, Ariaas was a skilled fighter. Though when Brenor stood, guarding an incoming attack, he moved with a natural fluidity that could not be taught.

Brenor held both hands high. "I am done for today."

Ariaas mocked, "A few days' rest, and you've grown weak."

"You slept in. I did not."

Ariaas leaned his sword against a post. "I suspect the soldiers will care greatly about your morning routine."

Realizing Lenora joined them, he approached and lay a hand over her shoulder. "I'm glad to see you out. I have to check the outer perimeter today. Didn't realize the hour. If I don't go soon, I won't finish by dusk." His brows raised, and he gave her a knowing nod as if he'd already read her growing list of questions. "We'll speak when I get back."

Ariaas departed without another word, whistling toward the horses and the tree line.

Lenora followed Brenor into the stables. Instead of a home for the animals, scores of weapons, traps, clamps, and snares littered the stalls. Targets, arrows, bows, and quivers lay beside a workbench, untouched for some time. Spears and swords lined the walls, carved in black and charcoal hilts, others in brass, and some with leather to ease the grip. The weapons bore the insignias of The South Sea, a few symbols of animals of the lineages, a raven, a snake. Opals and sapphires decorated these hilts, carved in delicate patterns.

"Do two men need so many weapons?" she spat in disbelief. "You could stock an army."

Brenor grinned—a smile of politeness, more than joy. He removed his leather gloves. "We have weapons hidden all over Aroun Vaer. And a good deal in the cottage as well. Ariaas has been training me since I was a boy. How to defend myself, how to escape confinement ..." Brenor hung his sword while his tone grew solemn. "How to kill should I need to."

Lenora's mind twisted, the questions magnifying. A cloud of mystery hung between them they both seemed unwilling to pierce—as if they both wished to start a conversation about too many topics, and neither knew where to begin.

"I wasn't around weapons. Not really." Lenora shrugged; the toy bow certainly didn't count. "My aunt and mother told me I would never need them."

Her heart fluttering, she trailed her fingers over a wooden bow, brown leather bound grips, with a golden feather hanging from the base. There were no toys there.

"Though when they weren't looking, sometimes my dad"—she squinted, shaking the aching thought away—"*Eran*. Sometimes, Eran would take me to the northern forest. Sneak his old bow and arrows into his pack. He taught me some. 'Just for fun,' he always said. Nothing like these, though."

"Did you know?" asked Brenor. "You were not their blood?"

"Yes. They told me as a child. Who knows now what parts were true or not? Ebigan, my uncle—as he called himself—brought me back to them from a small church with no family to care for me. My parents were killed in an accident. He gave no further detail."

"Did you piece together how we are related?" Brenor spoke slowly, choosing each word with careful intention. "When we first met? Is that why you left with us in the forest?"

She nodded, still finding this truth both pleasant and odd in one. "You're my brother?"

Brenor smiled, his cheeks raising. "Three years your elder."

"That makes you the wiser between us. The one who should torment me endlessly, particularly regarding potential suitors," she jested. "And perhaps play cruel pranks on me."

He chuckled. "We might be a bit old for that now." Brenor moved the swords in tall stacks, found one with a jaguar symbol, and handed it to her. The weight of the metal felt like boulders. "Was Eran any good with a bow?"

"He wasn't exactly bad. Though he let me practice more than he did. We made trees into targets. Once we began using them more, we left the arrows in the forest. It was better than trying to sneak them in and out. He didn't want my mother to see them. 'Not worth the scolding he would receive,' he said."

The memory warmed her, though she now wondered if Eran meant Ebigan or Areya when he spoke of being scolded.

"We found a boulder with a fallen tree to hide it underneath. It lived there for months. Then, one day, it was just gone. Taken by someone in the village. Or, now I know they were there, by the archers, maybe."

She paused to examine the intricate carving of the jaguar on the hilt of the sword.

"Will Ariaas want to train me?"

"Yes. He believes it is the only true way to keep us safe. He says he cannot keep us safe forever on his own. We must learn how to defend ourselves."

Lenora cleared her throat. "What exactly are we defending ourselves from?" She hoped this question would lead him to open like a bottle of spilled milk, delving into her thoughts in sequence: King Barrard, Ebigan, her mother, Eran, the archers, the perimeter traps, the desolate castle.

Brenor held his reply, his mouth opening while he attempted to form the proper response. "The answer to your question ... will lead to many more questions. Though I will tell you, we are leaving soon. The day after next. Maybe one more if you need another day for your wound to heal. I do not believe you would wish to begin training until we return. After understanding our situation, I assume you will wish to go with us."

"Where?"

"On a long journey to Jaisett." Brenor replied. "Do you know it?"

She shook her head.

"It is a small fishing town in northern Felreaon, on the shores of The Adlean Sea. We will not return until the winds change and the leaves begin to turn." He motioned for her to follow him into the training yard. "The woman we travel to see, Thaesla, found you when you ran. The one who led us to find you in the forest. Her price—if she ever asked us for anything, we would do it without question. We must oblige her request. That was the arrangement Ariaas made years ago."

"I hope you trust her. A job to be done without ever knowing the cost."

"She is our friend. One of very few we have," he assured her. They stopped in the shade below the tree Brenor had been hanging from. "How is your wound?"

"Better. Healing fast. I'm well enough now. I want you to tell me what's happened."

"Very well," he nodded. "Tonight, though. We will wait for Ariaas to return this evening. There is much I was too young to remember. Though he has told me much throughout the years, there may be many questions he would be better suited to answer."

This response was logical, though not the one she wished for. Her curiosity and patience were at odds.

"Wait here for a moment," he instructed.

When he returned, he wore a more devious grin. In one hand, he held two bows, the smaller wrapped in brown leather, emerald and golden scripted embroidery at the edges, the other larger, navy and deep brown. His other hand outstretched, full of arrows.

"Just for fun? I have not used one in years. I was never all that great at it. It is not my weapon of choice."

A bittersweet pang of sadness shot through her heart at the memory of Eran, intermixed with the thrill of being handed a real bow.

Brenor missed twice before striking the stump.

Lenora righted her posture and pressed her shoulders back, hitting one arrow after the next.

When she finished, Brenor gestured toward the bow. "You should keep it. It suits you."

Her heart fell into her stomach. Her very own bow? Not one she had to hide in the forest or sneak to practice with? Not a toy her dad bought in town? A proper, authentic bow she could call her own?

"Five shots," Brenor quipped. "Whoever hits the least makes supper?"

Lenora's grief, her questions of Aroun Vaer, and the strangers waned. If only for the moment, she thanked the stars she trusted Brenor in the forest.

"I'll take a roast," she jested, taking a fistful of arrows. "Potatoes with carrots. Honey cake for dessert."

ILLUMINATE

Mathett Marijem Jensett, Sengura of the Jolisard, The Wielder of Light, Eight Stars
Born: First Month of Winter, 1954
Deceased: Third Month of Spring, 2038
Children: Two

- Felreaon Official Ledger

At dusk, Lenora breathed in the redolence of roasting beef, cinnamon, and honey. Ariaas ate his fill and seconds twice before slumping into his armchair. She expected she might explode if she couldn't let her thoughts into the world.

"I want to know everything. Please. I want to know why I was taken. Why you need so many weapons. The traps. The archers. *Everything.*"

"Your patience was greater than I anticipated. I wouldn't have made it through the first night." Ariaas wiped his chin and pressed back his shirt, Taren rolling below his boots. "There's nothing I'll tell you of a pleasant nature—prepare yourself for that. Nothing of my past, yours, Brenor's. Nothing of any part of this family."

In truth, she was unsure what she wanted to know, pleasant or unpleasant. The hollow returned to her chest, as if the floor of reality had fallen out from under her boots. Sickness coiled in her stomach. She clasped her hands to stop their trembling. She lived in a lie every day of her remembered life. She craved so much more than truth.

She craved *real.*

Lenora nodded, unwavering. The truth, or nothing. No matter how unpleasant.

Ariaas continued, "You're the youngest of four. Arienne, the eldest, is thirty. Thealor, two years younger. Then Brenor. Your mother, Avaine"—Ariaas's forehead creased, almost as if it nauseated him to say her name—"she was my only child. I've lived at Aroun Vaer—between the castle and the cottage—for over ninety years. I moved here when I married Sarinah a lifetime ago."

Her stomach jolted. One of four? Arienne. Thealor. She had a sister and another brother.

"You've never been to Aroun Vaer, but the older three spent much time here. Your father—Gelhan—and I shared little in common besides the will to keep you from harm. You were born at the border of Hanielle and Tenuel in the northern lands. A Yurelan camp."

Lenora's curiosities piqued at the word, a name she had heard in whispers and nothing more, passing conversations of Ebigan and Dyan they never allowed her to join. "I ... I'm Yurelan?"

"No. No. Certainly not. A horrid bunch," he scoffed, waving the thought away. "They were a piece in the long line of people meant to claim you."

She winced. Again, someone spoke of her as property.

"The three eldest lived at Aroun Vaer for near two years, where I kept them hidden. Gelhan thought it safe for them to return after you were born. But Queen Navaera's men were watching. Spying. They came not long after and captured all four of you. Snakes, the lot of 'em. A battle ensued. The Yurelan fought, but they were still a band of renegades. Many died that night. A few hundred or more, I was told. Who knows for sure? The accounts are scattered, and I was a world away. A night I swear I saw the stars stain red."

She had a sister. And another brother. She knew this story connected—somehow—but she couldn't yet follow the picture the pieces of the puzzle created.

"For what purpose? Why did we need to be kept hidden?"

"They thought when you were born, you had ... great power." Ariaas ran his hands across Taren's long coat, and the dog uttered a satisfied groan. "Many attempted to keep you. Many attempted to hide you. Many will attempt to use you."

Ariaas and Brenor exchanged wary glances—an act not lost on her.

Ariaas inhaled, hesitating as if he wished to spare her from the following portion of the tale. "In the First Age, a prophecy was given by the Meiderie of Cascanvore after the end of The Great War. Eons ago. Foretelling five children born in the Third Age. Do you know it?"

"Everyone knows the tale. Where some old seers tried to make the world sound interesting and failed miserably." She shrugged, indifferent to childhood stories. "Canen Dera."

"And you know what it says the children of Canen Dera will do?"

Lenora frowned, digging into the far recesses of her memories to the stories she learned as a child: scattered history lessons, mythology, the birth of their lands, folklore. "It was a dark tale. Eight images were seen. The five children were savages. They would bring about an end of days, killing armies, bringing down land, mountain, and forest. It's a horror story they tell children to get them to behave."

Brenor interjected, "Do you recall anything else?"

"I believe there was mention of raging seas and fires."

Ariaas sighed, dragging a hand over his face. "The power the old tales speak of—the Canen Dera—it lives in your blood."

He waited, studying her reaction.

Lenora laughed, a short, sharp sound. "Absurd. I'm no savage."

She thought of the orchard, of her tiny life. The idea of bringing down armies felt more like a cruel joke than fate.

But Ariaas didn't smile.

"They feared the five children," he said. "Each one was seen in visions—burning armies, sinking cities, crumbling mountains. Terrible, apocalyptic things. And yes, each child had ... bright eyes. Eyes like fire in different colors."

She swallowed hard, picturing her own reflection—the unfamiliar glint she had seen.

Still, she shook her head. "That's *storytelling.* Myths to scare children."

"It doesn't matter what you believe. It matters what *they* believe. The South Sea. The King. The Yurelan. The hunters who chased you through the woods.

"We're fortunate, at least in one regard. In its original state, the prophecy can no longer come to pass. No fifth was born," Ariaas continued assuredly. "However ... the reason for the destruction has not varied. The five had more power than anyone had ever seen, not in all our history. It lives in your blood. Unfortunately, the quantity born does not change the individual's strength. The strength predicted to bring the world to its knees. The power is seen as immense and untapped.

"It also doesn't change how much idiots who think they control the world like to hold control over that power." Ariaas fidgeted in his seat. "The Yurelan and The South Sea have been fighting over possession of the four of you since birth."

"Who else plans to come and say they own me?" Lenora's belief on the matter was still in debate, though her stomach settled, and her brain felt satisfied with an answer more significant than she could have expected. "Where are Thealor and Arienne now? Are they safe?"

"Safe? It depends on your definition of *safe*. They aren't dead."

Her heart wrenched. What an odd thing to say. *Safe* and *not dead* seemed like quite a far departure.

"How did you find all this out?"

"A story for another night. It's longer than this tale still." Taren rolled under Ariaas's feet, rattling the table. Ariaas held it steadily without glancing at the dog, apparently accustomed to the routine.

"The evening before I ran, the man who called himself my uncle—Ebigan—was summoned to Islarourne for the business of King Barrard. The next day, my mother told me the letter had called me to Islarourne and not Ebigan. 'The new King means to reclaim his property,' she said."

Ariaas rubbed his chin as Lenora swallowed the bile rising in her throat.

"King Barrard thinks of me as his property?"

"Yes," agreed Ariaas. "Kept well hidden under a watchful cloak for decades. As we assume, at least. Not near his cities. The people. We suspect someone in your close circle was Qcaranen. A powerful descendant of the lineage, to have hidden you so thoroughly and for so long. Cloaked you. We think that's why we couldn't find you when Thaesla searched. Not until you ran."

"They wouldn't allow me weapons. Never allowed me to be unsupervised." Lenora recalled Dyan and Ebigan's stern rules and harsh demeanor when she disobeyed. "They did this because they knew what had been ... predicted?"

Brenor assured her, "Canen Dera, as seen, cannot come to pass. How you use your abilities is your choice, dark or light."

How ridiculous all of this sounded. How naive must the king be to assume a person who had never brought death or life or controlled the winds, or the rain was anything more than a common farmer from Valesove.

"I'm not worried Canen Dera will come to pass because it's a load of nonsense." She scoffed. "I don't have power." She did not even have the abilities of sharp sight as Ebigan and Areya.

Brenor leaned forward, voice softer. "You've never been trained, Lennie. You were hidden. Shielded from what you are."

Lenora frowned. "What I am? I'm just ... me. No different than anyone else."

"Everyone is born with lineage," Ariaas explained. "Some control rain. Some earth. Some fire. The difference is training. Those raised in the open, under their cultures, learn to use it early. You weren't given that chance."

He rubbed at the edge of his glass. "It's not about prophecy anymore. It's about blood and bone—what you *could* do, if pushed."

Her stomach twisted. *Could* was a dangerous word.

"But I don't feel anything," she protested. "No power. No ... whatever you think I have."

"They made sure you wouldn't," said Ariaas. "By isolating you. By never letting you train. By making you believe you were ordinary." He smiled grimly. "And still, here you are. Alive when you shouldn't be. Running faster and farther than most soldiers twice your size."

Ariaas let the words hang between them—a quiet, inarguable truth.

"Brenor spoke of a woman you travel to see soon. Thaesla? How is she connected to all this? Why do we travel to see her and not plan a rescue for Thealor and Arienne? The king will know I escaped."

"An old friend." Ariaas took a swig from his glass. "She's a descendant of many lineages; she searched for you with the Unvaerus lineage. Though, it's your choice if you wish to go or stay. She wouldn't ask us to go so far if she didn't need us."

"But what could possibly be more urgent than rescuing your family?"

"It isn't that simple."

She huffed. Perhaps yes, perhaps no, but she would not know if they did not let her in. But perhaps now was not the time to speak of rescue. "Brenor spoke of training?"

"I won't shadow you as Taren shadows Brenor, so unless you wish to be afraid all the time, I suggest tomorrow you learn to arm yourself and choose a weapon well."

Lenora answered assuredly, elated with Brenor's gift. "I already chose a weapon."

Ariaas drained his glass with a satisfied smirk. "Very well."

Brenor pulled on his boots at the cottage door, leaving the laces untied. "Grab your boots. I want to show you something."

Lenora rose, grateful to divert her attention. She needed to move, to *do* something. Anything to confine the tornado of new truths to a dark corner of her mind for a time.

When she reached her room, cool night air drifted from the cracked window, stirring loose papers on the table. She bent to retrieve her boots—but paused.

Folded parchment rested atop her pillow, an envelope she was certain hadn't been there before she left. The paper smelled of almond and vanilla.

She peeled open the folds, her fingers quivering.

Dearest Lenora,

I know you do not know me, but I grew up alongside your brothers and sister. Your family was once a home to me in ways words could scarcely express. Though they no longer welcome me as they once did, I could not let your return pass in silence.

I celebrate your arrival home. Your strength leaves me in awe.

It is my deepest, most abiding wish to see the Varan family whole again ... as it was always meant to be.

If you ever find yourself in need, I am but a letter away. I left a quill for you—crafted for a singular purpose. Should you choose to reach me, your words will reach no other.

Let this be a confidence between you and I, a secret whisper of ink.

Yours, always,
Oedd

As she finished the last line, the ink blurred before it vanished entirely. She stared at the page, numb, her heart hammering. Her mouth went dry. Whoever this man was—he knew her. What would Ariaas and Brenor say?

She shoved the letter and quill below her mattress and bolted for the door.

Outside, Brenor turned to the forest to the north. She rushed to catch him below the navy sky, eying for silhouettes of men in the darkness, leaving Ariaas in the kitchen scavenging for a third supper.

Should she tell Brenor of Oedd's letter?

They arrived at a weeping oak, long hanging strands of the vasse noves crawling over the branches. She expected the massive tree might house secrets when they arrived, but Brenor turned to the smaller tree beside it, covered in the same thick vines. Tugging back the heavy tresses, he looped them over the length of a sturdy, knotted branch. Lenora leaned over the depths to view what he had drawn her to, but her eyes met blackness. Below their feet appeared as nothing more than a cavity of dirt and roots.

"I know there has been nothing but unfortunate news since you arrived. News of our past, of our family. But not everything at Aroun Vaer is disconcerting." Brenor gestured for her to enter.

"You want me to go in there?" Lenora pressed her lips to control her smirk while she pointed into the dark abyss. "This certainly looks disconcerting."

"It looks much less ominous in the daylight." A statement, she assumed, of half-truth. But he beamed when he spoke, and her fears eased. "It is the entrance to a series of tunnels. One of many, though this is my favorite. They all lead to the castle; there are a hundred hidden doors in there. They all have different twisting paths. Different intersections. Some secrets still dwell in there, that much I am certain."

"You're going to take me inside the castle?" Excitement leaped from her voice, and she beamed in the darkness. The structure was fascinating, the trees and the vines, the way it seemed to shine even when abandoned. "This is a hidden way in?"

Seemingly amused by her reaction, he pulled the vines further back, exposing the tip of a ladder. "Just the tunnels for now. I expect you would be up exploring well past dawn if you made it into the castle tonight."

It appeared to be nothing; a deep hole where the mud caved in below the roots. How deep she did not yet know. Eran would say overthinking was a dagger in the heart of anything worthwhile. She lowered herself onto the ladder clinging to the side of the entrance.

Brenor aimed the torch overhead while she descended, dropping it after she reached the floor. The wood echoed as it bounced and rattled over smooth rock. She retrieved it, holding it to illuminate the walls. The flame only offered a small circle of light. She stretched it above her head, though it did not reach high enough to show the ceiling, merely the cold stone floor, echoing against her footsteps.

Brenor's voice reverberated, "Stand there."

At his request, she positioned her body toward the wall, inhaling the steep moisture in the air. He took the torch and returned to the ladder, rolling the flame into a few small puddles left by the night rain some days ago. It extinguished and the smell of char and stale water rose.

"Did you bring the balanser?"

"Yes, but we will not need it. Let your sights adjust."

Blackness pressed in on her.

She waited for her eyes to acclimatize, to find a sliver of light. Her finger touched her nose, but she couldn't see her hand even when resting on her face. The cool air raised bumps on her skin. Smells became more potent in the darkness: the water, the cave, the stone, the remaining smoke of the burnt flames. Her breath became loud in the hollowed emptiness, and a small drip fell in a delicate rhythm. In the far distance, a faint trickle.

"Reach your hand behind you." Brenor's voice echoed, "Hand behind you, behind you, you, you," traveling the length of the tunnel before it trailed into faint whispers. "Open your palm and place it against the wall. Against the wall, the wall, wall, wall."

This is insane.

Lenora outstretched her palm, extending her fingers wide. She moved forward until her hand met cool, coarse, jagged rock, as rough sand in the frozen winter.

Lights illuminated above her. First one, then a dozen, then thousands.

They stretched over the ceiling. Intermittent glimmers, fading in and out, as a diamond flickers when the sun moves over. Her heart leaped as the golden lights danced in her eyes. "I've never seen anything like this. A million stars live in this cave."

Her eyes widened in wonder.

"Ariaas tells me it only illuminates for us," replied Brenor. "Others have been here. They touched the walls, and blackness remained. I am glad to see it lit for you. He suspected it would."

"Why does it only illuminate for us?"

"Perhaps one day we will know."

The two walked through the cavernous lights and echoes, twisting, turning, limitlessness in their mysteries. The weight of her troubles evaporated. For a moment, nothing existed other than sparkling lights overhead and whatever awaited beyond.

RETURN TO WHERE YOU CAME

"We speak of matters of ill importance to our agenda. There must be a vote. Should you wish to keep the Larrone Duren watched by this new law, the law which governs the word, raise your right arm. As Dhaesreaon has not sent a member of their high born to the council the majority vote will be four."

- As recorded by the Head Scribe of Lesomen, 878

Sissel slipped on her sandals and descended the steep stairs of her grandmother's home. She ignored her usual politeness toward the merchants in the market, adopting blind ignorance of their presence.

Wandering through the cobbled alley, she arrived at the round, cobalt door surrounded by bright fuchsia blooms. Sissel gripped the round brass handle, numbers in Nieran surrounding a quail, and ascended Thaesla's stairs.

Inside, the books formed maze formations on the floor, trinkets perched on their rightful shelves, ash and caimeres shards swept away.

Thaesla's pleasant smile faded to concern. "Why is Idith not with you?"

Sissel's eyes welled with tears, and her words choked. "She's been asleep since we spoke."

Thaesla's words fumbled. "For two days?"

The room showed no signs of the young man from the day prior—no shoes, clothing, second saucer for tea, breakfast plate. The raging waves in Sissel's stomach settled. Her emotional turmoil would only be visible to family, not nameless, mute strangers.

Tears fell freely while Thaesla wrapped her arms around her tightly. A reminder she wouldn't face her grandmother's final days alone.

"It's time I go see her for myself."

+ ——— · + · + · + · ——— +

Near the eastern gate, soldiers of The South Sea assembled atop a platform for the theater troupe while a crowd congregated below. At Thaesla's side, Sissel slowed to study a heavily adorned woman in gray formal attire, slicked short black hair from her face, wet as if she recently exited the bath or perhaps coated in oil if she hadn't seen one in some months. Her shoulders were broad as any man's, and with each fibrous twitch of her cheek, she attempted a pleasant smile in place of the grim, downturned arrangement nature had gifted her lips. Her knuckles coiled around rolled parchment, waiting for the throng to calm.

When enough of a crowd gathered, the woman quieted their commotion with a raised hand.

In the lull, the woman began, "Good afternoon. I'm High Commander Ilija Ravaris of the Armies of Monera." As she spoke, the throng hushed their chattering. "I'm stationed in Islarourne. We've traveled quite a distance to meet with the Armies of Tenuel and Commander Tuyure."

Thaesla paused their walking, grasping Sissel's wrist, tilting her head to the side while listening to the High Commander's business.

"We wish to keep the city of Wesilea safe. We wish her people happiness."

When has The South Sea ever wished happiness on another people?

The High Commander continued, her voice projecting over the crowd, "Citizens of Wesilea fear people of The South Sea. This is understandable. Those with a bloodline of the ways of death are living amongst innocent, peaceful people of Tenuel, a people of senses and instincts. Those who possess more than one regional lineage, residing here as well—the mal'soniure. We are asking these people to return to their homes in The South Sea."

At Sissel's side, Thaesla sneered. Tenuel may be a region of senses and instincts, but they were not unsuspecting children. They possessed the abilities of intuition, insight, sound, flesh. Perhaps Tenuel's soldiers at the High Commander's back wore the pin of a falcon. The soldiers in burgundy, cream, and linen with thick leather boots resembled Seravis the Hunter. Tenuel were not warring people—as The South Sea—but they were not naive reeds.

"We've spent several days searching Wesilea for our own kind, those native to The South Sea. Now we ask them to return home." The High Commander turned to the next rolled page of parchment. "A list of our people who reside here will be read aloud. If your name is read, we ask you to gather your belongings. A caravan will be waiting to transport you home at first light."

Sissel leaned into her aunt, muttering, "It's not illegal to travel and work in other regions. Surely, she exaggerates."

She eyed the baker, her neighbor, the faces of men who taunted her in the evenings. Thaesla did not reply, her thoughts drawn with a piercing gaze toward the High Commander.

At Thaesla's intense fixation and reluctance to move, Sissel's fear multiplied. She gripped her arm. "Thaesla?"

A second soldier stepped forward, the list of names in his hand. He spoke with a deep booming voice. "By order of High Commander Ravaris, and by order of His High Royal Highness King Barrard the First, the natives of The South Sea shall be removed. They shall depart at first light. All mal'soniure will be detained."

Varying emotions raged amongst the chattering mass: some gasps, some fear, some nodding in shared approval.

"Rabril Basard, of the Noslarrar, The Breaker of Bones. Belahrok Nalorn, Remerard, The Dark Warrior."

The two men stood together amongst the gathering, friends, it appeared. Their mouths hung agape. Sissel did not know the first names they read, nor did Thaesla should the expression on her face speak.

"Berea Nasan Genosu, born a mal'soniure."

The throng prattled further amongst themselves in shock and whispers.

"Maternal descent of the Remerard, The Dark Warrior of The South Sea, and the paternal descent of the Tiortem, The Master of Sound of Tenuel."

A rising cloud of fear infected one after the next, snaking through the patrons.

A bystander shoved. Two more pressed forward. Varying elbows forced into one another, cries, panic, weeping—a contagion spreading. Every person was born of one lineage, one people, each powerful; but to be born of two regions, perhaps even three, made them an object of trepidation.

"The woman from the bakery," whispered Thaesla. They bought bread from her, sometimes petite vanilla cakes with cherry sauce on special occasions made fresh each morning.

"Thaesla, what's happening?"

Suddenly, Thaesla grasped Sissel by both arms; their eyes locked. Her knuckles whitened at her firm grip. She breathed each word, "Go. Get.

Idith. *Now.* Carry her if you must. Meet me at the docks. They'll let you in."

Dumbfounded, Sissel solidified, jostled by the mass of people. No matter where Thaesla wished to take her, her grandmother's condition had deteriorated so rapidly, she wouldn't make it to the docks.

The soldier continued, "Roseam Kalvye, a third-degree highborn of the Roscivis." The chatter increased to audible gasps, merchants shouting, children crying, eyes wide, fear rising. Arguably, the Roscivis were the most feared power in Monera, able to steal the breath of a dozen people in one swoop without ever laying a hand upon them. A simple whisper, simple words, and death conquered.

Sissel studied the stranger.

A Roscivis made their way to Tenuel? A highborn? Without anyone noticing? The Roscivis bore a black mark akin to soot smeared across their cheeks to improve recognition. Instead, this woman wore scarring so vicious, her flesh appeared to have met wild and torturous flame. Perhaps she attempted to peel away the marking herself.

"And lastly, Nerale Baradelle of The South Sea."

The gasping crowd toppled to utter silence.

Through the onlookers, Mr. Baradelle stood with his mouth agape and glasses at the tip of his nose—a statue of a man.

"There's a mistake." Mr. Baradelle stuttered, "I ... I am ... not from The South Sea. I've lived here my entire life."

"I wish I could detain people on the sole grounds of blatant ignorance, but such matters are outside my jurisdiction," Ravaris responded. "The name Baradelle alone is from The South Sea; no other proof is needed."

Mr. Baradelle's eyes widened. A low sound lifted from the far recesses of his innards, the soft gurgling of a stream from the saliva trapped in the back of his throat. His hand rose to his heart, a film of sweat on his forehead. His legs caved to the weight of his body, knees cracking when they met the stone ground.

The crowd jeered at his fall, one indiscernible from the next. Bystanders tripped over one another to distance themselves from the kneeling man. Though there was a Roscivis amongst them, the deadliest of the South, Mr. Baradelle's presence brought them greater fear: fear of the unknown. His lineage had not been read aloud, and what he might do in the theatrics of his taken knee was too much for them.

Mr. Baradelle was no longer their neighbor, friend, the odd gentleman who fixed their mother's ring, and their father's compass, or simply a man who struggled to find air. He was a potential dealer of death.

Sneers and boos echoed from the crowd. "He moves to kill us!"

An honest, reliable keeper of small objects, Mr. Baradelle deserved no such treatment.

"He's not trying to kill you," shouted Sissel, appalled. "He's dying."

Thaesla grabbed her arm, though Sissel wriggled away, driving her way through the bystanders. Her grandmother could sleep a few more minutes. Thaesla's shouting drowned in the commotion while the crowd closed the gap between them. Mr. Baradelle's body dropped to one side on the stone, his knees tucked below him unnaturally, and his round glasses lay crooked and shattered upon his nose. He attempted a futile inhale between labored sounds of suffocation.

Sissel skimmed face to face, seeking aid; each harrowed and horrified anyone would assist a foreigner. The masks of the people she once knew chattered against her. How could she help him? And alone? Only those who lived a world away, on the opposite shore, held a lineage that could heal impending death.

Suddenly, swiftly, Mr. Baradelle lunged, clamping Sissel's left forearm.

A current surged when their arms met—a jolt of searing pain coursed through her body—as if all her nerves blistered in the hot coals of a deep flame.

Mr. Baradelle took in a sharp, fierce, and wide-mouthed inhale as if he had never held air in his lungs.

A soldier of Wesilea crashed in a heap upon the stone, instantly lifeless. His burgundy cape draped elegantly over his fresh cadaver, his widened eyes elsewhere, as if deep in a dream of vistas in the clouds.

Mr. Baradelle regained his breath, rapid, panicked, and no longer at the bridge of death.

A commotion rose amongst the crowd: panic, pushing, screaming.

"She traded his life! Traded it for the life of our soldier!" A bystander shouted. The throng rattled, people shoving and shouting over one another to escape her proximity.

Mr. Baradelle released his grip; Sissel's forearm reddened, remembering his fatal touch.

Sissel raised her hands to affirm her innocence, reconciling the split-second series of events. In a blink, Mr. Baradelle lived, and another, died.

Guards of The South Sea hesitated, even with her physical show of assurances. Mr. Baradelle had performed fatal theatrics much as this mere moments ago. The fear was palpable, each soldier looking to the next to detain her.

What have I done?

Thaesla shoved through the small sea of people, shouting, clear she had no care for hurt feelings or bruised toes. The commotion rose, and the people merging created an impossible path.

High Commander Ravaris leaped from the podium. Her demeanor never altered, never swayed, not even in the presence of a swift and unexpected execution. With a motion of hands, soldiers in gray seized Sissel's arms, driving her into a submissive position on her knees.

"Your name?" Ravaris demanded.

Sissel's fear deafened the surrounding noises of Wesilea.

This cannot be.

In a meek voice, she replied, "Sisselara Vacarro."

The High Commander paused, her plump lips tightening to two white lines, her chocolate eyes darkening. A muscle in her square chin twitched.

Her stature loomed over Sissel as she spoke her words carefully. "It seems we missed a Roscidarra in our searches. Take her to the caravan."

The soldiers ushered her away in an instant.

Sissel's thoughts froze.

"Take the dead man away as well. Deliver him to Commander Tuyure." She focused on Mr. Baradelle. "And that one."

High Commander Ravaris ascended the stage in heavy black boots, a solemnness about her. "People of Wesilea. I am deeply troubled by what we have witnessed here today. I am sorry for the loss of the young soldier's life. Though the actions we have all witnessed have allowed us to find a further child of The South Sea hiding amongst you. She will be removed from Wesilea and receive due punishment. A punishment appropriate for the crimes she has committed against your people."

Against an eruption of cheers, Thaesla's voice cut through the crowd. "She is not of The South Sea!"

High Commander Ravaris nodded to the raucous crowd. "We are committed to our promise to restore our alliances with Tenuel."

Gray soldiers whisked Sissel away from civilians. Thaesla trailed them beyond the eastern gate. "I need to speak with her. Please do not take her!"

When Thaesla met her side, Sissel began to weep, the dense weight of death hanging in her throat. "I didn't. I ... don't know what happened."

"She is not of The South Sea. Please." Thaesla gripped the soldier at the end of the formation. "She is a child of Tenuel. She would never kill anyone."

The soldier did not meet her eyes. "Address your concerns with Commander Tuyure."

LEAVE HIM

If our brother from the mountains does not care enough to show his face to our council any longer, I should not care to remove his rights from where he sits.

       - As recorded by the Head Scribe of Lesomen, 878

L enora slipped the quill from her pocket, her pulse quickening. This was either brilliance or madness.

She unfolded the blank paper from the envelope. Oedd asked for confidences shared between them—a secret she would allow. For now. And perhaps, if he truly wished to help, he could prove it.

Only questions. Reveal nothing. She pressed the quill to the page.

What do you know of my brother and sister?

The ink bloomed fast, eager, curling across the page.

Ah, Lady Lenora ... I hoped I'd hear from you.

Her fingers tightened on the quill. She wrote, sharp and unflinching:

Answer my question.

The parchment trembled, then dark letters bled into view:

By all means.
Both breathe. They are not lost to you forever, Lenora. Some sands of time remain. But not many. You must move with haste ... before the world claims them.

Lenora's lips pressed into a hard line. She wrote, sharp and clean:

Anyone could know they breathe. That's not an answer.

The page sat stifled, lifeless. Then ink slithered out, slower:

They are both held captive.

A knot wedged in her throat.

Why should I trust you?

The reply came as quick as breathing.

Because I have never lied to you.

Lenora stared at the page, the words swimming. Some part of her yearned to believe his actions were benevolent—but the sharper part stayed coiled in suspicion. She pressed the quill to the paper one final time.

I appreciate your time, Oedd.
I must go now.

She set the quill atop the desk, the ink slithering away from the parchment. The empty space once filled with her words left so many questions hanging. Far more than she dared put to paper.

Her fingers brushed the edge of the parchment, restless.

She considered asking Brenor—pressing him for a name, a history—but something in her gut, that same wary instinct that had kept her alive in the forest, whispered Ariaas would not look kindly on such questions.

For now, Oedd would remain her secret.

+ ———— · + · + · + · ———— +

Lenora met Brenor outside, horses packed for a long journey. She put her hand on Luscan's nose, and he leaned into her embrace. She muttered her goodbyes to Aroun Vaer. It wasn't quite her home yet, and it was far more home than Sanrial.

Along the trail, Brenor gestured to a metal clamp partially buried beneath the earth. "The traps on the interior line, here, are more rudimentary. Ariaas built them decades ago. They do not catch much but watch for the steel wiring. They mean to grab your ankle." Lenora scanned the ground—detecting only scattered trees of varying leaves meeting open dirt.

When they met the split rail fence, Brenor cautioned, "This is where the real danger lies. Never leave the road within Aroun Vaer. Never. Not until you know where the traps are. This goes for tens of miles. I will show you more when we return. The traps here are meant to deliver a swift death. Since we cannot walk the entire exterior line in many days." His head dropped at the thought. "It is cruel to leave someone to suffer."

Beyond the split rail fence, she found warnings on signs and painted in black directly upon the fence itself.

Danger!
Do not cross unless wishing for certain and painful death!

"You've found people here? People who didn't abide by the signs?" Lenora had yet to determine to what level she was horrified. At least they had been given a warning. "People who've come for you?"

"Yes. That is the reason Ariaas takes to the exterior. He is better with the dead."

"I thought you took a vow not to kill?" asked Lenora, idly, scanning one trap to the next—the snares, the wires, the metal clamps covered by tall grass.

Brenor rode on in silence.

Did he not consider his traps killing intruders to be death by his hands? She chose not to press further. After all, there were caveats, she was told. And were Oedd's words true? Were Arienne and Thealor truly captive?

While Taren lay in the shade below a sycamore tree, they rested while the sun grew high. Brenor closed his eyes, drinking in the sun's heat.

Lenora avoided the most nagging question on her tongue. She needed the right moment. Instead, she asked, "Should we be concerned about the archers? Will they come searching?"

"It is difficult to say. Our trail would be hard to follow. Your horse remained in the forest. It rained the night after and there has been nothing in the traps. If they are friendly with those of Qabriah, they could bring in a kalthero to track you, but I highly doubt it. We should be concerned about King Barrard."

Lenora swallowed, nodding.

"Those were soldiers of the crown; they would likely not have those people amongst them. They are not friendly with their eastern neighbors.

"Ariaas possesses the bloodline of the Qcaranen—a distant relative—which is why he cannot be sought easily. It is why there are no people pounding at the door after you as we speak. The lineage is weaker in us. We host more power with less ability to hide. We long suspected you were held alongside a Qcaranen for that very reason. They would have to be highborn; most cannot cloak anyone other than themselves, though there are few who are powerful enough. Aroun Vaer is vast enough; it should protect us ... for a time. The more of us there are together, the less likely they will be to attack. They would not risk such a thing."

The idea of power, of strong blood coursing her veins, excited her. She opened her palm and closed it, taking in the sense of her hand, and wondering how anyone in this world willed their mind or their body to control something else.

"That's twice now, you two have talked of power. And yet, I've got a lot of nothing."

"Perhaps not. Perhaps your only power is beating me at contests for supper," Brenor quipped. "Let the soldiers think what they want. It only helps us."

"Won't we be vulnerable on the road?"

"We head west, away from those who can track us, sense us. Two unlikely parties crossing paths. We should be alright, should we stay off the roads when we depart Aroun Vaer lands. I expect Thaesla is anxious to meet you." Brenor leaned over his knees, resting his elbows. "Why did you choose to leave with us? In Say Livore?"

The fear returned, creeping and trickling into her mind. When she ran—dragging sopping wet boots through the stream, and he tore the arrow from her flesh, gentle as possible, pain searing through her body—she had not been afraid. Fear found her once she was safe, sleeping in another home, in an unfamiliar bed. This postponed fear washed over her then, realizing how close to death she was, crashing upon her as the surging waves of the sea.

"I suppose ... you didn't seem too menacing."

Brenor grinned. "Your instincts are strong."

Taren nipped at bugs in the grass while Brenor gathered himself.

"Those of The South Sea do not possess such instincts. They rely on violence, war, imprisonment. They make choices without a gut feeling to draw them in one direction or the other. They kill more easily, die more easily, are revived more easily. Death has always been a forgone conclusion, as was pain, as were battles."

Brenor led Belcen by the reins as they walked. "As Ariaas tells it, when he found us after the Siege, near two months had passed since we were taken. Arienne, Thealor, and I remained together. You were already lost. A single grain of sand into the wind. I am surprised we found you first when the winds turned. You came home so easily. And with nothing but a small flesh wound." He gestured at her side. "The other two will not be so simple."

A small flesh wound was a cut or a scrape, not an arrow through the gut. She must reframe her reality around Ariaas and Brenor.

Another split rail fence came into view, this one outlining a tiny square around a small home, comparable to the groundskeeper's cottage. In the yard, an old carriage grew vines much as the castle.

A round woman with a dumpling shape with a weak chin—nearly as wide as she was tall—waited on the lawn. She waved vigorously. "Hello! Who's this?"

Brenor faltered, his words trapped, much as Lenora remembered Eran. The thought pained her.

At his fumbling, Lenora interjected, "I'm Brenor's second cousin on his mother's side."

"Oh, you are family." The woman's cheeks glowed rose amongst the wildflowers and the tall grass in her small yard as she took Lenora's hand. "How is it you have come to visit?"

No need for questions she too was ill-prepared to answer.

"Merely passing through. You have a lovely home. Did you grow up in this area?"

"Oh, thank you! No. I grew up south of Ellace, near the Arden Reaon. I am a descendant of a highborn of the Argentirus. Heilara Favaelier Ansivor Ebrolie is my name."

The round woman beamed. Her fingers gripped one another in front of her waist, and she began to bow before realizing it should be the other person's responsibility. She adopted an odd stance, her shoulders pressed back, and her eyelashes batted, a smug smirk of importance smeared across her cheeks.

"How wonderful." Lenora smiled. "You must be proud."

"I am, dear, I am." Mrs. Ebrolie asked, "Do you have time to stay for tea and cakes?"

"Unfortunately, Ariaas is waiting for us," Brenor interjected. "Maybe another day."

"Will you be joining Brenor when he returns? You are welcome to stay for tea and cakes when you come for Taren. I would love to speak to you more."

"Certainly." Lenora nodded with genuine sincerity. "I'll plan on tea and cakes with you when I return to Aroun Vaer."

"Wonderful! Brenor, dear boy. Will you be back soon?"

"At least six weeks I would assume."

Her face rumpled.

Brenor hugged Taren against his will. When Brenor released him, he ran amongst the wildflowers biting at the swarming bugs, a smile on his face.

· + · + · · + · · + · ·

Lenora and Brenor spent the entirety of the day riding due west through the winding dirt roads of the forest to reach the border to Dhaesreaon, and to the edge of the Aroun Vaer land where they met Ariaas.

When they stopped for the evening, Brenor made a fire while Ariaas grumbled they had no proper meals. Lenora studied the maps of lands she had never seen.

"Why are we not taking the mountain pass through the Blackwood? Wouldn't it be faster? The pass between Mount Ohbrolis and Mount Yunosa is so far north."

Ariaas used his pack as a pillow, adjusting his head. When he was comfortable, he said, "We avoid The Blackwood."

Brenor inched in, whispering, "Ariaas met Lord Dumous of the Quparae many years ago. He still won't look me in the eye when I ask what happened."

Again, Lenora's questions multiplied. "Where are Qcaranen from? I hadn't heard that word until I met you both."

"It is a lineage of Qabriah—a chameleon, should you see the pin. They call themselves The Hidden." Brenor added, "You seem to know little of the ways of this world, even born within it and raised not far from us."

Ariaas shot up, half asleep, and pointed toward her. "Should I be a betting man, I should wager that was done with great intent." He exchanged a comical gaze with Brenor and said, "I don't know who I am fooling. Should any man or woman wish to place a bet, I would near stake the fate of Aroun Vaer on such a gamble! Wouldn't be the first time, nor the last, I tried to rid myself of the stone heap."

His point made, Ariaas curled back into the ground and within moments snored in sputters.

While she had further time with Brenor and no open ears to hear their conversation, she sat closer, whispering many questions in lieu of sleeping. The day's hot weather grew pleasant in the darkness.

"Tell me what you know of those of The South Sea," Brenor murmured. "The lineages of those of death."

"Well, I thought I knew a lot, but I knew nothing. I know most keep to their own people, within their own cities and villages. Some lineages in the West have the ability to control the earth and what dwells upon it, though the lineages' names escape me now. As you said, those of The South Sea are people of death; some can be revived after death, some can will death upon another."

Brenor nodded. "They are near all warring people in one way or another. Though their armies are built mainly of the Remerard, skilled with the blade and nimble as they come, with near no soul as I hear it. Though such a thing is mere speculation." He chuckled. "I shall find you a book soon. You will need to know all the lineages, though I will warn you, there are many. You will need to know who you should concern yourself with and who you should not."

Ariaas shouted from his sleep, "For the time, anyone not in this room is considered someone you should be wary of!"

Lenora fell back, upsetting the earth and a tin pot, startled by his sharp reaction.

Brenor laughed, lifting his arm, and allowing it to fall in a heap. "He is not awake."

After some time adjusting to Ariaas's odd sleeping patterns, Lenora whispered, "Where are our parents?"

"Ariaas heard—from a source of questionable reputability—they are both deceased." Brenor kicked off his muddled boots. "He had not seen or heard of them, since before the siege from the Queen's Guard."

She finally asked the question she'd been holding onto all day. "Where are Arienne and Thealor?"

He considered her question far too long for Lenora's liking.

Finally, he began, "Arienne is atop Mount Reldor, imprisoned at The Reldory. Within the hanging cage, as they call it. Theo, a servant, at Brouverg Castle atop Mount Ohbrolis. Not far from here. In the same location since the day they arrived twenty-three years ago. No need to cloak them when they are untouchable."

"They are held captive?"

"As were you. Though you seem to have been held under much kinder circumstances than we anticipated." Brenor offered her a knowing nod. "They kept each of us far away from civilians, and far away from one another." He added, "They wanted us never to find one another. Never to reunite."

Oedd had been honest. Lenora never witnessed such atrocities, let alone lived them, and she shuddered to think of what had happened to her mother and father, and Arienne and Thealor. When she discovered Ebigan and Dyan's intentions, she felt pity for herself—though now she sat baffled—hearing she was kept in the most pleasant of circumstances.

"If they had their way, we would never see one another again. They could have executed us then. Young children. Unable to defend ourselves."

Brenor unrolled his sleeves and dragged the patch of leather over his arms for warmth. "Queen Navaera certainly would not allow us to be raised by the Yurelan, her enemy. We were taken by her order—though I doubt what happened after was her intent. As I was told, the four of us were to be brought to her, so she should decide for herself our nature upon meeting us. Pass judgment if we were truly dark or light. Though none of us ever made it far enough south to see her. Death would've been better in the eyes of many, though she frowned upon the execution of children."

Lenora rolled her eyes and the dense hole in her middle. "How fortunate."

"Dare I guess the new king has the same feeling, lest the order to execute would have been given directly." Brenor's face flushed and contorted into a grimace.

"I could've told them. Should they have asked!" Ariaas shouted, suddenly awake. "If you wish to know the way to make a monster, imprison a child for yet committed sins."

Lenora would need to get used to his sudden outbursts. They had a long journey ahead.

Ariaas sat, rubbing the sleep from his eyes.

Her thoughts returned to Arienne and Thealor. "Have you tried to free them?"

"So many times, I've lost count," lamented Ariaas, a shadow casting over his eyes. "Many years ago, I stopped trying. When Brenor was a boy. I stopped when I finally understood I had no chance—not alone."

Brenor said, "Once King Barrard knows you are gone ... he may move to take them."

"You speak my thoughts aloud." Ariaas stretched and cracked his limbs. "Since we left Say Livore, the scenarios have been playing in my mind. Time won't be on our side to retrieve them."

"Will we try to free them?" A surge of excitement passed her. "How will we go?" The thrill of a valiant rescue, danger shoved to the wayside, called to her every instinct. "Will you train me before we go with a sword, too?"

"We must." Brenor nodded, equal parts amused and melancholy. "As soon as new information presents itself. As it sits now, we cannot get into either building. If you know anything about Brouverg Castle or The Reldory, we welcome it."

Her enthusiastic pace slowed. She shook her head. "I know nothing of either."

+ ——————— · + · ✦ · + · ——————— +

In the morning, after restless sleep, the three reached the mountain gorge. Brenor rubbed his neck, while Belcen stirred below his saddle.

The hair on Lenora's neck stood on end. Along the Ravine Road, they were trapped the moment they strode between the high rocks, she could feel it, with no escape until they pressed through the other side of the mountains.

Ariaas stood petulant, eying a small dirt path winding into the northern hill. "This is the trail to Brouverg Castle."

The three idled. Ariaas's jaw tensed while Brenor bowed his head in silence.

Lenora sat atop Luscan's saddle, horrified. Words eluded her. She sputtered to their departing backs, "You just leave Thealor there? You ... just pass by?"

Brenor lamented, "We have no other choice."

Lenora dismounted, her boots crunching against gravel. The path yawned before her—and her blood itched to follow the ribbon of dirt and stone. Somewhere behind those cragged slopes, her brother lived, shackled by chains she could not yet see.

And she was standing there. *Free.*

It would be so easy to go alone. To trade caution for courage.

Her fingers twitched at her side.

She clenched her jaw until it ached, forcing her feet to stay rooted beside Brenor. Forcing herself to believe that waiting—for now—was not surrender.

"I see your eyes. I had that look once," Ariaas said. "His time will come."

"We can go now. I can sneak inside."

"No." Ariaas answered sharply, rubbing his collarbone. "*Impulsive* is the last thing we need to be."

Gazing over the rocky path, Lenora swallowed the temptation to go on her own. There was a way, wasn't there? Certainly, there was a way they hadn't tried. Her thoughts moved as lightning in the night sky—sudden and swift—before she reluctantly accepted Ariaas's orders.

"You must leave him. For now."

Lenora grasped Luscan's reins. Though she had yet to meet Thealor—not that she could recall, at least—she had the nagging impulse to desert Ariaas and Brenor on the road and make for the mountain. If the man was anything like her newfound brother, he deserved to be released from his binds today—not some unspecified time in the future. He needed justice.

Ariaas interrupted her thoughts. "Hey—do I need to worry about you sneaking off in the night?"

"No," Lenora said, and even somewhat meant it. She clenched the quill in her pocket. "I promise."

ROAD TO TANES

I had seen it — he and I as teenagers, as adults, growing old together, our faces lined with time. Ours was a love unlike any other.

- Diary of Daisirie Cabredd Mire, Volume 7, Entry 2

Sissel awoke a third morning with her bare cheek upon the dirt. Her hands, at first bound by thick twine behind her back, bore blistering rashes, the skin stained wine-colored around her wrists. Over the long days, the rope had loosened while the soldiers ignored her.

That evening, the cord settled into her flesh beside the fire.

"Better not get near her," a soldier scoffed, his brutish voice to her back. Amongst themselves, the soldiers spoke of her during their meals. Almost as if she had no ears. One tossed a crust of bread onto the ground before her. "Go on now, little birdie."

They laughed while she learned to eat without hands.

High Commander Ravaris made no attempt to stop their abuse. She did not speak to them often or feed into their musings of Sissel, Commander Tuyure, or the mal'soniure. But something dwelled behind her dark eyes, a blackened sparkle or a pleasure at Sissel's suffering. Possibly—no, probably—Ravaris' disposition was worse than any of those under her command.

"Why not kill her?" a snide voice rose behind her. "Has the job not been done?"

"You heard her name, you fool," another shouted. They whispered, mocking her name—*Vak-ARRA*, pronouncing it with a hard *R*.

"Too hasty a decision if she is highborn. If you kill her, there is no one if they come to claim her. Then we're at fault."

A calloused female voice replied, "She should go to The Reldory. Better to make it near impossible to claim her."

Ravaris threw a silver pot, hot water splattering over the soldiers' black boots, silencing their gossip. They jumped and scattered as young children scolded by their mother.

The commander created a second fire built for one, claiming a branch from their flames and moving it to her own set of logs and kindling. While the soldiers cautiously chattered, she read a pocket-sized book and warmed herself.

Sissel overheard their musings—she would be hidden away at The Reldory for her crimes. The only prison in The South Sea suited to her. Her cheek twisted into the dirt while she tried to conceal her tears. The rumors of the cage and its torments twisted through her belly.

Within their band, they assigned Sissel to another soldier, Kaloyein. He reminded her of a vulture—a lanky young man, odd for a person of the South. Perhaps one day he would grow into his adult body and beak-like nose.

"As a fellow Roscidarra, you are immune to her curses," Ravaris had assured him. "No lineage can perform such acts on their own people." She gifted Kaloyein a second sword too heavy for his frame to carry alongside the narrow, delicate blade at his belt.

Still, Kaloyein moved too slowly for the High Commander's liking. She cursed and growled when he led the company. They could have arrived by the summer Uen'can at The Reldory had he not been so slow. Now, they would miss the day the bridge opened by a hair and be forced to wait another half year for the building to open again.

The following evening, the soldiers slept at the Inn in Tevacas. They left Sissel to sleep pressed into the mud on the ground outside the kitchen door.

When they gathered their horses in the morning, Sissel overheard, "Last night in a bed for a long while." She stretched as best she could through her binds, dreading their walk through the wild. Since their departure from the peninsula, she had held silent, futilely attempting to understand her circumstances and what had transpired. No part of her wished to anger them, and she obeyed their every command.

But the possibility of never seeing her grandmother again weighed heavy on her heart. What had Thaesla told her? What did her grandmother think of her now that she knew what had happened in the square? When she closed her eyes, she thought of the blue silk dress and her grandmother's joy at seeing the denmero. Each memory bruised her heart more.

Could she really have ... killed a man?

South of Tevacas, tensions rose amongst the company. No signs denoted where Tenuel ended, and Felreaon began.

"Stay drawn to the shore," High Commander Ravaris ordered. "People of the sea are kinder than those of the land in these parts."

As she instructed, the company hugged the soft sanded shore, following lines of small dwellings along the horizon and the slow simmering waters bordering them. Three or four civilians came into view—although Sissel could not see well at a distance—and High Commander Ravaris left the company at the edge of the beach to approach them. Ravaris pointed to her often during their conversation.

The civilians signaled for the soldiers to follow, leading the company into the town of wet stone streets where the air tasted of fish. When they drew in closer, they found wooden boats at the docks. Commander Ravaris' conversation with the civilians continued. They watched her outside a small structure Sissel assumed to be an old boat house.

Perhaps they were in Jaisett.

When she parted from their company, the High Commander held two papers with a crimson wax seal and a symbol Sissel could not decipher. One she tucked in her jacket pocket, the second she gave to Kaloyein, saying, "Permissions to travel south. Keep it safe."

The company was welcomed to move through Felreaon for the time, though it did little to ease the tensions in the group. Regardless of their authorization, they were not welcome enough to stay in a bed or under a roof. They traveled beyond Jaisett, hugging the shore until dusk. When they settled, they slept on the sand around the fire, the soft crashing of waves behind them.

As light broke through the sky, sea air rushed over her face. Sissel trembled in fear and wept in silence. Her hunger and exhaustion exacerbated her guilt.

High Commander Ravaris awoke Kaloyein by kicking his boot. "Here we separate."

"I ... thought we were all meant to stay together until Tanes."

"You thought wrong. A dozen soldiers don't need to attend a fragile child's transfer. If you can't handle taking her to Tanes yourself, I'll find someone who can."

He nodded, trembling upon his knees.

"Stay in Tanes until her transfer at the winter Uen'can," Ravaris ordered. "When she crosses the bridge and is secured, you may return to Islarourne. If you fail to do your job, don't bother returning."

The others did not address Kaloyein or Sissel further. They did not take their morning meal, quickly packed their belongings, and kicked sand atop the dying flames.

When High Commander Ravaris mounted her black steed, she addressed Kaloyein a final time. "Head straight southeast. I trust you know your way when you arrive in our lands." Her eyes narrowed as her eyes judged him. "Don't disappoint me further."

Ravaris spurred her horse, and the soldiers parted ways.

Kaloyein and Sissel watched them disappear along the shoreline.

His breathing remained heavy, and she heard the *thump thump* of his pulse. His fear struck her as odd. Did he not live surrounded by dealers of death as a boy? One of his own people? He fumbled, shook, and refused to meet her eyes. She supposed that knowing people possess power and seeing them wield such abilities are two vastly different matters.

When Kaloyein wished to walk, Sissel sat atop the back of his ashen mare. More often, she followed behind, bound by rope to the reins while he pulled at the slack so she maintained his pace. Her sandals broke in the first days, and her shirt ripped on the thorns of a caberune bush, tearing gashes into her abdomen. Her jacket protected her flesh from the harsh summer sun during the day and the cold of the night.

They traveled for several weeks this way—a journey which should have taken much less should they both have been on the back of a horse. She ate scraps of food he threw onto the ground she picked up with her teeth. Kaloyein called the mare by no name, hissing, and cracked his whip when she did not comply with his immediate wishes. Sissel could tell that the horse was agitated and exhausted, just as she was.

Kaloyein never spoke to her, not once in all the long days.

Crossing the border to Felreaon appeared to ease Kaloyein some. Sissel suspected he feared dirt, wind, and sea while within their lands— feared they would rise and swallow him whole.

+ ———— · + · ✦ · + · ———— +

Stray birch trees and scattered sparrows lined the road. By the time they arrived in Tanes, the midday sun sweltered, and the winds blew in warm air from the north.

Sissel ached from the hair atop her head, through her soul and out her feet. Was she even human anymore? Would they leave her with the slop and the pigs? Maybe she should allow the ashen mare to drag her. It might be more comfortable. Her hips ached as daggers replaced her joints, and the muscles were made of sand, grinding with every move. Tangles matted her hair; some had become stuck across her face, hardened by sweat or tears, and her eyelashes had glued together at the outer edges.

The sky silk dress would have been more comfortable, the light fabric, cooler. Urine would not have held in the seams like in pants.

Kaloyein only stopped when he needed.

They passed small buildings, dwellings perhaps, to find their destination. She assumed these structures housed the baker or the town healer. Two soldiers awaited their arrival—a woman in a regulated stance and a bearded man of statelier gray and black cloaks.

Kaloyein abandoned Sissel on the dirt road still bound to the mare.

The bearded man addressed Kaloyein with harsh tones, a dark, fierce glare, and a strong brow.

Kaloyein cowered.

The bearded man's tone grew crueler, louder, though Sissel could not decipher the specific words he spoke. The female soldier struck Kaloyein across the cheekbone with a closed fist, and he tumbled to the dirt. The bearded man did not flinch at his fall nor when he scrambled for a foothold.

When Kaloyein rose, the man spoke further, motioning towards Sissel. Kaloyein slunk toward the dwellings like a tail-tucked young dog; the female soldier approached.

Sissel expected her legs might buckle, the empty sensation inside her bones causing her to sway as if she were upon the sea. The bearded man stood, petulant, studying her. His eyes ran across her matted hair, once warm and golden brown, now patched in grime. She stared at the dirt, unsure of the nuances of their culture.

The air felt dense at his formal, composed stance and judgment over her. Across his chest, his fine gray and black fabrics were covered in pins and stately adornments, much like High Commander Ravaris'. The others did as he asked without hesitation.

Was he concerned about the well-being of his soldiers? Or himself? Sissel carried no weapons. She arrived haggard, far worse than Kaloyein, a stray dog beaten in the streets. Perhaps he, too, was concerned about the lineage of the Roscidarra.

Some time passed before he spoke in a stern, rasped voice, "I am Commander Benson of the Armies of The South Sea. Please accept my apologies for the nature of your journey. Soldiers are forbidden from using such barbaric methods under my command." He righted his shoulders. "Have you been fed?"

Sissel began to reply; however, the voice she expected to part her lips did not. The weak sounds from her own mouth startled her. When she attempted again, the words came broken and exhausted, hushed tones through thick sanded skin. "Day before yesterday." She did not dare to say scraps from the dirt.

Across the dirt, shadows of his hands gestured to his soldiers. The woman untied her binds. Sissel twisted her wrists, the aching pain of her raw flesh worth the price for their freedom.

Commander Benson asked, "Your name?"

"Sisselara Vacarro," she said, more manageable than the last words but still challenging.

"Hmm," he repeated, "Vak-*ARRA*." His pronunciation of her name was so heavily accented that it sounded foreign. The same way she had heard it spoken by the soldiers some weeks ago.

"We would not wish to receive you or accommodate you should it not be ordered by the High Commander. We only learned of your impending arrival yesterday, and details were sparse." He continued, "You were moved to Tanes because it is close to The Reldory, where you will be transported, as I understand it, on the next Uen'can. As the summer opening has passed, you shall call Tanes home for several months."

Sissel's shoulders dropped further at the mention of *The Reldory, home,* and *several months.* She didn't belong there, as a prisoner or otherwise. She didn't even fully understand her crime. Her chest rose and fell, irregulated, while she squelched her rising panic.

"Tanes was once a small town. Now it is home to the Armies of The South Sea and, on occasion, those of the other regions. It has no formal cells. It is not built for prisoners. I only have one small room with a washroom. It will be yours until you leave, should you abide by the rules I set forth for you." Commander Benson's spine stiffened while he waited to ensure she grasped his message. "It is the small room or chained to the tree outside it."

The two proceeded down the path, soldiers at their back, guiding the ashen mare. Kindness met her like a foreign tongue—unexpected, and almost impossible to believe. A bed? For her? She had seen nothing of compassion from the other soldiers she had encountered from The South Sea. Though Sissel kept her eyes on the dirt, she could feel the stares of those who passed her, glaring at her matted hair and sunken posture.

"Do not mind their glances," Commander Benson assured her. "Your tale fascinates them. One of our own, hidden away in a foreign land, killing a soldier of Tenuel with an ability of The South. This much excitement has not passed through this town in years." His voice, though dark and rasped, seemed almost humored. "I had meant to send Captain Kalory to your arrival, but I had to see whom they spoke of for myself. I must say, you are much smaller than I anticipated. You are almost a child."

Sissel had passed her twenty-third birthday, not near a child. She glanced at the passing women—tall, expansive, built of firm muscle. Besides these women, she appeared frail, and would have even before weeks of malnourishment.

"This village will be kind to you, should you be kind to it. You will be given a warm bed, meals, water. You will not be beaten or tortured. I do not believe in such practices without cause."

When they moved from dirt to cobbled streets, the ache in her hips deepened over uneven terrain. Commander Benson slowed his strides to match her laggard pace. Uniforms of varying colors traipsed around them, doors opened and closed to barracks; a fountain trickled water in the town center, and the smell of casting metal and heat permeated the air. The buildings were closer and taller in the center, a market, a tavern, a weapons station, their signs in faded birchwood swayed unpainted.

After what seemed like an eternity, they stopped before a simple wooden structure with a round brass handle and one modest window. The dwelling sat before a road, not near the center of the city, and yet not outside.

Commander Benson crossed his arms behind his back and said, "Should you attempt to escape, you will be executed."

Sissel's stomach twisted, and bile rose to her throat.

"We have no time for such matters. Nor for the matter of attending to High Commander Ravaris' agendas. Wait in silence for your transfer. You shall eat and have a warm bed. We shall leave you be. Are we in agreement?"

While Commander Benson opened the door, Sissel nodded, fixated on his unsoiled tight-laced black boots.

Sissel attempted to lift her leg, but her weak body trembled and collapsed. After righting herself, the Commander firmly gripped her bicep and steadied her up the steps and through the threshold. Once inside, she attempted to raise her sights to meet his but could not gather the courage. She had questions; those she was not brave enough to ask. Commander Benson did not seem like a man who wanted to give answers. He seemed like he wished for silent compliance in all manner of things.

A soldier arrived carrying a tray of food—an odd mixture of breakfast and supper—two slices of bread, water, an apple, a boiled egg, and green leaves. A feast for her starving body.

Commander Benson closed the gap between them, towering over her, smelling of cedar and mint as he lingered. He directed, "Bathe. Eat."

He turned to leave, but before he departed, he stopped himself. "My curiosity is getting the best of me, and I must ask. Did you intend to kill that soldier?"

The unbearable weight in her chest of stealing a man's life had departed for a time, replaced with a new host of issues and moral consequences to ponder: hunger, pain, justice. The heaviness of confinement and the circumstances of her future had distracted her like the horseshoes clanking in rhythm on the road.

But this simple question stabbed daggers of guilt into her chest. Tears streamed over her cheeks, a rushing river, and her face contorted. She covered the emotion unsuccessfully with her palms, choking on her breath.

"I did not expect so," he said sadly. "Good day, Miss Vak-*ARRA*."

✦ —————— · + · ✦ · + · —————— ✦

Sissel ate her fill until nothing on the plate remained. She did not want to bathe; she ached for rest but washed, nonetheless. No use in making such a beautiful clean bed muddled. The gray cotton pants and blouse, in a neat, folded pile on the bed, fit her well enough. She slept through the afternoon, through supper, and woke sometime in the darkness, not long before dawn.

One light dangled from the beam in the ceiling. The insignia of The South Sea, eight triangles, pointed to the inside—creating the negative impression of a star—littered the room. A small table and chair in the corner. When she stood at the bedside, she could see through the edge of a small window. This is where she might observe the world, the small world beyond her window in Tanes. The night breeze blew in, soft, fresh.

A few small animals scampered outside the window—squirrels, perhaps; birds chirped in the trees. Two soldiers walked by, on their way somewhere, alone and in casual formation. After the two others passed, Commander Benson walked the length of the cobblestone. A hint of darkness lingered when the new morning light surrounded him. She absorbed his entire appearance, bolder now than when in his presence.

This man appeared too young to bear the title of commander, thirty years at most. In the early hours, he wore less formal attire than yesterday. His glimmering gold and silver pins were missing: a long golden blade, the symbol of the commander, and a second, bearing the same star as on her sink.

Over his shoulder, he glanced toward her quarters.

As if I own it, and live here permanently. Maybe he simply glances this way to see if I remain in my confines.

Her intimidation faded as she observed like a bird perched in the trees. The other soldiers did not notice her this morning. Commander Benson might not notice her now.

For a moment, she thought his eyes met hers, but she could not be sure.

Commander Benson carried on. She backed away from the window and sat at the bedside, blood draining from her face. Would he rush the two wooden steps and scold her for watching him?

She glanced around the room, hoping for a distraction.

The door and the round brass knob bore the same emblem of The South Sea. They stamped the star everywhere. They used dark, heavy wood; many objects were embossed. Even the fabric chairs proudly displayed gold and cherry embroidery. Everything about The South Sea, even the women, appeared masculine, strong, and aggressive. Though, the room she would call her prison was nicer than the sofa she had slept on in Wesilea.

Commander Benson's blunt warning replayed: *should you attempt to escape, you will be executed.*

Her grandmother would have rescued Sissel when her body was less brittle and frail. She had cautioned Sissel to run to Aroun Vaer should she be in danger. An old friend lived there.

Her grandmother made Sissel memorize every detail of the journey:

Travel east until you meet the mountains. Travel the Ravine Road, the pass between the northernmost peaks—dangerous, but direct. When the land descends, travel southeast. You should find it after some days, the split rail fence. Do not go through! Wait until you see the road.

Never leave the road.

NEVER leave the road.

Even if she could find Aroun Vaer from this new location—even if the soldiers retreated, leaving the village abandoned and her the sole inhabitant—she was not brave enough to attempt an escape.

8 QERUS STREET

Five riders galloped toward Lenora, Ariaas, and Brenor. Under his breath, Ariaas instructed, "Move to the shade at the other side of me." He issued Lenora a clear warning. "And stay away from Brenor."

She guided Luscan below the branches of the tree as instructed, heart slamming into her ribs. Why didn't they flee at the same pace the riders dashed toward them? The riders constricted the gap, clashing a cloud of dust in their wake.

Ariaas ordered, "Shoulders high."

Lenora righted her spine. They gained ground, faster, faster, and now she could see the whites of their eyes.

"Don't meet their sight. But don't appear to hide. Never speak unless spoken to. Never glance up at the same time as Brenor."

Ariaas never thought to warn me? Instead of now, with riders thundering straight for us?

From what she'd seen, most travelers paid them no attention, passing with a silent nod, more caring of their own pursuits than the business of strangers.

She perched still as a statue and impending danger throttled forward.

A woman, spear in hand, stopped her steed in a violent skid. Feathers and jewels adorned her weapon, complementing her black hair and matching skin. The others stopped behind her lead, all bearing similar wares.

The woman addressed Ariaas. "Your name?"

"Othen Duekko, of the Khayernamen." The lie slipped from Ariaas's tongue. "The Warrior of the Mountain of Dhaesreaon."

The woman pointed with the steel tip of her spear. "And them?"

"My son and daughter, Ynasar and Ynaca Duekko of the Khayerna-men." Ariaas answered with charm. A lie he conjured in the moment or rehearsed and recited often?

Brenor perched high on his horse, his shoulders flaunting their width.

Lenora adopted a similar pose of a prideful posture, hoping her trepidation didn't leak. Against Ariaas's wishes, she eyed them, suspecting a visual of the strangers would ease the thrumming of her pulse.

The women donned twisting silks tied across their shoulders in tan, plum, and nightshade. Their hair, cut close to their scalp. They did not wear hides and furs of Dhaesreaon, meant for the cold of the mountains.

"People of the River Realm wear their lineage stamped upon their chests," said the woman, curiosity in her voice. Gold jewels, in swaying motion, stretched the length of her ears, clanking. "You wear no such charms."

"My sword is all I need," rebuked Ariaas.

The woman's face fell. "What business brings you, carrying arms no less, over the border of Felreaon?"

"A mistake of steps to the south, I'm afraid. We meant to ride the border toward Tessira. And we travel nowhere unarmed. Not in this climate," he said politely. "My daughter is the hunter amongst our party. The bow and arrow are for our meals." Ariaas leaned in, not bothering to lower his gaze or his voice. "Though in truth, all three of us are well armed for protection. Should we be so unfortunate to stumble upon the Yurelan in our travels."

At the word Yurelan, they chattered amongst themselves, their horses prancing. After some deliberation, the woman said, "The Khayernamen are not our enemy. Travel back to the border. An hour ride north. Take your journey there. The Ilnem Reaon does not accept travelers."

"The Ilnem Reaon—" Ariaas repeated, the first instant his calm demeanor faltered. His reply stirred them once more, their horses cavorting while they righted the grips on their weapons.

Sternly, the woman asked, "Is there a dispute?"

"No." Ariaas sat taller. "Your lady is a bold ruler. She may name her realm anything she wishes."

Lenora caught the flicker of grudging respect between them—an odd pissing match where neither side wanted to blink first. "Be on your way then, Othen Duekko."

After they departed, Lenora exhaled her held breath.

When they were far from earshot, she asked, "Who were they?"

Ariaas explained, "We wandered inside their borders. They patrol there, close to where the four regions meet. None enter their lands outside of their authority."

"The Lady of the Milnire is a bold ruler indeed," Brenor remarked, "that she would name her realm against the wishes of the crown. Did you see? The girl in the back, the one on the black steed? A Xentirie."

"I didn't see her." A tentative smile crept over Ariaas's face, as he nodded, processing what Brenor told him. "Lady Jareleine is wise to match. She sends a Milnire to patrol the borders, followed by a Xentirie."

"What *did* you see?" Lenora asked. In the instructions not to watch them, she had seen little other than the colors of silks and horses.

"Felreaon is one of the few regions which understands the balance of their talents; they understand they have more impact in combination than isolated. They cannot restrain the waters of the rivers, but they can influence the current of the seas, the rushing of the winds, the tumbling of the rain. They can affect the presence of flame, the Milnire, The Ruler of Flames. But I digress. Together, the talents of Felreaon can make matters unbearable for unfortunate travelers. They are known to not be friendly with the lineages of their own region. They hold claims on the entire northeast portion of Felreaon. The woman in the back wore the silver pin of an anemone—a Xentirie who controls the winds."

"We were not even close to her land, a half day at best." Brenor replied.

Ariaas mused, "Perhaps *she, too,* is expanding her territory."

"We ride for Jaisett," Lenora pressed, wishing she understood the world as they did. "That is in Felreaon."

"We will stay at the border inside Tenuel, and cross as we reach the eastern shore. Jaisett is a seafaring town. The Milnire do not dwell there."

✦ ———— ·✦·✦·✦· ———— ✦

Jaisett's damp, cobbled streets smelled of fresh fish pulled in from boats docked for the evening. The three wandered the long alleys for hours, a dark caste by the shadows of the roofs.

"How will we know where to find her?" Lenora twisted her hair into a knot at the base of her neck and drew her leather satchel over her shoulder. The letter Thaelsa had sent was vague at best, and their search had thus far unearthed no leads.

Ariaas groaned. "I've never been to Jaisett, and the woman didn't leave instructions."

Lenora tightened her grip on Luscan's reins. "Does she know anyone here?"

"I haven't seen her in a decade. And even when I had, I wasn't current on her acquaintances."

"There's a man there." Lenora gestured toward a man closing a shop door below an ornate sign. "I can ask him if he knows anyone who meets her description."

Lenora started toward the man, but Ariaas grasped her by the arm, yanking her back into the darkness.

"I told you before we left Aroun Vaer. I will do the talking." Ariaas left the two of them with the horses in the dank, thin road without another word. Watching him from afar as he spoke with the man, Lenora narrowed her eyes.

When he returned, she stood wide-legged, arms crossed, lips pressed together. "I'm not useless."

"I don't think you're useless," he whispered, ushering her into the dark alley. "I think there are a finite amount of people who know of your existence, and even a smaller amount who truly know who you are. I don't want to give these people a reason to remember your face."

Lenora's frustration waned. She hadn't thought of matters that way. He might agitate her, but he did have good intentions.

They wandered further as the skies turned to night until they found a small inn, as good a place as any to check. Once inside, Brenor and Lenora warmed themselves beside the fire while Ariaas approached the innkeeper.

"We are looking for a woman named Thaesla," he disclosed. "Do you have any guests at the inn by that name?"

The man's stretched, drawn face sagged; his mouth hung agape. His long boney fingers rang a small silver bell. When a young girl hurried in from the backroom, he spoke in a language of hands.

The girl rustled through a stack of papers, finding the one she sought and handed it to Ariaas. "No one here by the name Thaesla." Black ink, smeared by the moisture in the air, bled through the folds. "But we were told if anyone comes asking for her to give them this."

8 Qerus Street

"North a few blocks." The girl pointed. "Then turn toward the sea."

The northern portion of town held houses close together, the paint on the wooden walls fading from the salty air. Ariaas knocked with a firm hand on the door even at the late hour. A man answered, his skin deep umber.

"We have come seeking a woman named Thaesla. Do you know her?"

The man had a clean shaven face, with a wide nose, high cheeks, and short hair. He wore no uniforms; instead, he bore casual clothing akin to those of the sea. Lenora could see no visible weapon. He sat still, his eyes dark, both soft and hard all at once.

A deep voice rose from his thick lips, his eyes drawn to an unseeable horizon in the depth of his thoughts. "banah ... lain ... khoetath ... canua ... ne'routh." The words jerked, the language unnatural to his tongue. He spoke much as a child giving a speech he had memorized at his parents' request. "ea ... ve'lea se greaon."

Ariaas crossed his arms firmly. "You are slaughtering a beautiful language. *ea ve'lea se greaon* is the final line; it is not thrown in the middle."

The man's deep concentration refused to be waned. He continued though the words seemed to pain him, "... baell egeanan ever."

"*evir!*" Ariaas shouted, pinching the bridge of his nose. "I implore you to make this stop."

Brenor held out his hands. "That is plenty to prove you know her. Thank you."

"Do you even know what you are saying?" Ariaas spoke bluntly. "The correct version is *banah lain khoetath, canuan eise ne'routh. eind acelone thea uneh cairu. baell egeanan evir lea crymer hesu. ea ve'lea se greaon.* The words translate to 'Friend or enemy, today I am neither. I have only arrived with words. Whom I will be once you hear them is yours to choose.'"

The man's lips grew stern, his eyes less welcoming.

"Please ignore him," Brenor implored. "The gesture, however, is appreciated. I recognize you now, though it has been many years. We met in Wesilea at Thaesla's home when we were boys. Jahen, is it?"

The man nodded in confirmation.

"Thaesla said we would find her here?"

Jahen rubbed his temple. "She never made the journey across the Bay."

Ariaas's tone shifted from anger to concern. "What has happened?"

"Much."

"Do you care to elaborate?"

Jahen shook his head in slow motions, grasping his sandals from the floor. "I will take you to her."

The boat journeyed through the night while Lenora marveled at the stars' beauty, their reflection waltzing on the face of the sea. Some hours passed before she could stand on the vessel without losing her footing. Everything about the journey to this point, in hindsight, thrilled her now that she had quiet time to recount all she had seen of the world.

Jahen barely spoke, but his hand guided the ship as if the sea itself bent to his will. Watching him, Lenora felt as though she was seeing pure enchantment.

"I can't say the same for the winds, but it's almost as if the sea herself wished us a rapid journey. The currents have been kind."

Lenora watched Jahen as he spoke. His face carved a small smile, so minuscule it would have been missed altogether if Lenora would not have been watching for his reaction. She beamed. "*You* will the sea!"

Jahen nodded slightly before turning his sights to the sails, pressed rigid by the winds.

"You are of ..." Brenor hadn't taught her the lineages of the west yet, and she hoped he'd fill in the mystery.

"Jahen Jentaisar Marelis. *Tu'dende*"—he nodded—"dormant highborn of the family Jentaisar of the Xentirie. Dominant highborn of the family Marelis of the Marisaerson of Felreaon." He offered them his formal titles, as he wore no pins. "My sister, a Xentirie, as our mother. If she had been with us, our journey would have been shorter still. No Xentirie commands the winds as she."

The winds almost spoke through the sails, sending them rattling, their rapid gusts speaking their familial preferences as if they, too, wished his sibling was along for the journey.

Lenora was stunned he offered her more words in one moment than he had the entire evening.

"Highborn?" Fascinated, she rushed to sit at his side. "How do you do it? How do you control the sea?"

"I think of what I wish to happen." Jahen pressed his fist into his chest. "Feel it." He trailed his fingers into the briny waters. "And she listens."

Enchanted, she traced his every movement, captivated by the rhythm of the water he commanded. The world contained so much more than plucking apples from a tree.

Lenora leaned her head back onto her arms and watched the night sky. For the first time, she was truly living.

HER PRICE

His words haunt. "That name was killed in the Dire wars a century ago."
                    - *Diary of Daisirie Cabredd Mire, Volume 5*, Entry 223

N avy night morphed to black while the stars on the western horizon waned. Lenora wrapped her cloak tight, gawking at the cliffs before them. As they drew closer, white tips sloshed onto the rocks. The water calmed from the bustle of the day. A few lights burned in the windows at the top of the precipice, darkening as they neared.

Jahen secured the boat and led them up the stairs, then through the city of Wesilea in darkness. Lenora tallied the breaks in the road when they twisted west, north, and then back east again.

When they arrived at a cobalt door, Jahen nodded. "I leave you here. I'll be at the boat." He departed, disappearing toward the docks.

The three stood below bright fuchsia blooms growing in winding vines along the outside of the threshold. Ariaas twisted the handle. Locked. He struck the door, shaking the aurum flowers on the wall. Lenora grazed her fingers over the deep plum petals, fading to maroon and cherry at the edges, and smelled the sweet vanilla blooms.

A woman answered, her brown eyes illuminating. She grasped Ariaas's cheeks within her palms. "I've never been so happy to see your old handsome face in all my days. Come in, come in."

Thaesla.

She locked the door behind them. Upstairs, she and Ariaas embraced each other as good friends long departed, relieved to see the other unharmed since their last meeting.

Thaesla turned toward Lenora, extending her hands for her to grasp. "I can't believe I lived long enough to see this day." She held Lenora's arms wide, surveying her height, eyes, and hair. "And you're all right." She placed a gentle hand on her cheek. "I'm thrilled you're here."

Thaesla turned. "Oh, Brenor! I barely recognized you! You are ... *taller* than I recall."

"It has been too long, my friend." Brenor laughed, embracing firmly. "It is good to see you, as well."

When Brenor and Ariaas found her in Say Livore, their reunion was a flurry of rushing panic. In this haphazard room, for the first time she felt something resembling love. Thaesla behaved the way Lenora expected an aunt would behave after missing one of their own family for years.

Ariaas rummaged through the cabinets as if they were his own property. "Why didn't you make the journey to Jaisett?" He examined some dried pasta and tossed it over his shoulder. "Where's Idith?"

Thaesla's face withdrew, the joy in her eyes replaced by heavy lips and steep eyes. "Sit, please. There's much to discuss."

They stepped over piles of books in maze-like formation, making it to the sofa below the window. Thaesla brought a kettle with cups of tea and saucers on a tarnished brass tray. When each had their tea, she joined them, tucking her knees below the long fabric of her skirt.

"The eve we prepared to leave for Jaisett, a band of soldiers from The South Sea arrived. The rumor, as I heard it—a journey to attempt to renegotiate their tenuous alliances with Tenuel." Thaesla placed her worn hand on Lenora's knee. "That evening I found you, dear. The first search leading to a result. I nearly fell off my chair."

She turned to Ariaas. "After I sent your letter, I sent a second to Jahen. I planned to depart with Idith and Sissel and get them to safety further east." Thaesla then recounted how Sissel—a relative, perhaps?— attempted to rescue a friend, killing a guard of Tenuel instead, and The South Sea whisking her away in an instant.

Lenora's lips parted, as if a question formed—but it never left her mouth. *Arrest* and *accidental death* echoed in her ears.

Brenor stated the obvious. "Being from The South Sea and being in Tenuel is not against the law."

Thaesla raised a knowing brow. "They have Idith behind bars. Arrested for harboring Sissel. Still, she can't even get off the floor. I'm working with some locals, doing what I can, reminding them of what she did for them some decades ago. I hope they'll release her into my care."

Ariaas twisted a lantern on its hanging chain. "I bet she is happy to ruffle a few feathers in her golden years."

"I called you to Jaisett to help the three of us to safety. Idith will not make it to Aroun Vaer otherwise. But now you're needed for other matters. My caimeres was destroyed, or I would've sent the matter by letter, so you didn't need to make the journey. Now, Idith asked me to deliver you a message, stare you square in the eyes when I said it."

Thaesla held Ariaas's shoulders. "The rumor is Sissel will be moved to The Reldory." His face grew long at her words. "When you rescue Arienne, you'll get them both."

Ariaas's eyes grew wide. The teacup plunged from his grip, the handle severing when the ceramic collided with the floor. He growled, "I'm certain you aren't serious."

Lenora's stomach jolted—like a fall from a high cliff.

Brenor interjected, "Why would they move her to The Reldory for an unintended death?"

"Sissel is truly a native of Tenuel. They arrested her under the false pretense that she is from The South Sea. No trial. She'll be hidden."

Should Ariaas be able to breathe fire, he may have done it. "I haven't been able to retrieve Arienne for two and a half decades! How could you possibly ask me to retrieve a second?"

"Family is not always blood." Thaesla's voice hardened. "Idith told me to remind you."

Lenora's spine chilled and elated at the thought. Another prison. Another rescue. Though she knew nothing of Sissel, it made pure and logical sense to her—go in for one, leave with two.

"Absolutely not." Ariaas attempted to pace, though there was no place for his feet amongst the rubble. He threw his arms in the air. "I can't believe Idith would even ask such a thing."

"She suspected your answer, and I should tell you, she will hire someone with the last gold coin to her name to serve you the *gran dunos elmounay* and leave you this time for good. *ne'las duaeu!*"

A harsh laugh and a cringe of pain escaped his lips all at once. Ariaas ran his hands over his hair.

"*No regrets,*" he whimpered. "The woman would have regrets if she poisoned me, again. That I tell you." He sat on the sofa, smiling, knees twitching, tugging at his hair. Then he stood again, and growled, throwing his arms. "Why can't you stop the transfer before the girl crosses the bridge?"

"Summer Uen'can passed. And if she didn't make the opening of the bridge, we don't know where they're keeping her. My sands are gone. Unless you wish to gather me more in Lacasla. Though in the time you make it back from the southern shores, she will certainly be inside the cage."

Ariaas rubbed his brow. "Do you have anything stronger than tea?"

He did not wait for Thaesla to reply and tore through cabinets himself. When he found a dusty bottle of brown liquor, he took the stairs three at a time to the roof.

Brenor sighed. "I should check on him."

When the men were out of earshot, Thaesla asked, "How were you raised, dear? I never knew anything about you. Not until a grain of sand skipped across my map."

"I suppose I was raised well. In a family."

"Hidden in plain sight. Maybe they wanted the youngest to have a conscience." Thaesla's words piqued Lenora's curiosity.

"You're told to be the strongest amongst them, you know? Did Ariaas not tell you? As The South Sea calls you, the youngest is to be *Aerson Roscem*. The Master of Death. Each born stronger than the last. If your upbringing was intentional, it was wise to not raise you as a captive. Not make you angry at the world. Though I would've said that of the older two as well."

Lenora scoffed at the term *Master of Death*. She had no such power, no such ability. The matter still astounded her, the predictions of her future. And now, she grew annoyed by weeks of this talk without any proof.

"Has the truth been heavy on you?"

"I try not to consider it, especially since it's no longer possible. At least not the way it was originally seen." A matter Lenora thought was most easily spoken, not easily accomplished. The truth behind the lies settled like bricks on her shoulders, mirroring the weight of her worries for Areya and Eran. "I must admit—I'm surprised you know the reason behind our separation and aren't afraid."

"Oh, I've known your family's story since childhood." Thaesla's warm cheeks beamed. "Ariaas didn't tell you how we know one another?"

Lenora shook her head. Ariaas shared much of her past but not much of his own.

Thaesla continued, "I've known him my entire life. Even before he turned into the scoundrel you're acquainted with," she lauded. "My grandmother, and my mother for that matter, believed your family must be protected. A belief they passed to me. The past. The future. They intertwine in an ever-moving circle. Nothing is certain."

Ariaas told her much the night before they departed for Wesilea, but everything he mentioned was dark or ominous. She wondered aloud, "It's so odd to me the Meiderie would deliver the message they did. Especially knowing how much can change in so many centuries."

"We all use our gifts our own way." Thaesla sat her tea and saucer at the side table. "How much do you know of the Meiderie? Of the lineages?"

"Not much. Only the lineages of Valesove. My family never knew my lineage, or so they said. Areya and Ebigan, my mother and uncle, are Eslaolun. Sharp sighted. We never studied anything. They said I never needed anything else."

"Ah, everyone has a lineage, dear. Everyone is born of one people." Thaesla gestured up and down her body, winking. "Or many. And kept in the shadows, us *mal'soniure*. In the beginning, each of the eight regions had eight lineages of people. The gifts of the old gods, so the legend says. Though now some of those have gone by the wayside, such as the Juranen and Fenreos of Felreaon. The descendants of Qerusond of Dhaesreaon died out many years ago—or they were casualties of war, no different than the Meiderie. Or even still their blood was diluted by other lineages so much their abilities were lost.

"Most try to keep their people together and stay within their own. *Ah*, and the Endruas are near extinct, as well. Only *one man* stands alone, pure of the bloodline, the only *Sengura*. And not the man you know—Ariaas's lineages are so diluted, he's like a mutt on Jaisett's streets." She chuckled. "They came to arrest many on their name alone, nothing but a thin wire to stand on."

Lenora thought on this. Everything made such little sense. "If the Meiderie were so powerful to predict the fall of so many twelve hundred years before the time, how were they not powerful enough to see their own death by war?"

"Clever question," replied Thaesla. "As I heard it, they actually did. Though most don't understand the ways of the Meiderie. Their visions came to them in sleep. They could only see singular images, like a painting. Sometimes they would receive several in sequence. It was never as we sit—no conversations, no intentions. Just a simple picture.

"Certainly, it'd be simpler if several images presented themselves. The more powerful the individual, the more images they were said to receive. The highborn and those with rare exceptions could see many," she continued. "It's the Meiderie's discretion to translate the meanings of the images—witness and judge in one. They have no context otherwise. They must decide where and when and, if they must, who is at fault.

"As I understand, a rare occurrence happened in the case of Canen Dera. Hundreds of their people were given the same eight images after the end of The Great War. All on the same night. The elders of the Meiderie met before the sun rose and the council agreed on the verdict—that is to say, what was coming—would be dark. They departed for Cascanvore on large ships, across the Adlean Sea bound for Islarourne, to warn the king."

Thaesla rose to rummage through a cabinet. "Allow me to show you something."

When she returned, she laid a charcoal image before Lenora. A woman sat across a dining table from two men drinking tea, nothing else of note in the small room. "Should I show you this image, what would you think is happening?"

Lenora pulled her chair close. "Three people, talking and drinking tea around a table. Much as we are doing now."

"Now, you see that image first." Thaesla placed a second image of a throne room upon the table—a scene of mayhem which made Lenora's bones chill. "Followed by this one."

A man from the first image carved the king's heart from his chest with a dagger, the crown still on the king's brow. The woman held two swords, standing over two lifeless soldiers, both wide-eyed in a pool of blood. Even when drawn in black, the blood appeared a heavy, thick red. Holding a spear in the chest of a guard, the final man—also mortally wounded with a gaping hole in his stomach—fought on one knee. Others lay dead, their bodies scattered across the floor.

"The same three people ... they're ... slaughtering the king." Bodies of the King's Guard lay beside the throne, their uniforms and adornments the same cut as their executioners'. "The king's own soldiers planned an uprising?"

"Now, you know what it feels like to be a Meiderie. You must translate what happens in the drawings that come to your mind in the order they are received." Thaesla pointed at the first charcoal picture. "Would it be safe to assume you consider these bad people?"

"Yes." Lenora's hands ran across the minute details of the charcoal, so difficult to achieve in such small strokes. She studied them, the carvings of their rings visible, the light shining through the windows bright even in black and white.

"You assume as many of the Meiderie would. You see what is placed before you and you determine the meaning. Seeing one image in lieu of two would change your perspective dramatically. Or three, or five, or eight. Eight images were seen in the case of the Canen Dera. Visions are given for a reason. Offered, perhaps, that action might be taken to divert their course.

"However, you know nothing of intent. You mostly know nothing of time, lest there be a totem or method of determining. Here, for example, we see the rings of the kings on the throne. You can count them. He is the forty-second to wear the crown."

Thaesla's smile grew as she watched Lenora's expression. "And most especially, you know nothing of what came *before* the tea."

Lenora shifted her chair as close as it could reach. "Tell me."

"The younger brother of the king had taken him prisoner and locked him in the dungeon of the castle awaiting a public execution for a crime the younger brother himself committed. He stole the crown and slaughtered all loyal to the king."

Thaesla pointed to the first image. "The two men and one woman you see, they were the three surviving guards of his keep, able to escape unseen. Their positions so low amongst the guards, no one even realized they were missing. They were young, and though they were not in charge of the castle, they knew the king was a kind man, and his brother corrupt.

"They feared death. Both knowing they must kill and knowing they might meet their own end. Still, they mustered their courage to take the castle back, knowing they would most likely die."

Lenora sat back on her heels. "They killed the usurper. They saved their true king."

"Do you still consider them bad people?"

"No."

"Many would agree with you. Most would consider the three worthy of the highest honors. Though, these two images alone would have you thinking they deserved the sword themselves." Thaesla gathered the pages, tucking them neatly into her drawer. "It's merely an illustration in understanding the predictions of a Meiderie. Their gifts are powerful, but they, too, have their limitations.

"This is a lesson my grandmother used to teach me. A lesson to prove you don't know the entirety of the tale when you only see a few scattered pages from various chapters of a story."

What images had the Meiderie seen of her family? Of her own actions? What the plates looked like carved in brass—wherever they were, what they meant, how they had gotten there—Lenora assumed she might never know.

Thaesla pointed toward the ceiling and the roof above, her golden bracelets clanking. "How are they treating you?"

"They treat me well. Brenor's kind. I'm getting to know him ..." She hesitated. "Ariaas can be a bit ..."

"Brash?"

Lenora chuckled. "Yes."

"He doesn't look like a papa, nor does he act like one. Probably why he asked Brenor to use his given name." Thaesla continued, "You should know, though, he has a good heart. Somewhere in there. Sometimes I think he buried it under all the lives he took. He never wished for this life, just as you didn't wish for yours. He had to do much he never wished to keep you all alive." She winced at the mistake. "To keep Brenor alive. He grew a thick skin."

Lenora drew her fingers over the map on the dining table, trailing the mountains through the glass. Would her skin grow thick and brash like Ariaas if she had to endure what he had? Would she become hardened? She brushed the thought away. Two women lay captive in the southern mountains. It didn't matter what the future held—the wrongly imprisoned needed to be set free.

The injustice must be righted.

Stacks of Thaesla's books drew her. Lenora trailed their covers, seeking anything to help her discover how to break into a castle and an impenetrable prison.

NE'LAS DUAEU

Caela Dalian Dackene, Tu'dende of the Wrensten, The Intuition, The Cardinal
Born: Third Month of Summer, 1990
Deceased: Second Month of Summer, 2071
Children: Three

- Cascanvore Official Ledger

B renor leaned against the cold stone of the rooftop, watching the old man unravel thread by thread under Thaesla's steady gaze. He choked on the quiet dread of how long a path still stretched before them—and now The South Sea claimed another life.

"Tell me," Ariaas snapped, "why does everyone I know keep getting confined somehow?"

Thaesla draped Ariaas's shoulders in a thick wool blanket. "You're the only one who ties them. It must be your doing."

Brenor sealed his lips. This wasn't his fight—yet.

"Idith saved your life many times," Thaesla implored. "She never asked for anything, not once in all these long years. This is not my price; it's hers. But if I must, I'll call it my price as well."

Ariaas grumbled beneath his breath. Maybe they should've carved out a rule—something simple, something obvious: if you can save an innocent, you do. But this new woman ... was she savable? Or just one more name on a growing list of the lost?

Thaesla pressed, "You already mean to go there?"

"Yes, but I've never been able to get in. *Never.*" He paced.

Brenor shifted, crossing his arms. Ariaas needed something to break. Preferably not a bone.

She wrapped her arm around Ariaas's shoulders. "Because you weren't meant to do it alone."

Brenor straightened. He caught the word she'd emphasized—*weren't.* Not anymore. Ariaas might still act like a man shouldering the world, but he didn't carry it alone.

His training had always been about defense. A vow not to kill. But maybe there was more to his life purpose than simply restraint. Maybe protection wasn't just about defense—it was about action. Movement. Risk.

There were caveats, after all.

"You've led a torturous life. I know. It's not lost on me. But—Brenor's no longer a boy. Not one you need to protect. Lenora's strong. I see it in her eyes. If trained, I'd wager she'd be an unstoppable force."

"Three does not make an army."

"Better than one."

Brenor grinned. Perhaps it was finally time. It was the twenty-third year, after all. The year Ariaas had claimed they would find his siblings. And as much as he hated to admit it, thus far, the old man had been correct.

He'd trained diligently. He could handle the rescues and still uphold his vow.

Ariaas exhaled through clenched teeth. "What does she look like? The girl."

Thaesla's voice softened. "Sissel has long hair, and skin of deep gold. She reminds me of a butterfly. Beautiful, delicate."

Ariaas grunted. "Delicate things don't survive in cages."

"Neither do strong ones, if left too long."

He caught Ariaas's sharp glare.

Brenor knew little of Idith, only that Ariaas held favor for her he never held for another. "Who is Sissel to you? To Idith?"

Ariaas shrugged his shoulders.

"Idith took up arms with Commander Sermaris when he lived—when they defended northern Tenuel. In the years after the siege, when the Yurelan lost Arienne, Thealor, Brenor, and Lenora they were not kind in their search for power. In their pursuits, they saw to it that many more children were left without their parents, parents without their children. They took the ones they wanted. Killed the rest. It was a chaotic time."

"Why do these idiots keep doing this?" Ariaas lamented. "Why is power all they see?"

"We sat in the eye of the storm for a long while, my friend. Now, dark times are coming upon us once more." Thaesla turned to meet his eyes, securing his attention, any joy in her face falling to sorrow. "Ariaas, you should go to the prison. Before you leave."

"No. I'll bring the girl back. I'll see Idith then."

Thaesla sighed. "You might be hearing, but you aren't listening. If you succeed ... if you return Sissel, Idith won't be here when you do. She lives on borrowed time. You need to prepare yourself."

Ariaas barked a dry laugh. "Borrowed time? Idith would outfight the gods with a walking stick."

Thaesla's grin held too long. Behind it, grief seeped into the open air, thick as smoke from a wet fire. The weight burrowed into Brenor's chest in the stillness. Unspoken, but true.

"I can't promise anything," Ariaas argued, his arms flailing with disturbance. "I can't be certain we can get either of them. I can't even—"

"I know," Thaesla interjected, her worn hand patting his arm below a layer of cloth. "It's not a promise I expect of you."

How would they return, though? They have no Thealor. They have no Arienne. And now ... a third.

A third.

Ariaas sagged into a chair, appearing, for a fleeting moment, his actual years.

Still, he knew this man. The decision was made, even if Ariaas would fight with every breath he had.

"Rest is for the dead," Brenor pressed.

"Well," Ariaas responded, "I'm not dead yet."

PRIVATE CONVERSATIONS

In accordance with the Laws of Lesomen, set forth in the year 878 of the Golden Age, each region shall name its people, cities, and settlements according to a designated naming structure, that heritage and origin may be clearly traced. Primary Letters, assigned in pairs, are granted to two regions in succession, and all major names shall begin with letters thus allotted. No deviation shall be permitted without sanction from the High Council of Names. (See: Section IV — On Naming Structure.)

By decree of the Lawkeepers of Lesomen, in accord with the High Council of Names, this law is hereby entered into the Book of Kings.

     - *The Book of Kings*, Entry 3110, Year 878 of the Golden Age

Twenty-six days Sissel listened to heavy boots in rhythmic sequence trampling outside her window. Bare wooden walls and the noises from the other side of them were her only entertainment, the modest window her only view of the world. She wished for a book or quill and paper to ease the thrum of nothingness.

Most soldiers wore gray uniforms of The South Sea, silver and brass pins at their chests of varying natures. Others dressed in navy uniforms, a handful in emerald—though those soldiers only stayed a few days. She knew them all well now, their faces and the language of their walk.

A small boy in charcoal with sandy brown hair walked in formation with a limp he tried to hide. Obvious to her, he winced in pain at the weight of his own body. No one else seemed to notice. A woman, also in charcoal, a soldier of The South Sea with long braided walnut hair, stared at another soldier in formation before her. Her cheeks flushed when he spoke, and she averted her eyes when he turned toward her. Sissel could almost feel the girl's heart racing as if it were her own. The man never noticed her longing gazes.

On occasion, the female soldier who struck Kaloyein passed Sissel's window. She wore a severe face, and deep, harsh eyes which opened easily when she came upon someone familiar. Captain Kalory, she overheard.

Sissel's thoughts woke her early—her thoughts and the birds. *The birds.* The animals confused midnight for dawn. She'd grown used to them now, no longer groaning at their din every morning.

A sparrow flew to her each day, sitting for a time before it perched upon the silver tray outside her door, and tapped its claws against the metal. The bird danced before the remains of her supper, though never ate from the lingering crumbs. Some days it held a small stem of a young flower, the white tips of a bud ready to bloom in its beak when it flew west to wherever it stayed when it did not visit her.

At dawn, Commander Benson took his rounds. Each morning the man of routines walked before the soldiers and again before supper when the sun hung low. At the latter time, he returned in tattered clothing caked in sweat and muck. Sissel's barracks were not a stop on his routine. A fleeting glimpse at a closed wooden door sufficed.

She noticed the days he did not glance toward her door.

Commander Benson must see her as a frightened creature if her barracks required nothing more than an occasional glance. No need to check on Sissel when she is too weak-minded to leave—a mouse who would not dare dash through an open door to freedom. After some days, she stopped averting her sight, longing to know what he watched, be it her or something appearing to be her from where she stood.

Occasionally, Captain Kalory joined Commander Benson. Sissel imagined their conversations—mere voices on the air. A feeling rose inside her at the sight of him, though she struggled to place it: fear, intimidation, curiosity? In recent days, she wished the birds would wake her in an attempt to understand her thoughts. Her days became timed by his morning and evening walks, her gaze unable to divert from his presence.

Sissel's mere existence in Tanes felt like a cruel joke, a nightmare masquerading as a kind gesture. A woman alone, unable to walk, unable to speak to another. Her solitude did not seem terrible at first, especially the days after she arrived, exhausted and worn. Now, she was being driven to madness. Her body could only sleep so much. After she received her breakfast for the day and ate, she would sit and wait in nothingness until supper. If she were to talk through the front gates of Tanes, would anyone even notice?

Today, she ate a boiled egg, bread, and an apple. Her meals were brought to her morning and evening, the only time the door opened, and warm sun met her skin. When she finished, she placed her tray outside, observing the passing soldiers.

The gray soldiers disregarded her presence.

Sissel sat on the stoop, invisible yet still paranoid, waiting for whistles and panicked alarms. When none came, she closed her eyes, her golden-brown cheeks drinking in the sun. Sissel sat for a long while in the bright light, eyes closed, guzzling the heat. The sparrow, again perched on her tray, examined her, twisting its head from side to side. She reached a hand toward it as if it would allow her to touch its feathers.

The sparrow flew away.

She caught Commander Benson's eyes across the long path to the dirt square. He perched tall, intense, fixated as a hawk stalking unsuspecting prey. How long had she been sitting there? He charged toward her, his face not amused as it often appeared.

Sissel fumbled, standing with little grace.

Commander Benson did not halt, did not ease his rapid approach, did not mind if she was run over until they were both inside the confinement of the room. The door slammed closed behind him, and he hinged the brass lock across the frame. Sissel gathered herself, her sights locked upon the dark floor. He stood above her once more, closer than he should have been, his breath in her hair, even within the stunted confines. She waited for him to speak, residing in uncomfortable silence.

When it was clear he had no intention of speaking, she broke the quiet. "I've been in here for weeks. Alone."

"That means you are attempting to flee?" Commander Benson spoke through clenched jaws. "There's nowhere to go. This village was built at the base of the Dhenpara Mountains, and you are surrounded by soldiers. There is nothing for days in any direction."

"I'm not attempting to flee. I want to feel the sun." Her voice broke. "Maybe even speak to someone. Walk." Sissel wished she dared to speak aloud her true feelings: regardless of how nice the room, solitary confinement was torture.

"Can I please walk? Or speak with someone. I want to breathe the air outside these walls. See another human who isn't from my window." She braved meeting his slate eyes.

His posture righted. The harshness in his face eased, and his arms returned to their trained position.

At the change of his posture, she implored, "Please."

To her surprise, his rage redirected, and he unhinged the brass lock before he exited. "Keep the door *closed.*"

Hours drew on between his departure and the arrival of her supper. She had been torturing herself for her insolence for the better part of the afternoon when someone knocked on her door. The waiting guard held no tray. He gestured for her to follow him. She had seen his face but could not place him in the daily routine. She followed along the cobblestone road east before turning to the dirt path. The guard stopped before a large building, gesturing for her to enter.

Inside, Commander Benson sat in a chair at a wooden desk, bare-chested, his leg crossed at the ankle over his knee. His belt hung unfastened from the loops on his pants. He glared at the boy as if he might throttle him, his eyes black and boiling in the low light.

He growled through gritted teeth, *"Leave us."*

The boy cowered before he skittered away, slamming the door.

Sissel jolted at the harsh noise. Bumps rose across her arms and her hair stood on end.

Perhaps she misread the situation, misread his bare body. She suspected him noble, although irritable this afternoon, but not so brazen with a woman. When she was strong enough to look over him once more, he sat stoic. He had not moved, his leg still crossed, half clothed in the chair beside the desk. He wore harsh eyes, tanned skin upon his open chest, and muscles worn from training.

Sissel adjusted her sights to the rolling fire to obstruct her welling tears. "Why am I here?"

"I thought you were craving some conversation."

When she had the courage to meet his heavy gaze, needles traveled her spine. *"This* was not what I meant." She drew back toward the wall, a tight fist gripping the hem of her shirt.

He reached for a chair and pulled it close to his own. When he returned to his seated position, he gestured toward the seat, ordered in a firm voice, "Sit."

She closed her eyes, reminding herself she was not the weak mouse he imagined her to be. She straightened her shoulders. Along her cautious walk toward the chair, fear began transferring to resentment.

The day she arrived he seemed honorable, yet now he appeared nothing of the sort. She stood behind the drawn chair, holding the tears from escaping her eyes, and words to choke from her trembling lips.

"Do most women let you do as you wish with them? A hope to gain some safety or privilege amongst their confines?"

Commander Benson opened his mouth to speak, but Sissel raised hand to silence him. She expected to be struck or worse for her words, as Kaloyein had a closed fist to the jaw, but if only for an instant a wave of bravery passed, and she would not allow it to go unharnessed.

"You'd bring me in here for *this?* You'd expect this of me the instant I walk into your room, as my body is meant for your taking? I will admit, I thought you handsome, perhaps even honorable when I arrived. You seemed like a decent man."

Commander Benson closed his mouth. His eyebrow raised. The tears she held flowed over her cheeks, soaked to her neck, and salted her lips, heavy breath in a rising chest.

He paused as if he wanted to ensure she had nothing further to say before addressing her. *"My, my.* Perhaps not the fragile butterfly I assumed. Your mind wandered very quickly into dark waters."

She was right about his smirk. He was amused.

"When you arrived, I was angry because the orders I issued were to have you brought here *after* supper. I wished to discuss your sentencing with you. When he saw me, he realized his error. The reason he scurried off. It was not because I ... how did you say it? *Thought your body was meant for my taking."* He smirked greatly at the words. "You were to be brought here after I had finished my shower, eaten, finished my work, and most importantly, *gotten dressed."*

Sissel's face reddened, her flesh set on betraying her, heavy tears saturating her cheeks.

His tone softened. "Don't be ashamed. I would've assumed the same in your position. I apologize for the fear it created." His confidence did not sway, not even half clothed. He gestured to the chair once more. "Sit."

"Why didn't you correct me?"

"I began to, but you cut me off. Then you started speaking of how handsome I was, and after that, I had no intention of stopping you." His lips curled. "It's rude to interrupt. Particularly to interrupt a woman when she is so *passionate* about a subject."

Sissel blinked to keep further tears from escaping and he offered her a cloth from the table.

"You don't need to fear me. At least, not in that regard." Commander Benson examined her appearance, hair cascading over her shoulders, finally visible without cakes of dirt. He turned from her, tapping the ink from his quill, and writing at his desk.

"I prefer a strong woman. A woman that could handle me. I haven't determined if you'd break if the wind blew the wrong way. More importantly, I'd never take a woman who didn't want to be taken. Though, I did enjoy that speech." Commander Benson fixated on his work. "Did you have supper before he brought you here?"

"No."

A silver tray sat atop the dining table with a leg of chicken, a slice of bread, and a potato. He moved a glass and steel pitcher full of fresh water to its side. He commanded, "Eat."

Sissel pursed her lips, wishing she had noticed the food beside the chair earlier. Some level of ease returned to her—one part happy she could rest easy and receive no physical harm, the other part disconcerted by the oblique comments. "Why did you bring me here?"

"As I said, I wished to discuss your sentencing with you. And you get to speak to another human. It's a matter I've been planning to attend to, though I continued to get disrupted by other matters the past few weeks. After I spoke with you this morning, I cleared my business orders for the evening. That is, after I'd calmed down from your little ... stunt."

He wrote with long strokes on the parchment, replies to letters from what it appeared.

"Eat," he repeated, his sights glued on his task. "I've work to finish before we may speak on the matter."

Sissel had many questions but could begin with only one. "Commander Benson. Your shirt?"

"I wouldn't dare. Now I know why you like to watch me so much from your window."

Her eyes shifted the floor.

Commander Benson rose, leaving the room and returned, his cotton shirt tucked into his trousers. His belt locked into its intended position and his prideful grin vanished.

For an hour, he worked on letters in emerald envelopes, referenced rolled maps of Hanielle, and scribbled notes with a quill. She meant to leave her room to be freed from silence, yet she sat here the same. Though she could admire the new surroundings—his room was much like hers in decorating, though more substantial. A dining table, which likely held many meetings with six waiting chairs. A large bed covered in silver sheets and cherry embroidery. A high ceiling drew the room to darkness with long, heavy curtains.

When the sun descended, he illuminated the lanterns and joined her at the dining table with a candle.

"Tell me all that happened leading up to your arrest and what happened after. Every detail, even seemingly insignificant."

Sissel shared the tale of the day: how she had left to see Thaesla in the afternoon, how Sissel informed her that she and her grandmother could not join Thaesla in the evening due to her grandmother's failing health. How she had seen Mr. Baradelle two nights prior and given her grandmother the denmero. How soldiers gathered in the town square. How they read names. How Mr. Baradelle fell.

Commander Benson stopped writing after some time, no longer detailing the story when Sissel mentioned High Commander Ravaris. His eyes drew solemn. "Ravaris was there ... when the soldier of Tenuel was killed?"

"Yes. She was standing beside the soldier who read names from the paper."

Commander Benson shifted in his seat at the mention of Ravaris' name. He seemed to chew on his next words before speaking.

"It's unfortunate you and High Commander Ravaris should cross paths." He sighed. "You mentioned your grandmother, your *aunt*. Where are your parents?"

"They died long ago in the north."

"There should be no one to come to find you, then. None to try and claim you were wrongfully imprisoned? No one to ask questions other than Idith and Thaesla?"

"I don't believe so, no." Sissel had not thought much about the matter from his perspective. The thought saddened her. Her grandmother would have come, should she have been able. Thaesla may have come, too, though now she must care for her grandmother.

"You should not hope unnecessarily. If all is as I suspect, I will have scarce luck, but I will do what I can to see you are moved elsewhere. To a more suitable prison for the nature of your crime."

Commander Benson ran his hand over his neat, trimmed beard. "Commander Tuyure is a just man. I suspect he would not be pleased to hear of your placement, though you were not of his blood, you did grow to adulthood in his lands." He made a few more notes on his page, ideas which came into his mind. "The Reldory is not built for people like you."

Sissel cringed. Did he mean innocent people? Though by his tone, she thought he spoke of her feeble strength of character. She braved the question parting her lips. "People like me?"

"I've seen much evil in my days. Dark people who care not for human life, people who try to gain their own power. All I mean to say is—some people are dark by nature, and some people are kind by nature."

He held the quill between his hands, leaning back in his chair. "I'd destroy the hanging cage if it were my choice. In my opinion, only those who deserve execution for their crimes should be sent there. If they deserve execution, they may as well simply be executed. Though, according to some, it's more fitting a consequence to be in indefinite torture. I don't favor pain for the simple sake of pain."

The fire lowered, the birch logs shifting, embers spat into the air. Commander Benson rose from his chair and positioned new longs upon the old.

"What do you know of The Reldory? Are you prepared for your time there?"

Sissel almost chuckled at the question. "I can barely handle solitary confinement with a window and my own washroom."

Commander Benson's eyebrows raised; his head turned in agreement. "I haven't been cageside, but I've been to the landside of the bridge." His tone grew solemn. "It's barbaric."

She swallowed hard, trying not to let her mind wander to this man's definition of barbaric.

"I need some time to review the information you have given me, and it's getting late."

He opened the door to his chambers for her to exit. The young guard rushed toward her, fumbling over his own feet. "Take her back to her room. Bring her back here *after* lunch tomorrow," Commander Benson said, ensuring he drug the word *after* for effect. "I'm certain I will have some additional questions." Her face warmed as she glanced away.

Sissel wrestled with sleep, her mind pondering the nuances of their conversation: her sentencing, the barbaric nature of the cage, people like *her*.

She was not fed lunch, but the guard arrived when the sun was high. He would not misunderstand his orders again. She was uncertain what his punishment would be for his crime, though she did not expect it to be of a torturous nature after their conversation. Perhaps he had extra rounds, extra training in the fields.

Commander Benson sat at the dining table with his paper in a clean shirt and trousers, the belt and sheath which held his blade hanging from a hook beside the door. He asked her further questions of Idith and Thaesla. More about how she knew Mr. Baradelle, and if there were any other relatives, even distantly acquainted.

There were not.

The notes consumed him for a long while, his thoughts held deep within the paper.

After some time in his own mind, she interrupted, "Commander Benson?"

He wore a more serious mood today; he did not seem amused as he did the day before.

"Now that you know of what happened the day of my arrest, why do you believe they are sending me to The Reldory? When I had no intention of killing the guard?"

He sat with this question before he chose his words with great intent. "The relationship between Tenuel and The South Sea is fragile. A forgone alliance long built on fear of repercussions over willful partnership. The people of Tenuel are vastly different from the people of the South. They fear us." He corrected, "Most people fear us. Small gestures by way of the High Commander … your crimes in front of them … well, you may have given them more credibility in honor of a fragile alliance than would have been given for years otherwise."

Sissel studied the nuances of his face. The mood of his dropped brow resembled empathy—pity for a woman he barely knew, soon to be left to a destitute life. Perhaps, if he could help, she might have room to hope after all.

CHAINS IN THE STABLE

I arrived the same evening as he, seven days ago. He has yet to notice me following him.

- Diary of Daisirie Cabredd Mire, Volume 5, Entry 113

Lenora pressed Luscan past the split-rail fence and onto the edge of Aroun Vaer property. For all its ominousness and warning of death, the sign marking the border brought an odd sense of comfort. The horses slowed at the familiar ground, their hooves upon the dirt, the crickets the only sound in the darkness.

"We can camp here," suggested Brenor. "The sun will set soon."

Ariaas held silent. Perhaps the man slept with his eyes open.

Along the sluggish journey home, Lenora had trained with the bow, becoming the hunter of the party by their return to Ravine Road. Never in all her days did she expect to see the other side of Sanrial or breach the River Realm once, let alone return through it. Her stomach sank when they crossed the path to Mount Ohbrolis the second time. Thealor's presence nagged at her, a deadline long past, the guilt of her lack of action toward his freedom drawing her up the mountainside. In their many conversations about gaining access to Brouverg Castle and The Reldory, they repeatedly returned to Thealor in Brouverg Castle, the less fortified of the two. This fact took the sharp edge off her guilt.

Lenora shook her head. A few hours ride and she could sleep with something other than flies and regret. "No. I need a real pillow for once."

They pressed further without a word, weary through the darkening sky.

Eventually, the forest shallowed, and the cottage became visible, soft gray smoke billowing from the chimney.

Midway between sleep and awake, Lenora's mind slowly processed what her eyes witnessed. Smoke. The thin trail drew skyward until the single cone dispersed into the night sky.

All at once, her wits rushed back to her. Jerking Luscan's reins, she whistled for Ariaas and Brenor.

Silently, Brenor moved through the curving road to see the cottage through the trees, emanating light. "Ariaas," he growled.

Ariaas whispered, "I see it."

Lenora drew her bow.

The castle's once formal entrance, vast, luxurious, and woefully abandoned, stood boarded and unchanged. The windows, dark, covered in vines, still lay in desperate need of attention. She could not articulate what drew her eye, though the castle appeared changed somehow, almost shimmering beneath the moonlight.

"From this angle, it doesn't appear that anyone's in the castle," Lenora whispered. "Perhaps Mrs. Ebrolie?"

"She did not know when we would arrive. She looks in on the horses occasionally but only during the day. She fears Aroun Vaer at night," Brenor muttered. "It has always been our agreement we ride to her home to retrieve Taren."

Sword in hand, Ariaas crouched along the fence. "I'm not sure what we'll meet inside. Have your weapon ready."

"Ariaas ..." Brenor issued a wide-eyed glance at his grandfather. He mouthed the word *vow*.

Lenora crept, careful to avoid setting off any traps in the darkness, while Ariaas and Brenor made their way unencumbered to peer between drawn curtains of the windows.

"One man. Round in the middle. Old weapon. Asleep in my chair," mouthed Ariaas, moving to gain a better vantage. His jaw tightened. "His damn feet are on my table. And ..." He closed his eyes, rubbing the bridge of his nose. "He has Taren," he growled, pressing his way through the front door.

"Wait," whispered Lenora harshly.

Before either of them could move to stop him, Ariaas was inside, blade in hand.

He seized the old bow and quiver from beside the hearth, kicking the man's feet from the table. The man dropped sharply, whimpering onto the carpet like a bag of rocks. Taren scrambled while the man groaned and wriggled on the floor.

"Are you looking to be executed?" barked Ariaas.

Groaning, the intruder rubbed his sore knee. "What kind of person throws someone to the ground while they sleep?"

That voice.

Lenora shouldered her way beyond Brenor and toward the voice, finding the man wedged between the low table and Ariaas's chair in a tight knot. The air expelled from her lungs and her heart leaped.

Eran Hoeleck, squished amid the wood furniture, struggled to find footing while Taren nestled under his arm.

"Oh God," he sighed, closing his eyes and placing his hand across his chest. He rose to his feet, examining Lenora for signs of injury. "You're alive? You are alive, yes? And all right?"

"How did you get in here?" Ariaas growled, ignoring their exchange. "And why do you have my dog?"

"I didn't break in—I'll tell you that!" Eran positioned his body between Ariaas and Lenora. "The front door was wide open when I arrived."

The dense weight in Lenora's chest briefly lifted at the sight of him alive and well. But how had he survived? How had he found her when the archers had not? Was he still the man who raised her—kind, just, and always on her side?

Brenor asked, "Who is this man?"

Eran's mouth fell open at the question. "I'm Anse's father."

"You're most certainly not her father." The vein in Ariaas's forehead pulsed. "I'll ask a final time: how did you get onto the property?"

"A man who raises a child from infancy is indeed their father, whether by blood or not! Any decent man would know such a thing!"

Ariaas stepped closer, mere inches separating the two. "Abduction tends to void parental terms, I fear."

Lenora placed herself between the two; fearful Ariaas might use the blade he clutched onto so dearly. A pang of guilt or fear coursed through her—she couldn't be sure which.

Brenor interjected in a calm tone, wishing to ease the rising tension. "Can you please tell me your name?"

"Heneran Hoeleck, of Sanrial."

Ariaas shook his head, his nose wrinkling like he smelled something foul. "Your name does not sit well with me at all. *Heneran*. Your mother and father must have hated you the instant you were born."

"It's my grandfather's surname on my mother's side. I go by Eran. And, to reply to your previous question, I came by the road. I assume most men would get here by such means."

Brenor's jaw tightened, resisting a smile, a face of ironic laughter that was quickly squished by Ariaas's harsh glare.

Ariaas repeated, "Why do you have my dog?"

The weight of Lenora's arms felt like boulders. She, too, had many questions, none of which she wanted answered after bloodshed. Her two distinctly different worlds, past and present, colliding without warning.

"Can we please ... just ... sit? Keep your sword and his bow if it makes you feel better. But no stabbing anyone."

Ariaas paced, unamused, his blade at the ready, shooing Eran from his chair when he attempted to sit.

"I'd been here two days, and a woman came by. Mrs. Ebrolie, checkin' in on things. I told her I was mindin' the horses. Somewhat true. I'd been here for days, and I'd been feedin' them. And said she could leave Tarey with me." Eran scratched behind the dog's flopping ears. "She wasn't pleased. Left rather hurried. A few days later she came back—friendlier—saying she'd business and asked if I'd keep him. She was upset Tarey ate the honey apple pies she baked for the fall festival in Ellace. I offered to help make more but—"

Ariaas gritted his teeth. "His name is *Taren*."

"She thought the pies would win at least a third place ribbon. She desperately wanted to beat another woman, Mrs. Sal ... Mrs. Sar ... No." He shook his head. "That was about three weeks ago."

"You've been here *for a month?*"

"I didn't keep count of the specific days, but a month feels about right."

The fireplace smoldered with old wood and freshly cut logs stacked high along the side, dishes in the kitchen clean and tucked away. The aroma of a meal, something with cinnamon, lingered in the air. Lenora warmed herself by the hearth.

"How did you find this place?" She wanted to ask about her mother but feared the answer. Far too many questions mingled with her exhaustion. "How did you not know about the archers, and ...?"

Eran shook his head. "I've learned a bunch since you left. About what happened. Though there's still a lot I don't know. I'm still tryin' to find out why."

Lenora wished desperately for evidence he was still the man she knew. She would not be caught unaware a second time. The night she had departed played on a repetitious loop: his heavy boots trailing, his shouting after her. She begged anyone in the stars who might listen for Eran to be safe, for the blood spilled to only be her own.

"We'll hear your story." She eyed Brenor and Ariaas. "The company is safer than in Sanrial." At the painful reminiscence, she gulped. "I want to know everything you've learned. Then we can decide if you should be trusted—and if you truly knew nothing of what happened to me before I came to live with you."

Eran wiped his palms on his trousers, voice rough. "I ran after you that night. Lost the path in the forest." His eyes fixed on Lenora, desperate. "When I returned, your mother convinced me not to speak. Said we'd saved you from danger. She gave no proof. Only fear."

His voice cracked. "She made me swear. Said if you were found unguarded ... they would kill you."

Brenor and Ariaas traded a look. A Qcaranen had cloaked her—as they suspected.

"I believed her. Maybe I wanted to." Eran's hands trembled. "'If she couldn't be contained, we were to kill her,' your mother said. She made it sound like my order, too." He swallowed. "It wasn't."

He spoke of blood. Of waking tied to a chair. Of Ebigan's rage—and her mother pleading for his life.

Lenora listened closely, searching for cracks. But his pain was real. Slowly, her tension unraveled. She shifted to sit nearer him.

Eran had always been a terrible liar.

The scars bore the rest of the story: a deep gash at his temple, ragged burns at his wrists. Wounds healed without stitches, brutal and crooked. She wondered how he survived at all.

Ariaas cracked his neck, leaning over his knees before he regained his pacing beyond the sofa.

"This is the longest story I've ever heard. I agreed to a long tale—not one which would take years off my life or a meal from my belly."

"One night the details returned, Anse," Eran continued.

She bit her lip, caught between two people both meant to be her.

"You had family to the west. I traveled for a while before I fell into some sheer blind luck. I bonded with a man over stories and wine in an old tavern in Ellace. He complained about a dreaded journey he had to take at dawn. No direct route existed to circumvent Aroun Vaer, a land built of traps, and death and riggings, made to keep people out. Two men lived there, he said. The elder by the name Ebronds. The instant he said it, I knew. I knew. The name your mother said the day you left."

Eran nodded at Brenor. "I hoped if I kept the place in order, and tended to the horses, my intrusion may be greeted more favorably."

Brenor chuckled, whispering to Ariaas, "Where did you hide the good whiskey?"

Ariaas ignored him, and spat, "This story is much too long. I did not know. *The end.* That's how I would've told it."

The bookshelf drew his eye. Ariaas scoured the shelves, his hands trailing the leather bindings. "Where is *Revenge and the Long Lie?*"

His nostrils flared as he hunted. He found the title open upon the end table, a page creased in the corner to mark Eran's placement. Ariaas stared in disbelief at the shelves before turning back to the open novel.

"Did you rearrange my bookshelf?" He tore a misplaced book from the perch. He yanked one title after the next, throwing them over his shoulder, until a small pile remained on the floor behind him. "And you creased my—are they *alphabetized?*"

"It was all a tangle." Eran shrugged. "I chopped firewood. I cooked. I tended to the horses and the dog. I needed a way to entertain myself. There was no logical order."

"It was organized by the order I read them last!"

"Gentlemen, with all due respect, this is wildly irrelevant," Brenor interjected with another calm tone meant to ease tattered nerves.

Lenora grasped Ariaas and Brenor, pulling them into the kitchen.

Brenor mouthed across the room to Ariaas, "I am proud of you."

In some ways, she was proud of him, too. Eran was still alive. During his tale, Lenora remained quiet, listening intently for holes and gaps—for his voice to rise or his words to become rapid, none of which came. "I believe him."

"Well, I don't." Ariaas's eyes widened to saucers. "We can't have him snooping around. We'll chain him in the tunnels."

Lenora snapped, "Chain him?"

"I cannot imagine that to be necessary. He has been here for weeks. It seems the poor man has been through quite enough."

"Oh, for shit's sake. You can't be serious. He can't be free to roam about"—Ariaas snorted—"to warn the hunters if his stories are lies!"

She blinked, trying to imagine her dad in chains. "You don't need to lock him away. He's being honest."

Ariaas grasped her by the shoulders. "Answer me honestly—do you have a clear head right now?"

As he held her, her mind slanted by enervation, tumultuous thoughts, and the sudden collision of her worlds. Her bones ached, and the hollow of her stomach rumbled. Even while standing, the room moved.

Reluctantly, she turned her opinion. "All right. One night. Until we can think clearly in the morning. But there must be a better place. A room with a lock?"

"There's no room with a lock," replied Ariaas. "He can go to the stables. There are plenty of chains there."

"*No.* No chains."

In front of the hearth, her father played with Taren. The dog licked his face from his chin square to his eyes. The thought of chaining Eran nauseated her.

"Brenor will do it. There's nowhere else."

Brenor's cheeks puffed while he expelled his air. His face lost color as if he might vomit. He approached Eran. "It has been decided you will be chained in the stables until tomorrow."

Eran appeared both concerned and pleased he was not being expelled. "Oh."

This isn't right. But can I trust my own mind right now?

Brenor would aid her in the morning. Find a better solution. She would have him as an ally if she had to save Eran from Ariaas.

At least she hoped she would.

Brenor guided Eran through the old gardens and beyond the castle, Lenora and Ariaas following close behind.

"Are you of a lineage of Qabriah?" Brenor asked along the path. "I cannot imagine anyone other than a kalthero would find us in so little time."

"I wish. No, I don't know my ancestors' lineages. My family has been born of the lineages of Valesove for many generations," Eran said, his tone of shameful admonition. "I hate to say it, but ... I found Aroun Vaer by sheer luck."

Lenora leaned in to hear their low conversation. They seemed almost jovial, two men conversing after an evening's meal. Not one man walking to chain the other.

"Many might call such a matter *fate,*" said Brenor. He guided him through the stable doors, leading him to an iron chain. "I should not say such things, but I have been told to trust my instincts. I do not believe you should be chained here."

Eran asked, "You don't agree?"

"No," he whispered.

Her dad nodded solemnly.

Brenor held the cuff, the chain bolted to the support post. "I have a specific abhorrence for chains."

The iron—strong enough to hold a steed, wild and bucking—clamped around Eran's ankle.

VAK-ARRA

roscin cas baveell udecnt nent pacell ralok
un au cearion len launri eaime na miok
ea banior ere voreas teor ramer dim pallock

                                  - Battle Mantra from The South Sea

The bare-cheeked soldier returned after midday to escort Sissel to Commander Benson's quarters.

The first two days visiting his quarters were only a margin better than remaining in her own room. The man worked many hours, and she had nothing to occupy herself while he tended to business. Both days, a cold chicken leg, vegetable, and slice of bread waited for her on a single tray he instructed her to eat from. When she finished, she placed the lone shining steel outside the door.

Today, a long-worn book, smelling of vanilla and almonds, lay atop the tray when she arrived. Pages softened by age, delicate enough to wilt beneath her fingers, titled *Warrior in Black*, by Nascal Niedrin Nalorn. The inside cover bore thick black scripted ink, *To my Dearest Riera, with Love*. The owner, Riera, remained a mystery, and the reason for relinquishing a book dedicated to her puzzled Sissel. Although, she was pleased to have something to occupy her time.

Sissel read through a third of the book in one sitting, an autobiography of the author's life in the army of The South Sea some decades ago. It detailed a battle over the boundaries of the Rivers Converuan and Cuesuan. The Lavenas, the closest lineage Qabriah hosts to warriors, struggled to protect their own lands, hard pressed to stop warriors of the mountain staking claims without aid. Though she could not keep track of the names, the tale was interesting enough, and more entertaining than counting nails in the support beams.

The first day, Commander Benson asked her to tell him about Wesilea, then about Tenuel. The second, she asked about The South Sea, and he told her of Niera, and Tanes, and how the people of the lineages tend to live in their own cities together in all but Islarourne, which finds itself home to many people. When they finished their conversation, the bare-cheeked soldier escorted her to her room.

Today, when she made her way to the window, the bare-cheeked soldier no longer stood at his post across the road. No eyes on the door, not as he had the days prior, and another soldier had not taken his place.

"Commander Benson ..." Sissel began to ask why the soldier no longer stood waiting. Her thoughts wandered to his face, bare red with anger and embarrassment, on the day she first walked through the door.

His eyes locked on his work, he said, "Please, you may call me Ronan. No need for formalities when no one else is here." Sissel's heart fluttered at the familiarity, although did not understand his removal of propriety in her presence. However, she should not argue. He was trying to aid her. She would do as he asked. However, his given name did not readily cross her lips.

Outside the window, the female soldier with the braid stood beside a rippling fountain. The soldier she longed for not far behind amongst a group of men. They enamored her. How could the soldier not notice? Or was he simply indifferent to her?

"What do you watch?" Commander Benson asked, "When you gaze from the window?"

"It's been the only form of entertainment I've had these long weeks. I know each passing face and when. I noticed a man and woman; they walk in a group on the same rounds. The woman—she has feelings for him." Sissel observed the male soldier, laughing, speaking with friends, a tranquil time away from their responsibilities. "She tries not to watch him, but she almost can't help herself. I keep wondering if he'll ever notice her."

Commander Benson met her at the glass. He loomed above her small frame, glancing through the shallow opening of curtains. When he inhaled, with a closeness he seemed unaware of, the cotton of his shirt brushed against her back. "Who?"

"The girl, there." Sissel pointed. "With the long braid. Deep brown hair."

"And the man?" he asked. Sissel gestured to his position and his casual formation.

Commander Benson huffed. "The woman should say something. A direct approach is most effective."

"She spoke with him the day before yesterday, for a moment in passing. I couldn't hear them, maybe about the weather. She couldn't stop smiling when he left."

Commander Benson dipped his chin, turning his attention to her. "You find this spying to be enjoyable?"

"Finding a small bit of joy, even if I am borrowing someone else's, is not too much to ask."

A playful smile danced on his lips. "Watching me work does not bring you joy?"

Sissel's cheeks warmed while she concealed her amusement.

"What else do you see, when you watch from the window?"

Sissel turned to whatever else she might find through the glass—anything to divert her attention from his proximity and the tingling sensation rising on her arms. Soldiers marched in rows. Sparrows darted between birch trees.

"A young man missing from the formation. There."

"Hmm. Watching can have its benefits, if you observe with a keen eye." He stepped away from her, perching himself atop the dining table. Her back, suddenly cold with his absence. "What have you noticed of me?"

Her stomach overturned and she said the only words that could come to her mind, "That feels a bit like a trap."

"Not a trap." He chuckled and held his hands open in surrender. "You won't offend me, whatever it may be."

She met his slate eyes for an instant before she dropped her sights to the floor. Could he really want to know all she had seen of him? All she had witnessed the days she watched him walk back and forth across the street from her window?

Eventually, he said, "Very well."

When she dared to look again, he had returned to his writing desk. The weight of their silence tugged at her, a void she desperately wished to fill with any conversation, large or small. Any discourse other than what she noticed of him.

She searched for some time before she found an appropriate question. "Do you know the new king?"

"Since I was a boy."

"Do you think he's a good ruler?"

He laughed. "Thus far, he has done nothing to prove himself a terrible ruler, though his rule is still in its infancy."

"Do you agree with his decision to move people of The South Sea out of Tenuel?"

"I understand there are often diplomatic missions outside my titled authority, including removing the inhabitants from Wesilea." He answered plainly. "I have no opinion on the matter."

"What happened to the people not of The South Sea whose names were called? They are innocent people. They were not with the company on the journey."

"You speak of the mal'soniure? I cannot imagine they are imprisoned."

"He imprisoned me."

"Technically speaking, you are not innocent."

Am I not innocent? I aided a fallen man, as anyone would.

"Your King is making an example out of an accident."

"He isn't doing anything. He doesn't even know you exist." Commander Benson pressed his quill upon the table, the line of questioning removing his playful temper. "While it may be true it was accidental, you still practiced an illegal, high-level ability in a non-native region which resulted in the death of a soldier of Tenuel. You broke many laws. It may not have been intentional, but you are certainly not innocent. While close in meaning, they are not synonymous."

"Why did the soldiers of the South come to Wesilea? Why did they arrest people in our town who had done nothing?"

"Asking someone to leave is not equivalent to arresting them."

Perhaps tomorrow she would ask to stay in her own quarters.

He turned his attention to his letters. "He is your king, too."

"Hmm?"

"You said *your king*. He is not just my king."

"You can't possibly agree with what he's doing," Sissel sighed, imploring, "Mr. Baradelle is an innocent man. More innocent than I am. He is kind. It's not against the law to live in a region outside your birth."

"I'm a soldier of The South Sea. It doesn't matter whether I agree or disagree. I follow orders."

"Your people are dealers of death."

Commander Benson tucked his arms across his chest. *"Our* people." His chin tensed.

"I've always found it fascinating how some abilities are determined to be light and some dark. Some negative. Some positive.

"Valesove is the region of life. The South Sea, the region of death. Are those not one and the same? There is no life without death, and there is no death without life. What circumstances determine a second chance at life is darkness? Those of the Endruas can avoid aging, the Sarealium and the Sareoenti can heal themselves or others to avoid death. And the Anisirie can revive another from the brink a mere fraction of second before death claims them. Why are those gifts considered within the light, and the people who can breathe once more briefly after death has overtaken them be considered dark?

"I see no light; I see no dark. I see a second chance when there would be none otherwise. The Voreasus halts their own heart to avoid death when injured until they can be healed by another. Is it not the same as being healed primarily? Mere moments in which a heart beats should not determine which is of good intent and which is evil. Each of us fighting to stay alive with whatever tools we were lucky enough to be born with, whether it be an instant before death takes us or an instant after."

Fidgeting with her hands, she attempted to control the tone of her voice and not reveal her frustration. "Perhaps the dark and light lies within the intention of the use," she replied.

"Then you argue in favor of my position and not against."

"However, I do not believe there is a match from Valesove to the ability of the Noslarrar or the Roscivis. They can kill dozens without moving one muscle within their body. The Roscivis—willing it so—can snap the neck of anyone in the opposing army without ever touching them. That sort of power wields fear."

"Yes. But great power can be used with great intentions when held by an honorable person."

She mocked, shouting, "An honorable breaker of bones?"

"You cannot see the good it can wield."

"No, I cannot." Sissel allowed her words and thoughts unrivaled freedom.

Commander Benson drew close. She nearly felt the prickle of his beard, smelled the hint of mint on his face, his eyes a reminder she addressed the commander of her imprisoning army.

"I had a Noslarrar in my deployment many years ago when our small caravan was attacked by a traveling group from the Yurelan who had seen us on the road. They were young, following orders to attack without training, without organization. They were frightened; it was easy to tell. And some,

I would wager, as young as eight. They had the numbers to overtake us by force, not by skill.

"The four of us were well trained in battle. We would have put up a valiant fight, but we would have had the blood of three dozen children on our blades. My soldier followed her orders. She was instructed to break the right arm of anyone who came within twenty paces. The left if they still pursued. We called the warning, made it known long before they were close enough. She even called it in their native tongue.

"Those who came within the boundary were broken. One limb. Only three came close enough. Not one dared come inside the boundary after. Their leader didn't even pursue; sat atop his black steed like a coward.

"They weren't killed. There was no blood. They could still walk home to their mothers and fathers. They could heal. Her abilities saved my life, and the lives of the other two soldiers with us. And, with certainty, saved the lives of dozens of the children forced to attack us. Every ability has a positive use, so long as the person who possesses it uses it wisely."

"These are all rare circumstances."

"All weapons should be used in rare circumstances, yet I can think of many others. War is not always upon us. I know how to use my sword; I have used it many times, though I do not often kill a crowd of people because I felt like it."

She argued, "The South Sea are a warring people."

"Someone must be. When you need someone to protect you, I doubt you will call upon Qabriah or Cascanvore."

"You can't guarantee someone born into a lineage would use their abilities wisely."

"I could never guarantee such a thing—what a naive thing to say," he spat. "I'm merely asserting the ability is not what is dark. The darkness lies within the intent of the soul who wields it."

"And what of the Roscidarra? What is the use for that lineage? I see no light in trading the life of a healthy person for that of a dying one. That is certainly not needed in war."

Commander Benson's slate eyes glassed, as if they might shatter if she were to draw close. She had said too much. His eyes bore pain, and his tone drew long. "Using the ability of the Roscidarra without request or permission is the same as murder, as you well know."

She exhaled. "Murder is darkness."

"I am not sure if I should thank the stars or curse them that there are still people in this world as naive as you. You have a pure heart but can't see in front of your nose. Not unless it walks directly in front of your window."

Again, she lowered her gaze, wishing desperately to escape this room. He couldn't possibly have seen her watching him.

"The Roscidarra are held in exceedingly high esteem in The South Sea. One lives in the castle and serves the king or queen in Islarourne—the Gerive Aroun. People bow when they walk by, lower their heads to honor them as if they were a king or queen. They have the highest honors one can possess and live both a tortured and fulfilled life. They serve one purpose and one alone: they take the lives of those who request it to be done. I have seen many healthy individuals offer themselves for another. The act is done with the highest possible honor. There is even a memorial at the base of the castle, names etched into stone for eternity. In The South Sea there is nothing one can do which is more selfless."

Sissel twisted a strand of hair, processing the harrowing nature of this sacrificial act. "Why would someone wish to do that?"

"You should be thankful you do not know how it feels to be a mother, forced to watch her son dying of blackvein fever. To watch his blood become poisoned, take hold of the tiny body you brought into this world while he struggles for oxygen and his limbs turn gray. If you did, you would see light in trading the life of a healthy person for a dying one."

Commander Benson rose from his seat, his face illuminated by the orange flames of the fire, pain plain in his features. Below his cotton shirt, he gripped a golden chain around his neck.

"You've seen this?"

"I've lived it." He clenched his left fist, the veins beneath his skin swelling. "Though it took a few tries to take."

Sissel's tears welled while she processed his tale. This man before her would not be here had his mother not given herself for him. "What's your lineage?"

"In the South, it is disrespectful to ask, should you not wear the pin upon your chest." As he spoke, she remembered the pins on his fineries, including the silver symbol of The South Sea. "Should you not be a Sengura—not have pure blood—it's frowned upon."

Now she wished her ability lay in recoiling words once they departed her lips. "My apologies."

While she wished to speak to him, this conversation trail had moved far from where she intended.

Where to go from here?

After some time, he confessed, "I don't have a lineage which has ever made itself known. I don't bear the name of a highborn or anything that would distinguish my heritage. I was born in Islarourne. The name Benson is claimed by no lineages.

"I don't possess the will to break bones or the mark across my cheeks. My aunt was a Remerard, a warrior; that would be my assumption of my dominant lineage. Though, I had to work harder at it than others when I trained, so perhaps not."

Sissel's heart felt like a small vessel atop the raging sea. "Tell me something that isn't terrible to think about. How did you become commander? You seem so young."

Commander Benson wore a melancholy grin. "I'll save that tale for another time. It'll do nothing to improve your mood."

Sissel searched for any appropriate questions to keep their flow of conversation. "Do you know what has become of Mr. Baradelle?"

"Dear Mr. Baradelle, a man of the South living in Tenuel. Curious indeed."

"He did nothing wrong."

"Perhaps not, but a smarter man would've adopted a different name in a volatile climate. Surnames such as Baradelle, Vak'Arra. Those aren't found north of the mountains. Certainly not west."

"Why do you speak my name that way? The way you pronounce it, Vak-*ARRA*. It's Vacarro."

"There are many highborn families of The South Sea. The most predominant three, those said to be there when the world began, Naylanian, Vak'Arra, Era'Ourne. The Vak'Arra is an immensely powerful family, the name alone prestigious. Over the years, it was shortened to Vakarra. A strict Sengura family of Roscidarra. Though many still pronounce it in the old manner of speaking."

The weight in Sissel's chest lightened at the mere thought. A sense of calm teased the edge of her thoughts, a hope ready to clutch brushing the tips of her fingers. The words of the soldiers during her transport became clear. She had heard of highborns, though they did not live in Wesila, at least not that she had known. They were larger than her small life, a step down from royalty in The South. Maybe there was a way.

"Is that why you brought me here? To discuss my sentencing? You believe me to be of this family? Highborn of The South Sea?"

"That is a matter which requires more exploration. Though it does provide some evidence as to why you are being moved to The Reldory. You should wish to be of this family. That is, if there is any chance to have your sentencing moved."

WE DON'T MAKE FRIENDS

Kelreh Cedarn Bhailick, Tu'dende of the Dergenti, The Wielder of Metal, The Pangolin
Born: Second Month of Autumn, 1981
Deceased: Second Month of Summer, 2058
Children: Two

- Official Ledger of Dhaesreaon

I am a gentle ... man.

Gentle men don't hold prisoners.

The war waged inside, tugging and pulling, pulling and tugging. Eran spoke like a man with nothing left to hide—a man who bled for Lennie as surely as any of them would have.

But instincts didn't matter. Ariaas had final say.

A book slammed closed inches from his face.

Brenor jerked upright, blinking as Ariaas's face swam into view. "You alive in there?"

Brenor set his jaw and swallowed the words away.

He stayed silent while Ariaas had his first and second breakfast. While Eran sat chained like a wild animal in the stables. The matter tugged at him, keeping him from sleep, conflicting every fiber of his being.

Lennie sat at his side. They exchanged a knowing glance. She leaned in. "My opinion hasn't changed. He shouldn't be chained."

Brenor breathed for what felt like the first time since he clamped the chain. *Thank the stars Lennie is still on my side.* They both looked toward Ariaas.

"We cannot keep him this way," he argued, "and we certainly cannot plan Theo's rescue with a man tied in the stables."

"Quite the contrary, he serves us great purpose tied in the stables."

"He isn't a spy. I trust him." Lennie urged. "Maybe he can help us with Thealor or Arienne. Give him a chance."

"If he is a spy, I'll kill him," Ariaas spoke almost without thinking, clear he had no intention of believing Eran's tale. "If he isn't a spy, well—we need bait, don't we?"

Brenor pondered what type of bait Ariaas had been conjuring. He rehearsed in his head, *'My instincts say this is wrong. The man is no liar.'* All the words he wished to speak to Ariaas. Every other time he attempted to refute his grandfather, the words came out jumbled, never in the rehearsed, beautiful rendition they remained in his mind.

Ariaas's lips formed a small line. "We will discuss it after training. Go. Both of you."

Ariaas instructed Lennie, showing her in the interior perimeter, and the next three hours of the late morning, Brenor worked with her on her swordsmanship. The last hour, before she was allowed a short break, she mimicked the whistling sounds of the bluebird to little accuracy. Ariaas brought books and notes on loose pages so she might study the lineages in her free time.

Sleep was unnecessary; he reminded them they could sleep in death.

At the end of their training, Brenor and Lennie stood below the shadows of the stable. Perhaps she thought if she waited there long enough, Ariaas would realize he forgot something.

Finally confident in his rehearsed verbiage, Brenor shouted, his voice cracking, "Eran should no longer be chained." Not the rehearsed argument, but it would have to do.

"You trust too easily." Ariaas fidgeted with a gadget Brenor invented to keep the traps sharp as razors. "A good twenty to thirty years in there and we'll figure out Heneran's true intentions."

"I have trusted no one outside of you my entire life. But you also told me to trust my instincts. You said my instincts, if I truly listened, would never lead me astray. This is wrong. He is being honest. If he is honorable as he seems to be, and he loves Lennie, it would not be for nothing to offer him our trust in return. To unchain him. We could use someone who can vouch for us. Aid us if we need it."

"We don't make friends. We don't make enemies."

"Lennie believes him, too."

"I did." She shook her head, correcting. "I do."

"I am unchaining him," Brenor waited. Waited for Ariaas to chastise him for his outburst. Waited for him to shout or throw something, to which none came.

Lennie seconded, seeking his approval. "He needs to be released."

Ariaas finally said, "If you let him go, we must agree. He can't know who you are."

"Done," Brenor and Lennie said at once.

+ ———— · + · ✦ · + · ———— +

"I made supper," Eran exclaimed. "Took me a bit to catch one of the chickens. I found some potatoes and made some bread from letvisqel in the garden."

Ariaas sighed and slumped into his chair.

Brenor smirked. Perhaps this wouldn't be so bad after all. Without being prompted, Eran ranted about the weather, gardening, and told stories of Taren's antics while they were away. How he had twice caught him under the burgundy armchair from running in his sleep before his enormous frame sent it into the wall. He snickered at his own jokes in the story, even when no one else found it humorous.

The weather was his favorite topic—the weather and food.

Brenor found his quirky nature quite charming. Ariaas brought out whiskey early in the evening, tore the cork from the bottle with his teeth, spat it onto the floor, and guzzled from the open bottle. "Supper should be a silent, quick occasion."

Brenor opened a bottle of wine, the bottle he had been saving for nothing. Eran drank the glass he offered in one gulp as the three stared wide-eyed.

"I thought you didn't like wine?" Lennie asked, breaking her near silence of the day.

"Your mother doesn't like wine." Eran pointed the glass toward Brenor, who poured a second glass to the rim. "Said it dulled the senses."

"I prefer my senses dull." Ariaas's lips tightened though he ate twice his fill. "You should know. I am still adamantly opposed to him staying here."

Lennie grinned. "You are certainly not opposed to his cooking."

"Am I the only one who has not lost my senses?"

"I can help. I don't know how yet, but I will find a way. I will prove myself useful." Eran dried his hands on a dirty rag in the kitchen, his enthusiasm beaming. "I'm handy with tools if there is anythin' in need of repair."

Ariaas sneered. "Brenor fixes things around the house and the land."

"The land is vast. Seems a daunting task for one." Eran eyed Brenor. "I'll gladly help if you'd like."

"Your positivity is barred before breakfast." Ariaas sipped his whiskey. "Perhaps even before supper."

Eran created jobs for himself around the cottage without anyone's request. Each day, Brenor's work lightened. Eran tended to the horses. Mended a few broken items Brenor had in a pile upon the stable desk: a leg of the side table, a lock on the door to the kitchen, and the lip of the threshold which had split.

After days, Ariaas's slim grasp on something resembling patience had evaporated. He blurted out his feelings to Eran whenever they entered his mind, even amid a silent room while the Brenor read by the hearth. "We can't sleep indefinitely this way, Brenor all tossed up on the sofa and you on the floor. There's no room here for you. You need to return to wherever you came from." Brenor bit his tongue while Ariaas spat his anger. "Aroun Vaer is no place for you."

Brenor sighed with bittersweet relief. Lennie had missed Ariaas's outburst. His heart ached for Eran; he enjoyed Eran's quirky antics, his help, and the ease he seemed to carry. Brenor had not planned the future, not what *indefinite* meant, nor where Eran would call his home forever.

"Why do you stay in a place you are clearly not wanted?"

"Ariaas," Brenor finally interjected.

"No—I want to know—has Lenora asked you to stay? Brenor? I certainly haven't." Ariaas's volume grew. "Go home!"

Eran's eyes glazed. "What've I done to you?"

"You have done nothing to me. It's the *nothing* where the problem lies. Lenora and Brenor want me to trust you—a total stranger—who has done nothing to warrant said trust. You showed up asleep in my chair one day and that means you can live here? Petting my dog. Organizing my bookshelf. *Reading.* You're like a stray dog, you feed it once and it just won't leave."

Eran urged, "I didn't know what happened with Anse—*Lenora.* I had no idea."

"Perhaps not. Perhaps you didn't know. And then what? What if you truly knew nothing? That might even be worse! Your entire life was monitored, your house, your wife. The fields you tended, your very brother and sister by marriage, every nuance of your life—watched! Every. Day. You were being scrutinized without your knowledge for years. You never felt a hair stand up on the back of your neck as if someone watched you!" Ariaas slammed his palm upon the table. "You never felt anything amiss.

"That alone doesn't bode well for my trust in you. You're either one with our enemies or a bumbling idiot. There's nothing in between. A man keen on his surroundings, a man who is concerned for his well-being, doesn't turn a blind eye to such things. Even if I made a terrible choice to trust your intentions, I would certainly never trust your instincts."

Ariaas grabbed the bottle of whiskey by the neck. "You should go back to wherever you came from."

Eran closed the book and set it on the side table. "I had a happy life. A family was all I ever wanted. Children of my own. Flawed, of course. Every wish is, but I had it. A man with his dreams doesn't look for reasons to wake himself." With a heavy head, Eran met the threshold of the door to the cottage and departed.

"Eran, wait." Brenor rose from his chair, following close behind. He addressed Ariaas, "That was not necessary."

✦ ——— · ✦ · ✦ · ✦ · ——— ✦

Brenor and Lennie trained with the bow and a dense weight amongst them the following morning. No new plan emerged to rescue Thealor, Arienne, and Sissel. Ariaas had indeed become unbearable. They sparred when finished with the arrows in their rounds.

Eran stood patient, Taren at his heels. "I've seen you trainin'. Are you worried the bowmen will find you here?"

"Yes, I suppose." Lennie eyed Brenor. "Can I ask you something? Do you know anything of Dhaesreaon? About Mount Ohbrolis and Brouverg Castle?"

Brenor's insides curled. *We promised Ariaas we wouldn't say a word. What is she doing?*

"I know Mount Ohbrolis is covered in snow in the winter, warm in the spring, much like here, but harsher. Lord Brouverg died many years ago, ten or twelve, I believe now. Lady Brouverg lives alone in the castle now with her servants."

Brenor sighed—not much they did not already know.

"They collect things. Fine things. Show them off to other prestigious people to flaunt their status." Eran asked, "Why do you ask about Brouverg Castle?"

"Curiosity," Brenor quickly interjected. "She is so curious."

"Oh, and I always thought it odd, Lady Brouverg. The two of them, the lord and lady, living in the high castle," Eran continued. "So strange for those who control beasts to live in such a pristine space and not the forest."

"The Brouvergs are Quparae?" Two days earlier he and Lennie read about the people of Dhaesreaon—the lineages who control animals of the earth live in the forests. "I thought the Brouvergs were descendants of the lineages of those who control glass. The way their ancestors built the castle? You remember the passage we read?"

Lennie repeated from memory, "A sheer structure that falls into the snow by the right light built by the Cesurelear. The Quparaen live in The Blackwood. They are not people of gold and riches."

"My thoughts aloud." Eran raised a brow. "And the name Brouverg, a highborn name of the Quparaen, at that. To a superior degree, I believe. Though the name would be the lady's by marriage."

When Eran bent to pet Taren, Lennie whispered, "I promised I wouldn't say anything of our capture, but we didn't discuss keeping the other two to ourselves."

Brenor fumbled for words. "Ariaas will be furious." He pinched his lips tight, his eyebrows drawn together, equally curious and terrified. "You cannot bring secrets back into your lips once they are spilled."

"Do you trust my judgment?"

Brenor hesitated. The short answer—*yes*. The long answer—he still had a long life to live at Aroun Vaer and did not want it to be unbearable. Uncertain, he said, "Yes."

Lennie returned to Eran. "Out of curiosity, if you wished to get into Brouverg Castle, how would you?"

Eran stared off, lost in thought. Then after some time said, "At the first fallin' of the snow, the final winds of autumn in the north, they invite guests to the castle. The lords and ladies, that they might buy and sell fine things. They have a host of collections, jewels, art. I overheard Lord Ellsrhun speakin' on it long ago." He chuckled at the thought. "Though, he said he thought the Brouvergs meant to flaunt and not sell. They only seek to acquire status, somethin' remarkable to cross their eye. They do not allow people to stay unless they have somethin' of immense worth. If I were to wish to go to the castle, I would go then. Of course, I hold nothing of value."

How had I not known this? Does Ariaas know?

"They mean to acquire all manner of things?" Brenor thought through his next words, considering his own advice. Once spoken, thoughts could not be retracted. However, these words weighed the edge of his tongue until he was forced to surrender. "Our brother was sold to the lady of the house when Lennie was sent to you."

Eran's breath held in his lungs. Finally, he muttered, "Sold?"

"He's a servant, as I understand. Since the age of five."

"I ..." Eran stuttered, "I assumed it was the two of you, and no more."

Better not to lie. I am a gentle man. This is for the best. "There are four of us. The eldest is held at The Reldory in The South Sea."

"The Reldory?"

Ariaas would be furious, yet Brenor's mouth moved almost without permission. "We will move to retrieve them as soon as the opportunity presents itself. As we plan now, we will move upon Mount Ohbrolis first. We expect The Reldory to be our greatest challenge and wish to have our brother at our side."

Eran's hand covered his mouth, his fingers quivering.

Brenor considered this new information, the lords and ladies, and the items bought and sold. They needed no coin, but an object, something special.

"We need something of value, perceived at the least." Lennie seemed hopeful for the first time. "Then we have a way in."

Ariaas's voice boomed from the doorway, "Yesterday he was our chained prisoner, and today you welcome him into our home and share our greatest secrets?"

Brenor had not heard him enter and mostly didn't care. They had more information than Ariaas had in a lifetime.

"We unchained him two weeks ago." Brenor paced, the stress of leaning over the line of his promise consuming him. "And, not our greatest secrets. Merely, the ones with pressing urgency."

"Do you have anything? Anything we can sell or offer?" Lennie asked, her eyes alight. "Anything valuable?"

Brenor inhaled. *The books.* The books were worth a fortune, but they were Ariaas's prized possessions. "We have something."

"Not an option," Ariaas growled.

White as a cotton sheet, Eran's jaw dropped further. "What possession could you possibly have of more value than your family?"

"We do not need to sell them," Brenor argued. "Just give the impression we are willing to sell them. They will know if something is counterfeit."

"No." Ariaas yanked Brenor's arm, dragging him toward the training field.

Brenor rushed out the words before Ariaas scolded him, "The Brouvergs are not as their lineage would depict. They speak in wealth and coin, nothing less. He shares information we have never been privy to. They are of the Qup—"

"He shares information *you* have never been privy to. Their heritage isn't news to me. I tried to buy out Thealor's indenture. I attempted to sell them Aroun Vaer! The castle, the land, and many things within its walls! Lady Brouverg doesn't want a crumble of boarded up rocks! It's all the wealth we have."

"Then we do not use the money to buy his indenture. We use it to get in and see where he is, how he can get him out."

Ariaas eyed Eran warily. "Can you honestly tell me you want this man around here?" He held his voice above a scolding whisper. "You want him asking questions about this family? Knowing where we are going, what we are doing?"

"We are too busy here, too isolated. We know nothing of the news of the world." Brenor glanced toward the stable, ensuring no one listened. "I want our family returned. Thealor and Arienne—safe here with us. There has been no possibility with the two of us, and now even with Lennie. She was just as isolated. We have no new options with the three of us."

Brenor slowed his rapid words. "The Army of The South Sea has spent twenty-three years unable to find us. He located us in less than three months. *Three months.* There must be a reason he is here."

"Don't say it." Ariaas shook his head. "Don't use the f-word."

"It must be fate." Brenor beamed, the grin at his chin near ear to ear. He held Ariaas's shoulders in his wide hands. "I think we must at the least be open to accepting aid from others when we are unable to do something alone. I know for you ... trust is difficult."

"Trust is difficult? Stop speaking that way, your head up in the clouds. You're willing to let a stranger into our home, into our lives. If this goes wrong, it'll be on you."

"I believe he has good intentions. He loves Lennie immensely. He is no stranger to her. You seemed to trust him, too, or you would have harmed him the night we found him." He stared at Ariaas, a statement Brenor wished he would reply to.

Wide-eyed, Ariaas declared, "I took a vow."

Brenor crossed his arms over his chest. Ariaas only used such matters when they benefited his own cause. "Tell me the truth."

Ariaas stood silent.

A slow grin crossed Brenor's lips, and he repeated the line Ariaas's often offered him. "Your instincts? They will never lead you astray?"

"I briefly understood his pain at the loss of a child and gave him a chance to speak. Trusting him to know our plans, to stay in this house, is different than not killing him on sight. It's different than thinking him an enemy."

"I agree. Though, I also genuinely believe he wants to help."

"*Want* is the worst word in our language. I *want* a lot of things which will never come to be. He may very well want to help but only bring us further issues. He knows where we live. He found us. He has been here for weeks. What if he found the journals? What if he knows why you were all taken?"

"If he knew everything he would not be acting as he is now. You are being suspicious."

Ariaas pressed a finger into Brenor's chest. "My suspicions alone kept the heart inside your chest beating for the last two-and-a-quarter decades."

Brenor gripped his hand. "For that, I am incredibly grateful. However, this family will need allies in the days to come. We have one able friend in this world outside those who stand in this house, and she is weeks away at best, and unable to leave even if we needed her. Give him a chance. Please. Starting with one man who loves one of us dearly seems like a reasonable first step."

"You'll be responsible for him. It'll be up to you to ensure he keeps his word and speaks nothing further of us to anyone."

"I will be responsible for him."

LARKSPUR

We travel to Rabinor. Well, that is what Mother calls it still. They won't tell me why.

- Diary of Daisirie Cabredd Mire, Volume 3, Entry 308

Commander Benson forced the top off a cylindrical steel balanser with his thumb, illuminating an orb above him and Sissel in the otherwise dark room.

"Where did you get it?"

"I confiscated it from one of the boys in the yard. He stole it from a soldier of Felreaon who stopped here on his way home from Zyserar. The soldier was already gone by then—no one to return it to. I certainly would not allow the boy to keep it. A gift of a Jolisard, it would seem." He drew close, showing her the eight stars engraved in deep silver. "I thought it was useless for some time. But it reaches onto what it knows."

He placed the balanser into her palm. When his hand met hers, she delayed her withdrawal, holding onto the moment of his touch an instant longer.

"It reaches for the steel holders, not the brass," he continued. "I had used it in the yard, but apparently, whoever built this room also had one. I had to light the hearth by hand at home for light when the sun departed."

Lights rushed into the metal, and the room darkened behind drawn curtains before she opened them, illuminating it once more. "I saw one years ago. It passed through Mr. Baradelle's shop. He thought they were fascinating and wished he could keep it."

Such a funny thing, the fear she had of Commander Ronan Benson when she first came to his quarters. The man who now listened to the deepest thoughts of her mind, and she to his. "You asked me some weeks ago what I noticed about you."

Commander Benson's curiosities piqued. "I remember well. A question you didn't wish to answer."

"You have a bad left knee," she replied. "You can walk endlessly with it, but you never take the first step with your left. It doesn't bend easily to the side. You never cross your foot over your right knee, always the other leg. When you trained last week, you leaned in by your right that your left never was exposed, that it was not struck."

"Clever." His grin widened. "It doesn't hurt, but it's easily agitated."

Sissel finished the book he brought her and three more after, all bearing a dedication to Riera on the inside cover. Now, the two spoke at length instead of reading. They never had anything specific to talk about, but there never seemed to be a lack of conversation between them.

He stared at her for a while, seeming to decide something about her as he did the first day she arrived. After a lengthy contemplation, he said, "I need some fresh air. Would you care for a walk?"

He opened the handle of the balanser, pulling the lights back into their home, leaving them in darkness. Even in the black, Sissel's anticipation soared. The sun seldom touched her—only when she was led to greet him in this very room.

They wandered beyond the lengths of the buildings, toward the hills, and the lowering sun. Commander Benson—*Ronan,* she reminded herself—held his arms loose behind his back, not at the firm attention of a soldier, while they took a slow, meandering pace.

Sissel grasped his arm. "Last night, after you walked me back to my quarters, I saw the girl with braided hair walking with the boy. They walked alone. They were both smiling."

His lips curled beneath his beard. "This makes you happy?"

"Did you do something?"

"Not exactly."

Short of the birch tree and the edge of the rocks, Sissel stopped. The subtle movement of his lips was not lost on her, and she would walk no further without understanding the nature behind his grin.

He bowed to the silence between. "I said nothing of the girl or her affections."

She waited while the breeze caressed her hair. Certainly, a better answer lurked somewhere below the surface.

Commander Benson sighed. "Two weeks ago, I told him blind men cannot serve in my army. Should he wish to stay, he needed to learn to see. I said nothing further. What he did from there was his own choice. Though he clearly has become a bit more ... observant."

Heat crept into her cheeks. What could she say when he intervened in the attraction she watched from afar?

"Should he want her or not is of no consequence to me," he added. "His skills of observation, knowing his surroundings, which is a different story. It concerned me that you could see so much, and he could see so little. Not a man I would want at my side in battle, should I be lucky enough to choose."

Ronan tipped forward to investigate her reaction, arms crossed behind his back. "I'm certain it opened his eyes to many other things. Many things aside from her." His gaze met hers. A heartbeat later, a grin flickered across his face. "But—I'm glad it made you smile."

Her heart skipped. Unable to find words, she regained her casual stride.

Through the clearing of trees, the hills lowered, the fields opening wide as the dawn. In the clearing, birds chittered. The flora beckoned them with scents of fresh larkspur, the rolling hills dotted in lavender and blush, glistening against the sun like scattered jewels. She studied Ronan's features while he gazed across this new horizon, fixated through the field to the opposite forest edge. "What's beyond the field?"

"The border to Felreaon. A day's walk, through the birch forest." His jaw tightened and his gaze moved to her. "Their soldiers are welcome here. However ... Felreaon does not allow soldiers of The South Sea over their borders."

She perched upon a rock's edge, uninterested in talk of soldiers and borders. She yearned to be close to him and savor his presence. This moment with him and the shifting sky came as close to perfection as she could imagine. The horizon dipped and shifted from orange to bright pink.

"I've seen the sun rise many times. I haven't had many chances to see it set."

His slate eyes cast over her with sudden disappointment.

She could not place this shift in his energy. Why had he brought her out here to talk of the armies? She never wished to be alone with any men from Wesilea—never wished to watch the sunset, to walk through a field of wildflowers, to lose all track of the time of day. Ronan Benson was nothing like those men. They stared from her neck down her chest, undressing her. Instead, he watched her eyes with solemn curiosity.

Sissel's nose wrinkled into a frown. "Is something wrong?"

He exhaled through his nose and stirred with unease. Again, he eyed the sliver of Felreaon in the distance.

After some time, he sighed and sat quietly at her side. His shoulder pressed into hers, finally content to watch the rustling of the grass and the larkspur alter below the deepening colors of the heavens.

Desperate for understanding, she pressed for further conversation. "Do you miss Islarourne?"

"Sometimes, yes. But what I genuinely miss is no longer there."

"What's that?"

"My mother. She's been gone for a long time, but I still miss her terribly."

Ronan drew a golden chain from below his shirt. "She gave her life to save mine. I have long thought the act to be foolish." He dropped the chain into Sissel's hand. "She was too good a person to have left this world."

Sissel turned the ring in her hands, the stones each a different color, eight, between small round diamonds. The light danced and shone on their faces.

"That is all I have left of her."

"It's beautiful." Once she had finished taking in its splendor, he secured it again below his shirt. "Where did you go after she died?"

"My aunt was responsible for me then, my father stationed who knows where. She was the Commander of The South Sea at the time. She put me into the Aruvayuan Duem—where soldiers go to train. They often take children without parents. Sometimes the Remerard go in early, too." He withdrew into his thoughts, seeming to relive the memories.

"That is where I met Riera—Captain Kalory. She pulled me from being jolted in the chest by the hind hooves of a stallion who never wished to be tamed."

"Where is your aunt now?"

"She was a cruel woman. Family meant little to her. Very much in the likeness of Ravaris. Honor in the Armies of the South is an odd sort. Power, death, they all intertwine."

He opened his lips to speak twice and closed them.

"Many years after my mother died, once I served my time at Aruvayuan Duem, I was released into the Army of The South Sea. My aunt took me on a journey with her across the Adlean Sea. To me, she made some unforgivable decisions. When we returned, I ... went around the chain of command, told the queen what she had done. The next day, she arranged a battle between us in the tower.

"'The last Benson standing will wear the title Commander of the Armies of The South Sea,' she said. The former Commander Benson was well armed, the sword and shield in her arms. My aunt knew well what she had walked into long before I did, a favor to a standing Commander by the Queen."

Sissel's hand flew to her chest. He seemed a man incapable of such atrocities. "You killed your aunt?"

With solemness, he nodded. "It was a long time ago."

She wished she had the silk dress her grandmother had gifted her. Perhaps if she wore that instead of rags, he would speak less of the army and more of the soft breeze danced around them, carrying the scent of larkspur and birch while he eyed the western horizon.

"Have you found a connection to the family you spoke of some months ago? The Vak'*ARRA*." She beamed at the way the *RRs* rolled from her tongue in the way Ronan's did.

He smiled, both of pity and sorrow at once. "Not yet." The balanser twisted in his grasp, the steel reflecting the orange sun. "Tell me what you miss from outside Tanes."

How could she choose one thing? "I miss the sunrise from the roof at Thaesla's. On nights I couldn't sleep, I would climb to the roof. The sky was bright orange and pink. On a clear morning, you could see the land on the other side of the sea. At least I imagined I could.

"I miss the smell of the market in the morning, before it opened, when the bread was fresh from the fire of the oven and the morning air was cool. Before the bustling. I miss Thaesla's trinkets, her messy house. I had to step over piles of books to get to the sofa. In the pantry, there were piles of things"—she laughed—"but there was never anything to eat."

He grinned, listening intently to her tale.

"Most days, Thaesla fiddled with her trinkets and her maps. She never told me what it was, though. Always scurrying around." Sissel thought more on his question. Beyond her grandmother and Thaesla, other things seemed trivial. A reminder of a life she once lived. Her entire life.

"I miss my grandmother." The words burned on her tongue. "I miss her laugh, her voice. How she tucked her arm under mine when we walked. She was a warrior long ago, so she told me. She kept her sword even after she could no longer raise it to her hip. This huge thing with a black leather hilt, a golden rose at the top. As she told it, her father had it made for her. Perfectly balanced to the weight of her hand when she joined the army, etched and sealed.

"I think that is what I miss most, the stories she would tell. She had wild stories, those of snakes, and trackers, and lost loves, and adventure. She loved to tell them. She loved making me remember she was young once, too."

Ronan said, "She sounds like a woman after my own heart."

"I think some days, in recent years, a small part of her wished to die. I think she felt she was a burden to me, though she never was. Not that she wished for death, but she wished I might find a life elsewhere. That I would not stay in Wesilea for her. That I might have a life like she once had. A full life." Sissel sighed. "In two months, she will be ninety-seven."

The number alone pained her. Not many made it to see their ninetieth year; her grandmother would say it was a privilege.

"I didn't get a chance to say goodbye. She was not in the square that day. I checked on her sleeping before I left. I had no idea I would never see her again." Sissel let her thoughts escape her. "I doubt she will see another birthday, let alone a day I am not imprisoned."

"You should write to her." Ronan twisted his thumbs in his crossed hands.

"And how will I get it to her?" she jested, pressing her shoulder into his. "Do they allow prisoners the use of courier pigeons at The Reldory?"

"I'll take it to her."

She examined his face, seeking if his offer was earnest or in jest. "The journey is weeks ... just to get there."

He stared back at her; a sincere offer written in his eyes.

"Why are you being kind to me? The guard's barracks, the private conversations ... the long walk at sundown?"

She hoped he would say one thing: it was her. Maybe she was the reason he was kind—not pity or sympathy—but a mere wish to be at her side.

"You are one of my own people. And I feel you are being unfairly treated. There are many people who don't know their lineage, are not trained, don't know their capabilities. You meant to help your friend. And you did, the only way your instincts knew how. Accidents should not afford life sentences."

He pressed his boots across the dirt. "Living out each of the remaining days of your life in perpetual torture seems extreme. In truth, I can't think of any crimes which would warrant that type of punishment. The High

Commander and I are in stark opposition. It's a fate worse than execution. The Reldory should only be reserved for those who can't be contained elsewhere. You don't seem to fit that criteria." Ronan recoiled, seeming to realize he'd divulged too much.

"And ..." he added, "I may have also grown fond of your company." He grazed her cheek, moving the hair to her ear, the warmth of his skin against hers. "You're getting cold. We should go."

LADY ACALISARE

A crisp white blanket of snow covered boulders along the steady incline to Mount Ohbrolis, interrupted by a skeleton of trees. Lenora pulled Luscan to a halt, her heavy breath forming a cloud in the air. The road to Brouverg Castle twisted much like the one to Jaisett—cutting north, skirting the jagged line between Valesove and Dhaesreaon.

She reached into her bag, fingers closing around the quill. Still there. Still hers. One fragile piece of certainty. Maybe Oedd would know what to do.

Her family, new and old, had a plan. A good one. But it all hinged on her.

Lenora opened her mouth to speak, but words tangled in the sudden knot at her throat. She'd been so certain before—rushing toward her brother, toward an urgent heroic rescue. Now, doubt gnawed her ribs. What if she couldn't become the highborn lady this plan required? What if Brouverg Castle saw past the gowns, past the posture, straight into the soft girl raised in a cottage under Sanrial trees? What if she failed?

Brenor's brow scrunched while he twisted a torn cloth. "I wish I could go with you."

"We've discussed this," Ariaas hissed. "They'll recognize your face. You and Thealor are too much alike."

"I wish you could go, too." Lenora sadly accepted Brenor's absence from this plan, yet she had grown fond of his daily presence. She turned to her grandfather, the man who still held so many secrets. "You still haven't told me why you won't go."

Ariaas rubbed his collarbone. "Don't waste your breath on me. You should be sitting in the back of the carriage, not on top of the horse! You are supposed to be a *lady*. Not an archer."

He required her theatrics. The mountain did, truthfully. She righted her posture, lifted her chin gazing down upon Ariaas though her stomach knotted.

"You'll be alright." Ariaas patted her knee though his lack of eye contact said otherwise. "And you," he turned to Eran, "Don't touch anything. Don't talk to anyone."

Lenora exhaled, reveling in the cloud before her. Brenor grasped her hand one final time. "Will you ...."

"I'll be careful," Lenora assured. She raised her shoulders theatrically. "And remember, I was born to be a highborn lady." Without warning, Brenor wrapped his arms around her, squeezing so tightly, she thought she'd lose her last meal.

+ ———— ·+·+·+· ———— +

The mirrored face of Brouverg Castle vanished from some points of view, blending into the rocks and snow. Sheer walls rose in peaks and complex formations, invisible without the proper light. The entrance, a soaring, prominent bridge made of hand hewn stone—a stark reminder that lineages governing the earth comprised the River Realm—led to a long line of soldiers in fur stoles and crisp navy uniforms donning long spears. Beyond them was a company of highborn lords and ladies, chattering, giggling, waiting in their silks and fineries to present their articles.

The frigid air warmed.

Sheer walls blocked the polar breeze. Beyond women with elongated curls and glimmering tiaras, snow waltzed, and white mountain peaks stretched across every visible angle.

Lenora adopted the name of a lady of the Sareoenti, a matter she hoped they would not seek to prove. If Lady Brouverg carved into her flesh, there would be no quick mending.

Eran posed as her servant.

A mute servant.

Lenora's heart soared at the thrill of donning a charcoal silk gown with a steel blade tucked against her thigh. She was accustomed to keeping a weapon close. Ariaas allowed her to choose from any of Sarinah's gowns, all equally luxurious, all perfect for the highborn lady she now embodied.

A gentleman with a turned up nose in sapphire robes and cream trousers addressed the small crowd. "Welcome, lords and ladies of Monera to the Festival of Articles. Your wares must earn your place if you wish to stay amongst the company at the castle. You must have something worth the time of Lady Brouverg and the others in the room. You will present first; if your pieces are deemed worthy, you will be given a room for the duration of the festival, and your carriage and horses will be taken to the stables. This evening, a performance for your entertainment. Tomorrow eve, a game of beasts." His manicured hands clasped as he beamed. "The third day, a show of sport. When the shows are completed, bidding will commence on the fourth day."

First, a gentleman presented a painting of Lady Cyrina Bunmarhun, highborn of the Dergenti. Lady Brouverg slumped on a grand gold gilded throne as if she thought herself a queen, a well-fed woman with dark tresses of curls falling over her reddened cheeks. She wore fine silks of the purest ocean blue, though she appeared to have the gowns made at a different date or for a different woman, as the seams struggled to hold in her multitude of self. Lenora could almost hear the thread straining.

A flick of her haughty wrist, her gold bracelets rattled, and the man was escorted from the room. Apparently, the well-fed woman had no use for a portrait of a highborn of the Dergenti.

A carving of a woman's breasts in dance was offered next, her arm and neck flowing behind her, billowing ivory silks rippling without wind. They were afforded a chance to stay by slim margins.

An announcement rattled the air, echoing in Lenora's bones. "Lady Acalisare, giath'enlyn of the Sareoenti, the Heron of Valesove, from the Virdine Reaon."

Her stomach fell into the floor with a sheer rush of panic. She clenched her jaw, forcing her face into stillness.

Lady Brouverg spoke in lieu of the gentleman, righting her sapphire gown with her hands. Her voice echoed with displeasure. "What have you brought?"

Ariaas's warning echoed. *She can smell weakness, how a lion can sense the heartbeat of its prey. She will move to strike if she sees even a glimmer of it in you.*

"Pleased to make your acquaintance, Lady Brouverg." Lenora bowed her head. Eran opened the obsidian lid, hinges creaking, and revealed the eight leather bindings by Faiseus Auro to the gawking crowd.

Lady Brouverg waved Lenora away. "I don't deal in books; I deal in—"

Lenora raised her stance high. "You deal in rarities."

Onlookers hushed at her disrespectful display. She hoped the lady would not take notice of her eyes, not notice her resemblance to her brother, wherever he may be. "I present to the lords and ladies original copies of the eight novels by Faiseus Auro. In their original hand carved box, complete with notes upon the pages in his own hand."

The lady's posture raised, only a hair, and she reared her hand to stop the guard. Lenora's heart skipped. A famous author, long dead, words from his hand no one had seen. Perhaps she now understood the treasure Lady Acalisare presented.

"That would mean the box is over—"

"They date nearly four centuries." Lenora's courtesies evaporated into the wind, replaced by the manners of Lady Acalisare. "Their pages are too delicate to be handled by bare hands."

Low chattering echoed. Eran lugged the box closer to the Lady of the Mountain. Once she viewed their ancient bindings enough for her fill, the gold inlaid gate stretching across their covers, she slumped back in her chair. Eran eyed the floor, parading the box around the room. Lenora reminded herself highborns had no need to glance upon servants, though her heart thundered for him regardless.

Lady Brouverg asked, stark-faced and uninterested, "How did these come to be in your possession?"

Though Lenora could see something below her eyes. Lenora replied in stoic words, containing the grin rising at her cheeks, "They have been in my family for a century."

With the lady's motion of hands, they moved on to the next article without another glance. "Lord Ideran, giath'enlyn of the Wesilear, the Resistant of Tenuel."

✦ ——— · + · ✦ · + · ——— ✦

Lenora received north-facing quarters with an enormous thriving fire waiting in the hearth. Her windows gazed to the earth where the mountains faded, and the hills rolled as in a haze into the horizon.

She should have felt comforted by the warmth. Instead, heavy heat clung to the air.

"Once you have taken your tea, please meet us outside your room. I will be hosting a tour of the castle and Lady Brouverg's collections of articles." The steward's rounded cheeks rose high when he smiled, and his chestnut hair bounced. "Servants may stay in their rooms."

Tea. As if she could sit long enough to sip.

Lenora pushed her cup aside, her nerves taunting. Every passing second felt like a thread splitting through her grasp. Somewhere inside, Thealor lived. Silk and pleasantries wasted time.

As they took in the sights, she often reminded herself of the posture of her shoulders, the tilt of her chin, and the way she should hold her hands. She enjoyed the gowns and the shoes for a short while, until the silk stuck to her legs in the cold and the balls of her feet began to ache. The act of becoming elite slowly became beautiful, suffocating lies.

Once, her foot turned out naturally like when she sparred, and panic jolted through her. She quickly returned her stance to a delicate point. No time for mistakes.

Along their tour, they walked expansive rooms, passing dancing halls and walls of water full of swimming creatures with sharp teeth and spiked tails. Her fingers grazed the cool water's edge, skimming the surface, a weightlessness against her skin.

Lenora's calves burned from the length of time observing, walking, and scouring every room and every guard on watch. They arrived in a long hall of articles, a path through the center displaying fine jewels and sculptures. The floor shined ivory-colored tiles, reflecting her charcoal gown. No door to a prison or an unexplored tower; she hoped the tour would conclude in the basement, the only place left for Thealor to be held.

What if she'd missed something?

At the end of the long hall, a room sat empty, aside from a large podium with an embroidered carmine silk and velvet pillow and the guard overseeing it.

Please let this be it. Let there be a door. A passage. Something.

The steward rose to his toes with an impressive grin. "This room is solely for the display of the Coronam, Dhaesreaon's blue sapphire. Our lady's most valued possession, guarded day and night."

A beast of a guard positioned his broad shoulders taut, wearing an unflinching gaze, a stoic pale portrait of Brenor. He wore the same hearty nose, same square chin and wavy hair, though he stood two and a half heads taller than she. Instead of eyes of the brightest sky, his were ruby whose largest facet met the morning sun and allowed it to cast right out the other side.

Thealor—not caged as she imagined—but *trusted*. He worked in a clean, pressed navy uniform with neat gloves. Amongst the two ladies in front of her, one grew alarmed at the sight of him and rushed to the steward's side. The other fanned herself and diverted her eyes when her cheeks flushed.

"The stone is one of a kind. The Master of Dhaesreaon, as it was long ago told, sat beside the old gods of the River Realm. One of the oldest relics known to Monera, believed to predate The Great War. It can be deciphered from an imposter by trained eyes, reflecting violet hues in some lights.

"We have even collected many replicas which are displayed elsewhere, those that others have tried to pass off as the true Coronam."

Lenora stood below Thealor, attempting to meet his eyes, though his head did not dip from its forward posture. The others pressed forward, while she waited for the tour of the exhibition hall to retire into the next room.

She clutched onto the folded note in her palm. She exhaled. She had found him. This day his entire life would change. She sat with the realization that soon her brother would be a free man.

She placed the page into his coat pocket. She whispered, "Please read this, as soon as you can."

He dug into his pocket—his eyes cold and unswaying—and he flicked the parchment to the floor.

Gathering the folded pages from the ground, she implored, "Take it, please. Read it later." What could he possibly be doing? She pressed it into his hand, "I am—"

"I know who you are, *Lady Acalisare*," he mocked. "Whispers are swift in this castle. Whispers of bright eyes and the only article to turn my lady's sights for nearly a decade." His disciplined gaze fixated on the wide double doors before him, the deep blue stone resting comfortably on the carmine velvet pillow at his side. "I know where those books come from. I expected one day the eyes of fire would find their way into my home. I am surprised my lady didn't notice. There is nothing you could have written that I would wish to read."

If he knew who she was, why would he not want to go with her? She stammered, and uttered in a low voice as not to echo down the long hall, "We have come to get you out of here, take you home."

Thealor spoke through tight lips, "You assume I wish to leave."

Her muscles tensed. Of course, she assumed he wished to leave. She assumed he would wish to run through the front doors, a free man. Or bar the same doors, and within their confines, murder his masters.

Speechless, Lenora twisted the note in her fingers. The plan included his eagerness to depart. He should be grateful, relieved, ecstatic. He was supposed to run. Had she done something wrong? Why would he not want to leave? He spoke so flat, rehearsed, and never met her eyes. She tightened her grip on the note, crumpling the edges. She swallowed the bile rising in her throat and forced her chin high. She turned and departed down the long hall, heels echoing on the hard tiles.

Beyond the length of the second room of articles, she caught up with the gentlemen on high toes. Had they twisted his hand that he might never leave? "Might I ask, how are the guards treated here?"

"Very well, my lady. Should they be proper at their positions, they are awarded special accomplishments for a job well done." His cheeks were as round cherries as he spoke, proud of the way Lady Brouverg treated those who did as she asked. "Each is given rooms much as your own as they climb through the ranks of the house."

Thealor—stranger and brother—refused to leave. Maybe family meant little to him. Her breath caught, tight in her throat. The weight of her gown hung upon her like shackles.

He was a willing prisoner.

She reached her door, fingers trembling as she grasped the handle. They had destroyed his mind, hadn't they? Had they broken him?

But he was alive. That meant she still had time.

One thing was certain: she wasn't leaving the castle while he still served the Lady of the Mountain.

NO TIME FOR MERCY

Bhaisael Qeldouv Dumous, Sengura of the Quparae, The Master of Beasts, The Grizzly
Born: Second Month of Summer, 1980
Deceased: First Month of Summer, 2058
Children: Three

- Official Ledger of Dhaesreaon

Brenor sat along evergreen roots while Ariaas paced, snapping twigs and flinging them to the forest floor in his angst.

His grandfather ranted as he moved. "One entire day, and another half day, we waited at the break of the forest. *Thirty-six* arduous hours. How could we have left Thealor's rescue to those two?"

The words struck Brenor like cold water to the chest. Lennie and Eran, left to navigate the glass fortress alone. He conjured a million ways her plan could fail, his throat twisting as each played in his mind. Over the years, Brenor imagined Lennie's personality and resemblance to their mother. How Ariaas spoke of her, at least. They had a similar reckless spirit. Now, she had just learned the careful art of lying, and though she possessed some semblance of archery skills, she should not need them with the plan they crafted.

Ariaas rubbed the scar on his collarbone. "Heneran is a bumbling idiot."

The insult curdled in Brenor's stomach. "Why didn't you tell her? Why you can't go inside?" His voice sounded sharper than he intended. Many questions gnawing at him like rats in a barrel. The lady of the house knew the lines of Ariaas's jaw, the scruff of his beard, the curves of his face. A face that hadn't morphed or aged over the years while theirs surpassed his in time.

Ariaas reached for another branch, bending with suppleness instead of snapping with the desired intensity. He growled low in his throat. "I can't stand here any longer. I'm going to see what I can see."

Brenor gripped his arm. "Not a good idea."

"It's been five to seven days!"

"It has been one day." Brenor gritted his teeth. His jaw ached. He wanted to scream, to sprint into the pristine castle. To know anything of their status. Anything was better than waiting. Guessing. "I will go. Please do not do anything rash."

Ariaas tapped his foot, then started to pace. "Be quick about it."

Brenor clung to the ground, dashing between the long grass dotted with fresh snow and spattered white blooms. He descended the wall, careful to hug the slope of the hill. Eventually, Brenor made his way behind the castle.

Grunts and huffs filled the air. Hooves against stone. He raised himself onto the edge of the stones, grasping the windowsill by his fingertips and pulled himself to a better vantage point. Horses chained. Bears. Dozens of bears, some stags, and a corpse of a creature he could not identify in its state of decay.

The breath left his lungs. What was this place? His heart drummed against his ribs—too fast, too hard. He pressed his palm to the stone, half to steady himself, half to stay rooted. He had expected guards, maybe cages. But this?

Breathless, Brenor returned. "I could see nothing inside the castle. The Brouvergs, they—" He gulped, his eyes glazed in tears. "There are wild creatures kept there. Animals should live in the forests, not be held captive. All held together. Chained."

"Dammit." Ariaas rubbed the bridge of his nose. "That's all you did? Find captive creatures and go no further?" Ariaas silenced his tongue and adjusted the thick fur at his shoulders.

Brenor flinched. His brows fell, the realization washing over him. "You ... knew?"

Of course, he must have known. Ariaas knew everything there was to know about this glass prison. About the Cesurelear, about Lady Brouverg and how she acquired her herd of beasts. He just never shared the information with Brenor.

"They're used for sport."

Brenor's body slacked as the realization washed over him. "We could free them, open the doors, and allow them to escape. It could help—"

"No. We can't have any interference."

"But—"

"No. We have waited for this day for too long. Today you are not here for animals. You are here for your brother. Do not let your compassion be your weakness. Not today."

His throat burned. Not because Ariaas was wrong—but because he was right. He hated the idea of walking away from creatures as trapped as Theo.

Brenor's face reddened. This could be a clever diversion. "We could get Theo *and* the animals. Ariaas, I—"

"I said *no*," barked Ariaas. "Stay here. I wish to see with my own eyes. Certainly, there is more to be seen than just animals."

Ariaas trailed the same path, Brenor at his heels. "Just open a few of the chains." His voice cracked. Somehow freeing the animals seemed as important as freeing his brother.

At the rear entrance, Brenor and Ariaas met a brute of a guard. The man, perhaps close to Brenor and Theo's age, stared before him with a stoic, disciplined posture.

Ariaas surveyed him, boot to hat. The man smelled of wool and leather, a crisp winter cold tinged with a hint of horse manure.

Ariaas leaned in, whispering, "Bribe him for blindness."

Brenor listened to every one of his instincts. His hair did not stand on end; the bumps on his arms stayed calmly below his skin.

Swiftly, Ariaas yanked open the edge of the guard's suit, revealing his collarbone and the B burned into his flesh. The man swatted his hand away as one would shoo a fly.

Branded.

Ariaas unbuttoned the top of his shirt, revealing the identical scripted carving.

They both belonged to this castle.

However, they branded Ariaas for different reasons—so if he ever showed his face, there would be no denying why he came. But he could use the burned flesh to his advantage. They could show allyship.

Brenor swallowed the rising guilt.

Theo's captivity is wrong.

Chaining animals is wrong.

Bribery is wrong.

Ariaas interjected as if he knew Brenor would freeze. "I know you don't want to be here. We don't want to be here either."

Something in the guard's eyes or his forehead shifted, but it was minute to say the least.

"I ask for something simple. Something easy," Ariaas murmured. He shook his pocket, metal coins clanking ever so slightly.

Brenor's stomach twisted. This was wrong. All of it was wrong. But how else would they get inside?

"Do you have a place you can hide things?"

The man eyed the fabric. A long pause. Then he snorted through his nose and dipped his chin. Ariaas opened the guard's palm, placed three gold, and closed his fingers tight enough to feel the carvings in the metal. For an instant, his bottom lip draped open.

Brenor recognized that look. Wonder. Not even silver—gold. Enough to buy a carriage and a horse.

"All I ask is that today, you are blind and deaf. You do not speak to anyone or see what comes in or out of this hall. No matter who or what it is."

Ariaas waited. For what, he did not know. This brick wall made very little movement, and the little movement he did was quite stark. "Do we have a deal?"

The man exhaled sharply. He stared forward, shoving his riches into his pocket.

+ ———— · + · ✦ · + · ———— +

Inside the dining room, Lennie sipped afternoon tea in a gown Brenor had never seen. Not that he paid much attention to the ancient wares collecting dust in Aroun Vaer. Eran perched as an owl in the corner.

A guard in navy approached. Brenor tensed in his commoner's clothes he'd been in for days and smelled as much: worn trousers and scraped leather boots. He couldn't bribe one guard, let alone a second in a room full of nobility. He hadn't much considered his appearance or aroma in his haste.

The guard tightened his grip on the hilt of his sword but did not withdraw the blade. "Who are you?"

Brenor released his held breath. Fate was on their side. The second guard had not recognized Ariaas's face.

Lennie's voice thundered from behind. "Allow them to pass. They are members of our house."

The guard surveyed the three—Brenor and Ariaas in their smelly, week-old garb and Lennie's commanding, clean, wealthy appearance.

"Do you need further proof?" she barked. "Do you need him to gather the horses for us?"

Brenor controlled his grin, silently proud of his sister.

The man nodded, exhaled, stepping back and recalling his position. Brenor pursed his lips to keep from smiling. This guard indeed held no power over a Lady of Valesove.

Perhaps Ariaas had been wrong about her skill level. A lady wouldn't allow such behavior from an inferior, and his sister knew as much.

She commanded, "Follow me."

Lennie led the three men down the long hall, her shoulders and chin high. When finally behind barred doors, she pressed the folds of her swaying gown and dropped her deceptions. "What are you doing? This is not the plan."

Eran stood at his daughter's side, red as a tomato, sweat dripping over his brow.

"Thealor was supposed to be with you, in a carriage departing last night, or with me in the forest—he's neither—can you not find him?" Ariaas asked.

"I found him," she said sadly. "He won't go, won't even read the note. I tried three times. He doesn't want to leave."

Brenor's throat tightened. He could almost hear Theo's voice echoing down the long halls, see the flash of grief in his eyes. What had happened in all those years?

What could he do now?

At his silent contemplation, she urged, "I'm working on a plan. I need time to figure out the next step."

"We don't have time. We must be well out of the mountain before tonight. These people must be too occupied with the lords and ladies to pursue us." Ariaas rubbed his unkempt beard. "Where is he?"

"He guards the Coronam, but only during the day. The blue stone, the room at the end of the long halls of articles—"

Ariaas disappeared down the hall.

Lennie balanced herself on Brenor's shoulder, reaching below her dress to unfasten her shoes. She shoved them into Brenor's chest. He held them, his lips forming words his brain was too slow to recite.

"Don't say a word," she mouthed. She grasped her charcoal gown and dashed down the hall behind their grandfather.

Ariaas with his half-formed ideas and vague assurances had vanished into the corridors, chasing some phantom of purpose. And Lennie—Lennie, who should have known better, who always claimed to see farther—had followed him without hesitation.

And now Brenor stood alone.

No plan. No orders. No one to argue with.

The silence pressed in, thick and cruel. He clenched his jaw, trying to anchor himself in something—*anything*—but everything felt unmoored. They had left him the scraps of their resolve and expected him to sew it into strategy.

He paced two steps. Stopped. Turned.

What am I supposed to do now?

GUARDIAN OF THE GLASS HOUSE

Follow still, where the road no longer lies,
where twig and root, fern entwine.
- The Final Paradox, Faiseus Rancesla Auro, 1841

Thealor perched, straight spine. Each breath grated with guilt. Far too deep, his chest filled to capacity while no one stood before him to see his breach of protocol: silence. Ruthlessness. Invisibility.

Though his lungs refused to obey.

The door shifted.

His heart locked.

The footsteps were deliberate.

Papa.

The name slammed through him before his mind could calibrate; he named his betrayer with affection in lieu of rage.

The air changed when this man entered the room. Like the world turned cold and held its breath. Thealor tracked him from the edge of his sights, chills traversing his spine like daggers.

"Do you remember? Do you know me?"

With unwavering resolve, Thealor maintained his directed gaze. He didn't need to glance upon his grandfather.

The old man shoved a note into Thealor's pocket, just as Lenora had.

How naive. How childish.

Ariaas turned toward the door in silence.

Thealor grasped his spear and threw. The air separated with a violent whoosh. His weapon tore through Ariaas's neck, stealing a piece of his flesh. Blood trailed his collarbone, flowing onto his shirt. The spear's handle reverberated as it slammed into the wall, metal pitch echoing through the long hall.

Ariaas raised his hands, turning to Thealor, holding them outstretched in a request for mercy.

The blood fell from the wound like a warm bath.

Thealor's voice boomed, his fists clenched in a tight ball. "Did you think I wouldn't recognize you?"

"I wasn't certain," Ariaas said, his hands still held, requesting peace. "You were so young." He slowly, purposefully, moved to clench his wound, holding in the blood seeping between his fingers. "Your aim was a touch left."

"If I intended to kill, I would have." Thealor held his stern gaze, trailing his pins of honor with the edge of his fingertips. He ignored the blood trickling from Ariaas's neck, droplets dotting the floor. "You abandoned me." Thealor stabbed harder with his words than he had with his spear.

"I never abandoned you. The years eroded the good memories and the truth along with it. I never will. Brenor, Lenora, and I—we've come to take you home."

"Home?" Thealor scoffed. "The last time I saw your face, I thought you came to take me home." He released a sharp burst of laughter. "But you saved him and left me. You left me as I screamed for you. I called your name, and you watched as they dragged me away. A little boy pulled by his collars. You did not even attempt to save me. You didn't even move."

"We are your family, Thealor."

"You were my family. Now, you are nothing more than an old man with a guilty conscience."

"I couldn't fight the soldiers. I was alone; Brenor was a baby. Thealor, they would have tossed his body to the depths in an instant."

Lies. That's not how it happened.

"You had a chance." Ariaas grimaced, his hand holding his neck tightly. "I followed the odds."

Thealor nearly laughed in spite. "So eloquent with your words."

"I knew even as a small child you favored Brenor and Arienne. I thought for a long time it was because I looked the most like Father. But you left her, too. Your favorite. The two of you and your stupid little whistle thing. I have spent many years trying to understand how someone I loved so much betrayed us so deeply."

"You were five years old, Thealor. You don't remember things as they occurred."

"You have no right to patronize me, old man!"

The room quaked, and Ariaas slowed, outstretching his arm again. "Brenor is here with me. He waits in the forest. We want to get you out of

Mount Ohbrolis. We can speak about everything that happened whenever you want."

"You would send a stranger to fetch me like a package you don't care enough about to get yourself."

"She's your sister. We found her a few months ago. Well, really, she found us." Ariaas shook his head at his error. "Brenor found her in the woods."

"She is nothing."

"I did not want to risk being recognized. I failed you then. Let me save you now."

Thealor smirked. "Seeking redemption."

"I left instructions in your pocket on where to find us if you want to leave." Ariaas pleaded. "There are two ways out, if you cannot make those, we will find a third."

"I will go nowhere with you."

"Brenor has been trying to rescue you for a long time, as have I." He pulled his shirt to show the scar on his chest, the branded B across his collarbone. The scar danced and twirled like light found a home and coiled beneath his skin. "I never abandoned you.

"Even when he was three, Brenor wanted his brother back. He wandered the gardens for years looking for you. Trying to make sense of why you were gone. At least see him before we leave. He is at the break of the trees to the east. The reasons for your hatred of me should not affect him. More importantly, still, the reasons should not affect you if you are a forced servant for the rest of your days."

Thealor walked closer, evaluating the wound in Ariaas's neck. Once he had seen the man would live, he wrapped his hands around the spear. "Leave." With an easy grip, he peeled it from the door's frame. "You're bleeding on my floor."

Ariaas ran his tongue across the tops of his teeth. He turned and closed his eyes.

His bloodied spear held at attention, Thealor returned to his stoic posture, eyes locked upon the horizon and the long hall.

Thealor's teeth ground like a saw inside his skull, and he pressed a fierce wave of air from his nostrils as if he could force the hatred out of his body. Small pools of Ariaas's blood gathered on the floor, some of which had been smeared and turned a dried shade of brown in prints of departing boots.

The audacity of that man arriving with *her*—and to call her *his sister*, at that. They saved Lenora first and left him to rot. They hadn't even known her. She was nothing, a baby; Ariaas never held her hand or bounced her on his knee. They found her *three months* ago.

As the sun descended, the floor shone with a brilliant glow. Thealor diverted his rage to view the Coronam—his prize—an action he repeated near the end of his shift each evening.

If nothing else, at least he had *her.* His sapphire.

The reflection glowed blue.

Thealor rushed to the stone, his spear clattering onto the floor, his fingertips grazing the fissure lines while he shifted his body to view every affordable angle. The last ray of light shone upon the stone before the sun hid behind the mountain, the reflection a perfect navy.

Not purple.

At the thought of his prize stolen, in another's hands, in another's guard, the vein in his neck throbbed. A feral growl he tried to silence seeped through his lips. Thealor slammed the spear over his thigh, breaking it into two and sending metal spikes into his leg. He fell to his knees, pulling violently onto fistfuls of hair, doing everything in his power to muffle the sounds of his own screams.

◦ ⋅ ✦ ⋅ ◦

From Thealor's quarters, the view of the mountains and the skies were ever-changing, pale colors cast upon the sloping rocks. *Will my life ever take me to the other side of those peaks?* He needed nothing else besides his duty and his opulent room—the long sheer walls wrapping from the floor to the ceiling, a rolling fire, thick and high bed with sapphire silk sheets. He was respected amongst the servants. Revered.

Before he died, Lord Brouverg granted Thealor the gift of the day position for his dedication. The night shift was for a weaker mind; the man often said, "Darkness requires two."

Lord Brouverg brought Thealor to this room after he had proven his worth. "Think of yourself as my son, now," Lord Brouverg announced. "If you do as I ask, you shall be rewarded." He gestured around the room and its opulence; his hand rose to his round belly cloaked in silken robes. "And if you disobey, punishment will be swift. Goodnight, my son."

The painting Lord Brouverg commissioned after the pair hunted commanded the entire wall. The two posed in the snow; Lord Brouverg's hand proudly grasped Thealor's shoulder as he held his first kill, a giant elk, by the antlers. Thealor traveled out of the castle only once, but Lord Brouverg displayed the painting like the two partook in annual family rituals.

The lord was cruel.

The lady of the house was crueler still.

As a young boy, he had ruined a dessert as he carried it to the lady's chambers. The chocolate hazelnut cake with praline mousse slid across the silver tray. As he tried to balance the tray, the cake tipped onto its side for a mere second; chocolate curls shifted, and he muddled the glaze. Though he returned the cake to its upright position, the lack of pristine presentation dissatisfied her.

As a reprimand, he wore a steel-forged bridle for two weeks. The mouth guard forced sharpened spikes into his cheeks; the back formed for proper posture; the arm guards maintained his elbow at the appropriate angle for holding a serving tray. He wore this heavy steel even in sleep.

He learned.

He learned to never fail, never arch his shoulders, never falter, never say no to a request.

Failure was not an option.

Thealor mused on the unfounded possibilities of torture the lady would inflict if he admitted he lost the most prized possession of Dhaesreaon. In the low light, he weighed his options: remain in his perfectly curated cage or venture out with a man he despised every day of his life for twenty-three long years.

He grabbed the note and squeezed, hoping it would turn to dust in his grasp. Then he opened the page, seething while reading the words in Ariaas's hand.

We wait by two paths. The stables by the carriage or the forest to the east.

Depart by whichever you can come by easiest, and you will find yourself a free man.

A free man. What a strange concept. Was he not free? The doors were not barred. He had an illustrious room.

Thealor leaned both palms into the glass, ensuring the invisible wall remained where he last felt it and his eyes were not playing tricks on him.

The mountains felt ominously silent, other than to remind him in whispers from beyond their peaks of his failures. He had done his job quite splendidly until the old man distracted him. He saw no reflection of intruders in the tiles and heard no footsteps down the long hall.

Had he been so filled with rage he lost all his senses?

He would be hard-pressed (if he were fortunate) to choose between emotional torture or physical torture. The demon at Aroun Vaer would not offer him physical affliction, whereas Mount Ohbrolis valued anguish of the body. Thealor trailed his hand over the self-inflicted wound on his leg, wrapped in linens and stuffed with ground sage. The discomfort he endured now would pale compared to whatever the lady of the house would inflict.

Over the darkening horizon, he made his choice. A chance to escape whatever the lady might offer when she discovered his fault. He reminded himself he did not need to speak to Ariaas should he not wish, could leave them the instant they were far enough outside the border of the River Realm.

The letter was a door. Nothing more.

Thealor held a quill and ink in shaking hands, a note to Lady Brouverg. An apology. An atonement for his failures. A goodbye. The words sounded weak, timid. He shredded the paper, tossing scraps into the flames. The remnants curled and blackened under the heat.

Weakness cannot survive on the mountain.

He made his way to the basement, concealing his limp, hoping his wrappings didn't seep blood through his trousers. The guards paid him no attention, as he was their senior—all aside Duntaead, his superior. A Khayernamen. At Lady Brouverg's request, they sparred here and there, that the two might keep their respective titles. A match Thealor allowed to transpire, rigged, ensuring the Khayernamen would not be fed to the bears.

When he passed the length of the stone basement, Duntaead stood firm, a forward gaze toward the horizon. He paid Thealor no mind, did not blink as he strode toward him, or converse with him as he often did.

"I am checking the trees for an intruder," Thealor stated. None of the younger soldiers would pursue him, expecting he moved to retrieve a lost wolf or in pursuit of someone who entered the castle wrongly.

Duntaead held his forward glance.

Thealor asked, "Duntaead, did you hear me?"

He stepped back from the man's blank stare—the closest thing he had to a friend in his glass castle. Perplexed by his silence and now more resolved in his choice, he trekked from the castle.

Fear crept in. Had Duntaead already learned of his failure? Perhaps, now, he refused to be associated with an incompetent wretch no matter how many times Thealor spared his life.

In the distance, beasts roared while the crowd rumbled.

Duntaead's lack of attention baffled him. He thought of the man's unwavering stare as he took the eastern route, hopeful Ariaas had taken the carriages. Duntaead must know. Someone knew.

He hastened his pace.

But even with this knowledge, Duntaead was still friend and not foe, or he would not have allowed Thealor to wander through the gates under false pretenses.

Wasn't he?

At the edge of the trees, away from the sharp rock and shards of ice perched south, he came upon Brenor. No use in asking who he was, it was like seeing his own reflection in the bath. Thealor did not slow his steady pace, not even long enough to meet his brother's gaze, walking well beyond his presence and far into the thicket. The mountain knew he had failed them.

He could be cordial when he was well outside his lady's reach.

THE FOREST LUENUAN KNOWS THEIR NAMES

If this man tries to run away one more time, I swear on the Old Gods I'll throw him into the sea.

- Diary of Daisirie Cabredd Mire, Volume 5, Entry 141

T hree wanted men infiltrated Forest Luenuan, pleased and silent at the thick covering of trees.

Brenor walked through the night on foot for two days, his toes blistering, raw and weeping into his untied boots, opening the balanser only when absolutely necessary. They stopped for an hour, to rest their legs and eat the meat Brenor dried. Ariaas permitted each twenty minutes of sleep before the next could close his eyes.

Brenor barely noticed the meals or the sleep. He watched his brother instead—how he stared into the trees, barely breathed, and kept his shoulders pulled back tight.

Theo rarely spoke along the journey down the mountain and never beyond a warranted situation. Brenor thought well enough ahead to pack a change of clothes in his satchel for his brother. He would not make the same mistakes he had at Lennie's arrival. He had prepared for everything—food, clothes, plans—but not for this. Though he had freed his brother, this man felt like nothing more than a shell in his own likeness. A stranger dressed in familiar skin.

This was nothing like how he dreamed Theo would be.

The morning sun broke through the canopy of trees, the air clean, and the sounds of rushing water faint upon his ears. Brenor came through the final branches and through the dense bushes, the river was upon them—wide and rumbling over the rocks. Hours drew on until they came upon a small clearing beside the riverbank, large boulders to the northern curve and trees covering the south. The water flowed through shallow rock, boulders allowing a decent location for catching fish. Theo still bit his tongue while Brenor searched for questions he might get a reply from.

Though he didn't want to interrogate, he wanted to hear his brother's voice. Something real. Something whole.

Ariaas set his pack on the dry ground and filled his water on the soft side of the banks. "We will not find a better place to rest."

Blood seeped through the bandage at Ariaas's neck, desperately in need of fresh wrappings. Brenor met his side, investigating the damage. Ariaas had yet to tell him how he was wounded, and Brenor was too tired to press.

Theo appeared as no brother he expected—detached, brittle, irate. Not the joyful and emotional reunion Brenor imagined and replayed. Not the laughter, teasing, the arms thrown around him in relief.

Theo argued, rubbing his palms together well after they crossed into Hanielle. "We still have an hour of sun, at least."

A weight swelled beneath his ribs, a tight pressure closing in. He waited for so long for Theo to come home. *What can I do now?*

"The forest gets denser southwest of here, and the river more turbulent the closer it gets to the Valesove border." Ariaas grumbled as Brenor dressed his wound. "We will not be able to find food as easily." The three had not slept a night since they departed Mount Ohbrolis. Perhaps it was better to get a length away before allowing such luxuries.

When Ariaas was out of sight, Brenor plucked the courage to speak to Theo about more than necessities. "Do you remember me? From ... when we were children?"

"As much as one can remember their own shadow beneath their heels. You followed me incessantly." Theo held his firm stance, a wronged and bitter man. He ran a hand through his hair and the edge of his words softened. "It isn't you. I find it difficult to direct a pleasant mood at one person in the company and a bitter mood at the other."

Theo moved to sit at the northern end of the bank, Ariaas at the southern. Brenor walked a shallow perimeter around them, laying dried branches that he might hear should an intruder arrive as they slept. *How can I end this quarreling?*

"Two full days Brenor has caught all your meals and gathered all the kindling. Now, he sets all the snares. Do you help him ever?" Theo glared at Ariaas. "Or is he your servant like I was hers?"

Ariaas answered plainly, "We each have our duties."

"What are yours?" Theo rose, not waiting for a reply.

Theo waded into the shallow pools of the river and laid out a portion of net, throwing it from his perch on a boulder as Brenor had done the day prior. He yanked it in. Empty. He threw the net again, and again, growling, jerking with more ferocity each time. The stone he stood upon became wet from the net; his boots lost their grip and he fell into the water to his shins. Perhaps he would have gotten away with sopping boots and pant legs should he not have been so irritated he stumbled a second time and lost his balance.

Brenor waded into the water, offering his hand. Perhaps this was his chance. "The kindling you gathered was enough for the evening. I will light the fire so you can dry yourself."

If they were of the Milnire lineage it would come in handy during these times, should someone only show him how they willed flame.

Theo adjusted the dense fabric of his uniform.

The hairs on Brenor's arms raised. A whisper amongst the trees.

No.

The birds scattered.

Brenor searched the forest. He held a hand to his lips.

Theo's eyes widened and he held a hand out to Ariaas.

They were not alone.

An arrow soared into their camp, meeting the dirt ground beside the fire. A second followed, landing inches from Brenor's boot.

They scattered toward the shelter of nearby trees. Arrowheads littered the rough wood, wide and jagged, carved by an unskilled hand, not honed by those who willed metal or stone. Brenor closed his eyes behind the tree, pretending for a moment he was elsewhere and counting the rules of his vow.

Theo picked up the arrow, examining its adornments. "These are not guards of the castle."

Ariaas shouted as arrows rained upon them, his hands held high in surrender. "We are not your enemy! Please hold your fire!"

Brenor crouched in his hidden position. Whoever shot toward them bore little skills. Guards of the castle nor The South Sea would take such a shot, not into strangers, not when they were uncertain. An arrow shot into a camp of men, no weapons held, no confidence in accuracy or death.

Ariaas walked into the open, hands outstretched. One boy, one girl stood before them, weapons at attention amongst the trees, cloaked in shadowed hoods.

Theo threw the arrow back to the forest floor, whispering, "The Yurelan have been driving the Gerideard out of these lands."

"Exactly who I believe we are meeting," Ariaas muttered.

Brenor's bones chilled. Where The South Sea wished his death, the Yurelan wished to claim them. Now, more than usual, he would stay behind Ariaas's dutiful guard.

"We will not harm you! We are passing through on our way to Safia. I am a father with my two sons."

Silence.

"Your king would not wish us harmed," Ariaas barked. "I know him. You can ask." The name seared like poison when it met Brenor's ear, and a lump rose in his throat at the name from faded memories he had not heard in many moons.

At the name, a man stepped forward. His face covered in dark paint, eyes wild and angry with his bow wobbling at attention. The shadowed cloak fell from his brow. "You dare speak of our king?"

A second, holding her bow taut, stepped forward. "Identify yourselves. You are in the king's forest. His territory now extends the entire Forest of Luenuan."

Ariaas used his most trusted tone. "We were unaware your king's territory extended into these lands. We will depart from the forest at once."

"I said, identify yourself!" she shouted. "And your companions!"

"I am a father, traveling with my sons. We are bound for Safia and taking an early leave for the night."

The woman's cloaked hood dipped further, veiling her eyes. Pieces of her dark chestnut hair drifted below the shadows. The boy matched her in expression, drawn and irate at the disrespect of one of their own. "Make them rise."

Ariaas nodded that he and Theo should stand.

Brenor hesitated. His hand trembled outside of his control. The two of them, together, appeared too much alike—their eyes, their features.

The caveats. It is all right to kill to protect myself or someone in my family.

The girl peered over them when they stood—Theo wet from the stream, Brenor his copy in all things. She surveyed their eyes.

An audible choking sound split from her lips. *"You."* For a moment, her aim sank before she righted her arrow, aimed with intent at Ariaas. "You speak lies!" she shouted. "These are not your sons!"

Her eyes darted from Ariaas to Brenor and again to Theo. She turned to the boy at her side, his face painted, "danar, olamer ere val boain tecind therone, tu en te."

Brenor held still, his face blanched. Sounds were replaced by the rapid thundering of his pulse.

The boy faltered. She shouted in a harsh order, "danar! danar!" Her screams grew louder and louder until the boy realized his error and dashed through the trees as swift as his legs could carry him. Her bow held steady at Ariaas until he gained ground, and she pressed her own legs to flee. The two of them scurried through the trees, weaving.

"Do not let them escape!" Ariaas tugged his sword from his belt and raced in pursuit. "They run to tell the Yurelan!"

Brenor froze at the riverbank, much as the boy, blood draining from his cheeks. How long would it be, if they returned, to gather their people in their pursuit?

Their attackers owned the forest now.

Theo stared.

When he found Brenor statue-like with intent to move, he tore the bow and a few arrows from Brenor's pack. Still wet, he climbed high atop the boulder beside the water's edge, guided by the bend in the river. The girl dashed toward the northern cross. Theo released the arrow, glinting in the sun, sending the girl to the forest floor.

He adjusted his aim. The second arrow missed the boy as he ran behind the trees, the third met its target as the banks turned. He leapt from the boulder into the shallow water.

Theo rammed the bow into Brenor's chest. "Why did you bring this if you have no intention of using it?"

Brenor's lips formed words, though no sound rose to meet them. "I am a ... gentle ... man." He stood an easy target of a man, a lone tree in the forest, should their arrows be aimed at him. *How could I have frozen? How?*

Theo left Brenor in the clearing with his suffocating thoughts and followed the curve of the river. He didn't see it coming—their end—but he was glad they didn't suffer.

Brenor gawked at the river's edge as Ariaas and Thealor carried their bodies to the bank.

"I didn't say kill them," Ariaas said. "I would've restrained them long enough for us to get out."

"You didn't say that. You just ran with a blade."

Ariaas asked, "The lady of the castle taught you to use the bow?"

"It is difficult to guard a castle when you have no means by which to guard it."

"I had assumed the spear would suffice."

"I forgot the spear back where it tore through your neck," Thealor sneered.

"What else has she taught you?" Ariaas laid the girl to the floor in the clearing, tearing the seams of her shirt at the shoulder. She bore four black rings upon her bicep, a sign of status amongst the Yurelan.

Brenor's pulse, thick as molasses, coursed through his veins. Air would not reach his lungs. He mouthed, "You killed them."

Theo investigated the markings, sat back upon his heels. "She is fourth generation. Their king will not be pleased."

"Seems rather irrelevant, does it not?" Ariaas asked.

Theo reached for the sleeves of the boy, pulling, and tearing the fabric at the shoulder, revealing he wore the same rings across his arms. Fourth generation. "Power matters to them," Theo argued. "Sixteen blood lineages would matter."

Brenor choked, his hands over his lips. "What will we do with them?"

"You said the river picked up not far from here?" Theo asked, turning to Ariaas.

"Yes. Not far from the next bend, where the river bends south."

"Take the arrows, leave the Yurelan to the river."

"Will you leave them like fish you wished to discard?" Brenor argued.

"I don't care for the matter either, but we need to leave no trail." Ariaas pointed to the fire, the logs, the footprints in the muck.

He and Theo were both in agreement, though Brenor hated it, the bodies should be left to the river. "It will be difficult if they do find them to discover where they perished and any relevant trail to follow."

The matter here was fast. He could not think of what his best course of action was at the moment, and now the matter was done. More moral turmoil stood in the space in between life and death than it did once a road had been definitively chosen.

Anger bubbled in his ribs.

"Their death was in vain." Brenor spoke as Theo and Ariaas carried them to the pebbled shore. They carried the children's bodies with dignity, crossed their arms over their chests, and held their silence for a moment. At least there was *dignity*. When the time was over, Theo and Ariaas released them into the soft current.

When Ariaas returned, he commented, "They knew who you were. They recognized him, recognized you. They ran to gather the others." He turned to Theo, "Have you had contact with them before?"

"No." Theo watched the dead float in the current, their bodies jostled by stones beneath the rippling surface. "I have seen neither before today. I have only heard stories of this forest, never been in it."

"That is even more concerning," Ariaas paced along the banks. "We have found some level of peace in our hiding. Many are starting to know your faces."

The bodies pulled further along the river. Toward the bend, true to his memory, their pace quickened, pulled by a strong current. "We will need to be more cautious. We should not stop again, but travel under the cover of darkness and the trees."

"There will be no further rest this evening; there may be others on their patrol." Theo kicked dried dirt onto the flames with his boots.

"No rest for the hunted," Ariaas muttered, ensuring their boots left no trails in the mud along the pebbled edge. The running and exhaustion had caused his wound to reopen, blood blooming on his shirt.

Brenor rubbed his stubbled chin. "The other Yurelan will find out soon enough."

"We would have not made it until dawn. Never made it out of this forest. They would have killed me and taken the two of you. We would have been swarmed in hours, maybe less. We will not take this time for granted."

Brenor pressed onto the path in the darkness. He shivered, desperately searching for motion among the trees in the fading light. *I won't be able to rest until we're well beyond the split.* He had never been so fearful for his own safety, knowing he would not rest until he was well beyond the split rail fence and the safe confines of Aroun Vaer.

Am I a killer simply by being here? Do the caveats even matter?

LAMB BOUND FOR SLAUGHTER

"You favor the east. You give them everything and us nothing."
                           - As recorded by the Head Scribe of Lesomen, 878

S issel grasped the handle to Ronan's quarters, a sudden jolt in her stomach begging her to stop. Voices came from inside. She tempered her excitement to see him, leaning into the door.

Ronan barked, "Their passing whispers do not concern me."

"That is not why I came," a female voice replied.

"Spit it out, then."

"You're too close. You can't even see it."

"I'm not blind."

The woman cleared her throat. "I've served at your side for many years. I've been your friend longer. I'm worried what will happen to you when she's gone."

When she's gone? Who is 'she'?

The unsettling thought lingered. The prospect of her own absence—their lack of conversation, and his warm presence—gnawed at her. And worse, what if the female voice spoke of someone else?

"Riera, she wouldn't run for Felreaon," he said. "I gave her a chance, and she wouldn't run."

"If you aren't blind, you know why she didn't run. You don't give a lamb a name and invite it into your home when you know it's bound for slaughter."

Sissel's throat tightened as she thought of a lamb slaughtered for a Wesilean market.

She twisted the door handle.

Am I the lamb?

At the sickening thought, Sissel entered the tense room. Captain Kalory and Ronan quieted their conversation. Five letters lay on his desk, a line of gray and green against the dark wood. A lump rose in Sissel's throat as Ronan slipped one into an open pocket.

Captain Kalory adjusted her uniform and returned the chair to the table. Staring daggers into Ronan's eyes, she exited without addressing either of them further.

Sissel and Ronan meandered during their usual evening walk. Since she interrupted his conversation with Captain Kalory and he'd placed the letter in his pocket, his mood had darkened. Her mood, too, dimmed—drawn into the gravity of his silence. The weight he carried seemed to reach into the space between them and settle into her chest.

At the edge of the larkspur fields, Ronan's sights locked onto Felreaon. Why did he keep staring past the fields? She had so little time before she would leave, and his distance chipped away at their fleeting moments together.

Ronan spat, "Do you know how to defend yourself? You are most determined not to help yourself in any other way. You must at least know how to defend yourself."

His sudden abruptness wedged a knot into her throat. "What's happened?" The letter, Captain Kalory—well, Riera.

"You will die before you see a second Uen'can if you do not toughen yourself!" He reminded her of this thought often, and with each passing time, it ached more and more.

She lay her hand on his forearm, aching for him to return her touch. "I'm not a fighter. I'll be content to walk to my cell and serve my time."

"I despise it when you say that," he growled. "Do you think that's all they'll do to you? Do you think they will let you go to your room alone and close the door as you have here?"

He shuddered.

She lay a soft hand on his cheek, searching his eyes, begging him to meet hers.

Ronan righted his posture in one swift movement, brushing away her affections. He turned and left her alone amongst the long grass and lavender blooms.

The following afternoon, Sissel drafted a letter to her grandmother, a matter she had avoided for some time while Ronan attended to business at his desk. The words escaped her, not the way her grandmother's stories did, not the way they sat in her mind as if she herself had lived them.

She began with a standard greeting, sharing all she had witnessed since she left Wesilea. Before she finished, she placed the quill upon the fresh ink of the letter. Something about finishing the letter made her apprehensive, perhaps the finality of the matter.

Sissel ruminated on the matter of Ronan's request since the night prior.

She straightened the clothing and her spine. The act of him training her would do little, of that much she was certain. But more so than anything, she missed his playful demeanor. She missed their long conversations about nothing and everything all at once. And if training brought him back to her, then, she would train.

The quiet between them felt fragile, like breath fogging glass: one wrong word and his temperament would shatter. Still, she didn't want to feel like a stranger to him for one moment longer.

"All right," Sissel said softly, "At least ... teach me to defend myself."

He exhaled, almost as if in that moment all his fears left him.

For a week, Commander Benson taught her to spar.

If one could call it teaching. She learned the rhythm of bruises before she learned the rhythm of footwork. Her knuckles ached. Her pride stung. The only real result was a bloody lip and growing frustration.

Today, he adopted a wide stance before her, his arms open to block her strike. "Attack."

As he'd instructed, she swung from her center. He gripped her arm and pinned her to the floor. He jumped back onto his feet before she caught a breath, again adopting his defensive stance. "You're not trying. Get up."

The scab from her lip ruptured, littering her teeth with the taste of iron. She placed a finger against the cut which refused to heal. For a week they had continued this dance, and while she thought the act would return the man she had known throughout the months, instead it brought a hardened version of him.

The day had drawn to darkness. "It's late. Can we stop?"

His eyes widened and he slammed his fist onto the table.

She jolted at the noise.

"You will serve all your days!" he shouted. "Do you not care?"

"I know. I took a life." Sissel's spine raised, resolved in her choice. "Mine is what I exchange for what I've done."

Ronan raised his chin. "You stood up to me, the first day you came into my quarters. Was that all there was? Just words and nothing more?"

She froze, breathless, hands lifeless at her sides.

"Will you give up? Will you do nothing?" A deep tension settled in his jaw; it was a mere three weeks before she would leave for The Reldory.

Each day, rising and falling, she became more certain Ronan cared more for her circumstance than a passing guilt.

At her stillness, he tore a knife from a roast on the table, hurling the blade across the room. It landed in the wall, the metal reverberating. He moved above her, his breath against her hair. "I will ask you again. *Will you do nothing?*"

Still, she held her tongue.

He grabbed her hands, forcing her over the dining table, sending dishes spilling onto the floor. Steadily, he held her arms crossed over her head, his fingers intertwined with hers in a grip bordering on pain while her back arched unnaturally over a splattering of silverware.

"What if a man decides he wants you for his own? Will you lay back while your body serves another form of punishment?" He leaned in, his breath warm on her lips. "You've read the books on self-defense."

Sissel wriggled, futilely attempted to pull her wrists free from a body much stronger than her own.

"You can read, but knowing and doing are two vastly different things. You need to find a way to get your body to do what your mind learned."

Sissel tightened the grips of her fingers and relaxed her body. She savored how his hands felt intertwined with her own, relishing his touch, imagining he held her for reasons of want and not of impending suffering.

He shook his head. "You asked me to teach you to defend yourself."

At her stillness, his eyes lingered on her lips. His gaze drifted across her arms, and to their intertwined fingers. When he took in the sight of his own firm grasp, and the roughness which he had treated her, he released her fingers, pressing his palms into the table.

"I thought I saw something in you, for a short while. I thought maybe you had fight in you. Where is the woman who came in here, thinking she would be violated, and denied me regardless of the impending consequences?"

Sissel lay calm, begging for him to close the gap between them, her hands, cool from the departure of his warmth. "Perhaps you were wrong."

He leaned in over her, close enough she expected his lips might meet hers. "If it were me in The Reldory ... would you find some strength?"

She barely heard his words in the suspended moment. All that existed was the invisible thread of anticipation, the aching for their lips to meet, the flush heating her cheeks, and the soaring in her stomach at his proximity.

"Would you save ... *me?*"

The words hung between them, raw and unraveling. Of course she would save him, she'd die if it meant he'd live.

Her breath caught, heart tumbling forward. She whispered, "You know I would."

Ronan pressed his lips into hers—heat and certainty from months of silence breaking open all at once. His mouth found hers like a drowning man searching for air, fingers weaving into her hair with a desperation near reverent. She gasped—the sound vanishing into him as he claimed more, deeper, as if he could reclaim each second he hadn't touched her until now.

Her body reacted, rising to his grasp, clutching his shoulders like she might not survive without him. Sissel's lips parted and he groaned—low, ragged—as if her taste was his undoing. His hands slid beneath her back, to her waist, pressing her flush against him until no space remained for doubt, no breath left for words.

The world shrank. Just her and him, fury and fire, hunger, sharp and sweet, edged with all the words they'd yet to say. Her heart cracked open, and she yanked him tighter as if letting go would kill them both.

When they finally broke apart, breathless, dazed, his forehead dropped to hers.

Ronan straightened his spine, leaving her cold without his grasp. "I'm not wrong," he whispered. "You put your life on the line to save Mr. Baradelle. Apparently, you do not see yourself like you see others, not worthy of saving."

"I didn't think when Mr. Baradelle fell. I didn't think when I spoke up to you, either." She wished she could stop thinking now and close the sliver of air between their bodies. "If I had, perhaps I wouldn't be here."

Ronan recoiled, stepping away, stretching his fingers wide.

Now his behavior crystallized—a line dwelled between the man and the commander, and he kept one foot planted firmly on either side. He had never touched her further with less than reputable intentions, he had never tried, though he slipped on occasion.

The air between them thickened. "Will you go? With the transport carriage?"

"No. It would not be an assignment someone in my position would take. Nor do I wish to see you like that."

"You do not wish to see me like that?" She nearly laughed. "Tell me what you expect of me? Honestly. Should I learn to fight? Do you wish me to escape? Not cross the bridge? Do you want to train me, so I kill your own guards before the carriage reaches the precipice? Or just not get tortured while I am there?"

"I don't have an answer for that."

"Or do you just hope I do not lay back while another man takes me for his own?"

"Enough," he bellowed. "All I know is I cannot rest easy while knowing you are being sent there."

The words should have comforted her. Instead, they curled around her like smoke—suffocating and impossible to hold. The sharp edge of her question hung on his eyes. It wasn't just morality that burned. It was desire. A want he couldn't name without unraveling everything he believed about himself.

"I need to make sense of this. I need to understand why you are pushing me this hard, why you have grown so angry these last few weeks. No matter the scenario, it will not end well—for you or me."

Ronan eyed his desk while she continued, "If I did train, if I escaped, you would be required to send soldiers to find me. It would be your duty to do so. To execute me.

"If I don't escape, I'm still tortured and imprisoned and, by your admonition, will die quickly. There is no simple way out of this. Not in which both of us can find happiness." She wished to wrap her arms around him, hold onto the strength of his shoulders once more. "Please, can we enjoy the time we have left, the afternoons we can spend together? I don't want to spend our final weeks this way."

"I cannot sit idle knowing the minutes are fleeting and I am doing nothing." He turned to her. "As *you* are doing nothing!"

That struck. Hard.

"Say it aloud," she hissed, stepping into his space, her breath seething with fury. "You wish for me to escape."

"You know I can't say those words. You know I can't wish such things."

Her eyes burned into his, the firelight dancing behind him. All the aching, the hours of silence and buried feelings, roared to the surface. "If you wish so badly for me to be free, stop the transfer yourself. Don't pretend you're trying." She stepped closer, chest heaving. "Don't try to do anything you can to free me, yet only enough to free yourself from the guilt of your own accompaniment. Otherwise, you are the coward and not me. Your thoughts alone are treasonous."

She held her hand over the deep iron handle before she departed into the darkness. "Tomorrow, I want to be alone."

· + · ✦ · + ·

Thud. Thud. Thud.

Harsh rapping jolted Sissel awake—a boulder crashing into her door as the light of the morning sun touched the earth. She'd spent a sleepless night with regret for the harsh words she spoke, stumbling into deep sleep shortly before dawn.

The pounding belted onto the door so ferociously, she expected the wood might separate from the steel nails. She covered her eyes, groaning, wishing to silence the world.

Thud. Thud. Thud.

She removed her covers to answer the door, pulled her clothes tight over her chest, her eyes still blurred with sleep.

"Vak-ARRA, I will be your sole charge for the remainder of your stay here, including your transfer." Kaloyein stared above her forehead. "I have been given strict instructions as to your housing and care. You are being relocated immediately. Gather your belongings."

His cold demeanor and unflinching retort left her perplexed.

"I'm confused. Where are you taking me?"

Kaloyein repeated, "Gather your belongings."

Fear slithered into her mind. She shouldn't be leaving yet. It was still weeks too early to travel to The Reldory. Where could she possibly be relocated to? Had the fight been so substantial, Ronan wanted her as far from Tanes as possible?

Stepping through the old wooden door frame and the two stairs, she gripped the simple clothing she was given on her arrival. She took in the small room which had been her home for so many months, seeming so much smaller than the first time she had seen it.

Kaloyein stood at attention. "Follow me."

She trailed him through familiar streets of barracks, past the main gate to the cobbled road, turning toward Ronan's quarters. The fear then mingled with hope when they stopped before the familiar door. "You'll be housed here until your transfer."

Her stomach soared. She meant much of what she said yesterday, but she did not wish to be alone. Not today. Not any day. Not after she had calmed.

She resisted a smile. "Did Ronan send for me today?"

Kaloyein struck her with a closed fist across her cheekbone.

When she regained her posture, Kaloyein smiled at her shock and the rising rouge upon her cheek as if he had waited for her to make a mistake he could correct. The strike damaged her pride, rattled her bones and her senses, but was not enough to knock her to the floor. A late form of revenge it would seem, for his own lack of action some months ago. What would Ronan do if he saw from his window?

"You speak too freely of our commander," Kaloyein growled through veiled pleasure. "You need some reminding of your place here."

Inside the threshold, her relief and hope replaced her worries. She missed him. Even when he was away for the night, she wished to wrap her arms around him and sleep within the same sheets. She no longer cared for his professionalism, not when their time together was fleeting.

Kaloyein stepped inside.

The fireplace crackled, barely alive from the night, blistering its final embers. Lanterns hung from the ceiling with ornate designs. The dining table, cleaned from their fight, stood filled with fresh wine and delicacies, a roast, loaves of bread, and jellies with fresh berries and apples.

Sissel clutched her clothing. "May I please speak with Commander Benson," she asked in a manner she hoped would not warrant another blow.

From behind her, Captain Kalory entered. "Thank you, Kaloyein. You may leave."

The captain watched through the veiled curtains until Kaloyein was far from earshot. She turned her attention to Sissel with a grave expression. "A rider came last night with urgent summons from High Commander Ravaris. Commander Benson departed before dawn for Islarourne."

Sissel's stomach tightened. "When will he return?"

"He won't. Well, not of which you will see. The commander leaves for several months when he's called away. He won't return to Tanes until well after the year's end." Captain Kalory opened her mouth and closed it after eyeing Sissel's face. Her jaw tightened. "He shouldn't have gotten close to you. For either of your sakes. I think he genuinely believed he could alter your sentence. A year or less, in Islarourne, or Nyaruse. Time served for an accident."

"Why did you move me here?"

"His orders. Not mine. He did not tell me much of you, only that you were observant. You could see feelings in others. If that is true, you already know why he moved you here," Captain Kalory nodded solemnly, gathered a short stack of books, and departed.

Sissel's attention turned to Ronan's desk. She sat in his chair. A small sharp blade lay beside an old textbook. She examined the hilt—appearing to be the same knife thrown at the wall yesterday.

The book before her showed its extreme age, bearing a smoky, earthy aroma. The pages had begun separating from the binding, and the ink faded in some areas. A small, folded page slid out onto the ground.

Sissel,

Please accept my apologies for the harsh nature of my training. It is the way of The South.

I have no headway in the pursuit of the transfer of your sentence, though I have not exhausted all my leads.

Should we meet again, I never wish to say farewell.
RB

Sudden anger overwhelmed her for everything that brought her to this moment.

She had fallen for this man. She wished to lie on this floor in front of these flames in his arms. She may have even been brave enough to try if she had known they would say farewell much sooner than either had planned.

Sissel searched the letters, her draft to her grandmother missing, nothing within the desk other than the charcoal gray envelopes she often saw him fidgeting with. Hesitantly, she removed six letters from their perch, each addressed to Commander Benson, opening them in turn.

Commander Benson,

You of all people should know better than to circumvent the line of command. The girl's sentence stands.

Signed,
High Commander Ravaris of the armies of Monera
Second Month of Summer 2200

The only letter in an emerald envelope:

Commander Benson,

The Armies of Monera refuse to send troops to our aid. We cannot hold the borders much longer. The soldiers of The South Sea are needed in the North. Escenone stands between us and them.

Commander Aldis of the armies of Hanielle

The next three bore broken seals in silver and gold, variations of roses. Letters from members of the Vakarra family regretting they held no information on unaccounted relatives, the first signed Roscalie Remebron Vakarra, the second Ranaris Vakarra Vorescin.

Commander Benson,

Regrettably, no one in our family matches the description you have provided. We have only one member of our family who has ever gone missing, though the matter was three quarter centuries ago.

May the guards of Rabinor be at your back.
Vanard Tarouncan Vakarra

Sissel wavered at the final letter, deep gray, sealed in gold, a crown with a cherry-colored jewel. It appeared a seal of grand importance, one she worried to read. After some moments, she lifted the torn seal.

Commander Benson,

Your request for altered sentencing for the detained Sisselara Vacarro has been taken under advisement. I agree with the harshness of the sentencing given the detailed description of the events you have provided. However, at this time, sentencing is handled by High Commander Ravaris. As she was a direct witness, her judgment will be taken as the primary on this matter. Use the appropriate channels for any future requests.

His Royal Highness, King Barrard Nabirra Tavaroe I

Ronan had gone to great lengths, even so much as to plead the king himself for her altered sentence. It was all for naught.

She was alone, hopeless, and bound to spend eternity in the hanging cage.

OPEN THE BARRED DOORS

The caverns run deep, the orphaned living in groups, filthy, too long away from the sun. They call for help and he must go to them. He sets his pen atop the ledger. Though he wishes to leave his thoughts on life in the book, just as so many before him, he leaves the pages unfinished, gathering the children and ushering them toward the boats while the stone ceiling rattled.
-*The Book of Commons*, Faiseus Rancesla Auro, 1824

Taren barked wildly, pouncing through the long grass. He had yet to leave her dad's side since they arrived back to Aroun Vaer three days earlier. He shoved his snout below Lenora's hand and nudged her toward the cottage.

From the soaring glass castle windows, Lenora had watched Thealor depart Brouverg then she and Eran swiftly exited, telling the steward they couldn't bear to leave their books behind.

On the road, thoughts of Brenor and Thealor had haunted her. Had they been pursued? Caught by the guards on the tree line? Did either know what she had done?

Taren tripped over his own paws as Brenor, Ariaas, and Thealor strode down the long road toward her.

Lenora waited for them below the shadows of Aroun Vaer. Over the last three days, she had read incessantly about The Reldory, scoured the library for clues, trained alone with her blade and bow, and walked the perimeter lines.

Brenor rushed to meet her, hugging more tightly than he should, squeezing to her bones. Ariaas rubbed the hair atop her head as all three wandered into the cottage. Ariaas had never expressed affection, and this childlike behavior was equally annoying as much as it was pleasant. Thealor strode past. Her ... *brothers* ... lumbered into the cottage like two elephants attempting to squeeze through a mouse door.

She stood, uncertain. There he was—a stranger—and yet still family. Her heart sank a bit, unsure how she expected to be greeted. A word? A smile? A glance? "Thealor?"

Someone needed to bridge the silence, and if not him, who else but her?

He whipped around to face her.

Once she had secured his attention, she tripped for words. "I wanted to introduce you to my dad."

Thealor assessed Eran from ear to toe.

She corrected, "Well . . . my adopted dad."

He muttered something incoherent then said, "Nice to meet you," before turning his back on them both.

After taking a meal, Thealor and Brenor both slept for some time while Ariaas reclined in his chair. Thealor appeared a giant, unable to cross his leg between the sofa and the table.

Lenora waited until Ariaas was well enough rested and his belly full before addressing him with the obvious. "Ariaas, we cannot all sleep in the cottage."

Eran agreed. "Half of us will be on the floor."

"I'm sure there's still room for you in the stables." Ariaas did not divert his gaze from *Revenge and the Long Lie,* open in his lap for the untold time. "You said it was comfortable, if I recall."

"There are five of us," Lenora pressed. "The cottage was too small for three." As much as she wanted to move into the castle, she would not go above Ariaas's wishes. And while it certainly bore innumerable rooms, he'd boarded it up for reasons she did not yet understand.

Even though she sought her grandfather's approval, she suspected sleeping in a small cottage with four men and an overgrown dog could be deemed ... unfortunate.

Brenor came wearily into the conversation. "Truthfully, we need inside the castle for more reasons than the beds. We need a table to eat on, and chairs to sit in when taking a meal. We need a place where five could sit in front of the hearth, a table with books where five can plan for The Reldory. We could split, certainly, half in one place, half in another, but there is no purpose."

Ariaas grumbled, perhaps more so because he was tired than much else.

This pleased Lenora to no end. No answer was most likely the best she would receive. They had brought Thealor home; he was safe. Eran was here. Brenor and Ariaas were unharmed. Now they had good cause to enter the ethereal structure she had been dreaming of seeing since her arrival. Sitting back in her seat, she subdued her excitement.

They all gathered in front of the towering stone castle, the once shining crown of Aroun Vaer.

Thealor stood tall below the soaring walls. "How long has it been boarded up?"

"A few years after you were gone." Brenor replied with a long, drawn face at the rotting boards that had been nailed into the frame. "I remember it well."

Lenora gathered hammers and axes from the stables and dropped them into a heap in the dirt road. She stared, wide-eyed, and said, "We have about an hour of daylight."

The majestic structure enthralled her— a grand mystery, tunnels, secrets, which she was curious to explore. She pressed the rising excitement from showing on her lips. It was as if from the moment the structure was built, a slow battle waged between the structure and the earth, nature working steadily to reclaim her rightful property.

Thealor waited outside the doors. "It looks almost frightening in this state."

"Ariaas told me Father brought you here when you were young," Lenora said.

Father.

She said the word, and it fluttered in her stomach. The word she and Brenor might have called the man who cradled them in a different life. Sharing the title with Brenor was natural; sharing it with Thealor—in essence a stranger—was not the same.

Now, Gelhan was a shadow. A story, almost a fable. A man whose name passed in her thoughts and then drifted away again, replaced with more pressing matters of chains, captives, and servitude of the living, breathing family that remained.

"I have one memory of Father, though I have several memories of Aroun Vaer. In the heat of summer, we ran through the fountains." Thealor glanced over his shoulder toward the long-rotted gardens. "We'd hide in the passages in the castle, wait for Ariaas to find us. We'd run through the fields, pretending we were as wild as the horses." He gathered an axe and turned his boot in the dust of the road. "Lamenting over the past is useless, I suppose. Another life, now. I have no wish to sleep on the floor."

Once the last board was removed, they swiveled the door handle and Lenora stood before the open threshold. A surge of stale air flew around her. Her heart nearly leapt from her chest when her eyes met the inside of the castle.

The foyer was a large expanse, with a picture window spreading taller than any tower she had ever seen, gazing over the entirety of eastern Valesove. A crystal bulb spread light across the room like the small stars she witnessed in the tunnels. The building, even in its worn and tattered state, radiated enchantment.

Lenora felt she had come home despite never having set foot inside. The home they were meant to share together, the place they would reunite the last of their family.

Nature teemed inside the space, even below a layer of dust and webs. Two oak trees grew in the foyer and streams trickled through the expanse.

Lenora, enthralled, said, "This place is ... incredible. It is more splendid than Brouverg Castle. How did it ever come to be abandoned?"

Ariaas replied, "You'd be surprised how difficult it is to maintain a castle when you are raising small children alone." Lenora concealed her smirk at the thought.

"Ariaas, you must at least open it," Brenor nodded toward the large wooden doors to the southern wing beyond the foyer. "We need a place to work, and to plan for The Reldory. There is no better place in the entirety of Valesove."

Even when he and Thealor arrived home, Ariaas had not smiled with such ferocity—a grin so wide his teeth shone. Lenora found it odd in a way; whatever was behind the immense doors brought him joy.

They gathered below the doors, carved in intricate swirls and delicate vines. Handles of brass carved into swirling papers at the edges. The dust again twirled, but this time with much less ferocity, as the doors creaked open. The air smelled of old wood, vanilla—the earthy scent of well-aged books.

Even at dusk, the room flaunted incandescence. Windows stretched to the ceiling on the eastern wall. The western wall of books stayed far enough to be safe from the stretching light of the morning sun. Balconies awaited, wide and high, iron stairs to meet them in twisting circles and wooden ladders to reach the high shelves. Lenora's eyes stretched, but the height rose beyond her sight.

Lenora ran her hands over the face of an enormous gray table. "What is this made of?"

"A tree of Sus'Gaceteo. The only one made to my knowledge," Ariaas answered plainly. "The only piece Lady Brouverg was interested in purchasing before she found the price."

"It is one piece," Lenora marveled. "The tree must have been ...."

"The trees are enormous. They only grow there, in the skies of the hanglands."

"How did it come to be here?"

"This castle has many mysteries I am uncertain we will ever have answers to."

Lenora wandered on, gazing over the old paintings upon the walls, leather bindings of the books. Thealor perched himself in a crimson tufted chair beside the windows, watching the valley in the lowering light.

+ ———— · + · + · + · ———— +

That evening, Lenora could not settle even once the others stopped fidgeting. Between her excitement and the snoring of Ariaas and Taren, she would not be afforded a wink of sleep. She crept on the edge of her toes, careful not to allow the cottage door to creak as it often did.

Outside, a figure stood in the darkness atop the hill. By the wide stance, she assumed it to be Thealor. The two had rarely spoken, let alone while no one was present to hear. She walked through the tall grass to where he sat, his face in the soft breeze. Bitter, late spring air in Valesove nipped at her cheeks. He ignored the furs; she pulled hers close to stop from shivering.

She joined him in the grass. After some moments she said, "I am sorry for what happened to you."

"Your apology is unwarranted." Thealor replied, his eyes fixed before him. "Our lives were destined to be tortured from our birth."

"I don't think that's true."

"I am guessing they haven't told you much. You still seem to have a gleam in your eyes, something resembling ... optimism, perhaps?"

"Ariaas told you who I am, didn't he? I thought you knew in the castle."

"Yes. Although he did not need to. I remember well enough returning from Aroun Vaer to a screaming baby in my mother's arms."

She asked, solemnly, "Did he tell you of our parents on the road?"

"He didn't need to tell me of that, either. Lord Brouverg told me much throughout the years. They kept apprised on the happenings of our family, the Yurelan, the queen, the new king. Much to the crown's frustration. The queen preferred to keep her misgivings within a much tighter circle, although news did not travel far from Ohbrolis. Lord Brouverg would have kept whispers to his chest aware that he should only use their knowledge at the exact right moment."

Curiosity and guilt intertwined. "Do you remember them? Our parents?"

"I have small memories of them. I used to think of them often when I was young." He stared at her. "Where were you held, hmm? I assume it not in the same manner of barbaric propriety I was kept."

Ariaas had used the word *captive*. Thealor used the word *held*, and it sounded like a jail cell. And while she was, yes, captive, she wasn't really. She wasn't forced to serve a lady and lord on the high mountain day and night. She wasn't in a cell in the hanging cage. She wasn't required to walk perimeter lines and build traps that kill.

She was loved.

Not everyone in Sanrial loved her, of course. But Eran and her mother loved her. The woman who raised her loved her enough to betray her own blood and save her from the king of The South Sea. Eran loved her enough to trek across Valesove in her footsteps. They both loved her enough even though she was the youngest, the most feared—the Master of Death, as Thaesla said. She still shuddered at the title's sound even when it was trapped in her mind and wouldn't dare pass her lips.

But Thealor's first choice—to remain at Brouverg Castle with a cruel master—was lost on her. Why would he stay in a place that had broken him? Whether fear, loyalty, or something else entirely—it made no sense to her. Somehow that made it harder to bear.

"I was raised in Sanrial by Eran, along with his wife, Areya Hoeleck. Her brother, Ebigan, arranged for me to be brought there. There are still some missing pieces, but Eran was unaware of the situation. He thought I was left orphaned, a child who needed a home. The truth, I suppose. He still does not know of the Canen Dera. So, please, don't share with him."

"Raised in a family." Thealor affirmed, his interest piquing for the first instant. "Treated well?"

"Yes. Even though it was not real, I was treated well."

"You and Brenor, both raised in the Valesove, simple lives in the countryside. How quaint." Tension grew in his eyes. "Were you tortured?"

"No, I wasn't tortured." She shook her head at his apparent resentment. Why would she be spared from the tortures while the rest of them endured? It was a matter that constantly drew her thoughts. But this wasn't the conversation she wanted to have. She wanted to mend the bond that they had never had. "I have never had a brother until Brenor, and now you."

"How long have you known Brenor?"

"Some months."

"And you see him as your brother?"

Knowing well where his question led, she chose her next words carefully, twisting the truth. "We are still getting to know one another."

If she was honest, she would admit that she did see Brenor as her brother. Even though the reality—that she indeed had a sibling, let alone three—was so newly born. However, Brenor had taken to her in a way she expected of a brother. They laughed together. He distracted her when he knew she had been dealt too much. He knew her moods—when to talk, when to distract, and when to leave her be. He stood up for Eran. His behavior, and her quick bond with him, had taken even her by surprise. How they could walk along the perimeter lines each day and joke about nothing or speak of nothing at all, and the silence didn't feel awkward. She admired their relationship but also admired him. Brenor was righteous, and she was envious of his steadfast resolve.

"Blood does not make family." Thealor stood, brushing the dirt from the clothes Brenor lent him, an inch too short in arm and two at the leg. Pressing his hands against the pant legs, he attempted to manually remove the wrinkles which settled since he took his seat. When he finished, he set his sights on Lenora. "If you mean to speak with me as a means to build a relationship, do not bother. I am only here for Arienne. Once we rescue her from The Reldory—or die trying—I will leave. I have no desire to be your brother."

Thealor departed before Lenora could form a reply. Perhaps he would soften when Arienne came home. The edges of her fingers moved to her pocket, grazing the blue sapphire stone she had wrapped in cotton.

Perhaps she would tell him it was she who stole the Coronam.

Perhaps when he eased.

BY THE BELT

Telara Generoun Gebrego, Sengura of the Ghesotum, The One of Another,
The Butterfly
Born: Third Month of Summer, 1916
Deceased: Second Month of Winter, 1998
Children: One

- Tenuel Official Ledger

Lenora tapped her nails on the table. "We still have no entrance or exit strategy for The Reldory." None of the books she read aided her. Thealor offered no solutions. "We spoke about bringing the bridge down when it is not Uen'can, but such a thing has been tried many times before with no success."

Eran took a lengthy swallow from a deep cup of brandy wine. "Has anyone ever escaped?"

Ariaas muttered through his third helping of peppered fowl and carrot stew. "Only those who take the fall."

"It is a hanging cage, and you appear to have no wings," Thealor added.

Lenora's eyes drew to the flame, her mind twisting.

There was at least one way to get in. She knew it.

"I see your mind churning. Go on," Ariaas said.

Lenora met his eye.

"You have said it yourself many times. The Reldory cannot be taken from the outside." She stared at him for a long while, hoping he grasped her inference. "They close the bridge and there is no entrance. Like an iron door with no handles. We must be on the other side to open it."

"No."

"They will house the women together."

"*No,*" Ariaas growled.

"Two of us go into the prison on Uen'can, stay the full half year. The other three will be at the bridge the next."

Lenora sat, resolved in her choice. If she made it inside, if she knew the building inside and out, she could get her sister and Sissel out of their cells. The rest could take the bridge.

"Three armed assailants cannot take the bridge," Brenor argued. "Truthfully, I worry five cannot take it, either."

"Five cannot take The Reldory from the outside, alone."

But they could take it if half were on the inside.

Maybe.

"We have no allies. No one other than those who stand in this room. And Idith and Thaesla," Brenor thought aloud. "We need more to help us at the bridge."

"If more are needed, you have one year to learn to be nice to people and make some friends," Lenora replied.

"You will need longer than that," Thealor directed at Ariaas.

Her grandfather offered a derisive snort. Brenor chuckled.

Eran's finger rose to the sky. "I have some questions—"

Ariaas interrupted, "Who is the second? Who will be tortured for six months?"

"I had not gotten that far," Lenora replied.

Brenor spoke in a quiet, resolved voice. "I will go."

"No. Then we are right back where we began, three captive, one free. And in one place, at that. They destroy the bridge, and you are all done for. No. And Eran will get us caught the instant they ask him his crimes." Ariaas took a swig from his tumbler, holding the whiskey on his tongue. "It'll be me."

"You'll be executed for your mouth before you could do any good. Brenor is best equipped to go." Thealor propped his feet upon the table, one atop the other, staring pointedly at Ariaas. "Or you can send me. I'm sure you wouldn't mind throwing me into the depths of hell at that bridge one more time."

Ariaas pursed his lips but whether in frustration or guilt, Lenora couldn't say.

"Who is the other?" Eran asked. The room fell silent. After a beat, he repeated, "Who is the other?"

Lenora fixated her sights on the flames.

Eran was slow to grasp the inference of the stillness, of Ariaas's comments, and Lenora's plan. Finally, he spoke. "You cannot possibly."

"You need to stop thinking like a father for a moment." Lenora's plan was sound, the way the prison worked, the way they housed the inmates. "They separate the women and the men once inside. Every one of you would be kept away from them. That point alone makes your entire plan futile."

"How do you know you would even get housed with her?"

"I don't. There are two dozen rooms as you learned in your books. Assuming half are dedicated to women. One in twelve."

"I have heard they bunk them up." Thealor poured himself a glass of Ariaas's whiskey. "Allow them to kill one another for the food. Leave rooms unoccupied."

Lenora nodded. "Even better."

"You are left bare. They will take away all your weapons." Ariaas cautioned. "You will have nothing,"

"She will not have weapons, but she will not have nothing," Brenor argued. "Not many have so long to prepare for such a fate. We have half a year."

"It is settled, then." Lenora nodded solemnly, a plan she hated though the only one of sound logic. Her voice forlorn and cold, she uttered, "Ariaas and I."

Eran shouted, "This matter is far from settled, young lady!"

Lenora stood from her chair, pressing it back to the table. She turned to Ariaas. "We'll begin training in the morning."

✦ ———— · + · ✦ · + · ———— ✦

Lenora awoke before the sun and waited with her bow in hand until Ariaas gathered Brenor downstairs. Thealor sluggishly followed, as Ariaas led them to a dining hall fireplace. He twisted a lever and led them through a secret, thin, twisting staircase to an underground hollow. Lenora's heart fluttered in anticipation. They skewed and turned for some minutes through the tunnels, perched with flickering lights, until they arrived at their destination.

Lenora's voice reverberated through the colossal chamber, bouncing from one wall to the next in the darkness, the room near black as the tunnel she explored with Brenor. There were no streams of sunshine—a stark contrast to the light rooms of the main castle, appearing bright as the day itself. Brenor held the balanser, though the small flicker of light in his palm remained in its metallic perch.

"Not entirely certain." Ariaas touched his torch to a long passage in the wall. The flame poured in long lines as molten lava flowed from a mountain across the posts and stretched high to the columns, forming tall pillars of fire. An enormous, cavernous hall stood before them.

When enough light surrounded them, Thealor said, "It appears to be an old arena." An enormous chain with a cuff meant to bind an ankle coiled on the floor. The iron clamp, too large for him to lift alone. "Do you know what they keep here?"

"I never saw a man or beast in here. Whatever it was had come and gone by my time."

The cuff would fit a giant—should such a thing ever have existed. "What would this even fit?"

"The animals grow large in the North, and in the River Realm. Perhaps whoever lived here at one time kept prizes as the Brouvergs." Brenor added. The arena confines were kinder than the shallow ones in Mount Ohbrolis.

Thealor's voice trailed from the far end, echoing against the damp walls. "Was there ever treasure here?"

"If there were gold and jewels, such things are long gone. You are welcome to take the tunnels yourselves, see what my years may have missed." Ariaas ran his worn hand over scratches in the stone columns. "I couldn't ever figure out how to make a proper map, always found myself back at an exit or in the castle. I eventually took one tunnel from the north and one to the south. Never diverting. They twist and turn and lead you all over. I have not set foot in this part of the castle in many decades."

Moving the metal cuffs and the chains required all four of them. They left wide scuff marks and made a horrid shrieking when the iron ground into the stone floor.

Ariaas instructed, "Thealor, Lenora, take the floor."

Thealor disliked her, this much she knew for certain, and perhaps doubled her in sheer weight alone. He had already stolen a shard of flesh from Ariaas and killed two Yurelan in the forest. She expected he would not hesitate to harm her.

"You are going to teach me how to fight without a bow, right?" Lenora asked with rising concern.

"I wasn't planning on it." Ariaas motioned. "Toss your dagger over, too."

Reluctantly, Lenora tossed the blade to Brenor, who easily caught it by the hilt. She searched for anything to use as a weapon—a rock or a shard of glass—but the stones were planted deeply into the floor. Her hands held high to spar, she tensed the muscles at her center and guarded her face. Thealor did not bother to adopt the same position. When he stood over her, meaning to strike, his massive frame dwarfed her own.

"What you need to do is simple." Ariaas pointed to a small opening in the far wall, large enough for her body, perhaps a door for a dog at one time. "You need to get out of the arena by way of that small hatch."

Thealor drew his sword in one fluid motion, one he found in the stables; he wore a small grin across his wide, stubbled chin.

Lenora asked, her pulse rising, "He gets a weapon, and I don't?"

"That will be your reality; no need to dance around it. You need to get away from an armed guard." Ariaas took a firm stance, arms crossed over his chest. "remmer."

Thealor held his sword at his side. "What gibberish are you speaking?"

"Attack," Ariaas repeated.

"I have nothing ..."

Lenora turned her head to the columns and the flames, the stone floor. "Do you think I can conjure a weapon out of thin air?" she growled.

Think.

"You have more than they will give you there. And you ate today," Ariaas shouted as Thealor sauntered toward her. "You will be on your own, with two women who will be starved within an inch of their lives. This is your plan, remember? You must save yourself and them until the rest of us can get to you. Without a weapon."

Lenora subdued a scream. She did not wish to go, not inside the hanging cage. But there was no other way. The prison could not be taken from the outside; this much she knew for certain. Her pose was on guard, unmoving, legs wide, ready to move at any instant should he strike at her.

This may be a foolish plan.

Thealor tossed Brenor his sword.

He lunged, grinning when she startled at his movements. He struck her jaw with a closed fist, a blow slamming her to the floor. The hit seemed easy for him, as he would strike a young child.

"If you cannot take a hit, you will not survive," Ariaas groaned. She stood, wiping the fresh blood trailing her cheek where his knuckle had broken the skin.

A closed fist landed again, though she tried to flee. She again rose from the floor, though with less vigor the second time. Thealor knocked her to the floor repeatedly without mercy. She kicked, tossing sand at his face—which did not deter him in the least. When he drew closer, she could still see the granules in the whites of his eyes and across his pupils, though it did not make him wince or close his eyes involuntarily.

She again scoured the floor, finding nothing to aid her. No stones, no loose rocks, nothing upon the floor; the walls were smooth. She took the double wrapped belt from her waist which held her flowing shirt tight, holding the leather as a whip. She moved to strike him with it. He held out his hand, using his forearm to deflect her motions.

He struck her with a closed fist again. Lenora crumbled.

Thealor leaned in close to speak over her. "The old man is right. You won't survive inside The Reldory." He tore the leather from her hands, looked over it before he dropped it back on the floor. Her body was ravaged; she was too weak to use it. On long strides, he departed toward the door to the tunnel. "She yields."

Using the last of her energy, Lenora dragged her limp body to stand on quivering legs. Blood ran from her cheek and from the fresh wound at her eye. Her face swelled around her cheeks; her right eye closed. Her voice was pained when it creaked from her lips, "I did not yield."

Thealor turned to her, eyes full of rage.

She had struck a nerve, hadn't she? He enjoyed the minute conquering. He enjoyed the end of this dull game, forgetting it had a purpose. The aching pain surged through Lenora's leg. She expected it might shatter below her weight.

Stern and unrelenting, she repeated, "I did not yield."

Thealor crossed the space between them in a breath, meeting her face with the swift blow across her cheek.

Her ear crashed into the stone floor, her jaw cracked and shattered.

Then all went black.

✦ ————— · ✦ · ✦ · ————— ✦

Lenora jolted to consciousness to the smell of mint, pepper, and ammonia.

A man growled. A figure paced beyond her, before the burning fire in the kitchen hearth. "Was he trying to kill her?"

Brenor held a soft cotton rag to her eye, tempering the fresh blood. He laid a soiled rag upon the table. "She would not yield."

Eran paced, his hand covering his mouth. A father could not be pleased, seeing his child carried into the kitchen like a rag doll. His tone raised in anger and terror, he said, "Perhaps next time ... *ease* into it."

"I was not the one who asked for the final hit." Ariaas stood a few steps behind them, arms crossed over his chest. "Sometimes, though, it is best to know what someone's reaction will be. Then you know where they need training. Perhaps this is a good thing."

"A good thing?" Eran barked. "And what exactly have you learned?"

"She is not a good fighter, not without a bow or a blade." Ariaas leaned over Brenor's shoulder, glancing at her wounds. A small grin rose on his lips. "But her will is iron solid. Stubborn as they come."

UNANSWERED QUESTIONS

The caverns run deep, the orphaned living in groups, filthy, too long away from the sun. They call for help and he must go to them. He sets his pen atop the ledger. Though he wishes to leave his thoughts on life in the book, just as so many before him, he leaves the pages unfinished, gathering the children and ushering them toward the boats while the stone ceiling rattled.
-*The Book of Commons*, Faiseus Rancesla Auro, 1824

Lenora's mounting questions gnawed at her brain. *Canen Dera* burned behind her teeth and her pocket weighed heavily with the silent presence of Oedd. She hadn't been called property in some time, yet the nagging lingering thought of it hovered like a cloud over her mind. Ariaas had answers he refused to share about her fate. Now, Thealor's return—not the reunion she imagined.

The twenty-third year.

She sat by the alcove window, knees drawn to her chest, journal open. Lenora dug into her pocket and opened the blank letter. Her quill hesitated over her page.

Does Ariaas lie to me?

He's not a man of lies. Not to his family, at least. But he is a man who hides things.

How did Ariaas know he would find Thealor and I in the twenty-third year?

The ink paused, as if he was considering how to respond.

Your grandfather has many secrets.

Apparently, so do you. Look. If you are going to give me the runaround, I'm not going to write anymore.

Lady Lenora, it is never my intention to give you the runaround. For this particular query, I am at a loss, I'm afraid. Would you like to ask me something else about your family?

You were friends with Thealor?

Yes. He and I were good friends. Though I am Arienne's age.

Will you come to see him?

No. As I mentioned previously, I am not welcomed by your grandfather. He doesn't easily welcome many.

Abandoning the letter and quill in her room, Lenora strode to the library. The scent of old parchment greeted her like a second memory. Maps of western Hanielle lay scattered across the table of Sus'Gaceteo, their edges curled and soft with age.

CAGESIDE

I am alone now.

- Diary of Daisirie Cabredd Mire, Volume 3, Entry 431

Through iron-clad bars, the sun cast over jagged rocks, revealing The Reldory in new morning light. Sissel's transport carriage had trembled throughout the night, staked by wide ropes and enormous iron nails anchored to the stone floor. She expected it to roll onto its side each time gusts jammed hard enough to peel the wheels inches off the ground. A hundred feet stood between the structure and the closest ledge, with no path between them—old wooden doors perched at random increments with no way to reach their thresholds. The caverns dropped below where the eye could see, and the peaks rose high on the far precipice.

Bumps on Sissel's spine rose and fell, and a knot settled in her throat she might choke on. Attempting not to weep, she remembered her grandmother instructing her as a girl to be strong.

Weeping had its time.

Kaloyein had left her shoes in Tanes. Much as their first trip together, he left her to walk bound by ropes, this time to be yanked behind the carriage wheels. Her feet suffered the consequences of the ascent, bloodied and torn from the harsh terrain up the mountain road.

He unlocked the door.

"Get out."

When she did not promptly respond to his orders, Kaloyein grasped her hair, and tossed her to the rocky floor. "Soon I'll be done with you for good."

Stumbling, Sissel attempted to gain a foothold. He jerked her chained hands and lurched her shoulder blades taut. Against her will, her body stood at attention. The bitter winds tore at her open skin as the sun in the north burned flesh.

A sweet melody delighted the softer edges of the wind. A whistle.

For the briefest of moments, peace washed over her. The soft tune eased her tears and her hammering pulse.

"The winds are worse than normal, eh?" Kaloyein shouted to another guard. The man replied, though she could not decipher his words upon the air. He grasped her chains.

Her hair blew across her face, covering her eyes and cheeks, catching at her eyelashes and tangling in her mouth. She shook her head to release them, eyed the boulders, razors made of stone. Perched upon a thin stage, she braved the glance over, the fall into the abyss, weakening the strength of her shaking knees. Her stomach twisted and dropped as if she were already tumbling hundreds of feet into rolling and twisting fog.

The winds shrieked.

Death stood upon every surface, the wind pressing toward one demise or another. Now she regretted every moment she could have learned what Ronan meant to teach her. How had she willed a life to be traded many months ago? How did the ability of the Roscidarra truly work? She could run if she could kill Kaloyein, his hands tugging at her chains to balance himself. But then, where would she go on the torn flesh of her feet? She had lost the mental path to Aroun Vaer from her current location.

Guilt consumed her for considering his death.

The transport carriage for Cascanvore held two men—brothers, she presumed by the thin pale cheeks and wide ears. The carriages from Felreaon held a pair of meek brown eyes—a child with warm skin and tightly curling hair who could scarcely see over the opening. One man sat in the carriage from Dhaesreaon, which could hold no more. He bore one marled eye, staring at Sissel through the window with no regard for social decorum. The wheels on the carriage shook when he lumbered out, bowing to his enormous weight.

Kaloyein leaned in close to Sissel, snickering. His hot breath smelled like bile and copper. "If the High Commander has 'er way, when the bridge opens in the summer, it will be the last. Maybe by then, you'll learn to fly."

Again, bumps raised on her arms. She forced her eyes closed, imagining Ronan climbing over the jagged rocks in valiant resistance. When Kaloyein's calloused hands pushed her toward the bridge, she returned to reality.

Stone creaked, and the earth trembled when the bridge opened. Once tucked neatly below the mountainside, the earth extended from the cage in mesmerizing enchantment, growing and changing shape, branches of a tree expanding to meet one another. The sight would have been stunning had she not known she would be inside all the days before her.

She struggled to walk in the winds.

Kaloyein lost his balance. He tugged at her chains, and they stumbled together onto the bridge. Sissel's knees slammed against the stone, and she grasped onto the edge, steadying herself. The world unraveled below her. The air swirled in frenzied currents, shrouding the earth below in a cloak of obscurity. Her heartbeat shoved into her ears, ringing. She closed her eyes, regulated her breath, and focused on the high doors ahead.

The winds howled, again threatening her unstable foothold. Once they crossed, the gusts broke around the building, and the doors opened for her arrival.

Four inmates stood shackled to a thick metal bolt on the stone floor. A desk carved from the edges of rock sat in the corner. Three beds stacked high with wool blankets, and three chairs hovered beside an open flame.

A small room with three guards and those who had walked across the bridge to meet them. Nothing more.

A sturdy man with a long auburn beard, tied in knots at the front, sat at the stone desk. Wider than tall, he wore brown fur hides over his shoulders, a silver pin of a bison. He appeared busy, though he attended to nothing Sissel could see. The inmates looked mundane—all but the marled-eyed man. The young girl wept, grasping a sugar pink stuffed rabbit missing one button eye, the other hanging by a loose thread.

Kaloyein stood proud, while a guard investigated the locking mechanisms on their chains. The auburn guard eyed his colleague, nodding toward Kaloyein and the open door.

"Crane."

A tall, thin man, whose nose had been broken more than once, dropped his investigation, and grasped Sissel's chains. He bellowed at Kaloyein, *"Get out."* It seemed Kaloyein was doing something wrong no matter where he was. "You can't leave the door open!"

The third guard, well-aged, wore a black uniform with a silver serpent pin. The snake coiled inside itself, poised to strike. Should his uniform speak, he was in command, wearing similar fabrics and pins to those in Tanes, though built for the harsh cold of the precipice. The fur of a gray animal, a wolf perhaps, perched over his shoulder. Besides the small scar at the base of his left eyebrow, his dark features were utterly forgettable.

In turn, the well-aged guard asked questions of each prisoner Sissel did not wish to overhear. When he finished with the man with the marled eye, they stripped him of his clothing, then cut his hair with dull metal blades. In a roiling fire, his worn clothing burned as he struggled against them, his scalp repeatedly sliced in long shallow wounds.

Crane turned his attention to the bison. "Close the bridge."

The earth began to quake and Sissel struggled to recall how she stood upright on her own two legs. The girl fell to the floor, holding tightly onto her rabbit. One of the twins grasped for the other.

Through the sliver of the door, the stone bridge retreated.

Then nothing.

Sissel's breath clouded the air before her. They were suspended in the sky.

Kaloyein had barely enough time to make it to the landside. Crane stood behind her, tearing the jacket and shirt from her back. The rusted metal scissors screeched at the hinge while they cut her shirt away, still covered in the blood of the marled-eyed man. Jostled, they cut away the last of her attire, leaving her flesh bare.

Gooseflesh chased across her skin.

And so my eternity here begins.

Once they were certain she did not carry anything dangerous, Crane secured her hands to the chain. The floor quaked again. For an instant, she wondered why. The bridge had already taken the prisoners and closed. Then she recalled the doors with no floor to meet their thresholds.

The stone stairs creaked open.

The marled-eyed man was first to be unchained from the metal bolt. Crane held his chains like reins from a horse he would soon spur down the stairs. Without warning, the marled eyed man lunged for Sissel, a sharp and ferocious cry, slamming teeth as if he might tear at her flesh. Crane yanked him by his chains.

Her entire being stood, shocked and at attention. Adrenaline coursed through her veins, her need to flee more evident now than ever. Tears rose to her eyes, and she reminded herself to remain stoic once more.

Weakness had no place in The Reldory.

His teeth reeked of decay. The guard prodded him with an iron poker meant for herding cattle; he snickered at her fear. Her spine prickled. The marled-eyed man sneered, pinning her terror from her ears to her spine, washing her in the foul odor of months without caring for his teeth.

The well-aged guard continued his tasks. He approached Sissel, clipboard in hand. "Would you like your head shaved?" At her lack of verbal reply, he met her sights. She shook her head.

"You should reconsider. You have quite long hair. There will be no access to grooming tools once inside. It will become a problem."

Her voice quivered. "I do not want to shave my head." The sudden removal of her hair felt warrantless, but she hadn't time to think at length. Her clothes had already been lost; she did not wish to be void of all humanity.

He eyed her, irritated with her refusal of his secondary offer.

The twins pleaded and screamed, the tight control of solace lost. On his knees, one pleaded, "Please. Please don't put us down there."

The auburn bearded guard fumbled with their clothing, carrying far more than his short arms wished to hold. Then the flames stretched out, almost as if to clench onto them, swallowing her jacket and everything else along with it.

The well-aged guard said, "You will be taken to your cell as is. These clothes and any personal items you may have will be destroyed." His quill pointed. "Clothing will be in your cell."

A scream howled outside.

A man. He wailed—at first loud, then fading—down, down, *down,* until nothing remained. Her spine chilled, a cloud created upon the air by her deep exhale.

Someone had fallen.

When the doors opened, the auburn guard turned in his seat. "He fought you, *eh?*"

Crane shouted, using his entire weight to force the door closed against the shrieking air. "He seemed to be a good amount of trouble, anyway. I was not bothered when the boulder lost his balance."

This death amused the bearded guard greatly. "We usually lose at least two on Uen'can." Overjoyed, he slapped his hand upon the stone desk. "Who's next?"

Crane grasped Sissel, leading her by slacked chains to the double doors. The winding stone narrowly descended, wide enough for one body, the sides open to the heavens.

How would the guards know they imprisoned the correct inmate? The young girl watched her, a silent pleading of soft brown eyes, clutching her rabbit before the guard tore it from her grip. The last button eye detached, rolling across the cold stone floor toward Sissel's feet and settling between creases of stone as its soft pink hide met open flame.

While she eyed the steep descent, Sissel's thoughts escaped her lips, "He didn't ask my name ..."

"Five were meant to arrive." Crane pressed the iron poker into her shoulder blade. "*Five* are here."

The frigid air chewed against her nude skin. Sissel expected it might tear flesh from bone. Stone on her bare feet pierced like needles, and the first surge of wind pressed her to clutch the side of the building, her chains clattering. Slowly, she stepped, imagining the floor did not feel like shards of glass. The rock was steep and slippery, the footholds unstable. Every few feet, jagged protrusions threatened her balance if not navigated with care. When her arms rose to her chest, Crane swatted at her.

The fleet of transport carriages sat perched along the landside, the guards observing Sissel's every move as if she performed a distanced show for their pleasure. They taunted when she grasped for her life against the stone and cheered when her bare breasts returned to the open air.

When they arrived at an old wooden door, Crane yanked her rein of chains. Should the door even be called such a thing; it rattled, separated with age, and joined with rusted nails. Hair wound across her face spotted with melted snow. She pressed the tangled mat of hair over her shoulder with her chin. Crane shouted over the wind, "You will be kept in a single cell with two others."

Carved silver formed the intricate door handle into what was once a human being. The woman, on her knees, trapped between heaven and hell. Both flesh and clothing draped off her skeleton, her mouth unfurled in agony, her hands extended in prayer or mercy to the gods of the sea, mountain, or winds.

Sissel muttered, somewhere between a question and a curiosity, "There's no lock."

"Only the door to the main room you departed and the guard's barracks have locks. We encourage our inmates to end their suffering if they choose." His brown eyes gleamed with an almost pleasant aura. "One kindness we can provide."

Crane continued while she spun in her new reality, "The stairs will close into the walls when I leave. If I fall, they shall close indefinitely. If I die, or if I will it so. Are we understood?"

Her false confident position melted, and she tucked her arms into her chest again, providing a momentary shield from the thrashing winds the curve in the building had provided. She found herself thankful, if only for the time being, she kept her hair, even if it served no purpose but to keep her warm.

"We don't want to care for you. Prisoners push one another often to be the single owner of their meals. Also, I'd stay away from the *timaca*. The frail one. It's been here a long time. It used to kill anyone we put with it, but ... it's kept the last one alive for some time. At least it was alive last Uen'can. Perhaps you will be as unlucky as it was."

He opened the weathered wood masquerading as a door and unlocked her cuffs.

Two closed-lipped bodies huddled close for warmth—nothing visible but gawking eyes above a charcoal wool blanket and sprawled, matted hair. Crane thrust Sissel through the threshold. The wood clattered closed behind her as if it might shatter, and the squealing wind attempted futilely to pull the oxygen from the room.

One woman removed her hand from the cover and pointed toward a hole in the opposite wall. Sissel followed her instruction, finding a flat wooden tray suspended by thin ropes and a folded bundle of clothes. Without further thought, she pulled the mushroom gray fabric over herself, the stiff articles cracking. When dressed, she bent to the floor, holding her knees to warm herself.

The woman with black hair spoke through closed eyes and tight, chattering, rotting teeth. "When warm, I'll ... introduce ... myself ... honey."

As Sissel thawed, the room solidified. The stone had been molded from where the floor met the wall, and the wall met the ceiling. Perhaps a space honed by nature herself, much as a cave. A thin iron pipe, which she assumed was used for washing, two small pails, and three tin cups.

The wooden tray holding Sissel's clothing swung from the wall and lifted. The interior of the building, much as the exterior, was a circular fortress of negative space. Across to the other side, dispensary boxes were lifted, one still full of clothing. Though she feared him, her heart tightened. The marled-eyed man met his end before he found his garments.

The building trembled. Small stones bounced upon the floor. The door rattled, the old wood shifting and groaning to stay together. Sissel took a seat to keep from falling. When the rattling ceased, the black-haired woman pulled the blanket from herself, extending her hand to Sissel.

"Dy ..." She chattered. "Dy ... lia." Dylia appeared less emaciated than the other woman, with prominent bones and broader shoulders; her lips were a shade of plum, and her dark eyes still held some life within them.

"Nice to meet you." She offered her left arm in return. "Sissel."

"Don' ... you mind his words." Dylia glanced over the other woman with an abundance of kindness. "She's been here ... far too long. She'll talk to you one day ... ain't that right?"

Dylia nudged the woman's leg. When the woman offered no rebuttal, Dylia curled back into the blanket. "I talk to her all day long. Never get anything back. Hearin' my own voice all day can't be good for my mind."

The other woman glanced at Dylia, eyes sunken, cheekbones protruding, matted hair grown over her face.

"She spoke many years ago. Only in the last few, she went silent. Perhaps nuthin' to say but what hurts the soul. Better not to say nuthin' at all, I suppose."

Sissel evaluated the woman in the bed, remembering the guards warning. The woman stared with dead eyes and made no attempts to move. How could she be so frail and have killed others as he said?

Dylia interrupted her thoughts. "Why'd they bring ya here, Sissel?"

As always, the words pained her. "I ... killed a soldier in Wesilea."

"I didn' ask what you did, honey." She grinned coyly, her lips curving as if she knew how Sissel would reply. "There are plenty of confines for prisoners. I asked why they brought you *here.*"

Sissel leaned her head back against the rock, cool upon the back of her head, and closed her eyes. The stone was both uncomfortable, yet not—pressure to her head by the sandy sharp edges forcing into her scalp.

She tried to pronounce the word—the answer—in her head: *rosce. rosce,* to die. The word itself cloaked in darkness. She allowed it to roll over her tongue, the same way Ronan spoke.

rosce ... darra ...

A trade.

A trade of death. A trade of life.

"I am Roscidarran," she said, the first time she had spoken the words aloud. At the sound of it, her heart ached. The words sounded close to his voice, the sounds rolling off her tongue as they had his. "Though I did not know it myself at the time."

Dylia's face rumpled as if she smelled something foul. "That should make The South Sea happy. They love their own. Loyal even when they shouldn' be."

"There was a public gathering in the city center in Wesilea. A friend fell, and I tried to save him. It was an accident."

"Ah ... I see, honey. An example must be made." Dylia searched her with inquisitive eyes. "I mus' say, you don' wear the face of The South Sea. Women are taller, squarer. Darker hair, eyes."

Sissel raised her brows, she had been told this more than once. "Why are you here?"

"Ah. I saw something I shouldn'. When our father traveled, we snuck around. Empty buildings mostly. *Gotta' not be the slowest,* we always said. Not so much a joke now." She gave Sissel a knowing glance. "My brothers got away. I didn'. Faster climbing than running for some reason. Doesn' matter much, now."

The woman on the cot attempted to reposition the best her brittle bones could manage. Her body, much as the door handle, was suspended somewhere between life and death—skin finding nothing but bone to cling to.

She opened her eyes in a streak of sun from the cracks in the door, bright violet as wildfire.

Dylia cringed. "How rude of me. Sorry, honey. Sissel, meet Arienne."

BLADE OF THE KHAYERNAMEN

"Death and revenge do not a lasting couple make. They are one night of passion; as fast as the flame ignites, the heat extinguishes. The next morning you wake, wishing for more and wondering what you had just partaken in, feeling nothing but a void. Revenge only finds a lasting soulmate in torture. The two belong together and will withstand the longest night, growing old together. Torture can take many faces and never affords a chance for the two to grow tired of one another."

- *Revenge and The Long Lie*, Faiseus Rancesla Auro, 1839

Thealor twisted his blade, admiring the tanned leather hilt and crimson jewel at the crown. He swung at Ariaas, and the old man dodged before the steel struck him across his chest. Pleased with himself, Thealor said, "Your age is showing."

This time, Thealor swung with all the force he could muster, channeling the aggression he'd built over the years into the blow. While Ariaas cowered behind a shield, Thealor rained on him repeatedly, keeping the old man recoiling under the onslaught. When he had his fill, Thealor ceased.

"Your pride is showing." Ariaas stood and gathered himself. "It'll be the death of you."

Pride was one of the few things Thealor had left. He had no prize left to guard. With no weapon, keeping Lenora from the hatch had dulled to a chore. He only found contentment training with Brenor, the only well-suited adversary in this broken down land, both in size and skills the other found unaccustomed to defend.

Ariaas swung again, and their blades met, continuing this routine dance outside the stables. After a lifetime of suffering the weight of his betrayal, Thealor had little left for Ariaas besides hatred. He buried this loathing below his slashing sword and his gritting teeth. It depended on the day if he wished for Ariaas to die, to serve his same sentence, or beg forgiveness on his knees on shards of glass, a matter the months at Aroun Vaer had yet to erode.

When the two finished, they moved to watch Eran and Brenor sparring in rudimentary format. Ariaas leaned against the wall. "They look like two baby rabbits in a duel, pawing at one another."

"That's quite generous of you."

Eran rested his hands on his knees, easing his labored breath, his dark leather boots covered in dust. "I had a bit too heavy of a breakfast, I wager. Just the creamed eggs and the ham holding me down." Yes, indeed, it was the eggs, not the years of weight built around the belly.

"Enough," Ariaas instructed. "Brenor, take the rest of your training today with Thealor. Heneran needs a break. And Thealor needs someone else to hit."

Eran's eyes illuminated, pleased beyond measure. "I do need to attend to lunch."

Eran rushed toward the castle, clearly looking forward to his next meal while Ariaas departed for the cottage.

Thealor's gaze stalked Ariaas until he was well out of his eyesight, and all that remained were him and Brenor.

"In all these months, you have yet to tell me why you hate Ariaas," Brenor said. "You barely speak to him. Seems you are only happy when you are going after him with a blade."

"He left me and took you." He raised his chin, trying not to grind his teeth. "Not much else to say about it, I suppose."

"But you stay here with him?"

"Eh, you aren't all that bad." Thealor did not hate Brenor, but more so had nowhere to go. "At least not as far as brothers are concerned."

Aroun Vaer hosted many valuable weapons, books he'd never read, but also mouths that wouldn't shut up—mainly that of Ariaas. But two well-trained swordsmen and one decent archer were at his disposal if the mountain soldiers sought him to return to his post. Eran could easily be thrown before him as a shield. Brenor would fight to save him, perhaps, if he had time to study the caveats of his vow before an intruder struck him.

Truthfully, there was nothing of interest on the map of Monera from Mount Ohbrolis to The South Sea, Qerilan, and Tenuel, or across the Adlean Sea to Cascanvore. So why leave?

However, the matter that genuinely kept him at Aroun Vaer was more complex. "In truth ... if there is a chance to free Arienne, I ..."

He pursed his lips, battling with his words. The plan to rescue his sister had no true chance, but he hoped it would grow legs, regardless. He had walked through the gardens, recalling Arienne and her lavender blooms. Now, he wanted to rewind time. He would not tear them to pieces if she gave them to him now.

"She doesn't deserve the cage. She was the kindhearted amongst us. She always knew when I was sad or hurt and cared for me. Seems wrong she should receive the harshest punishment."

Thealor rummaged through the swords of the dead in piles in the stables. The inverted star of The South Sea on two blades, one large, one small. Many bore symbols of the Yurelan with feathers hanging from their hilts. He found a heavy sword, a brute of a thing, a lion of the mountain embossed on the grip. Only a few men could wield such heavy steel.

"I cannot say I believe the chances stand in our favor," Thealor lamented, swinging the broadsword. "The plan as it sits now ... a fool's errand. Lenora won't survive."

"She still has time."

"Not much."

Lenora will fail. She sparred fine with the blade. However, The Reldory allowed no weaponry. Despite her best efforts, she failed to pass him in the arena. Could she even pick a lock? Take a life? Pull his sister to freedom across the stone bridge? A piece of him wished to help Lenora—she was, after all, going in as bait to rescue his sister—but how do you train one to be better? To this question, a simple answer:

You practice until the blood runs dry.

You practice until pain no longer sears through your flesh.

You practice until you stop giving a damn what happens to the guard.

You practice until you are no longer *weak*.

Thealor tossed his leather coat across a boulder as the bitter chill of the morning dissipated. As the midday heat swelled, driving out the final gusts of winter, he drew his shirt over his head, revealing raised scars in rows, blades that pierced him years ago—flesh-carved, symmetrical art.

Brenor raised a fist to his mouth, perhaps about to lose his breakfast. "What happened?"

He held the large blade up in both grips, adopting his stance before he swung, a motion Brenor deflected. "The lady liked me scarred. Thought I looked more like a man."

The two trained together many days in the winter, but bearing witness to the remains of Thealor's tortured existence appeared too much for his brother. Brenor dropped his sword.

"She had you trained? Tortured you? She was not afraid you would escape or turn on her?"

"Lord Onalorn of the Khayernamen trained me at her request, yes. The lady treated me well when I did as she asked."

Brenor gestured to the scars. "And ... when you didn't?"

"It would seem I'm not always well-behaved." Thealor extended his arms to show his form, chiseled muscles, and broader stance to his brother. "Come on now—no need to lament over old scars. You need to have a tougher hide, too. You won't be able to do what is needed of you at The Reldory if not. You will need to slice through a man's throat. Watch him choke on his own blood before he dies. Skewer him in the belly with your blade."

Brenor's eyes drew wide in horror.

Thealor said, "Come on now. If you cannot hear the words, this plan is even more foolish than I thought."

He lunged. Brenor dove to the floor, deflecting Thealor's strike, their blades meeting.

"What are you afraid of?" Thealor leaned in to observe his brother's character, the room reeking of Brenor's fear like billowing smoke. "Afraid you won't be able to control yourself? Won't be able to rein the beast back in if you let it out?"

Pleased, he struck again. And again. Brenor dodged from his advances, motions of silk compared to his broader frame.

Brenor reserved his advances.

"You should yield," Thealor grumbled. "If you can't fight me with your full strength, why do you bother?"

"I do not want to hurt you."

"You seemed fine with it these past few months. You felt like a worthy adversary then."

Brenor eyed his old wounds. Thealor supposed viewing where blades pierced his flesh, his anguish and tortures where his skin healed over and over, was quite different than imagining.

"These scars are not from swords. One has never touched my skin. Though, I welcome you to try."

"Then what are they from?"

They continued their blows with less strength behind them, now more motions of a choreographed dance of planned strike and rebuttal. "The lady of the house had a jacket built for me. Steel spikes on the inside. It was rebuilt as I grew. She forced me to wear it to keep me from spilling her trays. To keep me from refusing the highborn ladies she sent to my chambers. To keep my posture straight.

"Lord Onalorn had other methods. Torture of the flesh that he would allow me to endure when I lost to him." Thealor pointed to other scars across his abdomen. "His whip was swift."

"And what happened to him?"

"I learned not to lose."

Brenor gulped. "What else did she do to you?"

How does one answer the tortures they lived for a lifetime? "It doesn't matter, now."

"I think I am done for today." Brenor dropped his sword to his side. Though Thealor suspected he would spar for hours had he left his scars to the imagination. "Let us go back inside. You are supposed to meet Lenora soon, and Eran is making lunch."

Thealor pressed through the kitchen doors, Brenor at his heels, the aroma of baked beef hand pies with warm buttered crust enticing him.

"You are halfway through the time we had to train you for The Reldory! More, actually." Ariaas scolded Lenora. "We depart in under two months. You have yet to complete the simple task of making it to the hatch. One task!" He slammed his hand on the wooden table. "You can't even get past one guard. We have not even moved to the hard part!"

Thealor sniggered. Ariaas shared his thoughts. How would she escape her cell if she couldn't escape the hatch? How would she get into Arienne's or the guard barracks?

"Find a new tactic. You have *today*. This plan is abandoned if you cannot make it by the day's end." Ariaas stormed out, the door swinging on creaking hinges.

Lenora turned her plate in circles as if the hand pies would morph into something new before her eyes.

Eran said kindly, "You should eat something."

Lenora shook her head, addressing Brenor, "What is our heritage? Our lineage?"

"Thank you for the warm welcome back," Thealor grabbed a pie, tossing it from hand to hand to relieve the burning heat on his fingertips. "I see you've had a fruitful afternoon."

Brenor sighed. "We are all mal'soniure, that much is certain. However, I do not know to what degree. I do not know all the lineages we are born from."

Thealor sat with his meal, concealing his deep curiosity at the question. Perhaps if he were more than a mere guard or warrior, he could swoop in and save Arienne himself before the others knew he was missing. Muscles alone cannot permeate the stone cage. If he were of the Aluadath, he could bypass all these theatrics, convince the guards to open the gate, and release Arienne without anyone the wiser.

"Can we not use what we were born to do? Should we not be trained in that manner?" Lenora stared at Brenor. "Flames or stone, metal, something useful?"

"Endruas is within your bloodlines," Eran added.

Thealor kicked off his shoes and propped his bare feet upon the table, eating in peace with Ariaas away. "The Endruas will be a stark disadvantage in The Reldory. They can torture you longer." Thealor had seen Lenora in the library with Eran, studying the lineages of Valesove and The South Sea, the ways of life, the ways of death.

Cascanvore's lineages were useless.

Lenora continued, "If we are descendants of Felreaon or Dhaesreaon, their lineages host abilities that might prove useful. If we could control stone, or fire, or metal."

"Perhaps if I knew Ariaas's mother and father's names, I could find them in the books." Eran's grin raised on his round cheeks. "Maybe they will provide some clues."

Brenor shook his head; he did not recall their names.

Lenora answered, "Fabirin Sarvor Ebronds and Lanealyn Dackene Ellnas." The room fell silent. "Ariaas told me in Say Livore the day we met."

"Oh ... right," Eran rubbed his forehead, and his brows squished. "Well, I will see if I can find their names in the library."

Curious. Thealor stopped eating to listen to their further conversation. Eran and Lenora could create a family tree; find his heritage and abilities.

Perhaps his time at Aroun Vaer wasn't useless after all.

YOU CANNOT BEST ME

Numara Lerent Eslar, Tu'dende of the Eternvis, The Ruler of Intellect, The Owl
Born: First Month of Winter, 2038
Deceased: First Month of Summer, 2118
Children: Unknown

- Felreaon Official Ledger

Lenora scrambled over the cavern's stone floor on bare feet, calloused and raw.

Above his head, Thealor swung his iron chain while the air whistled its warning. Their daily training for The Reldory had ruined her body, but she healed rapidly before she was ravaged again the next day. And now, she couldn't run as fast as she once could. He released his whip. The iron chain clasped her ankle, and her cheek collided with the stone floor while the rest of her body followed.

She lay upon the brisk stone, writhing, shuddering.

Thealor sauntered behind her. "You have no idea how boring this is."

"I thought you liked watching me fall," she coughed.

"Well, it was funny enough when you didn't see it coming at first." Thealor picked at his nails. "But now, it's just been done too much."

The first few days he struck her in the face. Now, he tended to strike her in the stomach or ribs with his fist, her ankles with the chain.

"Come on," he groaned. "Let's get on with it."

They were not nearing the end of today's torture. She had not stopped to think of what agony The Reldory had in store, but certainly, it couldn't be far worse than what she endured in this arena.

What am I doing wrong?

Her running pace slowed, but there would be no changing that with her injuries. The difference in their anatomy was irrelevant. The only difference was strength and weakness. He never swung the dual-handed sword, though he often admired it. Thealor took ten swings with the whip each day before his pace slowed. She counted time with her thumb and index finger, rubbed them together for each second, and calculated the lag in his movement. She knew how many bricks she could pass with each swing, marking her placement like a mental badge of honor.

When he slowed, the air whistled differently. She felt the whip's fading current. He would swing twenty times before he called it a day. Twenty-two on Sundays. In the days he trained with Brenor beforehand, he only made it to fourteen.

She contemplated the scenarios, her failures, what she continued to do wrong, how many steps it took to get to the door. How many swings he'd taken at her, how tired he was today.

Lenora growled below her breath.

Every moment a piece of her body ached.

He was interesting if nothing else, and often she used their familial connection to try to bond with him, an action that he swiftly cut down.

She used the wrong methods. It did not matter how often she could be struck and rise again, not if she could not get *out*. If she couldn't chain him. If she couldn't harm an armed warrior with nothing to her name, except her body and her wit. Pain with no reward.

Tomorrow she would find the lineages, if she could, train in that regard. And once that was done, if it could be done, how would she open the bridge from the inside? Or the stairs? Or rush through the windy abyss with no bodily strength? Or find Arienne if they were not housed together? Or Sissel? The thoughts multiplied. How many *what ifs* compared to even one impossible task.

On the floor, inhaling the dirt, she recalibrated.

This afternoon one task stood before her. Any remaining answers were a fringe benefit.

Lenora wore no belt—Ariaas claimed it after her first day. She was required to wear thin, loose clothing without hard objects or strings. All remaining were her thoughts, her words, her wit. She could not win by strength, a lesson she learned repeatedly but for months refused to heed. Perhaps her far-off abilities from some long-ago ancestors dwelled within her blood, though they were useless now.

"You cannot best me. Never once in all these little skirmishes we keep having." Thealor held his arms outstretched, taunting the longsword in his grips. He held the steel chain wrapped in coils at his feet. "It's been months," he mocked. "How many times must you take a hit before you admit this plan will not work?"

She rose to her knees, inhaling through the pain, rubbing a streak of blood from her nose.

Thealor was right; she could not best him in a match of strength. His skills with varying weapons—the blade, the bow, the spear, even the chain used as a lasso and on occasion a whip—far surpassed hers. While he held the chain, the hatch was impenetrable.

Every scenario sped through her mind in a repetitious loop. *You cannot best me.*

Suddenly, she knew all she had to do. A slow grin rose to her lips.

Lenora righted her posture, standing tall despite the aching. Her final chance. "Ah, but see, I have bested you. *Once.* You just didn't know it was me."

He exhaled a snort of a laugh. "When was this?"

After a second, his confident expression dropped a hair. "Certainly not in this arena."

"No." She stared into his scarlet eyes, pride reeking from her grin, watching his reaction as the words departed her lips. "Not at Aroun Vaer."

Her thumb and finger pressed together to tally the time of his strides. She counted. He would move to harm her intentionally the moment the words entered the arena. "I bested you in your own home. In the room you say you *guarded* for over a decade. Not the best at guarding, are you?"

Thealor's merriment ceased.

"Tell me," Lenora challenged, "Would you have left Ohbrolis otherwise?"

Rage grew, a visible fire building in his soul. Flames looped through his veins, the surges rising through every muscle. *"You?* You took the Coronam?"

"Not my taste, but still quite beautiful. Surely worth quite a lot."

The chain plummeted to the floor, and Thealor grasped the Khayernamen blade with both hands. The muscles in his jaw twitched. "I told no one of the stone's disappearance."

Thealor unleashed a primal scream. He dashed to strike her without thought of consequence, she could see as much in his eyes. She held her position, keeping time of his steps.

One.

Two.

Three.

Four.

From beyond his shoulder, he swung the blade. When the moment arrived, and he was upon her, Lenora ducked from the falling steel, rolling across the stone. She rose from her fallen knee, racing toward the hatch. The weight of the enormous sword pulled itself to the floor, Thealor along with it.

Thealor sprinted toward her. As she slipped below the threshold of the hatch, the swinging chain fell well out of range of her feet.

Thealor yanked the stable doors open. He roared at Brenor, "Did you know she forced my hand?" The horses scattered, dashing into the fields. "Did you know? You sat here. Tried to pity me. Tried to get me to share my secrets!"

Brenor set a rag upon the table. "Forced your hand?"

"Lenora," Thealor growled.

Brenor stood before him, blank as ever.

"She stole the Coronam. She stole it right from under my nose! So I would be forced to choose between torture or a life with you people."

Brenor's brows furrowed at the insinuation. "We are your family."

"Why does everyone keep saying that? You don't know me. You feel a kinship to me because you are supposed to. Not because you want to."

"I feel a kinship toward you because as a young boy, I knew I had a big brother waiting for me somewhere. And every year I dreamed I could find you and bring you home."

"You were close to the idea of me," he scoffed, "nothing more."

Thealor slammed his fist into the support beam, shaking the stable, sending dust from the rafters. Standing weaponry tumbled to the floor in a clanking heap.

A tear threatened Brenor's eye. "I did not know what Lennie had done. Though I cannot say I am angry. She tried for days and you refused to go."

"She put me between two impossible choices."

Brenor spat a laugh of disbelief. "Leaving forced servitude to be free, to be with your family, is not an impossible choice."

Thealor stormed from where he came, a tornado walking. He had his guard duties, his routine battle with Duntaead, his room facing the mountain. He had learned to behave. To be honored. "My life was fine before you people."

Thealor packed his belongings, finding little to his name. When he finished, he went to the kitchen, loaded the remains of the beef hand pies, all the hazelnut and chocolate cookies Eran baked. He bit through the last of the brambleberry muffin, stale and hard, the taste bitter and tart as they said it would be.

He threw the rest of it into the flames below the iron cauldron.

Thealor thought of Arienne, the only amongst them he considered his family. He held the detheron root in the glass jar, dried bits falling to the bottom. There was only enough for Lenora when she went and no more. Two months remained before she would walk the bridge.

Lenora would never make it. She would never survive even if she had an entire field of the horseshit plant. Their plan had failed before it began. Thealor would have more use of it in the mountain than she would. He opened the glass jar and dumped the dried root into his pack.

A mercy killing would better serve Arienne.

Upstairs, Lenora's room was his final stop. She sat upon the edge of the bed, book in hand when he pressed through the door and demanded, "Give it to me."

"Are you leaving?"

"I said, give it to me," he spat.

Thealor was in no mood for a negotiation. She had no use for the stone other than to torture him. His hand held the hilt of his sword, though he did not move to take it from the sheath.

Lenora set her book below her, took wrapped cotton from the inside of the window seat, and handed the large sapphire to him. In the light he examined it, the violet hue when the sun shone upon it at the proper angle.

On thundering steps, Thealor took the long nautilus shell stairs two steps at a time, quaking the floor below him. The enormous doors bowed when he opened them; the loud weight angry below rotting hinges. He left it open, walking the dirt road beyond the long dead peonies, the vines dehydrated and blackened, and his nose smelling nothing but char.

Thealor attempted a whistle, meant to catch one of the horses. Luscan trotted off beyond the stables and Belcen and Aurometti stayed far inside the fields. Disgruntled, he thundered along the dirt road on foot.

Jogging to catch him, Brenor shouted, "Theo!"

"I didn't want to be here in the first place," he said, his ferocious pace undeterred. "I'm free of my chains. If that's truly all you wanted, you won't stop me."

"I do not want you to leave." Brenor struggled to match his pace. "And, what of Arienne? You felt a kinship to her."

Thealor pulled the pack up onto his shoulder. "Arienne died twenty-three years ago."

Brenor stopped in the dirt, watching his back. "We are your family."

"I have no family," muttered Thealor, uncaring if the boy he once called brother heard him or not.

WHERE LIGHT FADES

The girl sat between her parents, bundled in her mother's shawl. Dust clung to the wheels, while the sun dipped low behind them. They spoke little as they journeyed north. The girl said nothing, watching the sky where she hoped to see the islands hanging like forgotten moons.
- *Walk the Vanishing Path*, Faiseus Rancesla Auro, 1836

Before Sissel arrived at The Reldory, she envisioned hanging chains, ropes to bind her arms, sharp blades, claws, clamps for removing teeth, spikes below the fingernails. Nothing of that nature lived here. The torture crawled—a crumb of humanity worn each day; a granule of your body, drained by the lack of food along with granule by granule of your sanity.

Knowing you were unwanted—despised, even—was an odd type of torture. Hidden away, no one wanted to remember you, no one wished to care for you, to ensure you survived. The South Sea hoped you would toss yourself into the abyss, end your own life, so they would not have to provide you food. Your life meant nothing. The black crow on the wall had more value. At least he offered a morsel of sustenance.

The rocks kept the room cool during the summer and sheltered from the frigid winds of winter. The room had one pillow and one blanket amongst them. Whoever the unlucky soul was destined to sleep on the floor received both the pillow and the blanket since the stone created such an inhospitable environment. During the coldest parts of the winter, the three huddled on the small cot of wooden planks, one curled into the next, trying to gain any illusion of warmth.

Sometimes the guards forgot to feed them. When they remembered, it was nothing but scraps, only enough for one. When an occasional crow flew overhead and lingered too long, the guards shot it with a bow, ravaging most of the body. They would eat the good parts and send the prisoners the innards. The raw vegetables from Uen'can lasted three lowerings of the tray. Now, all the food remaining was crusted bread which hurt to put weak teeth upon. They soaked the crust in a few drops of water from the leaking pipe to ensure it felt less like a rock when their teeth crashed upon it.

How long can I survive this way?

Sissel now understood why there were only two dozen doors and many unoccupied. Humans do not want to live suspended between life and death. They accepted the one courtesy the guards provided.

Struggling not to die was not life.

Death would be more forgiving.

Her own body had begun to waste away. The bones of her pelvis rose further each day, mountain peaks upon a previously even plain. She thought of when she first arrived in Tanes. Though the first few weeks provided no one to speak to, she was at least given food. Even when Kaloyein threw food onto the dirt ground she ate more.

Sissel was fortunate to have Dylia, though on occasion her optimism grew aggravating. She knew she needed to converse, lest she go mute as Arienne. Even still, Sissel talked to her skeleton often, a beating heart coupled with a thin layer of skin covering bones. Arienne watched Sissel when she spoke, her violet eyes engaged—and moving—on occasion even when her body was not.

Sometimes even that motion appeared painful. How long this woman hovered on the threshold of death's door without walking through was astonishing. Perhaps Sissel would leap if she had been there as long as Arienne—allow her body to feel the rush of air enveloping her for some seconds before meeting whatever dwelled upon the ground below.

Near every part of Arienne was gray, even her skin. When Arienne allowed her violet pupils to be shown, the whites around them were dark with broken blood vessels. It was hard to tell what color her hair would have been, now a matted and dirtied charcoal, though Sissel imagined it to be pale. She never washed it. Sissel wondered how it did not itch. Her head itched. Perhaps hers would stop, too, after long enough.

"Only a few more weeks 'til the winds change." Dylia grinned. "Then we can open the door and see the sun, honey. That's a good day comin'."

Upon her arrival, Dylia insisted she and Arienne track the days of their imprisonment. They tracked the weather, and Uen'can, growing ever accustomed to its patterns. Upon Sissel's arrival they carved their traditional notches upon the floor. They often discussed a time when the beauty of the etchings stretched across all their available space. Dylia spent her days ensuring each line matched in perfect depth, length, and width to the others, allowing her eyes to rest upon a peaceful piece of art and not the haphazard scribblings of a child which had been there in earlier days.

When they dared to check for spring weather, the open air nipped, the wind stealing their warmth. After Uen'can, it took six and a half days to warm themselves from the bitter cold. Sissel still felt the frigid bite of the stairs against her soles.

Now, for the first time in many weeks, she had something to hope for.

Every few days, Sissel used the pump in the wall to force clean water into the bucket. She pressed the lever repeatedly, until the water swelled in the pipes, and her arm grew fatigued. She had no soap, but the water was clean and refreshing, as if it were pumped directly in from the mountain spring. Although she longed to bathe in a warm, ceramic pool, and she was not truly as clean as she wished, the frigid waters eased her tension.

The light gray and cream fabric darkened in color. She was determined to wash her clothes as well, regardless of how cold she would be while they took their time to dry in their dwelling. "Why do they not provide a change of clothes?" Sissel scrubbed the clothing in the confinement of the bucket, careful not to allow water to drip out onto the floor. Her jaws chattered and her arms struggled to react to her repetitive motions, expecting her fingers to crack like ice shards.

Dylia huddled into Arienne for warmth, tucking her knees into her chest. "They don' offer any kindness to livestock, either."

Sissel offered to wash Dylia and Arienne's clothes. Arienne's violet eyes grew harsh, her brows creased. At least she understood when Sissel spoke. Dylia accepted after some prodding, removing her clothing, before she returned to Arienne's side below the warmth of the blanket.

"Does the smell bother you?" Sissel asked.

Dylia shrugged. "I can't notice, but that took years."

Sissel finished her task, wrung them out with her bony and aching fingers, and set them across the floor to dry. Dylia held out her arm for Sissel to join them below the wool blanket.

It seemed to not take the two women long to adapt to her company, almost as if she has always been there with them. At first, she had been self-conscious, but fearing to use the washroom in the waste bucket, soon faded. A new normal was realized. Nudity was irrelevant; her body was no longer her own, born of a raw need for survival in which any proprietary tendencies were lost.

The rattling winds returned memories of the day Sissel arrived. "I could've sworn I heard something on Uen'can before I took the bridge.

As if the wind itself sang. But it was so faint, soft. Almost calming." Sissel slipped down the side of the wall and sat upon the cool floor.

Dylia smiled, pressing her lips, and whistling a soft melody.

The song was real and not a melody her mind created to ease her. "That was you?"

"Arienne told me long ago she used to whistle the song, a tune she played on the strings when she lived with her papa. When they were in the forest, they'd whistle to let one another know they were close by."

Dylia glanced over at Arienne, asleep, curled in the ball she was often tucked into. "She whistled the melody every Uen'can when I arrived ... when she still could. I started doing it for her when she was unable. It's a silly ritual. Like carvin' the notches on the floor. Nuthin'll ever come of it. But it makes her happy." Dylia ran a tender hand over Arienne's side, like a mother nurturing her baby asleep in a crib. "She told me when she was in her first years here, the whistles returned from the landside. She swore it. Every Uen'can. Then after a few years they stopped."

"It's hard to believe she ever spoke," Sissel said.

"She did. She told me many things. Things in small pieces. A story of her life I put together over the years. But that's when she was strong enough."

"How long have you been here?"

"I came in the Uen'can of winter, as you. Eighteen years ago, now."

"Eighteen years," Sissel gasped. "The guard made it seem as if it was only a few." She had never taken the time to count the notches, thousands displayed across the walls, assuming perhaps others calculated their time long before Dylia and Arienne.

"Time's funny here. Moves fast an' slow all at once. Arienne was almost twelve. I was nineteen, honey."

"The guard said she killed all those who came before you. He called her *timaca*. Do you know what it means?"

"He thinks she's a demon. *Timaca* means tiger. That's the old way of speaking. Though, what he told you was true. She told me from her own lips." Dylia snickered at the thought. "Even starved within inches of death, she's a tiger amongst swine. She told me those who came before claimed to be her friend, but they meant her harm. Whispers inside her head told her they spoke lies. Told her right away if they were friend or enemy. She pushed them back out the door from where they came long before the guards pulled the stairs to their home."

Sissel sat dumbfounded. She found it incomprehensible for a pulse and bones to be so terrifying.

"The whispers are on your side, or you'd be in the fog with the others. The stairs are put away." Dylia ran her hand over the notches. "On my Uen'can, I had the same guard. He told me he put the ones he wanted to die with her. She does his work for him. He has less mouths to feed and he don' have their dead souls on his hands. She never told me how many—only said the guards smiled when they brought the prisoners here."

"Ah," Sissel lamented, wide-eyed, now understanding the wishes of the guard who led her to her cell. At least they had not put the young girl in there with them. "How have you come to live so long, then? The two of you together?"

"I can't ease her pain, not the pain of her body. But I can calm her nerves." Dylia smiled. "She feels at ease."

"You can calm her nerves?" Sissel thought of what Ronan had said—it was considered rude to ask someone their lineage, though she wanted to know what people Dylia was from.

Dylia heard her silent plea, replying with a smirk before Sissel had the courage to ask the question. "It is alright, honey. Nothin' much offends me. Perhaps a proper introduction is long overdue. Dylia Canhenti Umbrovetck, of the Meresavas of Cascanvore ... amongst other things."

Sissel grinned; she had never heard Dylia speak so well mannered. "The Meresavas placate people?"

Dylia nodded.

"I only know of the lineages of Tenuel, and some from The South Sea. I have heard the names over the years, but I do not know them all." The door pressed, wind seeping in. Her thoughts ran away from her, expecting shards of wood upon the door might crumble before her. "What if you get hurt or sick?"

"I assume that's another reason they don't put locks on the doors." Dylia raised an eyebrow.

"A young girl was brought in when I was. I did not know they brought children here."

"The same reason you were brought 'ere. It's for the hidden, not the villainous. Though, at times, the two may intermingle. Arienne was seven when she was brought here."

"Seven?" Sissel shuddered to think of it, though she thought the girl with the stuffed rabbit would not be much older.

Arienne was now awake, her face despondent.

"The girl that came the day I did was close to nine, if I were to guess. They burned her rabbit." Sissel could still hear the button meet the stone, the sound of the wood rolling before it twisted and found a place to rest still fresh in her ears.

"Kids are more dangerous than adults in some circles. They speak freely of matters they shouldn'. Can't control their abilities or their tongues. Lucky, though, they are often less powerful than adults, trained in the ways of their lineage before they grow."

Dylia turned to Arienne. "She's fadin'. More the last five months than the last five years. I don' know what to do for her."

Sissel held the crust of bread, wet with the drops of mountain water. She learned to count the drips below the pipe—four drops, each side, and it wouldn't fall apart as wet sand between her fingers. Below the blanket, she tucked her knees under herself, holding the soggy crust to Arienne. "You need to eat. I've barely seen you eat anything for weeks."

Somewhere deep a shred of a human hid behind the violet eyes. Sissel waited, hoping she might reply. "Do you understand me when I speak to you?" Arienne offered no answer, but Sissel knew she could. "Do you want me to tell you a story?"

"Is it about a man?" Dylia interjected, curling closer, her knees tucked into her chest.

"No, a story my grandmother told me long ago. How she took on seventeen soldiers of the Khayernamen in Mount Yelnaone by herself and lived to tell the tale." It was one of Sissel's favorite stories her grandmother used to tell, though she was unsure of the validity. She did not know if it had been stretched miles high over the years.

Arienne's eyes lit, and though Sissel could not tell with certainty, she suspected a muscle of her lips curved. "You need to take a few bites, though." Sissel held the bread out so that she might agree.

Dylia sat at her side, taking the bread from Sissel's hand. Arienne dropped her lip, and Dylia fed her tiny morsels, tearing the crust and pressing them into her cracked mouth. They dissolved against her tongue. Arienne drank from the tin cup Dylia held while Sissel told her grandmother's stories. Stories she prayed would make Arienne forget her pain for a moment.

Stories of adventure, danger, and lost love.

Stories of sunshine in the darkness.

THE ODDS

"Henceforth, let it be decreed: no child shall be born of two regions. Should such a union produce issue, the punishment shall be death of the child, carried out without delay or exception."

- Law of Larrone Duren, 841

Lenora's chest tightened. She had yet to eat.

Four—not five—sat around the small fire in the kitchen, burning below the wide iron pot. The flames cracked and popped, loud in the silence her family refused to fill. The space between them lingered, the way no one spoke his name. Her stomach clenched, but she didn't flinch.

I made the right call. He wouldn't leave Brouverg Castle.

Justified or not, the silence felt like punishment.

Ariaas eyed the flames crackling in the hearth. "He just wandered off. Into the darkness."

Brenor nudged Lenora with his elbow. He pressed at her with his boot when she did not speak, pressuring her with a knowing glare. Lenora did her best to ignore him.

Brenor pressed again.

Ariaas addressed their silent bickering. "What is it?"

Lenora bit her lip. She did not wish to discuss why Thealor departed—did not wish to own up to her role in his indignation. The news would likely send Ariaas's temper flaring. She had seen Ariaas enraged, but he had never been furious with her. She'd sprung at the chance to twist Thealor's hand at Brouverg Castle. They had little time to free Thealor, and she had one more chance to get to the hatch. However, her actions had an unforeseen outcome.

Ariaas stared at her, lips drawn.

After some time dwelling within their silent gaping, Lenora conceded. "At Brouverg Castle, Thealor would not leave. Time was not on our side. I thought he needed some ...*pressure.*"

Ariaas's spine straightened. "What kind of pressure?"

"While the two of you argued ... I ..." Lenora's sights ran to each of them in turn, wishing to avoid their reaction. "I ... took the Coronam. Replaced it with one of the replicas on display."

Ariaas's lip fell open. "I didn't even see you."

Lenora gestured to his neck, the wound long healed and scarred in tattered pink and tan flesh. "Both of you were busy with other matters."

"You didn't think you should help me?"

Lenora replayed the day's scenarios, prioritizing the direst situation. "It didn't look fatal." Though, at his stark expression, a pang of guilt shot through her. "Are you angry with me?"

"I cannot decide. On one side of the coin, Thealor is free. He might not be otherwise. On the other hand, our chances with Arienne are nearly gone. Gained one, lost the other."

"And Sissel," Brenor added.

Ariaas muttered, *"Shit,"* his fingers rubbing the bridge of his nose. He kept forgetting her, didn't he? Ariaas pursed his lips and scratched the scruff on his chin. "Perhaps, it would have been better if you kept matters to yourself and not told him."

"You told me it was the last chance I had to make it to the hatch. I had to do something I had not done before, and I decided to ... make him angry."

"Did it work?"

She grinned a sad grin. Ariaas rubbed his temples. Her tactics had been clever, though they did result in some unintended consequences.

Eran asked, "Will we go after him?"

"We?" Ariaas countered. *"We* went to Mount Ohbrolis so he could be a free man. Going after him would only make him feel more caged." Ariaas shook his head. "If he does not wish to be here, he should not be forced. I hope he returns once he has had the chance to calm."

"Will we still go to The Reldory as planned?"

"I found the detheron roots. I found a way to keep you strong in there." Eran nodded, seemingly warming to the idea.

Ariaas scrubbed his hand down his face. "It's impossible to take the bridge with two on the outside. Even if I stayed back, not even three. Not without two on the inside." He swirled the bottle of whiskey, eyeing the brown liquid turning inside the glass. "The plan barely worked with two on the inside, three out. We have found nothing new in these long months. The plan to put the two of us on the inside was the only one of any merit."

"We still must go." Lenora sat straight in her chair as the realization of his relinquishment washed over her. "You cannot abandon them."

"You cannot truthfully believe we can get in and get out unscathed with only the four of us."

"They know I am gone. They know Thealor is gone," Lenora urged. "How long will they leave Arienne be? They will kill her for the simple fact we do not get to her. *This may be the only chance we have.*" Blood boiled in her veins.

"Thealor was a highly skilled warrior. As skilled as Brenor. Without him, matters are significantly more complicated." Ariaas turned the bottle after each sip as if it would speak wisdom to him.

Lenora turned to Brenor. "I know you, of all people, will offer a direct answer. What are the odds of success at The Reldory without Thealor?"

"I would say, before, when he was still with us, if we went ten times, we might succeed one. Now, one out of a hundred or worse. There will be three dozen people, guards, prisoners, soldiers at the landside. That does not include who is on the inside."

"What is your vote, then?" Lenora asked him. "Will you go? When you know the odds?"

Brenor twitched his untied boots.

Lenora turned to Eran and Ariaas. All three men refused to meet her eyes.

No. Her stomach clenched, and her lungs tightened.

She could not recall Arienne, yet in the near year she had spent with Ariaas and Brenor, she found pieces of her everywhere. The secondhand stories Brenor told, the old clothes she found in Arienne's room, the dried violet flowers woven into a crown. They could not abandon her.

They could not.

Ariaas was accustomed to it—twice a year deciding to leave her another six torturous months—but Lenora was not.

"I won't go unless a new plan is agreed upon," Ariaas lamented. "It's settled."

"It is not settled," Lenora argued. It was not right. Nothing about this was right. "We must still go this Uen'can as planned." She turned once more, hoping they would second her refutation. Not one met her eyes, no one willing to speak aloud.

She shouted, "We must!"

Ariaas grasped his whiskey by the neck and departed.

Brenor and Eran stood to follow, the latter patting her on the shoulder before he left. "Tomorrow we will search for a new plan," he said.

Lenora stood alone beside the hearth—defeat weighing thick in her chest.

✦ ——— ·+·✦·+· ——— ✦

Lenora pressed quill to paper.

You said you'd be there if I needed you, right?

Eternally.

She clenched her fist around the quill. Was there any other way?

They've abandoned her.

The response was immediate.

Abandoned Arienne? Then they've abandoned us all.

She swallowed hard. If Brenor was willing to leave Arienne and Sissel, who else did she have now? Lines weaved beneath her hand.

I need you.

Oedd's script appeared before her ink was dry.

I'm already on my way.

MADDENING ENIGMAS

"For when you arrive to view yourself, your natural instincts will betray you. For the only one who knows your instincts better than your conscious mind is your subconscious mind. You will never win a battle against yourself without behaving with complete and utter disregard for your instincts' instructions."

-*My Self Reflection*, Faiseus Rancesla Auro, 1828

L enora tossed in her bed, watching night rain shadows shift like smoke—unreliable, just like their plans. Every time she closed her eyes, the image Brenor painted of Arienne flared behind her lids. She tapped her foot.

Oedd is on the way. He will help.

But ... what if he can't? What if I am wrong about him?

She stripped the blanket from her legs. The hallway to the library yawned before her. If there was something—*anything*—that could answer this enigma, it was hiding there, between the pages and half-remembered margins.

Something she missed.

Her fingers trailed the spines of novels and histories she'd studied endless times. She knew of the warring lineages and those of Cascanvore. She knew more of Dhaesreaon than anyone would ever wish to know, and secrets held by ancestors in Niera. She knew the ways of death and so many of Monera's pins. But no matter how she'd studied the text, no path revealed itself to the hanging cage.

She sighed.

Is it all for nothing?

A low *click*.

A segment of shelf slid open with a breathy *shhnk*, revealing a narrow gap, soft golden light seeping out like the sunrise through fog.

Lenora stared. For a moment, she couldn't move, couldn't believe after all the hours, the searching, the doubting—*something answered*.

Her legs moved before her mind caught up.

A desk, small and warped with age, was littered with jagged rows of half burning candles and strewn with parchment. The air smelled of ink, wax, and something faintly metallic. Papers hung from the high walls—pinned or nailed—holding scribbles and annotations. A winding iron staircase led upward into darkness. Dust floated like ash in the golden light. Notes overlapped diagrams, dates scratched out and re-written.

She approached the desk, focusing on a note written in a familiar hand.

Faiseus Auro knows. He knows.

Her pulse jumped. She stepped closer, brushing dust from the hanging pages. The parchment greeted her in three languages—one familiar, one she assumed to be Nieran, and one veiled in etched symbols.

This was no simple archive.

This was *obsession*.

A page in scribbled ink caught her eye.

scattered twenty-three western winds,

old man for years attempts in vain

She read the final portion of the passage aloud. "Reclaim our darkened, weary fate. Seek truths beyond the gilded gate. Of captive children, none remain. All now released from tortured pain. Now go, the freed, journey in haste. Seek me, the stars, and gilded gates."

Lenora swallowed. *Had Ariaas written this?*

His notes beside the verse read, "Twenty-three years. Twenty-three years. Twenty-three years. I am not old, and I will not wait in vain!"

The door creaked open behind her. A gust of cooler air swept in, stirring the parchment. Somehow, she knew it was Ariaas.

His eyes moved from the chaos on the walls to her face. For a breath, neither of them spoke—only the quiet hiss of burning wax between them.

"How long have you been in here?"

"The door to this room opened. It opened so intently I thought someone was on the other side asking me to come in. I expected to see you or Brenor, but ... instead ... I found ..."

What have I found? Her finger searched the notes and crumbled pages nailed to the shelves, trembling. She raised a page littered with symbols, parchment so old it might crumble and decay beneath her grip. "What is this madness?"

"The truth," Ariaas muttered. "And if you hold it like that, it'll be lost forever." He grasped the page as delicately as he could.

"I'm unsure what I expected. Where you snuck off to at night." Lenora stiffened. "Is this it?"

"I know how mad it looks. But how else could I connect these dots, the lines of text, the intricacies of the works left for *me* to find?"

She shook her head. "What was left for you to find?"

Ariaas stared into her eyes, seeming to judge her. For the first time, she felt like he didn't trust her the way she thought he did.

"There are too many pieces. I can't make sense of it." Lenora trailed over the image of a tiger and the coded symbols. She moved to the obsidian box and the scribbles in Ariaas's hand. "This poem—The Gilded Gate. Did you write this?"

"That poem outdates me by many centuries."

"*Centuries?*" Lenora crossed her arms, her tone deepening. "Why have you been keeping this from us?"

"It's difficult to predict how people will behave. Most want an interesting topic of conversation for their next dinner party."

Lenora shouted, "You meant to make me a fool!"

"I never wanted anything from you," scoffed Ariaas. "The tales of the long dead need not affect your choices with the living."

"There could be something here we could have used! How did you find this? Where did the box from Faiseus Auro come from? This says there's a fifth!"

"There is no fifth."

Lenora frowned, and waves of hair fell over her brow. "I have many questions."

Ariaas snorted a laugh. "Well, that much is quite obvious."

"Do not answer my questions that way. Tell me." Lenora held the tiger sketch, crinkling the parchment beneath her grasp. "What is this madness? A straight answer, this time."

Ariaas skimmed the corridor of books and windows lining the eastern fields, grasping an iron bar. The shelf twisted and closed, trapping the two behind the confines of the private office. He struck the winding staircase frame with a closed fist, and a bottle of whiskey revealed itself. A thin layer of brown liquid swirled at the bottom, and he twirled it until it mixed to his liking. "I'll kill you without hesitation if you breathe a word of this to anyone. Do you understand me?"

She bit an ironic laugh. "No, you won't."

Ariaas sighed. "I know." He gulped the elmounay, exhaling the burn. "Eran would pass out if he found this."

Lenora flew to the shelf, tearing a poem from a tack. "This is in your handwriting."

Her heart thundered as the image of beasts in war littered her mind. One letter, one poem, one word after the next connecting a series of events that had already transpired and some that stood before them in time. "I don't claim to be the wisest, but this poem alone speaks novels."

Lenora trailed the scribblings. "If you didn't write it, a Meiderie must have seen this if it is as old as you say? The author knew we would be taken. How long we'd be held?"

She waited for corroboration. Instead, Ariaas drank the last of the bottle with a large swig. Lenora cried, exasperated, "The Meiderie died out centuries ago!"

"Sit. And stop panicking. I can only answer one question at a time."

"Telling someone not to panic isn't helpful." Lenora stomped her weathered sock. "Don't dance around the answers. From the beginning."

"What to do?" he muttered to himself. "When I first moved to Aroun Vaer, I explored the tunnels. I found the box we took to Mount Ohbrolis—the original books from Faiseus Auro. Inside was all you see here." Ariaas gestured about the cluttered space. "Lest a few notes and translations in the Old Tongue. Those I wrote. Findings. Research of the writings." He tore a page from a nail splintering into the wood, handing it to Lenora. "This letter was on top."

Dear A.H.E,
When you are ready, find me.
Signed, F.R.A, First Month of Summer, 1850

Lenora whispered, pausing with each befuddled word, "Ariaas. Haran. Ebronds."

He opened the brass hinge, revealing the eight novels, on their covers, vines formed a gate in gold foil. "I thought it was a coincidence for many years. I even embarked on a journey to *find him* after Sarinah died. But I never found his remains.

"When you came of age, the King of the Yurelan planned to use their predicted power to conquer The South Sea. The number of children never mattered. Canen Dera didn't matter. To them, you are weapons ... deities of a sort. But The South Sea would never let a group of illegal renegades wield something so dangerous. So, under Queen Navaera's order, you were taken—scattered across the land and peaks. Now, you stand between two sides of a silent war."

Lenora exhaled, his eyes locked on the floor. *Power. It was always about power.*

It was almost as if Ariaas spoke her thoughts aloud.

"When I found the others, you were already gone. I watched the wealthy claim Thealor; The Reldory swallowed Arienne. After that time, I eventually returned to the works. The box. The letter."

With Ariaas's drink finished, he picked up a sharp blade meant for opening letters and pressed the tip firmly into his thumb. "The poem then made sense. All the words as if they were meant for me to hear. Dear *A-H-E*. That's how I learned you would find freedom in the twenty-third year. And *I* would not be the one to set matters into motion. Though, it was impossible to sit by while some lunatic dead author tells you what to do. Or what not to do."

"Brenor thought you were a descendant of a Meiderie."

"No. No. This centuries-old hogwash told me. I have no gifts. I have an old box with poems and scribbles made by a corpse—a box that made me question my sanity many times."

Lenora slumped to the floor at his side. "Then what is the purpose of all this? The scribblings. The maps, the symbols. This poem, speaking of what happened?"

"I'd be guessing," Ariaas huffed. "I have no proof."

"Please. Guess."

"Someone had answers, but of course, they'd die before they could spill them. Answers maybe to questions even we don't have. They left their secrets the only way they knew." To survive prying eyes, looters, The Army of the South Sea, the Yurelan snakes, the decay of time, the weathering of the written word, along with the weathering of anyone's care to read the long-dead history."

"How long have you had all this?

"Not long." Ariaas's lips downturned, calculating, his hands resting peacefully on his knees. "Ninety years. Give or take some months. I took some years away from trying to solve its messages somewhere in the middle. My skills are not well suited to coded letters and hidden languages."

"Ninety years." Lenora studied the leather bindings, the gold embossing of a gate spanning their covers. "These books ... I thought you were so cruel not to sell them in Ohbrolis if they bought Thealor back."

"And what would be the point of that? Buy his present, lose his future."

"They're just books. Adventures."

He smiled faintly, but his eyes remained hard. "I know. I've read them."

"The Meiderie delivered the prophecy at the end of the First Age," Lenora recited what she'd learned. "More than a thousand years. The story depicts us as savages, beasts."

Ariaas leaned forward. "Ah, see, there is a key difference. Canen Dera is certainly ancient. Twelve hundred years predicting our doom with eight cryptic images." He dramatized with his hands the fanfare, the bullshit. "But Canen Dera doesn't mention beasts. Never mentions animals at all. Just a bunch of pictures the geriatrics spend ages deciphering.

"However, *the story* does mention beasts. Another old fable based on the prophecy. The paintings depict the writings of the fable." Ariaas dragged out a drawing, a tiger amongst a chaotic battle of beasts. "Each child meant to be symbolized by a different animal." Ariaas gestured to the pencil sketches of animals fighting amongst flames, the blood, the carnage. A bear. A stag. A cardinal. A wolf. A tiger.

"Beasts in war."

Lenora recounted all she knew. "The fable was written nearly four hundred years ago. In 1834. The story of *A Tigress in the Wood* was written by ..." Lenora followed the mystery, eyeing the works hanging by their rusted nails. "... Faiseus Auro." She stumbled on her own words. "And if he wrote this, and the fable, and left the box, perhaps the author sides in our favor."

"Yes, there's that," Ariaas added. "Or he's a dead madman laying an elaborate trap for us. Enjoying his spoils from beyond the pyre."

Lenora's hands trembled as she sifted through the pages, each line unraveling a thread of narrative she'd now been told was her truth. These writings weren't of ruin or inevitability; they were splintering paths, branching from darkness into possibilities. Something new. "What am I missing? I can't see how this all comes together."

Ariaas shook his head. "This labyrinth had already bested me."

"Does Brenor know?"

"No. Certainly not."

"Why have you not told him? He can handle it."

"Knowing this is as useful as putting butter on a broken bone. You want him to live with more predetermined choices? More than you already have? No damn free will? You want to be puppets on strings? No. *No.* I've lived that way far too long. I've seen it eat the life out of Brenor. It's no way to live. It's its own cage, I'll tell you that.

"Over my dead body will my grandchildren focus on this maddening enigma while Arienne lingers in squalor. Plus, I have no desire to delve into a never-ending abyss of questions. Not when we have actual priorities to focus on."

"We will seek the truth when Arienne is free?" Lenora asked, though she already knew her own answer. Her insides tugged at her, begged her to find the answers *now*.

Ariaas sighed. "Perhaps."

She asked the question that had been biting at the edge of her tongue. "What purpose do you think it serves? The colors of our eyes being so bright?"

Ariaas pressed his lips into a thin line. "There are animals of vibrant colors, those born in the South and the West. In nature ... it serves as a warning."

"A warning of what?"

"To leave you be."

NOTUME

Naen Belsrem Ramunan, Sengura of the Noslarrar, The Breaker of Bones,
The Raven
Born: Second Month of Summer, 1984
Deceased: First Month of Spring, 2062
Children: One

- *Official Ledger of The South Sea*

Thealor clutched the Coronam in his pocket, questioning its authenticity.

Lenora's demeaning theft of his sapphire must have been a ruse—a belittling ploy meant to rattle his senses. And yet, each time he focused on the stone, violet reflected from the sun's rays. Hourly, he repeated this process, a wave of fury crashing with every repetition of this addiction.

Lady Brouverg might forgive his long departure if he returned home to Mount Ohbrolis, claiming he followed the thief until he retrieved her prize. If not, where else would he go? He only traveled outside Mount Ohbrolis once prior and owned no map after his brash exodus.

He followed the dirt road beyond Ebrolie's small cottage. Lines of sheltered green leaves lay in a pristine curated sanctuary.

Vegetables. No meat.

Thealor grasped the stems and yanked the plants from their burrows.

Carrots. Radishes. I loathe radishes.

Grumbling, he stole the orange stalks and the red bulbs—better to have more than less—abandoning the green remains to the earth.

Hours he wandered through the forest while the trees condensed, the foliage clumped, and nature commanded he veer around an old grove of evergreens. His innards hollowed. He reached a clearing at the base of a mountain. Rocks wound through the trees from their tumble from the slopes before they found proper resting places. Snow piled up the crumbling face. He had reached a mountain.

But not his mountain. Mount Ykkoro.

Behind him, footsteps crunched on the forest floor. Someone followed him—a fact that became clearer the further he stepped from the thick trees.

First, he suspected Brenor before the knotting in his stomach spoke otherwise. Few options dwelled amongst the trees. Stay amongst the evergreens to veer south, or turn further north toward the mountain's base.

After a short deliberation, Thealor pressed north. His shadow would be easier to lose in the peaks.

He trekked toward the base, the snow, and the frigid air, his toes numbing. Eventually, he lost trace of the shadow's sounds and sheltered himself in a small cave. He stayed in this cavern, shivering, hiding, growing in his rage at the woman whom he reluctantly shared blood with. The trees provided little branches, and he took them all to create a small flame.

Eventually, as if he had forgotten the need, his body craved nourishment. Eran's root had worked wonders to satiate his appetite. He opened his pack to find the hand-pies squished, squandering the carrots, saturating what remained of the detheron root with days-old gravy. He screamed from his core. He launched the rotted vegetables from the cave, dotting the evening's pristine fallen snow in rotted muck.

Food was scarce in the snow. A hunter can only be skilled in a land with prey.

Below Thealor's feet, snow melted by the midday sun and froze again by the cold of the night. As the fire dwindled, his toes lost all feeling, and his hunger morphed into deafening nausea. He marched to find food, but the further he departed from the cave, the more numbness crept up his appendages.

After three days, he caved to the snowy floor on his knees, digging for the remains of the detheron root. He retched and gagged several times before he forced the slop into his stomach. When satiated, he dragged a stick through the muck, intending to write a scripted letter B, the emblem of Brouverg Castle. Though he repeated this action, he could not make it appear the same or place what was incorrect. After several attempts, he scrawled over it, snapping the stick.

He burned parts of the shirt, first the cuff, then the sleeve, to keep the embers alive.

Mountain dwelling calloused him. He moved his hand, trying to touch his nose without success. Staying on the mountain much longer would claim his life. Few options lay before him. He needed to brighten the fire, but just as yesterday, there were no trees, no more kindling.

Would the Lady of the Mountain take him back? The jacket wouldn't fit anymore. She would construct another. He grazed the scars beneath his cloak, recalling metal crawling into his flesh.

The rumors of his family replayed: the *power*, the *power*, the *power*, the *destruction*.

Horseshit.

Power only existed in his fighting skills. And in fighting, he learned all he ever needed.

Thealor attempted to will the fire in front of him many times.

"Dance," he commanded.

The petite flame ignored his wishes.

Many years earlier, a visitor to Lord Brouverg spoke in Nieran when he willed walls of air into glass. Thealor stared at the flame intently. He barely knew words of the Old Tongue, though he attempted many variables and accents. He groaned. His memory failed to recall any translations.

A word came to him, not *dance*, as he had wished. The word *rise*. He crouched before the small flame. *"notume."*

His petite flame rose at his instruction. He scrambled to his feet, summoning from the depth of his core, the embers to grow from their infant state. He shouted, "notume!"

The flame burst to the ceiling in a fierce and thunderous column. It bowed to the stone above, winding itself over the roof in an orange-domed sky. Thealor stumbled onto his rump.

He righted himself, warming his toes with deep satisfaction.

Suddenly, all had become clear. He would depart south at first light.

+ ——————— · + · ✦ · + · ——————— +

Rivers dashed aside Qerilan's stone streets between the glass high-rises. The people of these lineages were not shy about showing off their gifts, and Thealor might have appreciated the splendor had hunger not overwhelmed him. A woman passed, shielding her children's eyes. Two other parties encountered him this same way: fearful. He supposed his general appearance frightened them—the stature of a giant with the eyes of a demon.

Thealor followed the scent of baking bread, finding a shop full of pastries and sourdough baguettes. Outside the window, half a crust of burnt bread lay tossed from the baker's window. But, with his newfound abilities, he refused to eat like a dog. He walked inside.

"I'll take a fresh roll. Actually, make that ten." When the baker gave him the same fearful, down-turned lips as the passersby, he smiled. "And I won't be paying."

An hour he observed Qerilan's sights, warm and full. He sat on a bench admiring the canals. From behind his back, he heard, "You, there!"

Behind him, two men rode horseback in gray cloaks. The baker must have summoned the authorities. How uninspiring. However, these were no men of Dhaesreaon in furs and leathers. Some of the crowd thinned against the soft flowing canals, while others shielded themselves behind the corners of the buildings.

Thealor turned himself back to admire the view.

"I said, you, there!" the soldier shouted. "What is your name, boy?"

"Boy?" With an annoyed chuckle, he stood, allowing them complete visibility of his size. Thealor's stature made the men appear as children, regardless of age. "Do I look like a *boy* to you?"

The older of the two wore a silver raven pinned to his chest, shining against his black cloak and black hair. He'd seen Lenora study this in the library: the raven, Noslarrar, The Breaker of Bones. "We seek a man who escaped from Mount Ohbrolis in the north. Tall like you," he spat. "Scarlet eyes."

Thealor pretended to examine their pins, though he knew the symbols of The South Sea well. "Who seeks this man?"

"Orders of King Barrard I," the old raven said. "Come with us."

"Where are we going?"

The younger spouted, "Come with us; no fighting, now." The Roscidarra raised his fingers to the hilt of his blade. So delicate, this young rose, he might as well have petals for hair.

Curiosity outweighed any fear Thealor might have with this young rose and old raven. Was he one of them? Able to control bone and life? No one lay dying currently for the Roscidarra to trade him with. And Thealor had broken bones in his past, not that he wanted to relive them. But he desperately wanted to know ...

Thealor pressed away his heavy cloak, revealing the large sword of Khayernamen at his side. "I'll go wherever I please."

The two drew their arms, holding their swords at attention. He waited. They would use their abilities on him, wouldn't they? Sure as the rising sun, the old raven whispered, "larard reh renues."

A sensation rose across Thealor's left arm, proliferating, dull aching akin to those he felt in sleep as a young boy. When his bones did not bend, the old raven's eyes widened, and panic spread across their hollowed jaws.

He pressed his lips taut to hide his rising smile, but a breath later, gave in and beamed. "Did you mean to break my arm?"

The old raven dismounted his steed, drawing his blade. "I don't know who you are, but you'll come along. No fighting, now."

Thealor grasped his longsword and swung over his shoulder. He had no further use for the Noslarrar. A swift death was merciful. After a brief parry, he sliced into the stomach of the old raven, spilling his blood onto the street.

He shook his head. Aside from Brenor, Thealor had yet to meet even a half-worthy adversary.

The young rose seized his companion's arm, sweat beading his brow. *"alus avem."*

He quivered and grasped tighter, repeating with great ferocity, *"alus avem!"*

Warmth radiated through Thealor's core, and his heart suddenly raced. "Did you mean to kill me? To trade my life for his before he died?" Now, he was pleased to have met them. "I suppose I owe you a thank you. Now I know the abilities of the Roscidarra and the Noslarrar bear no power over me."

Thealor slipped his longsword between the young man's ribs. Blood pooled in his mouth, gurgling as he drowned. As the life drained from him, Thealor lamented, "Your king should have told you who you hunted."

Thealor tore the pins from their bloodstained cloaks.

How exhilarating. In two days, he learned more than Lenora gleaned in all her months in the library. She could learn a thing or two from him. His plan may come to fruition sooner than he anticipated.

The onlookers gathered while the charcoal stallions snorted, agitated and riderless. No need to leave such beautiful creatures uncared for. Thealor mounted one of the beasts and calmed him as best he could.

Thealor departed through the city gates, riding until he reached the southern border of Dhaesreaon. The golden statue of an inverted star hung beside the road—before him stood the edge of The South Sea. Across the border, he secured the pin of the raven to his chest and stopped in front of a lone cottage, fire burning in soft billowing smoke from the chimney. A dark-haired man with crooked eyes answered the door.

"Pardon the intrusion, sir. I'm a soldier from Islarourne, sent on assignment from King Barrard to Qerilan. There was a skirmish, and I barely returned to the border unharmed." Thealor delivered his pitch with effortless confidence. "I managed to gather my horse before I escaped. I had hoped I could take shelter here. Gather myself. Perhaps share a few of your meals before I return to my post?"

Reluctantly, the man let him inside. The South Sea cared for their own, especially a soldier in blood-stained cloaks. The crooked-eyed man fed him and gave him fresh cloaks appropriate for a Noslarrar of The South Sea.

"I will stay for some days." Pleased with himself, Thealor ate pheasant and warmed himself beside the hearth. "And I need you to find me a book on the Old Tongue."

SHADOWED PROPOSITION

"Tell me why you follow me. I want to know who you are, and why my name
is in these books. The truth."
"I have spent many days, years even, imagining how the two of us would
meet for the first time. I must admit to you, this was certainly not within
those scenarios."

Aroun Vaer castle seemed to weep, the skies above Lenora morphing gray, solemn since the plan to rescue Arienne had been abandoned. Oedd had remained silent for days. Eran continued his search in the library for another plan. Every evening, he recounted his research to her over supper, obviously hopeless he could not aid them.

Her training continued with Ariaas and Brenor, and she hunted for their meals. In the dark, she practiced with her bow, her aim sharper by the day. Brenor threw objects into the air, first an apple, then a berry. They both celebrated the day he tossed an old gold ring he wore on his finger into the air, and she met the center into the waiting target.

Brenor had grown close to her over the months. They walked the interior line together, aiding Taren when he grew tired and fell over in a heap upon the grass. They built him a carrier the two used together to bring him back to the cottage when he grew weary, made of leather and metal clamps they could wear to suspend his weight between their shoulders.

The improvements to the castle were slow but steady. Eran had grown in his skills in the kitchen with books on recipes from every region in Monera, an act which seemed to please him immensely.

The four had settled into a gentle rhythm of life.

The air was still warm in the late setting sun, early summer upon them, when Eran moved a small table onto the terrace that they might eat outside for the evening overlooking the fields to the east. He prepared braised beef with baorguan cheese, soft loaves of buttered bread, olives, and berries.

The others joined him, exhausted beyond measure from their day. Ariaas shoveled food into his mouth, barely civilized enough to use a fork.

Lenora asked Eran, as she had every supper for weeks, "Did you have any luck today?"

"Not today," Eran lamented. "Tomorrow, I will move onto the books on the highest level. Who knows how long it has been since someone has been up there." Eran turned to Ariaas, but her grandfather merely shrugged through a mouthful of food.

The hair on Lenora's arms stood on end. As one, she and Brenor glanced up to the northern end of the terrace.

A slender man in a brown leather cloak and an arrogant smile sauntered in from the shadows. A long strip of muddied hide decorated his shoulders, a dozen gold rings pierced his ears, and his hands outstretched with peaceful intent.

Lenora stiffened. Ariaas reached for his sword.

As one would correct a young child, the man shook his finger, *tsk tsk*. "I mean you no ill will, Ariaas. No ill will." His voice resembled a sly crow, doused with awe and contentment. "I needed to see her. I needed to lay my own eyes upon her."

Ariaas pulled his hand from his hilt as a chill coursed through Lenora's body.

This man gaped, eying her from her knees, waist, chest, and shoulders, finally past her chin and to her eyes as if he savored the spectacle of a spring feast of delicacies he would soon consume. He closed the gap between them, his lips curving.

"My dark queen." Black paint coated his cheeks in fine lines, arching over his angular nose. He reached his quivering fingers to touch her cheek.

Lenora drew her dagger, pressing his hand with the blade's edge—a touch far gentler than he deserved. A caution not to anger an unknown enemy. His black eyes wandered again, first her eyes to her cheeks, then her flushed lips, her chin, the soft skin of her neck. Lingered far too long upon her flesh. His general appearance chilled her—something in his stance, manner of walking, gaze, and arrogant confidence in another's home.

Eran matched Ariaas's guarded stance, grasping a candelabra as a weapon. His voice trembled. "Who are you?"

"Who I am is of no consequence to you, Mr. Hoeleck. At least, not today." The angular man grinned. "You can return the candlestick to the table. You do not strike me as one to bludgeon."

Brenor pulled his sword from the sheath. Lenora expected he meant to truly use it should he be given the opportunity. "You cannot take her."

The man chuckled. "You mistake me for someone else. I am not in the business of procuring people against their will as the man you call king."

His sights returned to Lenora. He deeply inhaled through his nostrils. "You are quite stunning. I now see why they wished to tuck you away for their own. Your features are a perfect blend of Avaine and Gelhan. And those eyes." He smiled, enamored. "If flames burned green."

Lenora maintained her neat and confident posture while her knuckles whitened around the grip of her blade.

"Go on, now. Speak of why you have come," Ariaas barked. "I have no time for your games."

"I have come to offer you a gift."

Ariaas threatened with the bottle. "There is nothing you could offer we would take."

"Put that sad bottle down. No need to waste the stuff. That's a prime vintage."

"How many are with you?" Ariaas growled.

"Today, I am alone." The angular man shifted the tail of his long cloak to sit upon Ariaas's chair. Once comfortable at the table, he tossed a grape into his mouth, tore a piece of buttered bread, and slathered it with a large cut of baorguan cheese. He ate with soft bites, chewing and swallowing, as if he was enjoying a dinner with friends.

When he finished, he wiped his chin. "How many years has it been, old friend? Twenty-four, no? Did you recognize my face? I was so much younger then. Unlike you, never changing."

"Whatever you have come to give, we want no part of it."

"You have not even heard what it is. You may reconsider," he claimed. "I have been watching for some time. Watching all your comings and goings. I know your traps, your defenses. I know the lines of the perimeter. My people tested them for years. One ... by one ... by one ..."

His sinuous smile curled further. "I know you found the bodies, old friend."

Ariaas's eyes widened.

How could this man defy their traps, the perimeter, the safeguards? This man could not have eluded their safety measures, their land, could not have been wandering free, could not have sent his people to die.

"Ariaas, please," he implored, holding his hands to affirm his innocence. "I realize our last meeting was … less than pleasant. You may think of me as your enemy, but I believe we do still have some mutual interests. Which is why I have come in person. I knew you would kill anyone else I sent to deliver my message."

"And yet, I want to kill you more than any other human on this earth."

Eran whispered, "Why are you not?"

"Not for lack of trying." The angular man unbuttoned his shirt; a considerable scar trailed his lower abdomen. "One day, perhaps, I will tell you how I came to live through the gutting."

"If you know where we have been all this time," Brenor asked, "why did you leave us be?"

"All I cared about was your safety. Your dear Papa would never let anything happen to you. Especially not when he failed so many times with the others." He chuckled. "Simply a matter of pride at that point. I knew when the time came, you should be the ones to find them. Sister and brother, finding one another, reuniting to save the other two. It is so heroic, so poignant. Don't you think?

"Now the time has come." He clasped his hands, turning his attention to Lenora. "The final child remains. I've waited exceptionally long for this. As you all have. The year is upon us. The time has come to reunite this family. All I have ever wished for.

"You are incredibly beautiful. And there is so much wild behind your eyes." His sights trailed to her shoulders, the nape of her neck, the curves of her lips.

"Are my words in your pocket?" he whispered, eyeing her trousers. His gaze then traced the chest pocket of her jacket. "Or are they closer to your heart?"

His words? She gasped.

Oedd.

She was certain in her bones.

"There may soon come a day where you no longer wish to stay here. Always hiding, training, running. The hiding has not been in vain; soldiers of The South Sea have never found this sanctuary. Though, it is exhausting, I'm certain.

"I'll be waiting for you, should the time come. Your messages will always reach me. There will always be a place for you, at my home. At my side. Always." Oedd gestured. "As Ariaas and Brenor, we, too, knew of the whereabouts of Thealor and Arienne. But we could never find *you*. And here you were, right under everyone's noses. A simple word of your abduction and you would most willingly leave. No deceptions, no elaborate rescues. So beautifully simple.

"With one tiny act, everything was set into motion." He beamed. "We never braved their rescue without knowing where you were. I was incredibly pleased when I heard of your and Thealor's return."

He almost spoke as if they had not had private words in the dark. As if he had not spent months tucked at her side. As if the distance in his voice was theater—a performance meant to bury their truth they both carried.

He addressed Ariaas. "Now, there remains only one. *One*. One which poses the most difficult challenge. Most difficult, indeed."

Ariaas's rage boiled below the surface of his skin as if it would burst through his flesh.

"Do not be concerned. Reuniting this family is my top priority. I think you know, when you really think about it, you had no chance at The Reldory. Even before. Even if you waited, made another plan. And another ... and another ... and another."

He paused, chest heaving slightly, then lifted a finger. "It is not a comment meant to offend, merely a pragmatic observation. The four of you against a fortress of death. The four of you against the hanging cage.

"Which leads me to my offer." He walked to Ariaas. "We depart tomorrow. We take the bridge. Together. The force of the Yurelan's best at your side."

Her breath hitched. *He's helping. He genuinely came to help me.*

Ariaas's eyes grew wide, tightened his grip on the bottle.

"My soldiers will be in the carriage from Tenuel and Felreaon, as well the prisoners inside meant for transfer. A half dozen or more will hide across the rocks at the peak. I assume the four of you to be in the carriage from Valesove. I sent a message ahead to Mount Reldor, that Valesove would arrive with two prisoners." He winked at Brenor. "I have been told Cascanvore and Qabriah have no inmates for transfer. That will leave the carriages from The South Sea, Hanielle, and Dhaesreaon, as well as the guards from the landside and the penitentiary itself."

He reached for another grape, lofting it into his mouth. While chewing he said, "You need allies in this world, old friend. Those of which I am honored to provide for you. Once the bridge is taken, the prison will be simple."

"We will not accept your aid. We will not pay the price for your gift."

Oedd stood tall before Ariaas, his tone at odds with his apparent gentle nature. "You misunderstand me, old friend. Lenora and Thealor have already been removed from their confines. I hear whispers. They mean to bar the doors indefinitely. Fate is with us; they have not done so yet. They will open the bridge once more before The South Sea tightens their grip on her. This may be the last chance there is. You may be willing to take such a chance with Arienne, but we are not.

"We take The Reldory with or without you. My gift is the chance to join us. If you are there, she may come back home. Home to Aroun Vaer, to heal her wounds with her family. I only want her freedom. If not, well …" A broad smile crossed his cheeks. "She will find a home with me."

Lenora's hold on her blade loosened.

The slim hole they needed into The Reldory, the bait, was being offered.

"Leave. Now."

"Perhaps, if only for a short while, Ariaas, we can be friends again." The man chuckled. "Your weapons couldn't kill me last time and I was only a young boy. You do not have the strength to kill me now."

Lenora raised an eyebrow.

"As an offer of good will, I would like to share a piece of information on The Reldory." He straightened his cloaks and offered Ariaas his own chair. "One which is not written in the books you have in your collection. Perhaps once you realize we are on the same side, you will take the aid."

Ariaas growled, "Say your peace and leave."

"The Reldory has been given some new refurbishments regarding security in the last decade since those books were written—the ones Eran reads in your old library. They have updated the bridge and the stairs. The building knows who is on her side and who is not. If the guards stationed fall, or they die, or they call for aid, the building will close. It senses fear. They must be rendered unconscious; they must not call for help, and they must not die, and they must not fall from the sides. Not even one, or the bridge will close indefinitely.

He straightened his jacket, removing dust from the edge of his hem. "That is from what I understand. The information came as a favor from the Dhaesreaon in exchange for a release of one of their own from a prison in Nyaruse some years ago."

"They do not have the power to give a building consciousness."

"I merely tell you what I have heard," he replied. "Remind me, old friend, what path did you take? When you departed Mount Ohbrolis?"

"Why would our path be of any consequence?" Ariaas offered a sharp reply before Brenor could speak.

"Two of my people went missing around the same time. Curiosity leads me to his escape."

"We took the Ravine Road, and we did not come into contact with any of your people."

"Hmm." His head cocked to one side. "Curious."

Again, the angular man returned to Lenora. "If you hear nothing else from this visit, please know others are on your side, regardless of what your dear Papa tells you. If you ever want to leave and go to a place where you would be treated like a queen, find me." His fingers caressed the white cotton at her shoulder. "You know who I am.

"I live to the west of River Gaulle in Hanielle, at the crest of The Forest Luenuan. If you choose to seek me, I will not be difficult to find."

The grin at his lips spoke of the genuine nature of his words. He winked that only she might see.

He turned to leave, tucking his long coat behind himself.

Through gritted teeth, Ariaas said, "Wait."

Oedd turned, his movement almost rhythmic, seemingly pleased with Ariaas's need of him.

"I need to know." Ariaas lowered his bottle and righted his stance. "Thealor—is he with your people?"

"Sadly, no, he is not." Oedd's joyful grin warped into a sour frown. "My soldiers tracked him into the mountains the night he departed Aroun Vaer. He sheltered in a cave along the south side of Mount Ykkoro for some time. My men were ill-equipped to stay in the cold weather without proper equipment." He continued, "Amongst my people lives a woman of the Rentiriat; she tracked him through the mountains for some time and kept his location while he lived atop Mount Ohbrolis. However, once the group returned, she could no longer find him. I am not confident, but there are speculations something unfortunate may have befallen him."

He admired the patchwork on the exterior of the castle—the hole large enough for the branch of the oak tree but not the birds. "I do love the updates you've made to Aroun Vaer, Brenor. It is starting to feel better. I can see some of the old life returning to it. It's beginning to feel like home again."

Oedd crossed his hands before pressing them to his mouth. "I have been waiting alongside you these long years. I do, most sincerely, wish to see this family reunited, healed of their wounds, and at full capacity in the near future. Please pass on my warmest regards to Arienne; I have missed her much throughout the years."

He found amusement in Ariaas's stance and tried to hide a chuckle at the bottle perched over his head. "We all need friends, Ariaas. We cannot survive this world without them."

As a reminder of his offer, he nodded to Lenora before he slipped below the terrace from where he came. The light in his eyes and the grin at his lips the most ominous warning he could provide.

Lenora stared into the distance, watching the place where Oedd had vanished.

There had been no way to reach Arienne or Sissel. Now, the path had landed square in their laps.

"What just happened?" Eran held his tight grip on the candelabra. He screamed, "You told me Aroun Vaer was safe! You said no one knew we were here!"

"Oedd knows his way around this land, and the castle. He lived here for some time. All the Yurelan had to do was get into the library, the plans are all over the tables, the desks, the books are on The Reldory." Ariaas's rage surged as he gripped the table, using all his strength to flip it onto its side, and hurl the glasses and cheese smashing onto the floor. Spilled meat and grapes rolled the length of the balcony.

Lenora paused. "The Yurelan?"

Eran asked, "How worried should we be?"

"Save your worries," Brenor replied. "We will need them for other matters. Oedd can be a problem for another day."

"He is not the kind of man to be indebted to," Ariaas warned.

"But he can help!"

"Don't even think about it," he cautioned. "We cannot use his aid."

Lenora walked toward the edge of the terrace while Eran, Ariaas, and Brenor's argument intensified. The men threw terms into the debate: Yurelan, extremists, attacks, savages, allies, enemies.

Oedd's silhouette appeared in the cotton pink light along the northern rolling hills. He turned, waving before continuing on his way. Taren caught sight of him from the terrace, his loud bark thundering at the back of his departing silhouette.

"Who is he? Really?" How could Ariaas hate someone so much who offered to help reunite his family?

"Lennie. He's king. He's the King of the Yurelan."

A cold bloom of nausea threatened her gut. She clutched the letter in her pocket. The words they'd exchanged—carefully chosen, topically trusting—and he had been in control of those who wanted to own her. "That cannot be."

"And yet it is."

Ariaas paced. "What to do? What to do?"

Her pulse pounded in her ears. Did she never want to speak to him again or run to his side in battle? A part of her trusted him now. He will hold his word of aid. But it was a twisted deal.

"What do you suggest? We go beside them? Or abandon their plan? If they fail, he will send them again. And again. Every year. If the bridge holds," Ariaas argued. "There will be a price. He will come back and demand one of us go with him. I know it. No one is going anywhere with him."

Brenor crossed his arms over his chest. "I do not want any price on my family."

The matter needed no further consideration. Lenora solidified her choice. "We take the aid. Deal with the ramifications later."

Silence.

A breath later, Eran dropped the candelabra.

"You know nothing of this man. You don't know his nature," Ariaas argued. "You wouldn't consider this deal if you knew you were climbing into bed with our enemy. The price will be heavy. And you don't even know that price yet."

"If what he said is true and they mean to close the bridge, how can you even consider walking away? Use his aid to retrieve Arienne and Sissel," she urged. "If it was my daughter, or my granddaughter, the number one priority would be getting everyone out alive. Not to mention the four of us. Anything after can be dealt with at that time."

Lenora continued, "It's not even one. We need to safely rescue *two*. Allow these soldiers to lay down their lives. Better them than friends we make and lead to slaughter. Better still, Ariaas and I won't be bait for six tortuous months."

At their drawn stares, Lenora solemnly assured, "I'll pay the price. Whatever it may be."

Ariaas huffed.

Lenora grasped him by the shoulders. "I know this isn't the plan you wanted. But we need to take it. It's our only option."

Ariaas stared at the food covering the floor, his thoughts drawn, appearing to calculate something.

"Ariaas," she said, garnering his attention. "I'm going. With or without you."

Eran rubbed his temples. "What do ya need?"

"Can you pack food? Water? Brenor, the horses? And the wagon?"

Ariaas sighed. "It's not gonna work."

"But we are still going to try."

Deep sadness settled over the creases in Ariaas's forehead. Finally, Lenora saw past the hard exterior to the life of love and loss this man had long lived. Eternal bonds with his family he could not break no matter how many times the world knocked him down. Perhaps the plan was not the best; perhaps they would owe more than they could repay or die in the process. But they still had to try.

"Can you gather the weapons? Hide the swords below the wagon benches with the extra quivers? And grab the chains and cuffs with the trick pins Brenor built?" Lenora asked, her eyes pleading. "I don't want to do this without you. But I will if I must."

After a beat he nodded, solemnly, and the knots in her stomach receded.

"I'll gather the whiteroot." She rushed to the glass jars of fine powder in the kitchen, hungry to watch the flames burn away the last bonds of Monera's wrongdoings.

FIRE AND SILENCE

Siara Pencanh Tanilar, Tu'dende of the Tiortem, The Master of Sound, Two Stars
Born: First Month of Autumn, 2003
Deceased: Unknown
Children: Unknown

-Tenuel Official Ledger

I slarourne stood tall against the horizon.

With the black jacket of The South Sea and the dead rose's emblem pinned to his chest, today, Thealor would be a young Roscidarra.

He strode through the colossal sandstone gates of Islarourne with a pompous bearing most only wore when well-connected and wealthy. The city's outskirts were an assault on his senses, everyone everywhere. Sounds of rushing attacked his ears. Unpleasant aromas of sweat, lack of personal hygiene, and a musk clinging to everything pressed heavy on his tongue. When he passed a tavern, the odor morphed into stale whiskey and even staler vomit.

He covered his mouth and made for the peaks of the castle.

As he entered the next rung of gates, the musk faded into a more tolerable aroma of steaming metal paired with the ripe smell of sickness. There was coughing everywhere. Singing. The guards on patrol grazed over him with the same discernment they gave to an elderly man hobbling past with a cane. His appearance had been well known on the mountain—either by the guards he worked alongside or the women he was told to please. He chuckled to himself. How very delightful to sink into a crowd.

On the street, passersby traveled to and from work or the taverns or wherever the hell they went, each day the same, never having to watch themselves to see if someone trailed their movements. If he abandoned his plan and took up work as a mason or a butcher, he might be just as they were. Common.

He sighed. What a ridiculous thought. He was anything but common.

The smells altered again when he passed the fourth gate—this time, stale earth followed by lingering bittersweet citrus. The King's Castle perched magnificently above the city—ethereal towers dwarfing Aroun Vaer. Following winding pathways, he sought the most direct passage to the gates. Some alleyways ended in homes, redirecting his path and adding fuel to the fire of his agitation.

At the fifth gate, he smelled sweet, fresh air. He hadn't realized how good the simple smell of *nothing* was. When he arrived in the expansive courtyard of ruby rose bushes, he entered as a man who belonged there, as his pin depicted. He approached the gate.

"I'm here to see King Barrard."

"Have you been summoned?"

"No."

"You must be summoned to seek an audience with the king."

"My apologies. I misunderstood you." Thealor shook his head. "I have been summoned. Please tell him I have arrived. Mister Varan, from Mount Ohbrolis."

Since his time in the caverns, Qerilan, and the peasant's cottage studying the Old Tongue, Thealor had deemed himself near indestructible. Four guards escorted him through the castle, donning coats much as his own with fine pins. The large blades at their belts did little to impose fear.

"Where will we meet him?" Thealor jabbed in whispers along the walk. "The throne room? A back alley in the shadows?" Had they truly told Barrard who came to see him, the man wouldn't greet him as he greeted a lord from a high kingdom.

Thealor debated with himself as he passed labyrinth-like halls, an empty grand ballroom, and grand portraits. *How should I enter the presence of a king? With a show of force or a kindhearted greeting?*

He made his choice as they approached two wide and grand doors.

Thealor no longer needed accompaniment.

He grabbed the closest guard by the neck, heaving his head into a stone column. The three turned to strike, but a blow to each of their heads—one by the jaw and two by the forehead across his broad knee—left them unconscious on the floor next to their comrade. Perhaps he should be offended they gave him such little fanfare.

Thealor strode through the double doors in an arrogant strut.

King Barrard sat poised atop the throne, a stately man with gray silk robes, holding an audience with civilians.

How is it so easy to gain an audience with the king? Should there not be armies guarding this man? Or is no one else quite so audacious? Where are his advisers? His head of committees?

The reasons were irrelevant. Thealor made it to this room. All the hard work he'd carried out in that cavern and the cross-eyed man's home was all worth it. The freezing fingers and the rage he still felt on the edge of his mind.

King Barrard regained his regal composure. "Why were you not escorted by my guards, Mr. Varan?"

"They are in the hall." Thealor gestured behind him. "They were quite tired. Such a long walk."

Barrard eyed the silent hallway, his regal facade dwindling ever so slightly. He gestured to a young girl with a brass pin of a raven. "Summon High Commander Ravaris. And Commander Benson, if he has not yet departed. And Captain Reid, immediately. Take the rest." King Barrard tapped his ring against the wooden throne while guards escorted whispering civilians.

The advantage was his. Thealor couldn't help but smirk.

"I take it by your whispers and the accepted summons request that you remember me." The adrenaline of the act, the studied words, his immunity, his abilities, and the lingering feeling of an unconscious guard upon his knee fueled him. "And you sent so few guards, I suppose I should be offended."

"Yes, Mr. Varan. I know well who you are. I recall your face from my nightmares. The demonic eyes."

King Barrard's lip hung low over his beard, and his eyes widened. The fearful gaze was familiar, dancing as wildly as the day they met at Brouverg Castle. Of course, he was not king then. The queen had traveled to see the prize Lord Brouverg was not willing to part with, even by order, not without war at their door.

"I presumed—should I offer polite regard to your visit—you might show the same to me. I see now that idea was foolish." Barrard replied, adjusting his jeweled crown. "Tell me, Mr. Varan, why do you seek my audience?"

"I have information. I've come to make an arrangement."

"What type of arrangement?"

"Full amnesty and my alliance to the Southern crown for the information I possess."

Barrard shifted forward in his chair, spilling his silk robes. "You removed my guards from their posts to request a peace offering?"

Thealor held his hands wide. "Perhaps I have a flair for dramatics."

"What is the nature of the information? You must believe it to be quite valuable. This act is bold, to say the least. Leaving your confines," King Barrard continued, "walking directly into my castle, knowing well you would be arrested on sight."

Thealor spat a disgusted laugh—the audacity. "I escaped my captors. I was never yours to claim, nor theirs. I don't believe forced servitude is within the laws of the crown. Perhaps you mistake my imminent arrest for a portly woman in the far north mountains. Or perhaps you enjoy imprisoning people before they commit the crime as your mother did." He must control the hatred spewing from him, lest it take hold and destroy every bit of his offering.

The doors swung open. A woman with short black hair and broad shoulders entered, followed by two men. The High Commander. The latter bearded man wearing a commander's pin, but no lineage, eyed him warily.

"High Commander Ravaris, Commander Benson, thank you for arriving so quickly." Barrard nodded in his direction. "Mr. Thealor Varan. He requests amnesty and alliance. I want your witness and your ... protection should it be required. Mr. Varan has come to us from Brouverg Castle in the north, excusing a short respite."

Barrard addressed Thealor. "Should I ask where you took respite? And how should I know what you say is the truth? I may make a deal with you only to find you possess little power, unlike what I've long been told."

Thealor's lip curled. The moment he had been desperately wishing for since he willed flames in the Mountain. "An evaluation, then, eh?"

King Barrard waved a hand and the girl with the short hair stepped before him. Thealor hoped it would be her he called upon—the gold pin of the raven at her breast.

She murmured.

His femur prickled with far sharper force than the raven in Qerilan. The aching stretched down his thigh, well below his muscles, morphing into deep throbbing. Wise for the king to keep the stronger Noslarrar at his side. Thealor maintained his apathetic stance as the pain reared and then settled. "What a silly test. Did you mean to snap my leg?"

Pleased, Thealor grasped the bony raven before anyone could stop him, pulling her toward himself. He whispered to her, "Are there any here who you wish to hurt? Those who harmed you, those who you wish to suffer?" He hushed her whimpers. "Quiet, now. I cannot break your bones by will alone, but I can with my hands. I can do many other things. I can make you break their bones."

Thealor whispered, "notume."

Flames upon brass-banded torches folded in unison as if they felt the same breeze at the same instant, perfectly synchronized. The fire rose from the stands, growing, stretching into wild spears of violence before them. The act would be uninspiring to a true Milnire of Felreaon, but to men of The South Sea, it was witnessing foreign sorcery. The Southerners diverted their eyes while the room sweltered like a desert in the summer sun.

The orange tunnels fell back to their natural stance upon the metal pegs.

"moiremvis hesu," Thealor uttered.

The surrounding clamor muted eerily like the rush of stillness after death. Barrard rose from his wooden throne, his lips moving, yet mute. The High Commander's lips conveyed angry, bitter conversation while the room remained silent. Thealor clapped, reveling in their bewilderment.

Exhilarating.

The king slammed his fists against the armrests of his throne, mouthing, 'Enough!'

Thealor spoke again in the Old Tongue, removing the plague of silence he'd cast upon them. "Did I pass your test?" he asked. "Or would you like to kill one of your commanders and see if I can bring them back from the depths?"

Barrard's eyes twitched ever so slightly, displaying his deep, implanted fears.

"You possess abilities known from Tenuel, Felreaon, and The South Sea lineages. You have proven enough." Quite plainly, the matter startled this dear king—the loss of sense, the flames, the resistance. "Release her."

Thealor forgot he still held the whimpering girl in his grips. "Don't be mad, dear," he said, as she stumbled warily behind the commanders.

Some part of him was surprised his show of abilities frightened them, each grasping weapons, blades steady in their waiting hands. The act was such a small show. Though the people of The South Sea were severely unaccustomed to the loss of senses, and more importantly, loss of power in the room they held in sole dominance.

What if I had been trained from infancy? What could I do with flames or with words or with the earth I have yet to understand?

"Mr. Varan, what information do you have that makes you feel you are worthy of a pardon?"

"My information will provide you with my alliance and two more of my kind."

Barrard's lips turned down. "You would betray your own family?"

"Blood means little. They are no more my family than you." Thealor continued, "I know you can feel what is happening. Or perhaps you possess no skills in the ways of instincts, so let me help you in that matter—you will be helpless to stop the shift of power if they all reunite. Or if the Yurelan get even one of them. Not without my aid."

"Before I determine if I will make this deal, I want something from you." King Barrard eyed him warily. "Your motivation. Why an allegiance to the crown? I stand in direct defiance of your very being."

"The months since my departure from Mount Ohbrolis have proven many things." Thealor perched at the edge of the window's stone arch, watching the people walking below. He had no home. He belonged to no city. He certainly belonged to no family. Not now. Not after all Lenora and Ariaas had done.

"I'm a pawn—to you—I know this much. And to everyone else. The matter is not lost on me."

Ariaas and his family wanted him back out of obligation. Lady Brouverg viewed him as a prized possession. The Yurelan wanted to burn and break the world to get their way, anxiously holding reins they meant to buckle to his neck.

He rubbed his throat as if it were already collared in thick leather. "Every street I step onto, I'm a wanted man. I can't see a guard without wondering if they are the one person who will sound the alarm of my presence. I want to live out my days in peace. I want to walk the street a free man and sleep with both of my eyes closed. The way I see it, a deal with you is the only path to a marginally normal life."

Barrard glared at him as if he might read more than his words revealed. "Very well," he said cautiously. "Amnesty and your full, unwavering allegiance are a fair exchange for information leading to the death of your siblings." King Barrard asserted, "Should you show proper respect to the throne."

Thealor chuckled. Theatrically, he took a bent knee, bowing his head, and waving his arms as if he were a gallant performer. "Yes, my king." Any person in the room could see his show was void of sincerity, though Barrard waved a hand regardless for Thealor to proceed. "I will be blunt—"

"Have you not been blunt already?"

"I'll live where I choose to live. I won't be guarded. This is a mutual agreement between the two of us. I'll answer to no one and deal directly with you."

"At least address your king with honor and proper titles!" High Commander Ravaris growled. "Even at your taken knee, you disrespect the crown."

King Barrard ignored his highest commander. "I agree to your terms."

Thealor rolled the sleeve of his arm and offered it freely that Barrard might take it.

Ravaris shouted, "Do not take his hand!"

The king pressed back his robes, and the two men shook open forearms. Thealor's plan, his deals, and the fear he could create went far better than he'd imagined. Someone, and not just any someone—the king himself—shook his arm as a man, an authority, and not a houseboy. He stood firm with valid opinions in this room instead of a chained beast guarding a prized rock for crumbs. Freedom would soon be his—not just freedom from chains, but from hiding and cowering.

"My siblings are attempting a rescue at The Reldory on Uen'can. As you know, my sister, Arienne, has been imprisoned there for some time." A pang of anguish settled in his stomach as he spoke Arienne's name. The dense weight seemed to possess gravity, drawing him to the floor at his betrayal of her doomed impending rescue. Even along the road from the man's cottage to the sandstone gates, he had reminded himself of the nature of his choice. Mercy. Offering to end her suffering, her turmoil, her perpetual starvation—was a blessing. The others would never make it inside. They would die trying.

"My brother, Brenor, and the youngest, Lenora, have reunited." He pressed beyond the pain of Arienne, and the thread of guilt for not calling Lenora his blood. "The two will journey together to ensure her freedom. Brenor will pose as a guard, Lenora an inmate, and imprison herself until the following Uen'can."

In a harsh voice, High Commander Ravaris muttered, "As we suspected, the youngest has reunited with them."

Long silent, Commander Benson's eyes widened. He bellowed, "You're a twisted snake!"

The man had been evaluating Thealor since he stepped through the doors. The only one not to draw his sword at his show of fire.

"Why did you bring this information to our king now? The Reldory is several days' journey, and the day after tomorrow is Uen'can. We will never make it there by dawn." Commander Benson addressed his king, "I don't trust this man's alliance request is of honorable intention. No man would betray his own flesh. How long has he had this information? He arrives now, knowing we cannot get there in time. You should not trust this man."

"You betrayed your own flesh to earn your title," Ravaris retorted. "Does that mean he should not trust you?"

Commander Benson lowered his head.

"There is no need to make it by dawn," Barrard replied. "Allow them to complete their plan. Allow the youngest inside. The two women will be trapped." Barrard returned to his throne, adjusting his silk and velvet robes at his collar, and gathered himself. "What other information are you withholding? Who else will be with them?"

"That is all the information I have. I wish I knew more; however, I was not privy to further specifics of their plan."

"Do they trust you?"

He chuckled at the thought. "I sincerely doubt it."

THE BISON

aiel tecu enathone taod.

- "The Gilded Gate," Faiseus Rancesla Auro, Unknown Date

All Sissel had in The Reldory were thoughts of Ronan, Dylia, and the bones of Arienne.

One hundred seventy notches, circles, and lines had been etched into the stone floor. Sissel lived in Tanes for a shorter duration, but the days she slept in that room with the mediocre window felt like a lifetime ago. She had been born and grown into an adult, aged, and died in the time since. Her memories reminded her of her time in Tanes, both years ago and yesterday, when Ronan pressed his lips into hers. She smelled mint and cedar, bumps rising on her skin, and her stomach dipping like a soaring bird when he spoke her name. However, her mind played cruel tricks. Her sense of smell departed many days ago, not in the years Dylia predicted.

She closed her eyes, recalling the feeling of Ronan's fingers intertwining with hers, his breath in her hair, his hips pushed into her. The warmth of his skin against hers grew challenging to remember, but her pulse raced, nonetheless. She should not think of him in such a manner—her body was not strong enough to make her heart thunder in such a way.

Now, she admitted to herself—though never aloud, never in words for others to hear—she loved Ronan.

"Who do you think of?" Dylia smirked. "When your cheeks flush?"

Embarrassment overcame her. Sissel shook her head. Matters best left unsaid. Somehow, speaking of him, what happened, or what did not, made the situation all too real.

"Honey, I have nothing but time and love your stories." Dylia's dark eyes illuminated. "Your husband? Your lover? Let your mind run wild and tell me all about it."

A wave of aching pain crashed through Sissel's ribs.

Husband.

Lover.

No.

Dylia's joyful expression sank. "Someone you wished to be."

"It was nothing."

Thoughts of Ronan flooded her mind constantly, though she never braved speaking those thoughts aloud. Daydreams of an optimistic mind. In truth, there were no real stories—none of their relationship besides words of stolen glances, moments they stood too close, and unwarranted acts of kindness. None other than his lips pressed into hers; the grip of his fingers tight in her own, his hips pressed into hers as she splayed across the table.

"Another life now."

"Hope is all you have in here, honey. Don't forget it. Don' let it slip away from you. Even if your only hope is that you see him again ..."

Sissel opened the rickety door to the outside, her muscles quivering beneath her frail weight. A rush of air swirled into the confines.

In the shadowed opening, Sissel coveted the sun's rays on her skin. She found peace in the gradually warming air. Two hopes remained—two people in varying corners of the world she wished to see desperately. How odd she had yet to speak Ronan's name aloud to either woman in this room, even Arienne while Dylia slept, a woman incapable of spilling her secrets.

"I was wrong to say it was nothing ..." Sissel said. It hurt to begin to speak of it, but it felt more real, perhaps. He wasn't nothing. How dare she say he was? "A man who took favor on me, in Tanes. As a child of The South Sea, he sympathized with my plight. He helped me—tried to have my sentence changed."

The guilt tugged at her stomach for speaking of him in such a way—*nothing* and not calling him by name. Even the thought of it brought a haze to her eyes. She wished to speak of anything other than what made her heart ache. "You told me some months ago you were a mal'soniure. What other lineages are you born from?"

Dylia frowned at the change of subject. "Well, I don' know my entire heritage, but I do know I'm descendant of Meresavas ... and Ucelentrie, and—"

"Ucelentrie?"

"Fairly useless trait, I'm afraid."

"Can you tell if I'm Roscidarran or not? With certainty?"

"You told me you were a Roscidarra, honey. How you traded the life of that soldier." Dylia's lip fell open. "I thought you knew for certain?"

"It doesn't sit right that my grandmother wouldn't tell me. Can you try? Please. She told me I was native of Tenuel." Sissel never questioned anything her grandmother told her, not until the time they became separated.

Dylia offered a cautious nod. "I'm not used to it though—"

"How does this work exactly?"

"Doesn't hurt, if that's what you're askin'. Gimme your left arm." Sissel sat on the floor beside her, extending her arm. "The lineages each have color. The South Sea—shades of gray. Though that's where I stumble a bit, where one needs trainin'. I know where some of the colors are from, mostly those of The South Sea, Tenuel, and Hanielle. Those are simplest to remember. A lot from Felreaon and Valesove are too close for me to tell, the blues."

"Do whatever you can."

After a few moments Dylia opened her eyes, pleased with her discovery. "It's beautiful. Like you, honey." Dylia patted her hand. "A deep red, maroon. Color of a ruby. And, red only comes from one place."

Sissel whispered, "Tenuel."

"It looks like Grams didn' deceive you after all."

"What does this mean?" Sissel reeled. *I am from Tenuel. Why would they arrest me? How could I have killed the guard of Wesilea?*

"You said you touched the man you saved, yes?"

"Yes," she said. "My hands were on his chest. I tried to help him." Digging into the recesses of her mind, Sissel reached forward, recreating the moment fate changed the course of her life. "I moved my hands, thinking he was having a heart attack. He reached for me, grabbed my arm. There were ... vibrations, pain. The guard fell. Mr. Baradelle sucked in a huge breath."

"You told me Mr. Baradelle was from The South Sea." Dylia's cheeks carved a smile, appearing to know the destination of her line of thoughts before Sissel. "Did he speak?"

Sissel shook her head. "No, not that I recall."

This made no sense. None of this made sense.

Sissel's spine chilled. The realization washed over her like a frigid river sweeping her away. "Mr. Baradelle was the Roscidarra."

Dylia nodded, assuring her theory. "You know then what your lineage is?"

"When he grabbed me … he *used* me. To replicate his own abilities." Sissel's thin veins coursed below her skin. She recalled High Commander Ravaris' words: 'No lineage can perform such acts on their own people.'

"A lady of the Ghesotum." Dylia's mood became somber. "Mr. Baradelle couldn't save himself. He used you to do it. Ghesotum are considered a harmless people in most parts; butterflies. You can become anything you want—but only for a moment. I wish you would have known before they had you imprisoned here, you are not one to be feared, honey." Dylia spoke with sincerity. "I hate to say it, but Tenuel wouldn' stand for a native of their region to be sent here—not like that. Baradelle made you do the work, take the fall." Sissel reeled in the weight of the truth, the pain of the knowledge unrivaled by the agonizing pain of the act. Deep inside, she never felt one with The South Sea, even though parts of her wished to be.

"You should've been sent to a small prison, in the city perhaps, to serve time for a short while for an accidental death. That's if you were locked up at all. The killed guard was from Tenuel. It should've been handled by Tenuel."

"I was never from The South Sea, not born and hidden away."

Ronan. He aided her, gave her a room, attempted to alter her sentence—all because he thought they were one of the same people. What would he think of her now? A true native of Tenuel. Not one of his own, certainly not highborn of the Vak'Arra. He wouldn't look deep into her eyes, their shoulders wouldn't linger, or brush the hairs from her face in a way that made her insides tumble. Their lips wouldn't meet with such urgency.

"The South Sea could arrest you and still remove Mr. Baradelle. They would not dare put you somewhere else, honey. If it came out, you were native to Tenuel … whew! Can you imagine? They'd be in the wrong for your arrest. No alliances hold strong that way.

"Not many Ucelentrie live anywhere near Wesilea. Most don' dare leave Qabriah or your name could've been cleared. They whisk'd you away on purpose. They could've held ya in Wesilea until Uen'can, but they transferred you that instant—to a place no prisoners are kept—so you wouldn' speak to anyone."

"And I did nothing to try to stop them." The air weighed thick in her lungs. "I took the punishment."

A sudden realization washed over her. How could Ronan rescue her now? How could he pull her from the other side of a vast abyss for which he had no wings? His lingering presence comforted her in sleep long enough to brave another day. But this—*this*—the notches, the stone walls, Dylia's words, and Arienne's mute frame were all she would see.

Sissel now knew in the depths of her soul Ronan would never enter this frigid room with the circles and the notches. She felt it in her bones as sure as the winds tore through the peaks and the sun rose each day. Despair washed over her, and she allowed the wave to crash. Hope accompanied her these long months. The thoughts sounded naive now—her being saved.

Tears coursed her cheeks. "No one is coming."

Sissel wept for the life she lost. The hope that she would see her grandmother again washed away like footprints in the sand. Ronan would not arrive at the landside, rushing the bridge. The grounds he had to save her were gone; she was not of the family he suspected. Perhaps, at one time, he had the means to save her. Though, if he wished to, he would have done it months ago, under much more manageable circumstances. He would not come when she had been locked in the hanging cage for months.

This building was created for embarrassment—for hiding shame.

She certainly felt shameful and embarrassed. Never questioning anything, never learning to fight, not training with a weapon, not trying at all. Pressing the back of her skull against the rock, she wished to feel pain.

"I need to find comfort in the presence of suffering," she instructed herself. "It's a part of my life."

Sissel moved to the door—the disheveled rattling wood—should it even be called a door. The threshold of death. Life dwelled on the landside, death in the fog, and they were perched in a delicate in-between. The South Sea wanted them to leap. A kindness to end the suffering.

The air caressed her face as she gazed into the abyss below.

Hunger consumed her. Her body ached everywhere: her mind, her heart, her bones, her joints. Even if Ronan had taught her to fight, there was no one to fight now. No one left to defend her in the hanging cage except ... herself.

Dylia spoke into Sissel's despair. "I wish I was from the River Realm. If I was of the Dlearbrond I would wait until Uen'can, tear the stone from below their feet while they descended the stairs. I'd watch them all fall, honey." She eyed Arienne, the torture she had long endured fueling her hatred. "It's what they deserve for what they've done."

How does she have the energy to speak so much? Sissel barely had the energy to stand at the precipice without falling. Birds flew amongst the fog.

Sissel leaned into the abyss, imagining the Forever Fall. What would it feel like to be free? To fall from the height. Fly for a moment. The choice would end her anguish. A rush of instantaneous pain, not years of aching bones, and slow, agonizing starvation. Her hand rested on the doorknob—the body of bones, the flesh dangling muscleless. It reminded her of Arienne. Her hand now morphed to match, bones painted with skin.

She whispered, "Should I step out?"

Dylia made no attempts to dissuade her. This dangling survival was not built for most. The despair at her circumstance was not a moment for unwarranted positivity. Instead, Dylia said, "It's rumored some buildings have a consciousness, you know? They can sense fear and betrayal. That's how they say the stairs work."

Sissel scoffed at the thought. The building did not have a consciousness. It didn't have a soul. If it did, it was a dark soul, cold and empty as the stone she slept upon.

As she studied the void, she reveled at the taste of salt on her cracked lips and the plummeting feeling in her stomach. The breeze tugged at her damp cheeks.

Though—if the building had no mind of its own—how did they control the stone bridge?

The Reldory bore stone armor, as a body protects its flesh by steel plates. Raging winds none could climb. Even if they should breach the armor, a bridge contained them, a bridge which would not open for their wishes. Only one lineage could will stone and they did not dwell in The South Sea.

"Dylia," Sissel muttered. "What is the symbol of the Dlearbrond?"

"A bison."

She wiped her tears, the hair from her cheek, dirt spreading over her skin. She slammed the rotten door closed, the wood splintering at the force. As quickly as her malnourished body could muster, she rushed to the inside wall. She climbed through the small opening, past her torso, making sure her hips fit. The floor, a dark pit, held a few bodies, light shining off bones in the corners.

Sissel examined the ropes dangling from the top floor, twenty paces above. The edges of the rocks lining the opening were stacked neatly, their cut edges attached by thin grooves. Unlike the perfectly smooth walls of their cell. The guards assumed they would try to climb; there were no footholds.

"There are three guards on this side of the bridge."

Sissel returned to Dylia and sat before her, beaming. "One of the guards wore a pin of a bison. The guard with the auburn beard." She grasped Dylia's cheeks. "Dylia, the building does not have a consciousness. It has a Dlearbrond. *One.* One man who makes the bridge rise and fall. One who opens and closes the stairs. The others wore pins of a snake and a rose."

Dylia's lip fell open. She shook her head while she wrapped around the news, but more importantly, how the news made any difference. "We have no way to reach them, and even if we did, what would we do then?"

"Use the ability of the Meresavas. You can placate him, as you placated Arienne."

"And then what? He is numb and nothing more. He won't open the stairs, honey."

Sissel stood, her eyes gleaming with the rush of her newfound lineage. "He won't need to."

Dylia's eyes shifted to the floor, the stairs, and the bricks inside the building. "You can replicate his abilities." Dylia rubbed her chin. "But there's no way to get up there without the stairs. Nothing to hold onto. The walls are solid stone."

"The walls are smooth on the outside. Inside is brickwork. Made by human hands." Sissel motioned to the small opening where the food was dropped.

"I can't grab onto grooves between bricks. It may as well be one piece. There aren' footholds. No place for fingers. There's a reason for the skulls on the floor. Even if we had something to help us climb, I'm not strong enough. The years have made me weak, honey."

"No one is coming for us. The whistling stopped for Arienne. No one has come for you." Her heart hurt, punching into her ribs. "No one is coming for me. The guard who brought me in said when the bridge opens in the summer, it will be the last if High Commander Ravaris has her way. I left Wesilea a year ago. And in all those days, I did nothing to help myself; I succumbed to what others told me to do. I never once thought of myself, what would happen, what I was being used for.

"If I die here, I'll be at peace. But I don't want to die by doing nothing. You've given me hope these last few months. Hope that the sun will meet my skin again, that I might see the sunrise once more. Now, I'll return the favor to you. I don't know how to climb. You must help me. We can't, either of us, do this without the other. I don't know how to placate the Dlearbrond. You can't open the bridge."

Arienne lay asleep in a serene cocoon atop the wooden frame covered. Dylia eyed her, tears coursing her cheeks.

"There is only one man, two others on guard," Sissel implored. "I see the way you watch her. Plain since the first day I came into this room. You love her. I can see, as if you said it aloud to me. If she survives to this Uen'can, she certainly won't survive to see another. You wish her to be freed, don't you?"

Dylia nodded in desperation. "And what do we do with the others? What do we do to cross the bridge?"

Sissel moved to the notches on the floor, ran her hands over the notches, counting each one by one. "We have two days." She considered all they had—two buckets, three tin cups, clothing, a rotting wooden door which barely keeps out the wind.

A door which might break if the wind blew the wrong way.

She trailed her fingers along the frail wood, breaking by age. Shards ran along the grain as a tree which had sat inside a river and was left to blister in the sun. She pulled one small slice free though it tore open her palm and wedged a splinter the size of a coin below her thumb. She used it as a wedge, tearing at the next piece. "Help me get the door apart."

The first iron plate was the most difficult, tearing six nails fully off the fingers between the two of them. Two of Dylia's teeth broke before they peeled back enough to separate the iron. Blood pooled on the floor as daylight dwindled. The honed rock, used to carve notches on the floor, hammered into the tin cup when the wind blew forcefully enough to muffle the sounds. The rusted iron bar in hand, long and thin, Sissel leaned into the opening, shoving the bar like a climbing post between the stones.

The iron held, inches deep between vises of rock.

"When will we go?" Dylia asked, her voice rising in astonishment.

Sissel took in a deep inhale, counting notches on the floor. She held the air in her lungs to calm herself. "Now."

"Now!"

"Your adrenaline won't last. And there is food up there," Sissel assured her. "Some of the guards watch when they perch at the landside. They'll see if we go tomorrow night. The guards must be sleeping. You go first, placate the auburn-bearded guard," Sissel pressed. "Go now, before you question yourself."

Dylia rushed to Arienne's side, brushing the hair from her cracked lips. She kissed her forehead.

She exhaled her worries and followed orders. She grasped the iron bars, squeezing herself through the slim opening, the stone scratching at her flesh. Sissel watched until Dylia moved one post to the next, her muscles quivering, until she slid through the slim opening two stories overhead.

Sissel heard a short struggle, a man grunting. A wail outside. Fading, shrieking, grew softer as the fog swallowed its dinner. Then nothing but silence and her own panicked breath.

Eventually, the tray lowered, inch by inch until the climbing posts were hers for the taking.

Sissel climbed on quivering legs, muscles not ready for the pressure they endured. She grasped one hand on the rope, the other on her posts, gripping onto the irons, her toes sliding upon their edges, pleading with the heavens that her grasp would hold.

Dylia struggled to hold a portion of her weight against the rope. "Hurry."

Breathless, at the top, Dylia pulled her through the opening, and the two collapsed onto the floor.

The auburn bearded guard sat in his chair, stoic. Crane lay near asleep in his bed, eyes to match. Sissel searched. "The older guard?"

Dylia lamented, "I pushed him."

Sissel pressed his death from her thoughts. There was no time for sadness for their captors. "How do I open the stairs?"

"I thought you knew. This was your plan, honey."

She hadn't had the time to think that far. A problem for now and not then. Dylia threw old odds and ends out of the storage room while Sissel sat with the bison. She tried a hundred different ways, maybe more, to will him to open the stairs. Dylia brought her bread and dried meat the guards had hoarded. The meal filled her stomach with a depth of satisfaction she'd never experienced.

Hours dripped by while she tried to open the stairs.

Sissel closed her eyes, pressing the breath to leave her lungs. She would need to will him into action, feel it from her core. The same way she had felt the need to save Mr. Baradelle with every ounce of her being. She offered the most direct order she could muster. The words rattled in her soul an order she willed with all her might, her hand held tight in his.

"Open the stairs."

Pebbles on the floor convulsed.

The ground trembled.

Dylia smirked, preparing to carry Arienne's meek body up the sliver of stone. "They'll all come up, honey."

The twins, the girl. All of them.

"Let them come."

RUNNING BONES

kalilar tus thevay
sarr rialvis, yores giath, dahmous entiru
larard hesu rhineru
- "The Gilded Gate," Faiseus Rancesla Auro, Unknown Date

On the eve of Uen'can, their carriage arrived at the landside of the Reldory. The four—Ariaas, Eran, Lenora, and Brenor—had barely spoken since the horses pulled into The South Sea.

A knot the size of a chasm settled in Ariaas's stomach. He'd lost count of the times he'd been at this precipice, but this time felt different. This time, he felt hope. And that simple difference terrified him. The slapping winds haunted his dreams. The fall into the void haunted his waking mind. The image of Arienne screaming, her butchered hair, her lavender crown falling while they pulled her across the growing bridge replayed whenever it wanted his attention.

The four climbed the winding road through the mountain peak for many days, gusting winds at their backs. The carriage hugged the stone walls at some junctures where the path retreated so deeply, Ariaas expected it to disappear. The horses drudged on, slower than human legs could walk.

Ariaas and Eran anchored the carriage to the stone floor by colossal metal spikes and ropes.

Lenora and Brenor slept inside the carriage. At least, he hoped they did, unsure how in this god-forsaken wind. Brenor had built the shackles that now bound both his grandchildren's wrists and ankles, crafted as perfectly as anything he'd ever made.

Ariaas reminded himself they would be able to escape.

But would it matter that they didn't follow Faiseus Auro's plan? The author had been right on every detail up until this point. Ariaas forced the thought away. He couldn't muddle his decisions with the words of the dead.

After a long thirty minutes of sleep, Ariaas sat against the carriage in the depth of night, clutching the chained cloak beneath his uniform. Eran's teeth chattered in his sleep. When he ensured no one was looking, he covered Eran with his cloak.

The two donned traditional uniforms of Valesove, the fabric shifting in the light from amethyst to jade. They appeared polished and professional, as they had done this job many times prior. Ariaas had even shaved his speckled stubble. They disembarked and waited at attention as dawn approached, their prisoners held captive behind the door to the carriage.

This moment was familiar and not at the same time. He half expected to see Rarrk cross over the edge of the rocks with his tattoos and straw legs. But Ariaas had far more than he had that day. He had more than a half-ally. He had two full allies, one dolt, and however many Yurelan Oedd could spare.

He desperately hoped it was more than one.

And this day held no auction. This was Uen'can. Not a backhanded deal with broken, unethical soldiers who betrayed their orders for a bit of gold—not a rogue opening of this colossal hanging moon against all reason and against all orders for the betterment of terrible men.

It was scheduled. It was routine.

Soft indigo light saturated the sky.

The winds twisted and slapped his face. Ariaas pursed his lips, and his insides flipped. When no sound parted, he wiped the edge of his mouth with the fold of his sleeve. Then, choking through, whistled the soft melody into the wind. The song was like a far-off dream—soft and low, drifting upon the air.

A melody calling his dear Arienne.

He waited.

A soft sound drifted upon the wind, a higher tone, the whistling returned to him. His legs trembled, and it took every ounce of his strength not to fall to the stone ground on his knees and weep.

Arienne lived.

Below the doors, the earth across the long abyss creaked and groaned like growing stone. The frames dragged apart, minutes passing as years while the bridge inched toward them. Then the rumbling of their own stone floor began. The bridge from the landside opened, guarded by a half dozen guards at the edge of the rocks, donned in gray cloaks, swords at the ready.

Stone from both the mountain and the prison extended like branches of a tree to meet one another, their stretches echoing against the sharp peak.

Eran stood at Ariaas's side. The dolt hadn't panicked yet; that was positive. If he stayed beside the carriage and didn't speak to anyone, perhaps he wouldn't have to lie and give them all away.

Guards held their blades close, three on each side of the bridge in tight formation. A small valley of sharp dagger-like rocks surrounded them, leading to the mouth of the bridge, black and deep gray against the new light of the morning. Ariaas surveyed them over and over, ensuring he missed nothing.

This was the moment he waited for. The moment he had forced himself to be patient for.

Once the bridge had opened fully extended to meet its counterpoint, one of the soldiers called out to them. "Valesove!"

Ariaas's eyes widened. No. "We are last. We are supposed to be last."

"We'll adjust." Eran attempted to calm him while Ariaas fumbled with the key at the back of the carriage. "I can take him as well if need be."

"No. No." Ariaas shook his head. "I will do it. I'll take him."

Eran drew the keys from him, unlocking the iron and holding the door ajar. Lenora exited first, followed by Brenor, his hands bound behind his back. They had roughed her hair and dirtied their clothes. Ariaas pressed his blade into Brenor's shoulder blades.

Lenora's hair twisted above her head into knots, even with the long braid at her back. Ariaas leaned into her before he departed. "I trust you'll do what must be done. When the bridge is taken, and the two are free, you have no allies outside this family. None. The enemy is anyone who is not us."

Lenora nodded.

The guards must be taken first. The Yurelan, if necessary. Two dozen surrounded them, perhaps more.

His granddaughter's finger rested steadily on the waiting pin below her chains, as she eyed the bow and arrow, and the blade hid below the carriage.

Ariaas forced Brenor forward, one hand on the long iron chain, the other on his sword at Brenor's back. The guards from Felreaon exchanged eyes as Ariaas took to the edge of the rocks—a caution, as he read their glances.

Brenor stumbled the long journey over the bridge. The metal chains clanked with his heavy steps. The pacing of his blood, holding his nerves, was apparent, as they inched closer than he had ever been to The Reldory. Ariaas's voice trembled when he announced, "Valesove!"

The doors groaned open.

A red-bearded guard made no motion toward them—his back to the door, busy at his desk. Ariaas led Brenor to the bolt on the floor. A thin layer of dust covering heavy metal swirled as the doors closed behind them. Two ratty, emaciated prisoners stood at one side and one at the other, prepared to fight with anything they had found.

At the sight of prisoners behind the door, makeshift weapons held at attention, Ariaas muttered, "Brenor."

The two extended their arms in a symbol of peace.

"I won't harm you," he called. "I'm not a guard. I'm here for a member of my family."

Frantic, Brenor pulled the pin, releasing his chains. "We seek a woman named Arienne, please. Do you know her?"

When none replied, Ariaas asked, "Are there others?" The boy pointed. Brenor found several prisoners trembling behind the walls, huddling behind the stacks of beds, waiting for repercussions. Ariaas held his hands to his lips, signaling for their silence.

"I am looking for a woman named Arienne," Brenor pleaded, scanning them each for anyone who might meet her description. "Please. She's my sister." Each silent prisoner bore sunken eyes, souls broken from years of confinement. The more he spoke, the more forlorn their faces became, knowing they were not the ones he came to liberate.

"She has bright violet eyes," he implored, one after the next. "She has pale hair and pale skin. Please?"

A woman's voice came from the corner. "I knew I heard it, honey." She leaned against the stone wall, cradling a body. "I heard the sound—I thought I was mad—but I heard the song." Gesturing to herself, she said, "I'm Dylia." She lay the body on the floor, crumpling as a sack of bones. "She's still alive."

Ariaas crouched at her side. A choking sensation rose in his throat before he swallowed it.

This can't be her. Can it?

After all these years, they'd come to rescue a corpse.

Brenor stood over him, placing his hand over his sister's head, moving the hair from her face, broken black teeth visible by her gaping mouth.

Suppressing a sickening sensation, Ariaas asked, "Where are the remainder of the guards?"

Dylia gestured to the bearded guard. "There were only the three."

A woman stood at his side, having risen from her hiding. The guard stared idly into the abyss.

Dylia pointed at the second body in the corner, the man wriggling against his binds. "The third fell."

A dozen prisoners stood ready to flee across the bridge. Ariaas's eyes trailed from gaunt man to gaunt woman, some in tattered rags, some nude. His eyes traveled to the woman, fearful and focused on Arienne, with hair once a lush gold and skin to match.

Brenor spoke pointedly as if they noticed the same thing at the same moment. "You are Sissel."

Ariaas stepped forward. "I'm ... a friend. Idith and Thaesla ... they asked us to bring you home."

"Are you—are you the man from Aroun Vaer?" Sissel gaped. "Ariaas?"

He nodded.

"Ariaas. We can't leave all these people," Brenor pleaded. "We can't—"

Ariaas rubbed the bridge of his nose. "How did you all get up here?"

"We climbed the walls. The two of us. It was her doing." Dylia nodded toward Sissel. "I handled the guards. But she opened the stairs. And the cageside of the bridge just now."

Brenor's eyes gleamed. He nearly laughed at Lenora's carefully-laid, voided plan. "You took the prison from the inside."

The guards were waiting for Ariaas at the landside to send the next prisoner. But how would he and Brenor get all of these people out if he went back now?

What to do?

What to do?

What to do?

The guards would bar the landside if they charged now. He had to believe Brenor could get them to safety when the time came. He had no other choice.

"Stay with Brenor," Ariaas directed Sissel. "I'll whistle the call when we attack at the landside. Be ready."

Dylia grasped Brenor's arm. "When the call comes, will you carry her, honey?" The words seemed to pain her as they parted her lips. "I don' think I'm strong enough to take us both."

Brenor nodded, cradling Arienne in his arms. "You need to go, Ariaas," he ordered, "Now."

Ariaas turned, leaving the three of them on the stone.

✦ ———— · + · ✦ · + · ———— ✦

Dylia grasped Sissel's arm. "You'll keep the bridge open?"

Sissel feared nothing when they rose to take the bridge, not when they climbed, or when the rusted metal sliced her hands. When Dylia shoved the old guard, and he lost his footing, Sissel had not even seen him since she had not yet risen to the floor. That night was silent. If she failed then, then her failure would have been swiftly ended, her body resting with the other bones. Now, if she failed, it would be on open display for all to see. Failure meant the death of every set of eyes peering back at her.

Everything was quieter suddenly.

"It's going to be alright, honey." Dylia embraced her. "Let me calm you." Sissel gazed into Dylia's eyes, her left arm outstretched. She needed anything at all to stop the coursing fear.

Her muscles and her mind soothed at Dylia's touch.

Gaunt prisoners peeked through the gaps in the door, gathering their courage for when the whistle came. An arrow flew, rattling, bowing against the wind, appearing to miss its target before the sharp air returned it, slamming into the back of the guard of The South Sea.

The whistle came—first loud, then drowned by the sounds of clanking metal.

Brenor bellowed, "Now!"

Dylia helped the twins open the doors.

The prisoners fled. They dashed as hundreds of bones and bones alone, falling and crawling and holding onto one another for dear life against the raging air. A dozen men and women scrambled for the last chance at life.

The last audible words Sissel heard through the wind was Dylia shouting, "Hold the bridge!"

One twin fell to his hands and knees, the second strained, pulling him to his feet.

"The wind is too strong," she said to no one. "They cannot make it."

The auburn-bearded guard rested while she held the bridge, her hand on his shoulder. He murmured to himself in his peaceful state. Though he held abilities to control the bridge, this man was no Xentirie.

Battle surged on the landside.

A dozen bodies donning umber-hooded cloaks rose from the rocks. Clashing metal drifted through the air. Prisoners swarmed to reach the safety of solid ground. Bodies stumbled, desperate, to cross to the half outside The Reldory's control while Sissel watched, helpless from the cage.

One fell. The body drifted into the abyss, growing smaller. Smaller.

The air quieted.

A second fell.

The wind itself seemed to reply, *stop, stop, stop.*

An object glimmered against the new sunlight, perched between two stones on the floor: the wooden button in the same position where it rolled to rest months ago. Sissel picked it up and dusted the face. She searched the running bones, but the young girl was not among them. The winds died, and the gaunt bodies ran with a chance, faster, and with more assurance. She scoured the room, Crane now fighting his binds, growling through the old rags tied between his jagged teeth.

The bridge on The Reldory side began creeping, sluggishly inching toward its home. She grasped the auburn guard, instructing, "Keep the bridge open."

A voice whispered from the corner, *stop, stop.*

The girl had tucked herself into a ball in a furrow of stone. Hidden.

"Please, the wind, please," she begged, clenching her hands over her ears to drown out the sounds.

"Is it you who wills the winds?" Sissel asked. "You who has given them a chance?" The girl did not answer, rocking herself to and fro. "You have done them a great service. They made it because of you," Sissel assured her. "But now we must go, too."

The girl murmured, "Afraid to fall."

"Take my hand."

The deep fear faded. What other choice did she have? Die trying or die by slow starvation.

Sissel extended her arm, pleading, "I won't let go of you." She scooped up the child, holding her like a toddler. Her legs wrapped around Sissel's waist, her arms around her neck. Far too large to be carried, Sissel's weak arms already felt the burden of the child.

Sissel examined the auburn-bearded guard. With Dylia away, he stirred. Meeting his eyes, she commanded, "You will extend the bridge again. It won't move until she and I are safe on the other side." Soon, he would be lucid. "Please."

Turmoil unfolded on the landside.

"Close your eyes," instructed Sissel, holding her own closed for an instant as if the order was for both of them. She pleaded, "Hold the wind for us. Please. Just a small bit longer."

The air stiffened. A pause in time.

Sissel surged forward as if no abyss yawned below—as if there were no fall into eternity should she step one foot out of line. She ran for the hope dwelling beyond the rocks, beyond the old wooden doors, beyond the bridge. Her limbs moved as a broken body could—clambering to balance through weakened muscles, weights pulling at her arms, the girl's bones pressing into hers.

She swelled forward into clangoring havoc.

When her feet met solid ground, the winds returned with less ferocity. The rocks of The Reldory quivered as the Dlearbrond returned to his senses too late to stop her fleeing.

Mayhem lay before her: uniforms of varying colors, umber cloaks, swords, arrows, wailing, blood, prisoners, soldiers, civilians, visible bones, and alliances misplaced amongst colorful chaos in the morning light.

She tucked the girl behind a sharp boulder. "We need to get you hidden away."

But equally, Sissel needed to breathe. She needed to move. To find Dylia and Arienne. Anyone familiar. Anything.

· + · ✦ · + ·

True to Oedd's word, two dozen shadowed Yurelan rose from the rocks, ringed tattoos at their arms, honed blades at their belts, their orders plain to Lenora: rescue the eldest sibling *at any cost*. Along with the guards at the carriages, their numbers were substantial. Today was no simple escape from a prison, no easy removal of two bodies awaiting the passage of death.

Today was a battle to claim The Reldory.

Lenora ignored the calamity—the noise, first, the harsh clashing of metal, now, numbed to low sounds as she plucked arrows from her quiver in rapid succession. She scanned the crowd, seeking Ariaas and Eran, who had already taken a substantial blow.

A Noslarrar broke the bones of several Yurelan, their location unknown. Seeking cover behind a rock, she listened intently. The sounds divided and she heard whispering in Nieran. Following the words, she found the hidden body, a figure in a shadowed cloak, and met his belly with a blade.

Though the Yurelan's numbers were depleted, The South Sea's were as well. They were not prepared for an onslaught of prisoners armed with blades of the fallen. Rocks were slung from the precipice, crashing across the ground, crushing limbs, though their origin was difficult for Lenora to place.

Lenora's next broadhead soared through the neck of a soldier of The South Sea. She expected to feel remorse, pain, or sadness, or a dense weight in her chest when the arrow met his flesh, but she felt numb. She faltered for a moment at the life spraying from his veins, and when his eyes rolled and fixated in an open position, his blood pooling along the stone ground.

Her training with Ariaas proved invaluable. She bore an effortless stride, pulling arrows from the quiver as if she had been a skilled marksman since childhood.

As the skeletons surged forward, Lenora slung the bow over her shoulder and ran her fingers over the chains below her blouse to ensure her safety should a sword aim at her flesh. Drawing the steel blade from her belt, she sliced through the back of the knee of a large looming man from Dhaesreaon who struck Eran.

Her blade met the belly of a woman from The South Sea.

Bodies were everywhere, some in uniforms, some in rags, so varied, it was difficult to know who was on each side.

She now understood Ariaas's warning. *The enemy is anyone who is not us.*

The reason for her lack of remorse became clear. The soldiers with pins of jaguars at their chests were her enemy. They kept a member of her family hidden away, and though she could not remember her sister, Lenora was compelled to rescue her and Sissel beyond all logic. The fire within her chest that had surged the instant she learned of Arienne's fate still burned.

Brenor sprinted over the edge of the precipice, a skeleton covered in flesh in his arms. Prisoners fought a guard who had lost all but a small blade, one of two brothers and one of the teen boys, holding loose rocks and sand they found on the floor. They all fought for a last chance at life with whatever their hands could find.

Brenor had taken cover behind boulders at the northern edge to get Arienne to safety, moving close to the edge to circumvent the rocks. He held her safe, and his hands covered his ears at the screams of men in agony as he grimaced. Lenora took in what he must see from his vantage—death at every corner—a plummeting fall, an arrow, a dagger, a rock, a sword.

The air sounded of clattering metal and smelled of blood.

✦ ——————— ·✦·✦·✦· ——————— ✦

I am a gentle man.

Brenor clutched his sister's frail body. "Caveat five: it is ok to protect myself or someone I love."

He repeated the conditions of his vow that would protect him should he use a blade, or a push or a rock to bludgeon someone who meant to harm them. It would be all right if he had to take a life. *It would.* His insides twisted violently at the thought. The sounds were too much, too many, coming from various locations and he couldn't single one out.

Dylia stood before Brenor as a guard approached in a weaponless defense of he and Arienne. He wished to stay hidden, to be concealed. The steel from the guard's short blade pressed into Dylia's abdomen and the air rushed from her lungs. She crumbled. Losing her footing, her dark eyes widened, and she collapsed into the fog in a hushed slump.

The guard grinned with pleasure.

Brenor, covered in a cold sweat, did his best to process the death of someone he met mere minutes ago. Someone who knew his sister better than he. He held a body and nothing more at the edge of the cliff. No open hands for weapons even if he were willing to use them.

He placed Arienne's bones on the ground and gathered the dagger from his boot. The soldier lunged for him, removing a chunk of flesh from his forearm before he could rise from the floor.

From a defensive stance, Brenor carved a gash out of the soldier's shoulder. He inhaled, reminding himself of the caveats; there was nothing he could do in this moment that would make him a monster. It wouldn't turn him. Brenor held his position with the petite blade and only swung when forced to retaliate—the weapon too small to be anything but a slight deterrent.

Lenora met Brenor's side, her bow drawn and aimed. "Put it down."

The soldier twisted his blade in his fingers.

His murder would be difficult while he held a steady position.

He lunged for Brenor's intestines.

Lenora pierced his neck above the collarbone before his blade could meet her brother's flesh.

In an instant, without thought, Brenor grasped the hem of his shirt. A gaping wound at his neck and eyes wide with panic, he glanced at the dropping abyss below his shoes. Brenor surveyed him, the murderer of the woman who sacrificed herself for Arienne. He held on fast to the man's shirt; his fingers, caked with sweat and dirt, slipped on the velvet fabric.

The man held his gaze, his eyes fearful and hard as obsidian. He would still strike if given the chance, if given a moment of freedom.

If Brenor released his hold, the man would tumble. He wouldn't see him die, but he would hear his screams. He could almost hear him now, as another fell into the abyss, first loud and terrified, then shrinking into the swirling air. His chest rose and fell, his fist tightening, knuckles white around the blade in his palm.

A tear fell from his eye and his voice shuddered, "I am a … gentle … man."

Which caveat was this? He didn't have time or the capacity to think of each in turn. But this was certainly covered, right?

Ariaas's voice came from behind him. "Caveat number five," he said as if he read Brenor's thoughts. "You can let go."

The man chuckled as salty tears escaped Brenor's eyes, his future not decided. As a warring man, he could find a way out of this, given a moment more, a second more, a rock, a hair, a blade he had hidden in his belt, something. Something.

"Let go."

Brenor shook his head.

Ariaas grasped his dagger by the hilt, pressed his left arm into Brenor's torso, and slammed the blade in his right down into the man's chest, separating the two as one would during a small fight at a tavern. Brenor's slipping grip relinquished to the force.

The man tumbled.

As the body drifted through the fog, Brenor's guilt of the death fell with it.

The caveats flew from his mind. The choice was no longer his. He no longer stood at the boundary between life and death.

The final three soldiers fought valiantly against Ariaas and two of the Yurelan disguised in tattered prisoner rags.

Lenora shouted to Eran amongst his fury of swords, *"Set the whiteroot!"*

Brenor collapsed on the stone.

Eran, breathless and bloodied, placed the bags in rows over the edge of the stone bridge. Whoever the Dlearbrond was working on this side of the land, they had not yet pulled the bridge back in, be it by death or otherwise.

Lenora shouted when the bags were set and threw the torch upon them, bystanders scattering. *"Take cover!"*

Brenor covered his ears.

The flames reached high when the torch met the dust, extending and gripping like the vines around the base of the stone. As the plant itself grew roots made of flames before it squeezed forcefully, breaking rock beneath it. The explosion lurched the hill, killing a woman of Hanielle and a prisoner, along with the two guards of the Yurelan in uniforms of Felreaon.

The hill thundered and jolted.

Eran crashed to the floor with a thud. "That was too much whiteroot!" he shouted. "I see that, now!"

✦ ———— · + · ✦ · + · ———— ✦

Sissel searched for sanctuary, keeping the girl well hidden. She scanned the crowd, the deceased and the dying, and those still fighting for control. Her stomach twisted and, for the briefest of moments, she caught sight of slate eyes. Was she still in the cage, dreaming of the man she loved rising gallantly over the peaks? She had the same dream when she closed her eyes on the cold ground and hoped to fall asleep.

No.

Those were his eyes, his uniform, his beard.

Ronan stood not twenty paces from her.

His eyes locked onto a woman, her arrow firmly aimed toward his chest.

This was no dream. The screams were too harsh, too visceral. Blood coated the dirt and the rocks. Metal clanked.

It was only a moment. A flicker.

The green-eyed woman was ready. Ronan was not.

Sissel reached for the bow, her soul determined to thwart impending tragedy. Time slowed like the fluttering of a hummingbird's wings. The arrow released before her; her fingers grazed the bowstring. It reverberated against her touch, but not swift enough to divert the path of the shaft. She lunged further, hurling herself at the woman, striking her with unwavering force and sending them both to the ground.

The air parting created a visceral sound.

The broadhead struck him, soared between his ribs, and shredded through flesh into the caverns of his chest. At the force, Ronan stumbled, grasping the shard of wood wedged within him as he fell, plummeting back to where he had come.

Sissel screamed—a shattering of glass and scraping of metal knives against one another. The sound echoed through the precipice. Arms lunged for her as she ran for the edge—firm and unyielding. She tried to escape the grip, but the man held firm, keeping her from tossing herself over the razor-sharp rocks to Ronan's side.

RELDOR ROAD

I had never heard of a denmero until today. What a fabulous piece to add to our collection.

- Diary of Daisirie Cabredd Mire, Volume 7, Entry 125

Sissel broke against the hands holding her as if Lenora's arrow had pierced her own flesh, her knees cracking into the rocks. She shrieked, grabbed cloth, tore at clothing with her broken nails. Brenor did not move, allowing this girl's grief to surge, letting her grips pain him.

Lenora froze on the precipice.

Ariaas rushed to Brenor. "Take her to the carriages," he instructed as arrows flew, they took shelter. "She can grieve on the road!"

Everyone but us is the enemy. Lenora shot a man plain as day wearing a uniform of The South Sea. He was not *us.* How could Sissel have known the same man? She diverted her gaze from Sissel's grief. She couldn't witness the heart wrenching from this girl's chest.

A single shooter breached the precipice.

Lenora aimed and let her arrow fly as he tucked himself behind a boulder. She aimed again through rising smoke of the whiteroot, char, and blood—he dared peering around the safety of the rock. It was enough to see the destruction, the chaos, the death. Who would dare to fight her alone when three dozen bodies scattered along the hill?

A half dozen armed assailants now turned their attention to him.

The bridge was theirs.

Lenora ran toward the boulder. By the time she reached the edge of his hiding place, the soldier had scurried away. Only stone remained below the sharp drop. No bodies were visible, not of the man Sissel mourned for or the second.

Ariaas met her side. "Did you hit the second?"

"No," Lenora said regretfully. She could not curve the arrow around a boulder.

"The first will die before the other soldier can help him, if he did not already," Ariaas assured her.

Lenora returned to address Sissel. *Does she want the first to die? Who is he?*

Ariaas addressed Sissel as she choked on her tears. "They arrived to put you back in the cage. Why did you try to stop her? The final soldier will flee back to retrieve more soldiers to follow us. Where we should have had a week to flee undetected, we now have mere *hours*."

Sissel fragmented before Lenora's eyes.

Lenora no longer felt numb. The weight of death crashed upon her, her heart ached, and char filled her lungs. In her brokenness, she eyed the landside and the sea of bodies left in their wake. Left in *her* wake. Then she swallowed the grief as quickly as it had risen.

Brenor pressed his lips, also taking the many bodies upon the floor. "We need to leave. I saw their pins. We released an entire prison." He met Lenora's eyes, and suddenly her actions became clear. "And we murdered the Commander of The South Sea."

We. There was no *we.*

Lenora murdered the Commander of The South Sea.

Half the prisoners scattered along the sharp cliffs, ambling toward the dirt road.

Arienne lay in the carriage from Valesove with Sissel, her head upon an old, itchy blanket they found below the seat. Eran and Brenor attended to them, walking when necessary. Eran had taken a blade to the shoulder during the skirmish, and had a wound over his forearm, one he neglected to tell the others about. Brenor noticed the lack of movement of his arm, the way he winced when he went to the door.

Alone, Lenora rode atop the carriage of The South Sea.

She reveled in the solitude atop the carriage, though she missed Luscan's calming nature. In her isolation, she had time to revisit what had transpired. She had never taken a life until this day, and now she had claimed many. When her arrows soared, pierced their flesh, she felt nothing. Their deaths were justifiable, a goal, an innocent; they stood in the path of her righteous resolve, between her and someone who must be saved.

However, when the commander fell, Lenora sensed something different. An emotion was not easily placed. Guilt, perhaps. She had felt guilt many times—a cavernous hollow within her stomach. She would call it guilt for lack of a better word. Perhaps because he was the first life she claimed who had a name, a person who knew him, a person who loved him.

Though, for an instant, she could not place if the feeling rose before or after the arrow released.

Lenora drew her attention to the road as the wagon lurched, turned, weaving through the narrow path. Her thoughts moved from the men who had risen over the rocks to the meaning of their arrival.

At the base of the mountain, they stopped to determine where the path split on their next course of action. The remaining prisoners left them there, parting their own respective ways at the young birch trees and the large boulders denoting the path south. The young girl was the only one who remained. Her knees curled, her face was tucked away below the blanket beside Arienne.

"We should not stop, not even for nightfall," Ariaas urged.

Lenora's brows pressed, her thoughts churning since the pinnacle on one matter she could not right in her mind. "They sent two soldiers. They sent soldiers from The South Sea to arrive after the bridge was meant to close. They were late."

"If they knew of the Yurelan's plan, they would have sent an army," Brenor said. "There were no informants of their people."

Lenora's insides twisted when she thought of Thealor, the only person outside their circle who knew of the plan to place them inside The Reldory. "Do you believe we were betrayed?"

Ariaas thought for some time. "We were betrayed, or they meant to blow the bridge to ensure we did not get to Arienne, as Oedd claimed."

"Did anyone see Oedd?" Brenor asked. Eran and Ariaas shook their heads.

A handful of Yurelan returned to their own people, more than Ariaas had planned to allow free. Though murder seemed extreme when the chaos died. Lenora was pleased they had not taken the lives of the Yurelan with intention. She understood Brenor's list of caveats, now. Better than she ever had. With the exception of the commander, Lenora had only claimed the lives of those who attacked their family.

"The soldiers of The South Sea will be sent to all corners of this mountain. Especially now they have lost their commander." Ariaas pressed the reins into Eran's hand. "Take the carriage. Get Arienne to Aroun Vaer."

Eran returned the reins. "Arienne will never make it to Aroun Vaer."

"You wish us to make it over the base of Mount Ykkoro to Aroun Vaer?" Brenor pleaded. "Soldiers from Dhaesreaon were killed; they will seek us as well."

Lenora asked, "Where would you have us go?"

"I do not have the answer. I only know she is at the door of death. I agree with Eran, she needs care, *now*," Brenor argued.

Sissel's voice came from behind them in a drawn tone. "Felreaon."

No one had seen her leave the concealment of the wagon. She stood haggard, wrapped in the gray blanket, drawing their attention from their argument. "Go to Felreaon. The border is not far, due west. Felreaon does not allow soldiers of The South Sea over their borders without permission."

"They will not allow us over their borders, either," Ariaas pressed, his tone inquisitive along with his typical gruff. "They will send us right back to the south."

"They won't." Sissel turned her gaze back to the carriage. "You have a child of their people to return home." The young girl had not left the safety of the small walls, curled at Arienne's feet. They had forgotten her, hiding out of sight on the floorboards.

Lenora and Sissel met eyes for the first time. And, just as fast, Sissel turned away.

"The long way, then," Lenora spoke after a few moments, the space in her chest aching. "Around Dhaesreaon, before Aroun Vaer. We will clean and regroup the first chance we get."

BRIGHT AS THE MIDDAY SUN

S issel found a range of emotions to navigate, unable to stay on one for long before the next took hold: grief at the death of Ronan, grief at the death of Dylia, caution at the stranger who wielded a bow against him, wariness tainted both with hatred and understanding.

In a battle for life, death is a given—but why did it have to be him? Why did an arrow have to pierce his chest? And then her thoughts would turn to the lost, forgotten girl belonging to those who perhaps knew not where she was or how to reclaim her, that is, if she belonged to anyone at all. Then she would turn her sights to the bones of Arienne, still breath in her lungs, somehow. Again, how could a body cling to life for so long without crossing the threshold of death? And then, to the journey before them, to the days, the weeks, she would spend traversing Felreaon, then around the peninsula, just to see if those hundreds of days, that entire year she had been away, if death hadn't overcome her grandmother.

And Ariaas. All the stories she heard about him were nothing like she expected. A man her grandmother had known long ago, so long ago, he should not look like he could be her father. Only a little salt around his temples and his worn beard.

A day's ride beyond Lake Madinne, they arrived in Paisiria, only questioned by two passing farmers about the nature of their journey. They bathed in a stream, ate the fish Brenor caught, and changed into the fresh clothing they had hidden in the carriage seats.

The girl remembered little about how to direct them to her home, but when they arrived near a friend's farm, she smiled, recognizing the woman in a long line of pecan trees. "She will help me home!"

The young girl wrapped her arms around Sissel's neck and bound off without another word. In the line of pecan trees, the woman fell to her knees in the grass at the sight of her, her chest rising and falling from their vantage. The young girl leaped into her waiting arms.

Arienne refused food. Sissel attempted to feed her bread from the market with little headway.

The carriage rode the following week on slow wheels toward Jaisett. They arrived at dawn, hoping Thaesla could ease Arienne's suffering.

·+· ✦ ·+·

In Wesilea under the cover of darkness, they crept onto the stone docks, wet with the lapping of the waves. Eran and Brenor carried Arienne in turns, snaking the steep stairs carved into the cliffs and through the winding alleys. Lenora, eying the paths before they turned.

When Sissel found Thaesla's cobalt door, she opened it abruptly, taking the stairs three at a time. After what Ariaas told her on the road—her grandmother's imprisonment and the length of time since she'd been home—she had little hope her grandmother lived.

Inside, Thaesla's mouth fell open. She stumbled, knocking into a pile of books and sending them crashing to the floor. Sissel wrapped her arms around Thaesla's waist and tucked her head into her shoulder without a word.

The others rose over the stairs: Heneran Hoeleck, Lenora Varan, Brenor Varan, and Ariaas Ebronds, Arienne in his arms.

At the sight of her, Thaesla's joy shifted suddenly. She instructed, "Lay her on the table."

Lenora pressed away the loose pages, plates, and cups from the table; they rattled and scattered across the floor.

Thaesla whispered in the Old Tongue, "agheue dih yilnu."

They lingered, hoping for a miracle, wondering how her heart continued to beat in her chest—but it held on, a rogue vine amongst the long-dead garden.

"You told us you would care for Idith," Ariaas spoke as she worked. "Where is she?"

Thaesla raised her arm to the back bedroom. "Today is not the day I stop holding true to my promises, old friend." She turned to Eran, no time for pleasantries toward strangers, "Get me that bowl there and some warm fresh water. Towels as well."

While Thaesla attended to Arienne, Sissel stood before the threshold to the bedroom, a deep hollow aching in her chest, a weight she could not escape. Grief surged from the recesses of her mind before it crashed into the forefront again. She pressed the door open.

Grandmother lay tucked below white cotton sheets. When she opened her eyes, Sissel threw herself on top of her, hugging her so fiercely she knocked the air from her lungs. Grandmother touched Sissel's cheek, her eyes wide. Sissel held her tightly against her face as she wept.

✦ ——— ·✦·✦·✦· ——— ✦

Ariaas waited—impatience gnawing at his bones, making him restless and twitchy—until Sissel said her peace to Idith.

He needed to meet with her alone.

He inhaled through his exhaustion. *I can rest when I'm dead.*

The concept of Idith's impending death pained him, a matter he refused to think about until he stood on this threshold. He would need to say goodbye, as Thaesla warned. But could he see her like that? His inextinguishable flame? After decades apart? Could she possibly be at the door of death?

Shit. Breathe. Just breathe.

"I know you're there," Idith shouted. "I could smell that unbathed stink from Jaisett! You didn't bathe in the creek with them, did you?"

Ariaas raised his shirt to his nose. *Do I stink that badly? Or is she just being ... her?* He chuckled, pressing his way into the room.

"I never thought I'd live to see this day." She smiled, a far different woman than the last time they'd met. "You, standing here in Wesilea." She took him in—his peppered chin, unkempt hair, clothes worn from the long journey. Gesturing to herself, her deep lines, her paper-thin skin, she muttered, "After all this time, I'm glad to see one of us still has their looks about them."

Ariaas spat a laugh. There she was. "Admit it. You've missed me."

"I have missed you. Very much." Unmoving, she appeared one with the bed, sprigs of white curls at her brow. Her grin settled, and she regained a serious tone. "I cannot say with words what you have done for me. Truly. For Sissel. For all of them. There are no words. *Thank you* must suffice."

"How long has it been? Twenty years? Thirty?" Though he knew the number of years in his soul, down to the very day. He inched forward. After all these decades, what should he say would be appropriate? "Do you wish to meet Brenor and Lenora? I don't believe Arienne is currently taking visitors."

"Not today." Idith shook her head and whisked a tear from her eye. "You saved Sissel. You saved them all."

"It's not quite what you think. My gallant days may be behind me. We held the soldiers at the landside. The rest was Sissel," he said. "She saved Arienne. None of us had the ability to get across the bridge without her."

Idith smiled warmly—as if she had told him many times, just as that lunatic author had—he couldn't do it alone. And he'd finally learned that lesson on his own in a harrowing, drawn-out matter. A matter he would never admit aloud.

"I need you to do something for me."

He raised a brow playfully. "The last favor you asked was ... quite large. Not sure I can survive another one of your favors." At her serious expression, his raised shoulders fell, and he abandoned his banter. He sighed, grasping her hand in his. "Anything."

"Take Sissel with you. You came to say farewell and have, or at least you will. As has she. She can't stay. Too many know her face, know her story." Idith's voice hoarsened, her breath laboring her every word. "Take her to Aroun Vaer, please." She coughed and spat. "Let her stay until she finds a home elsewhere."

Ariaas's chest tightened. Idith strained, laboring for a simple thing such as oxygen when her emotions soared.

How could this have happened? How could time have passed for her while it stood so still for him? His duty, the push and pull between Idith's wishes, the prophecy, the knowing of what is to come and living one's life regardless. He knew what he needed to say, words he may or may not abide by in the coming days. He still needed to think on the matter. But he'd be damned if he let Idith cross into the great beyond with worries on her soul.

"I'll take Sissel to Aroun Vaer, for you. So long as you promise your last dying wish is to not poison me again."

Idith's cheeks raised with a grin, and she tightened her grip on his hand. She appeared far too fond of the ludicrous memory. Perhaps her dying wish would be to poison him again for the sheer joy of it. "Deal."

· + · ✦ · + ·

Lenora slept across the floor, Brenor in the chair. Arienne had yet to eat, though she slept comfortably atop the dining table. Ariaas moved a kitchen chair into the doorframe of Idith's room so that he might watch both places, unsure where he was most needed. Or perhaps he was not needed at all. But he would be there, regardless.

In the darkness, Sissel awoke Brenor. Ariaas, thinking he was dreaming, leaned in to hear her words. "Sorry to wake you but can you help me take Arienne upstairs?"

Brenor bumped into Lenora, waking her. The three carried Arienne's limp body to the roof. Curious, Ariaas fumbled between sleep and wake, taking the stairs to find the four sitting amongst the waking night sky. What reason could they possibly have for moving Arienne? He could scarcely believe people were awake at this hour.

Lenora asked, "What are we doing up here?"

Ariaas wondered the same.

"At The Reldory, I told Arienne stories of the sunrise." Sissel gazed over the eastern sky as the black changed to navy. "Of the sky from this roof. The stories distracted her, and she ate. I want her to see it for herself. See the beauty of the skies. I want her to know the stories are real."

The sky bled orange and vibrant pink, the salt of the sea upon the fresh morning breeze. Waves could be heard in the silence, faintly crashing upon the rocks. Arienne opened her eyes, bright and wide for the first time. Her face drew long in enchanted awe, the sunrise glowing against her skin.

There was something about the four of them—Brenor and Lenora on one side, Arienne on the other, Sissel between them smiling wide as Arienne ate. How had he not seen it? They looked—so very similar.

What to do? What to do? What to do?

Sissel's eyes sparkled in the new dawn, golden amber, bright as fire. Bright as the midday sun.

ACKNOWLEDGEMENTS

To Julia, Miel, and Laura—my first critique partners—thank you for your thoughtful insights, your generous hearts, and for showing me how to develop my writing with both precision and courage.

To June—thank you for editing this manuscript. Your insights and guidance have elevated this story in all the best ways.

To Erica and Anita—thank you for cheering me on blindly, taking the kids when I needed time, and standing firmly in my corner no matter what. You are my chosen family.

To Katie—though *Hanged by Fate* was written before I met you, your immediate support of my vision, my work, and my life has meant more than I can say. You've helped me believe in myself during the moments I struggled most.

To Nic—thank you for supporting me in every way that mattered, for helping carve out the time and space I needed to unleash my creativity.

And finally, to you—the reader. Writing this series has been and will continue to be a labor of deep patience and love. This story holds my heart, and I hope it finds a place in yours.

Rowan Wolf is a writer, publisher, and dedicated caffeine addict living in southern California with her family and two golden retievers—her most loyal (and occasionally disruptive) coworkers. Originally from Ohio, she has a background in design, which mostly means she spends an unreasonable amount of time obsessing over fonts and rearranging things that were probably fine to begin with.

When she's not knee-deep in publishing (or trying to convince herself that one more spreadsheet will solve everything), she's lost in the world of her epic fantasy series, Canen Dera—a project that's been with her so long, it might as well start paying rent. She survives on an unholy amount of coffee in the morning, cabernet at night, and is even trying to step away from the desk, training to hike El Capitan in Yosemite, because, apparently, fresh air is important.

ROWANWOLFAUTHOR.COM

MORE FROM ALEX PARKER PUBLISHING ON THE WAY...

THE LIGHT OF LÚNASA:

Laura Foley

Powerless meets The Hunger Games, in which a woman with a powerful curse opens a portal to ancient Ireland where children are vanishing. Seeking redemption for her brother's death, with the help of a local hero, she enters the annual games to save the children before they're gone forever.

"A gorgeous fantasy novel perfect for readers seeking dark romance, mystery, and magic."—*Kirkus Reviews* (starred review)

"An imaginative, genre-bending gunslinger tale with a compelling queer protagonist."—*Kirkus Reviews* (starred review)

GAS GIANT GAMBIT:

E.S. Raye

On the run and seeking refuge, beamslinger Gus arrives at a desolate fuel mining station, where once thriving machinery lies silent and those in power hold dark secrets. Reluctantly drawn into the town's strange happenings, Gus must confront her own greed and decide if this fight is worth risking her life.

The 2nd Book In Rowan Wolf's Epic Canen Dera Series Is On The Way

Coming Soon